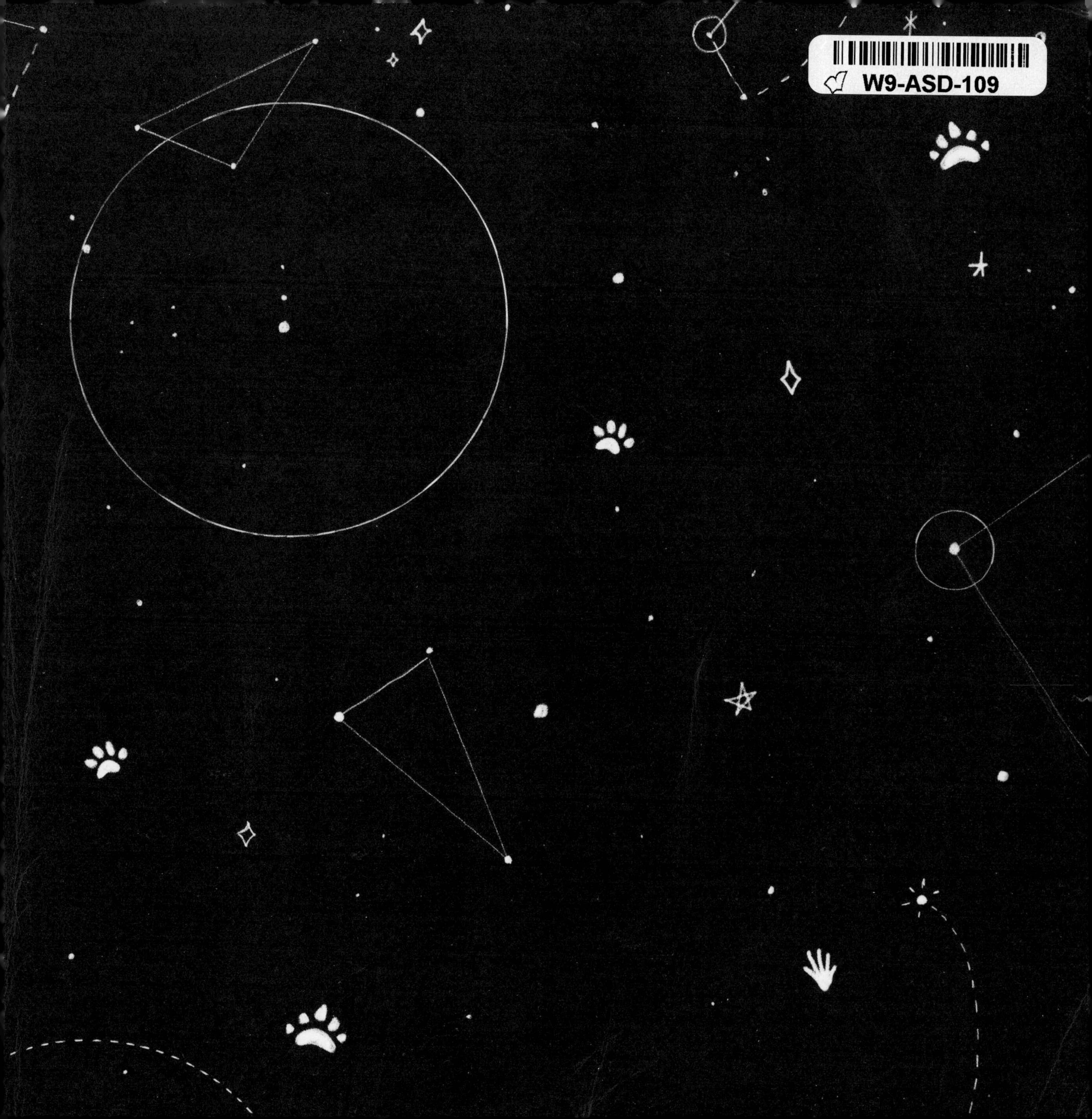

Ben Queen + Joe Todd-Stanton

BEAR ™

Published by
ARCHAIA ™

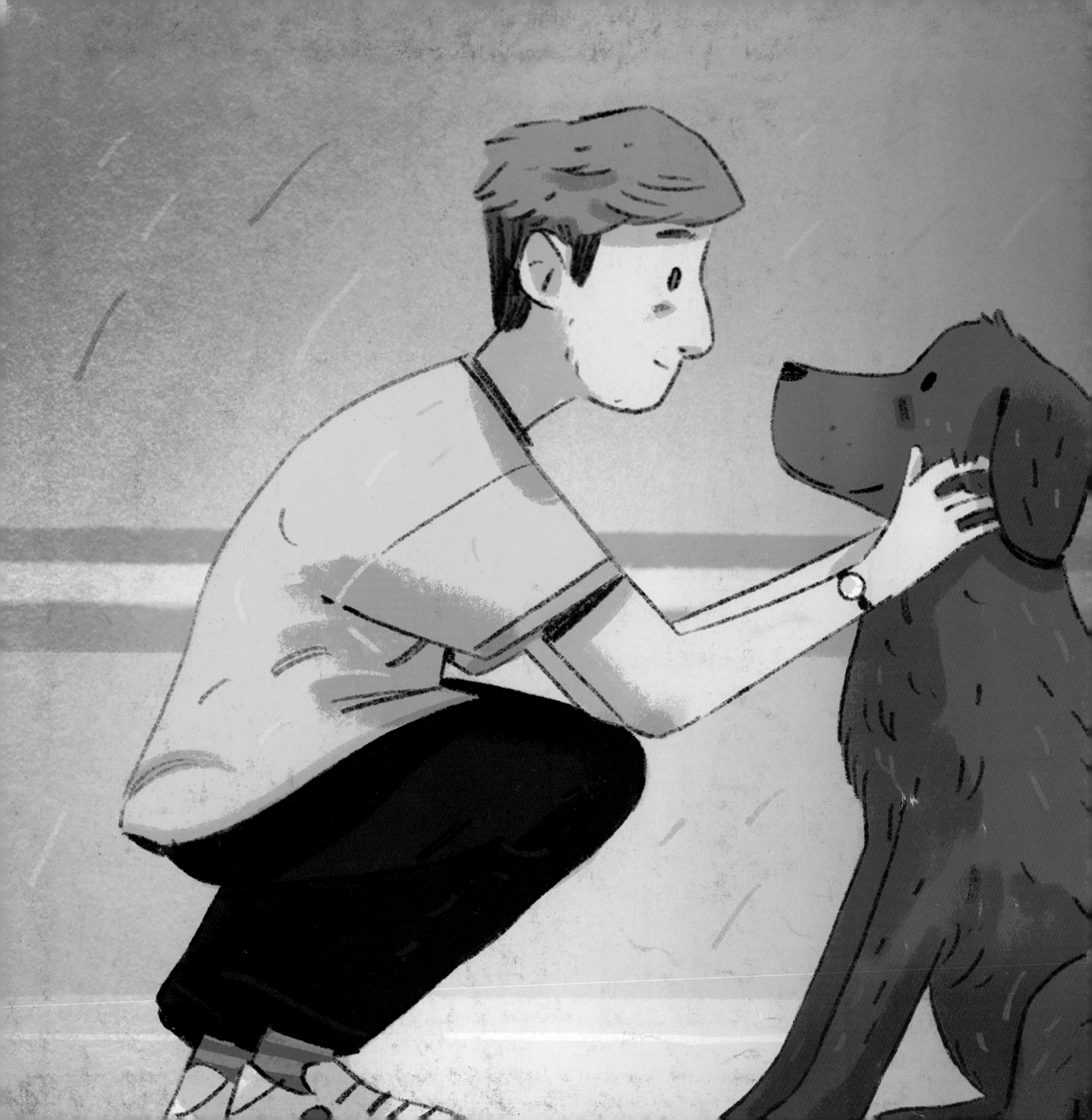

BEAR™

Written by Ben Queen

Illustrated by Joe Todd-Stanton

Lettered by AndWorld Design

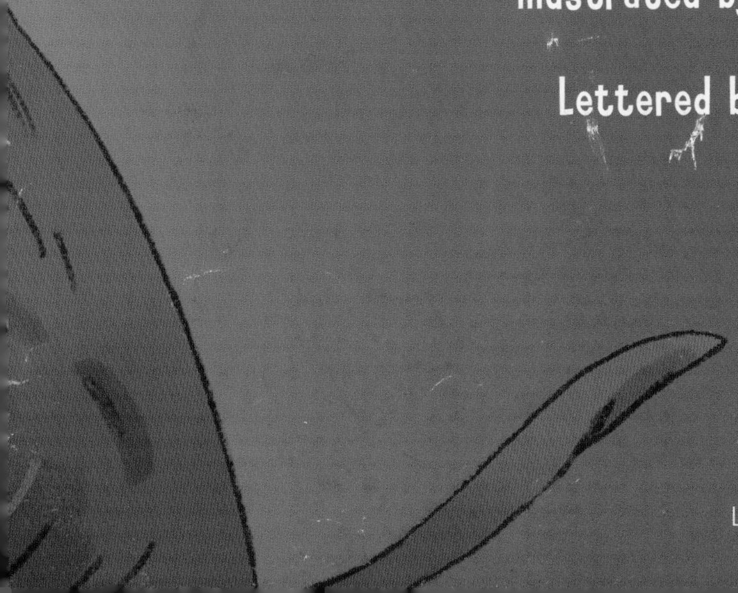

ARCHAIA™

Los Angeles, California

Designer **Scott Newman**
Editor **Amanda LaFranco**
Executive Editor **Sierra Hahn**

Special thanks to Stephen Christy.

Ross Richie CEO & Founder
Joy Huffman CFO
Matt Gagnon Editor-in-Chief
Filip Sablik President, Publishing & Marketing
Stephen Christy President, Development
Lance Kreiter Vice President, Licensing & Merchandising
Arune Singh Vice President, Marketing
Bryce Carlson Vice President, Editorial & Creative Strategy
Kate Henning Director, Operations
Spencer Simpson Director, Sales
Scott Newman Manager, Production Design
Elyse Strandberg Manager, Finance
Sierra Hahn Executive Editor
Jeanine Schaefer Executive Editor
Dafna Pleban Senior Editor
Shannon Watters Senior Editor
Eric Harburn Senior Editor
Matthew Levine Editor
Sophie Philips-Roberts Associate Editor
Amanda LaFranco Associate Editor
Jonathan Manning Associate Editor
Gavin Gronenthal Assistant Editor

Gwen Waller Assistant Editor
Allyson Gronowitz Assistant Editor
Ramiro Portnoy Assistant Editor
Shelby Netschke Editorial Assistant
Michelle Ankley Design Coordinator
Marie Krupina Production Designer
Grace Park Production Designer
Chelsea Roberts Production Designer
Samantha Knapp Production Design Assistant
José Meza Live Events Lead
Stephanie Hocutt Digital Marketing Lead
Esther Kim Marketing Coordinator
Cat O'Grady Digital Marketing Coordinator
Breanna Sarpy Live Events Coordinator
Amanda Lawson Marketing Assistant
Holly Aitchison Digital Sales Coordinator
Morgan Perry Retail Sales Coordinator
Megan Christopher Operations Coordinator
Rodrigo Hernandez Operations Coordinator
Zipporah Smith Operations Assistant
Jason Lee Senior Accountant
Sabrina Lesin Accounting Assistant

BOOM! Studios, 5670 Wilshire Boulevard, Suite 400, Los Angeles, CA 90036-5679. Printed in China. First Printing.

ISBN: 978-1-68415-531-6, eISBN: 978-1-64144-697-6

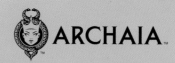

"For M, N and O."

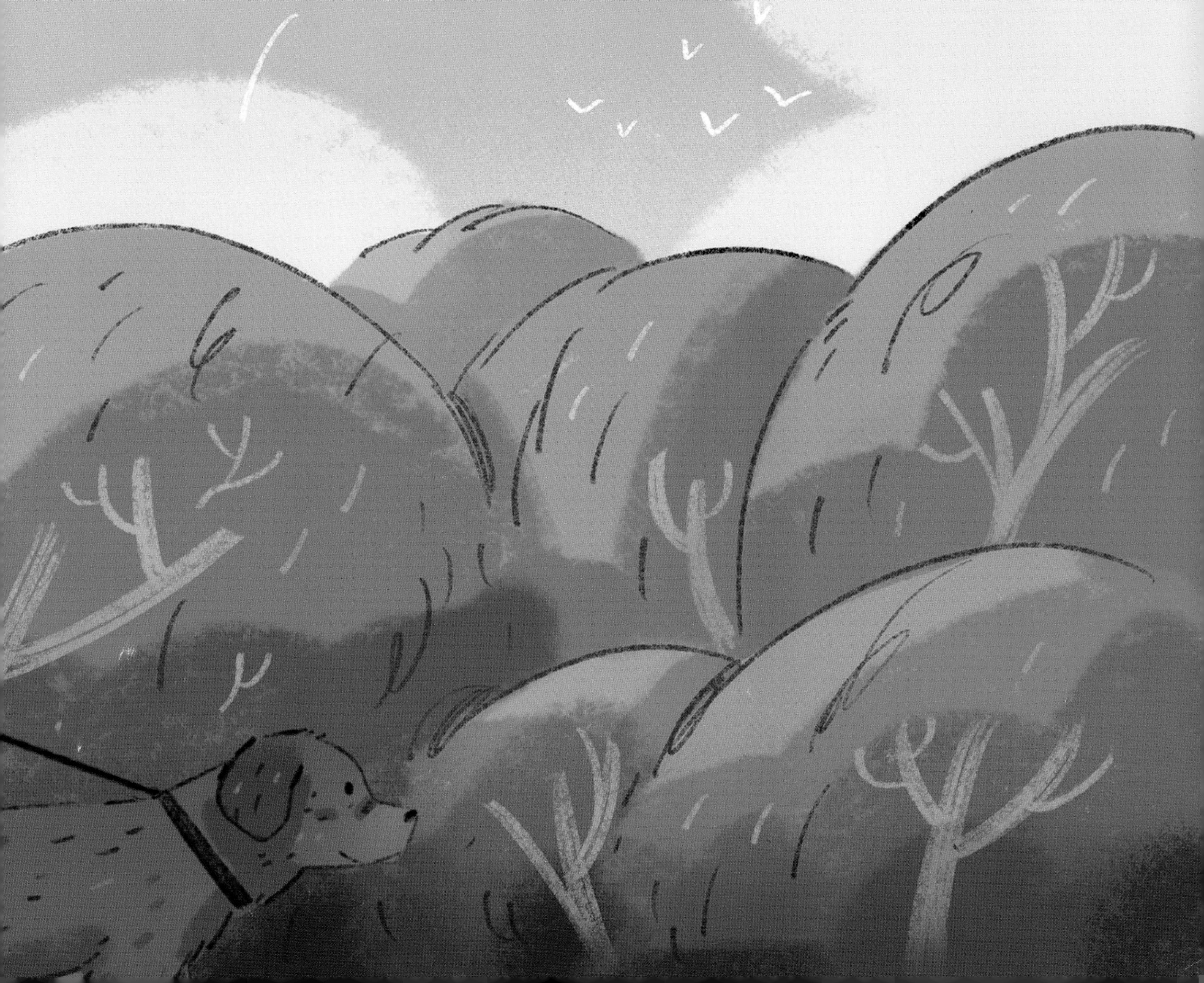

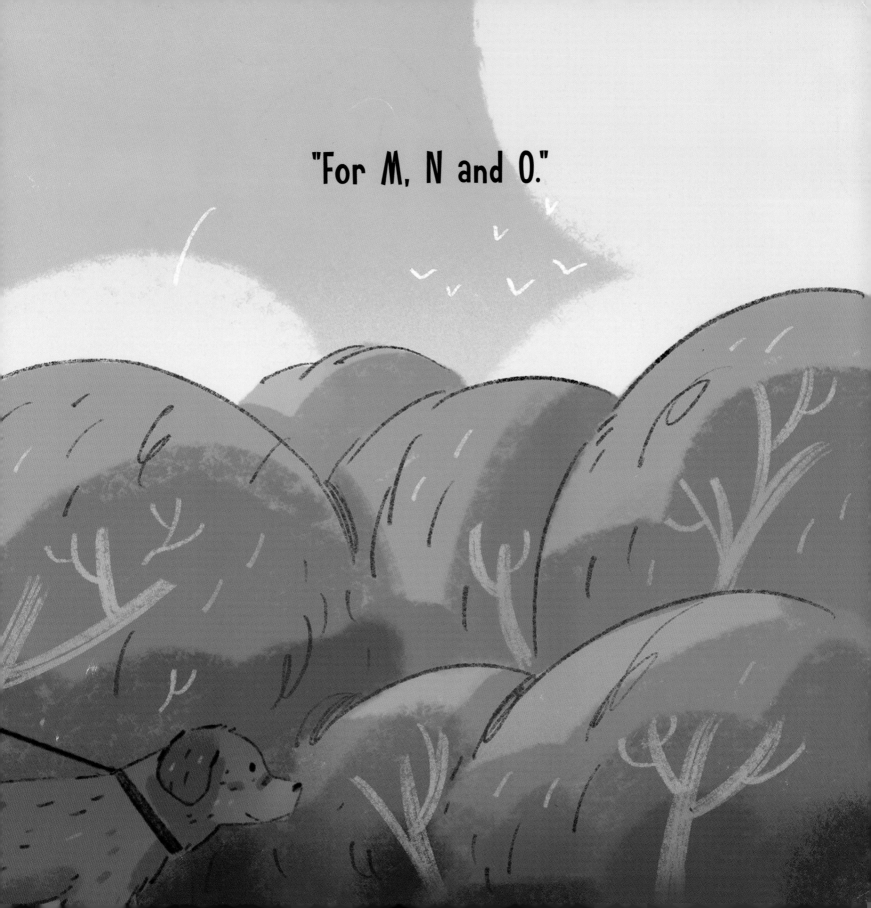

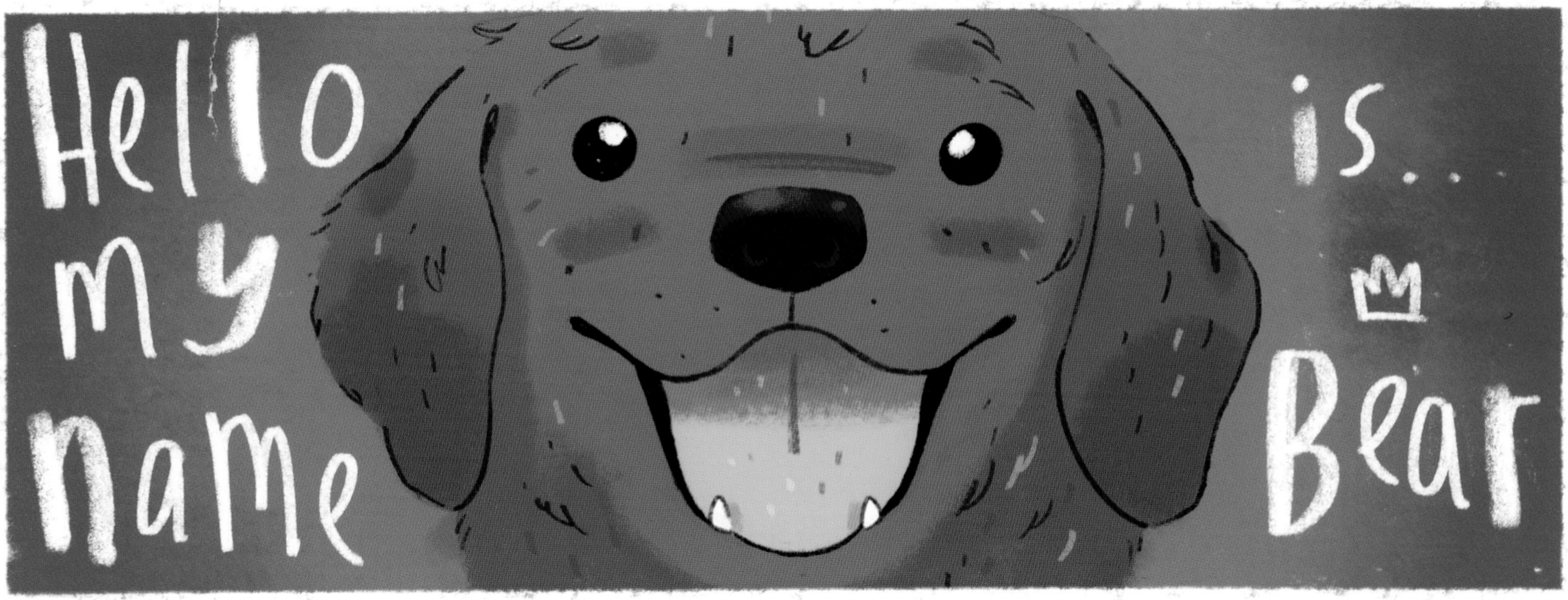
Hello
my
name
is...
Bear

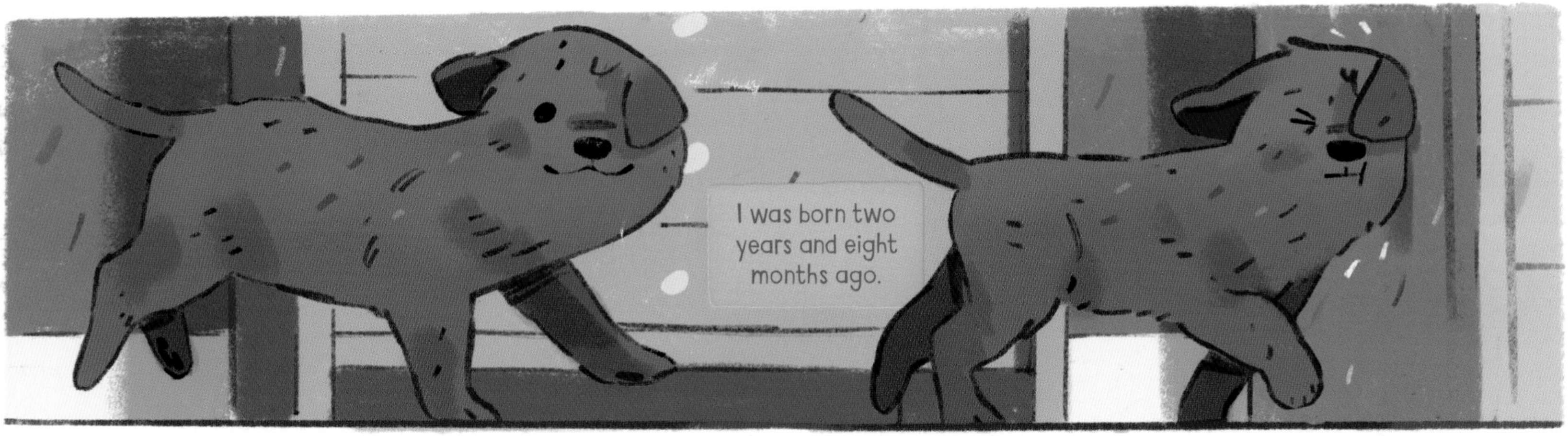
I was born two years and eight months ago.

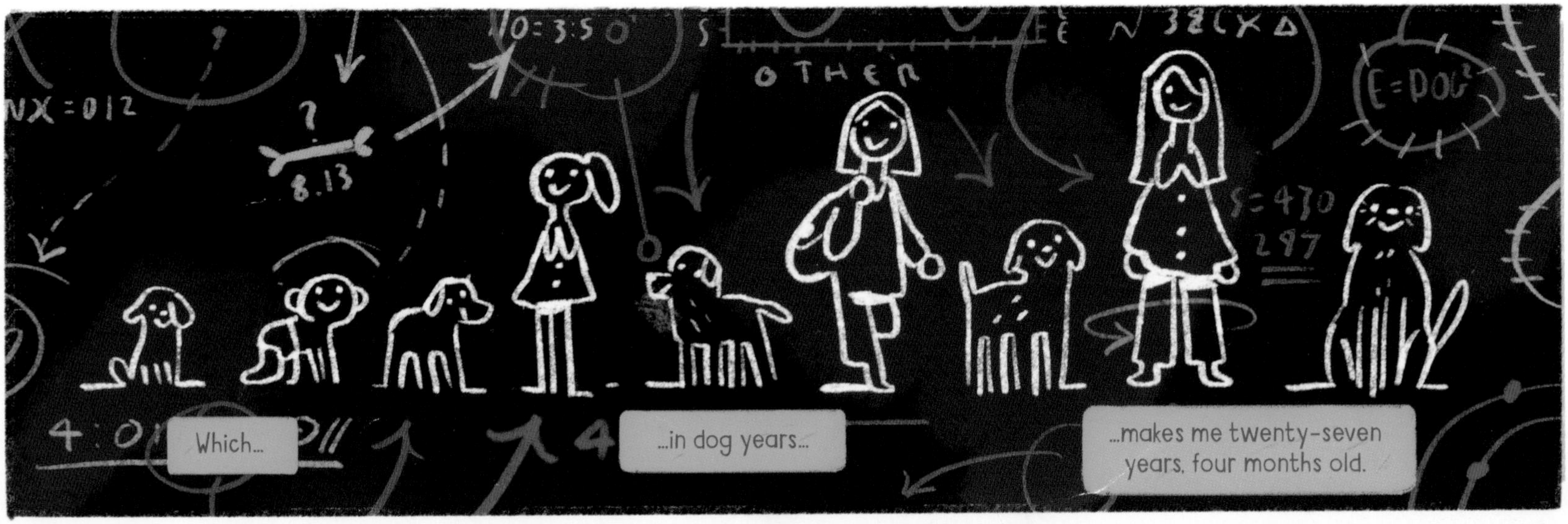
NX=012
8.13
OTHER
E=DOG²
Which...
...in dog years...
...makes me twenty-seven years, four months old.

I am not a biter or a barker...

HOOOOWL~ WOOF! BARK!

...I am a bit of a chewer, though.

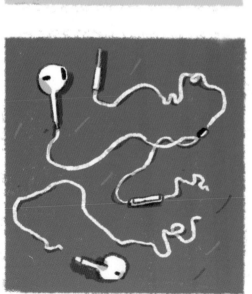

Once, I even bent a coin with my teeth!

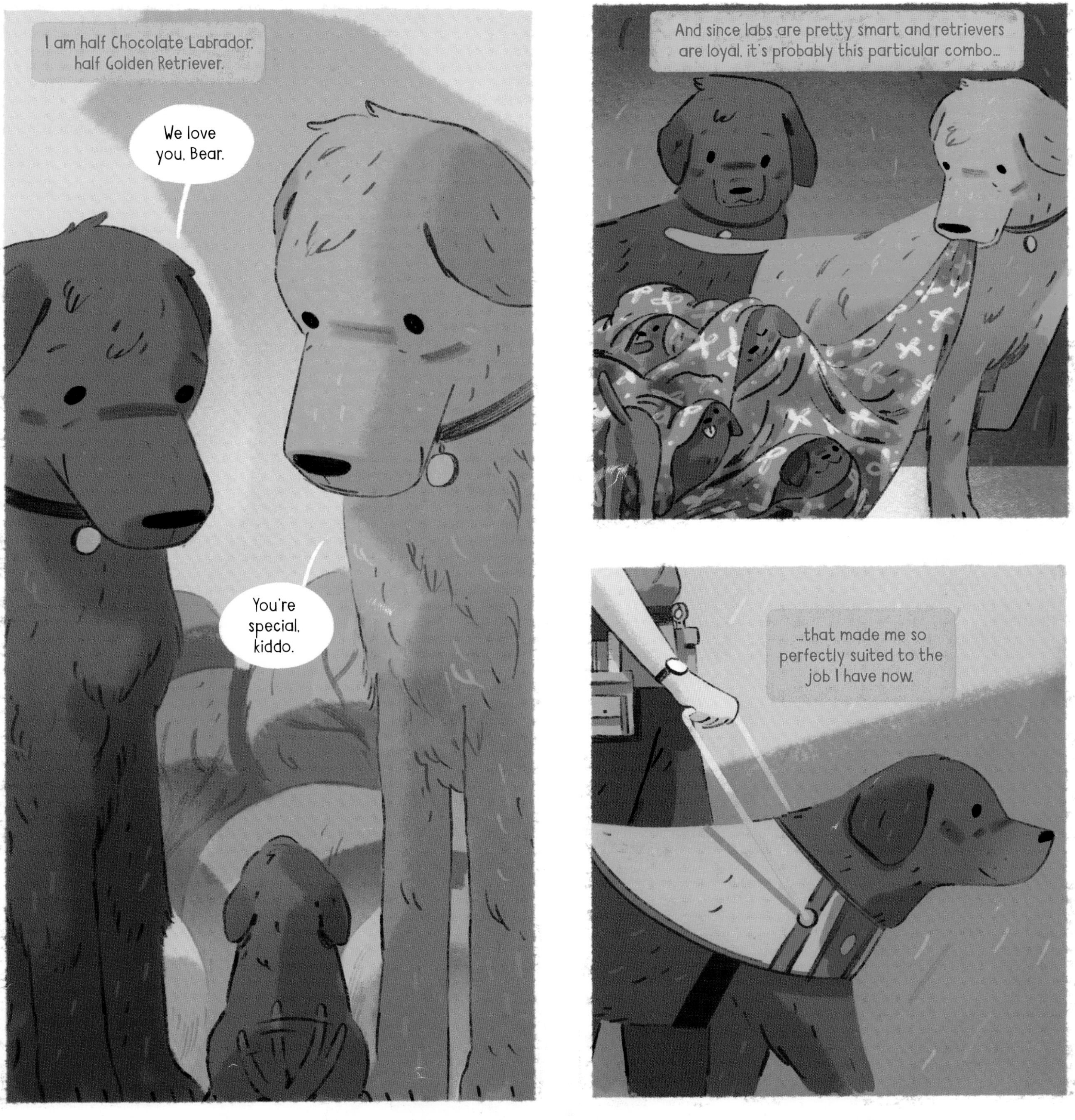
I am half Chocolate Labrador, half Golden Retriever.
We love you, Bear.
You're special, kiddo.
And since labs are pretty smart and retrievers are loyal, it's probably this particular combo...
...that made me so perfectly suited to the job I have now.

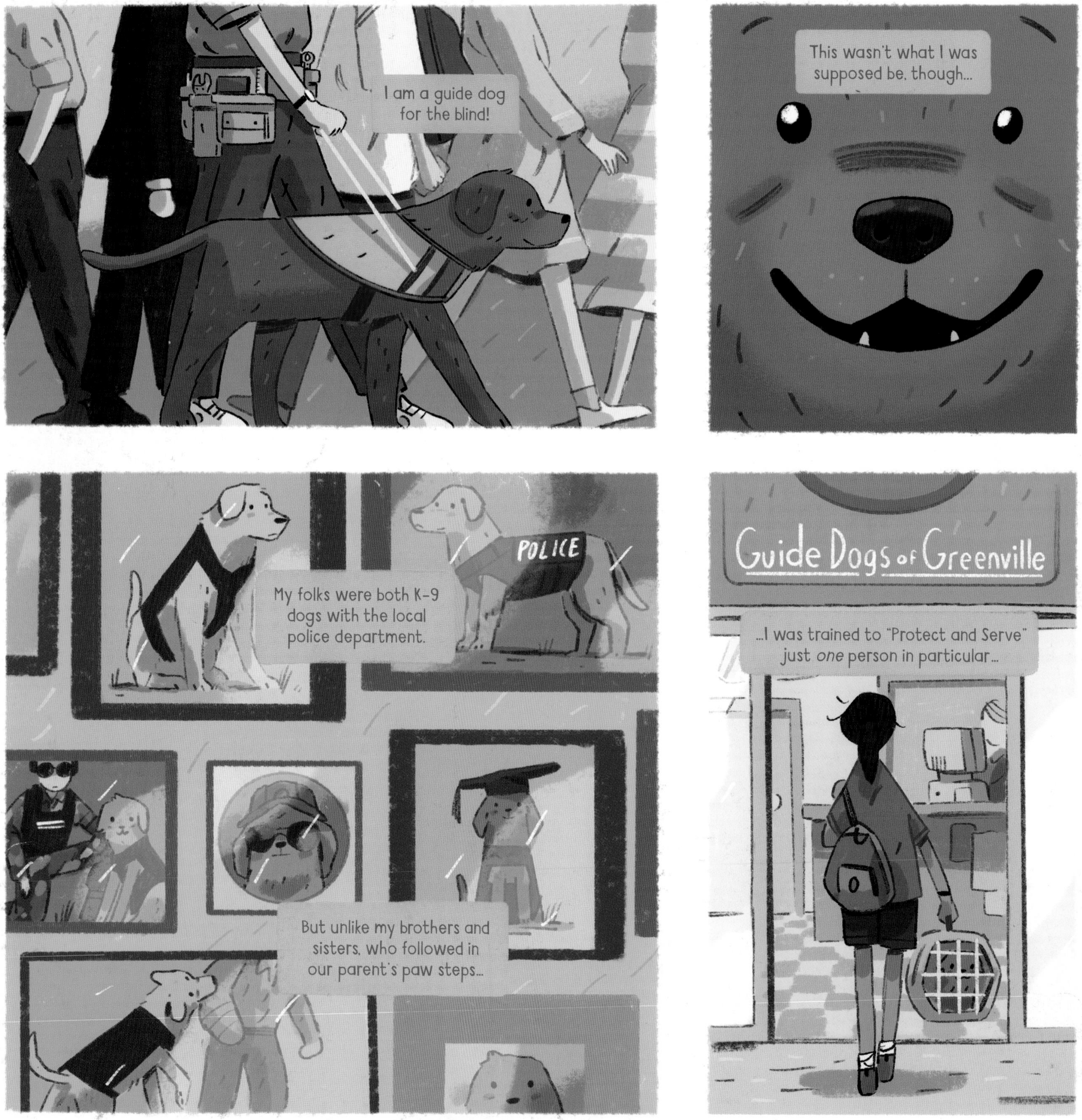
I am a guide dog for the blind!
This wasn't what I was supposed be, though...
My folks were both K-9 dogs with the local police department.
POLICE
But unlike my brothers and sisters, who followed in our parent's paw steps...
Guide Dogs of Greenville
...I was trained to "Protect and Serve" just *one* person in particular...

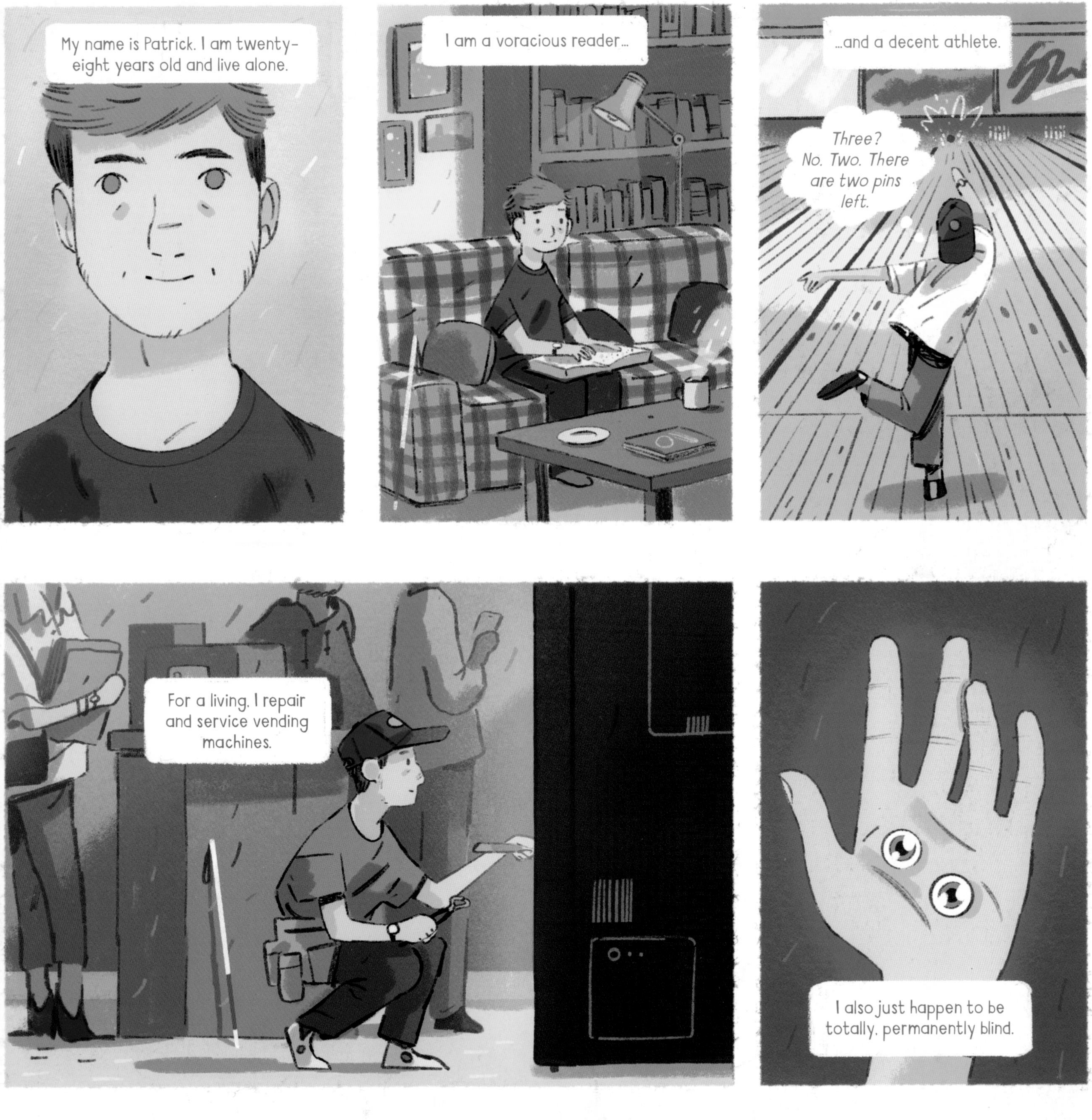
My name is Patrick. I am twenty-eight years old and live alone.
I am a voracious reader...
...and a decent athlete.
Three? No. Two. There are two pins left.
For a living, I repair and service vending machines.
I also just happen to be totally, permanently blind.

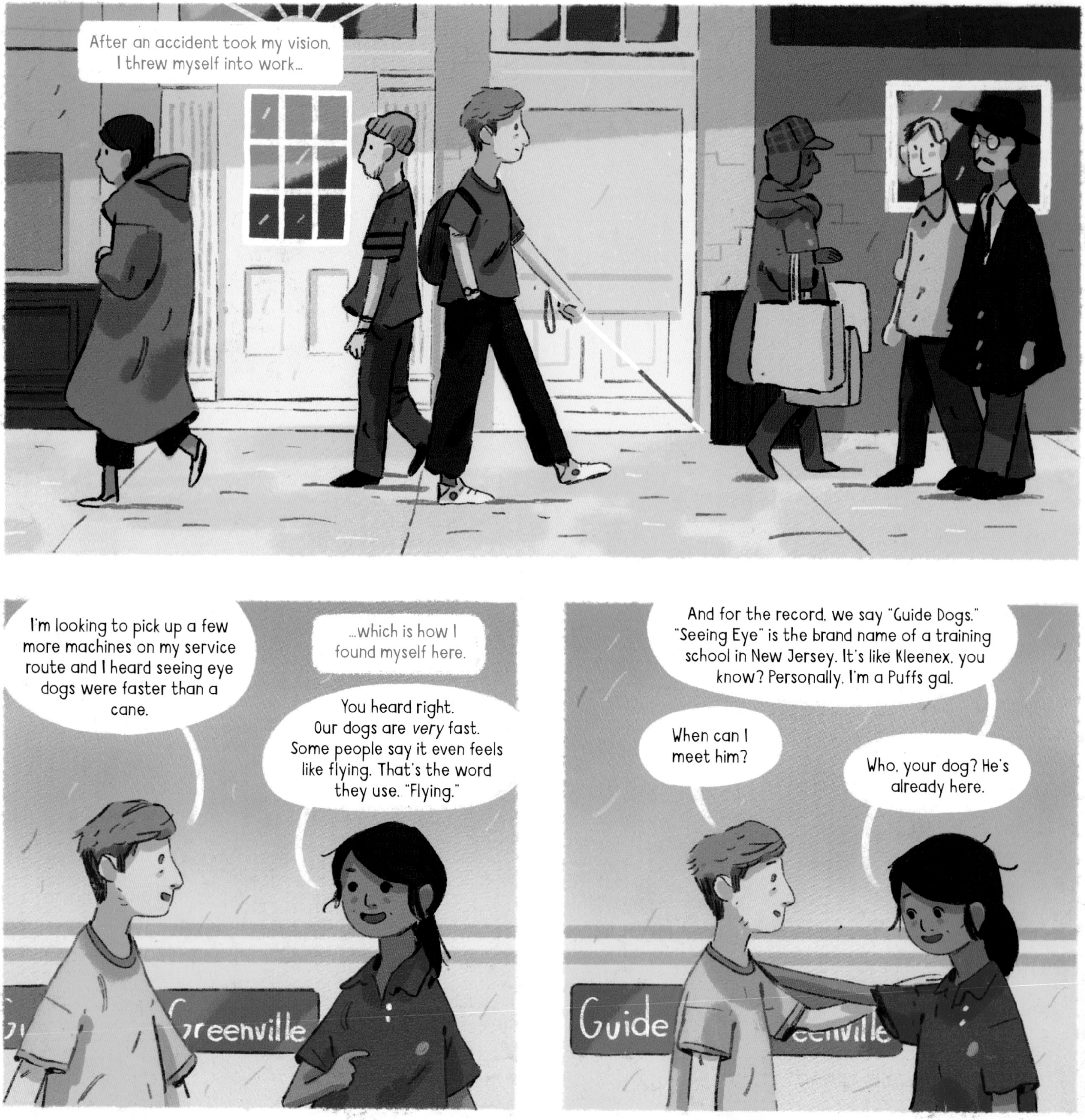
After an accident took my vision, I threw myself into work...
I'm looking to pick up a few more machines on my service route and I heard seeing eye dogs were faster than a cane.
...which is how I found myself here.
You heard right. Our dogs are *very* fast. Some people say it even feels like flying. That's the word they use. "Flying."
Greenville
And for the record, we say "Guide Dogs." "Seeing Eye" is the brand name of a training school in New Jersey. It's like Kleenex, you know? Personally, I'm a Puffs gal.
When can I meet him?
Who, your dog? He's already here.
Guide

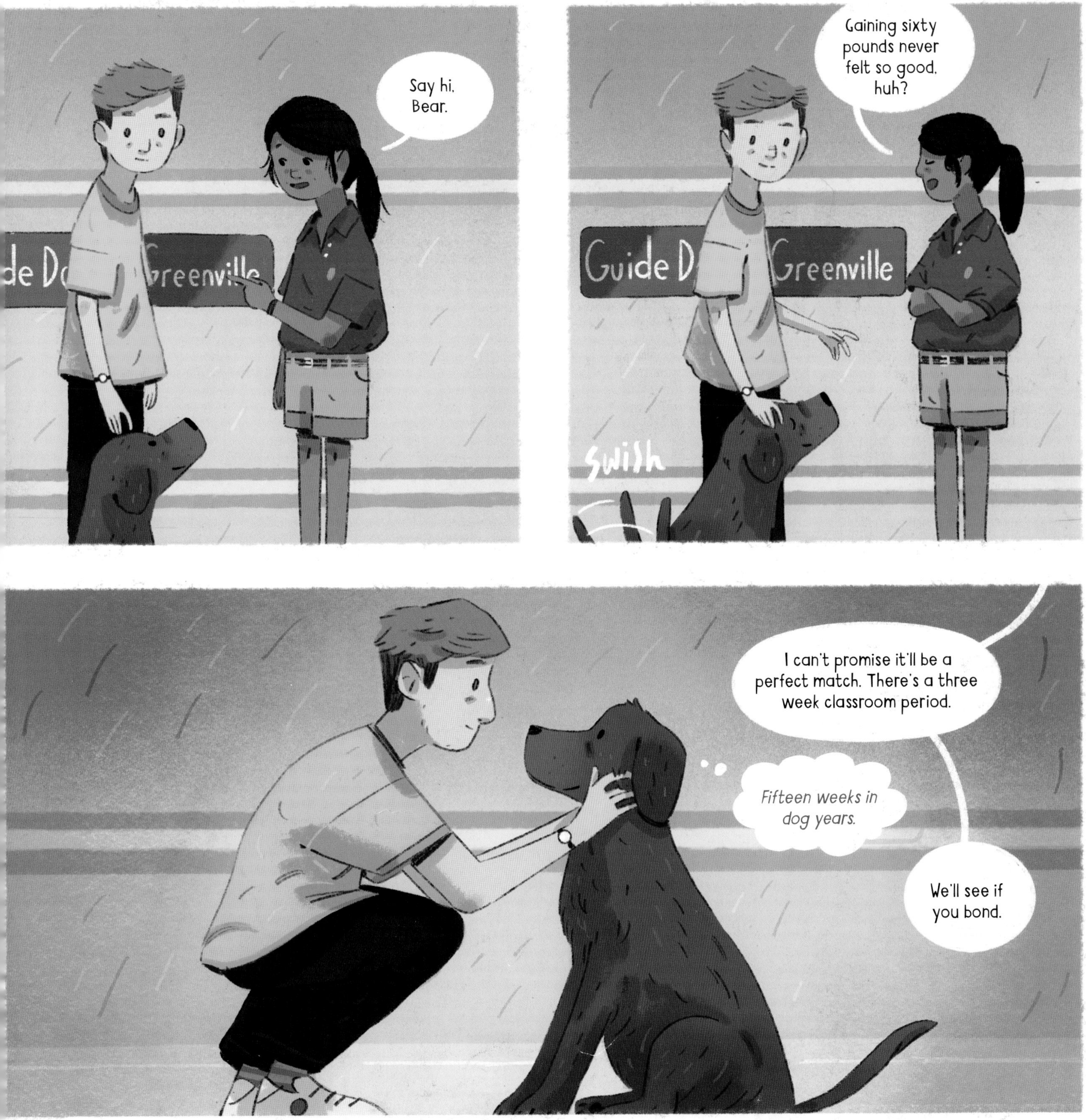
de D
Greenville
Say hi, Bear.
Guide D
Greenville
Gaining sixty pounds never felt so good, huh?
SWISH
I can't promise it'll be a perfect match. There's a three week classroom period.
Fifteen weeks in dog years.
We'll see if you bond.

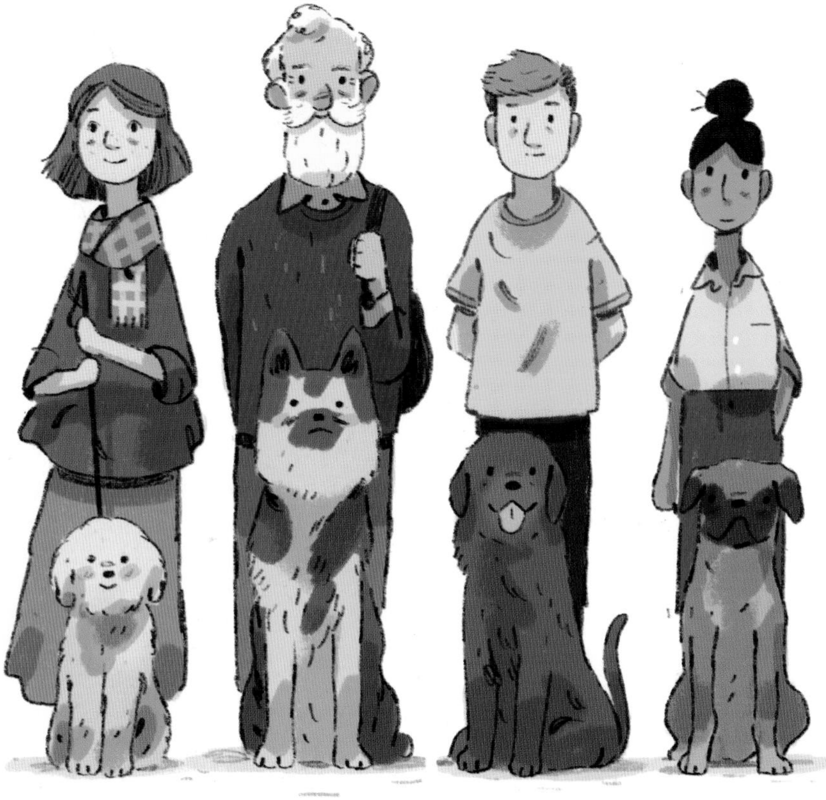

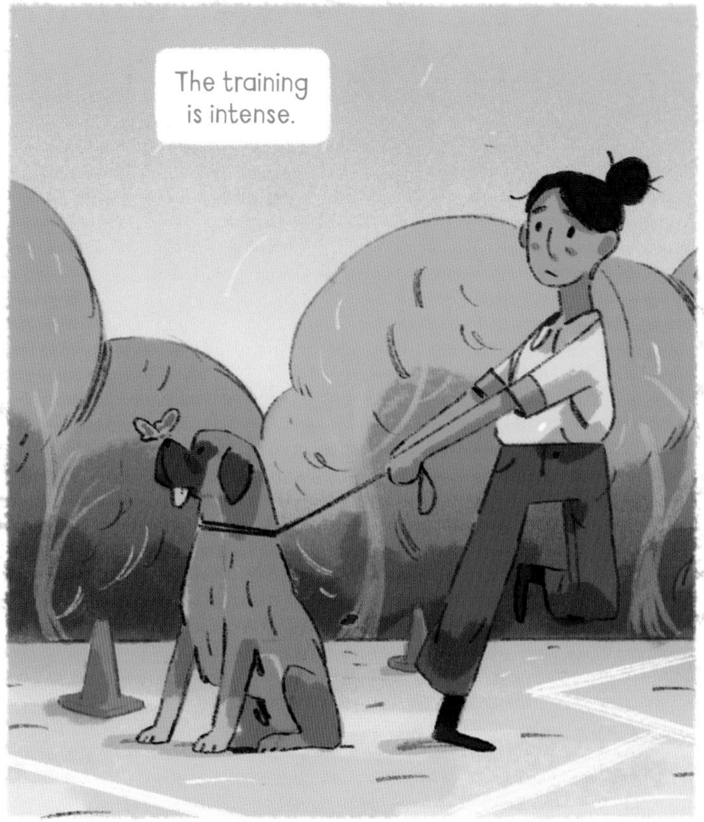
The training is intense.

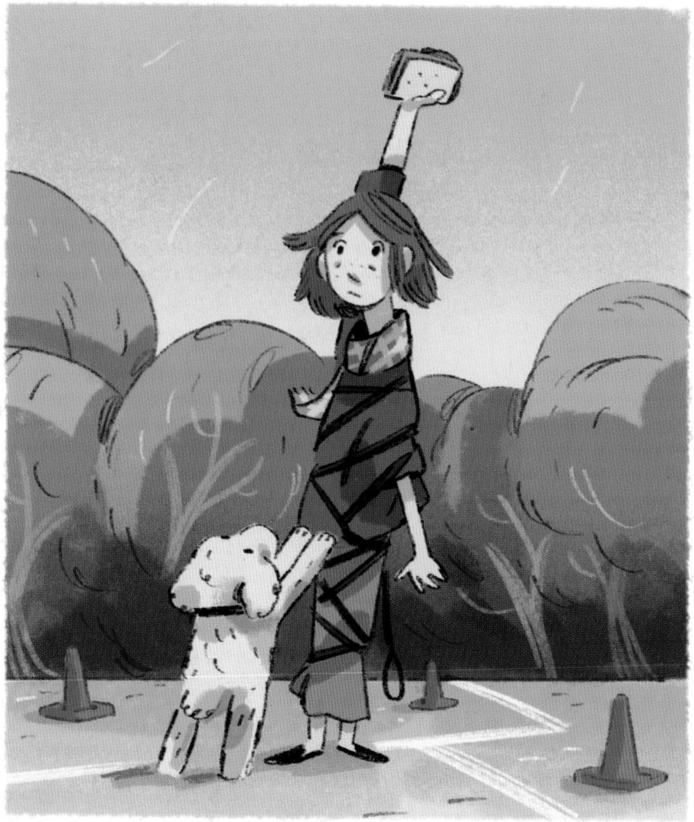

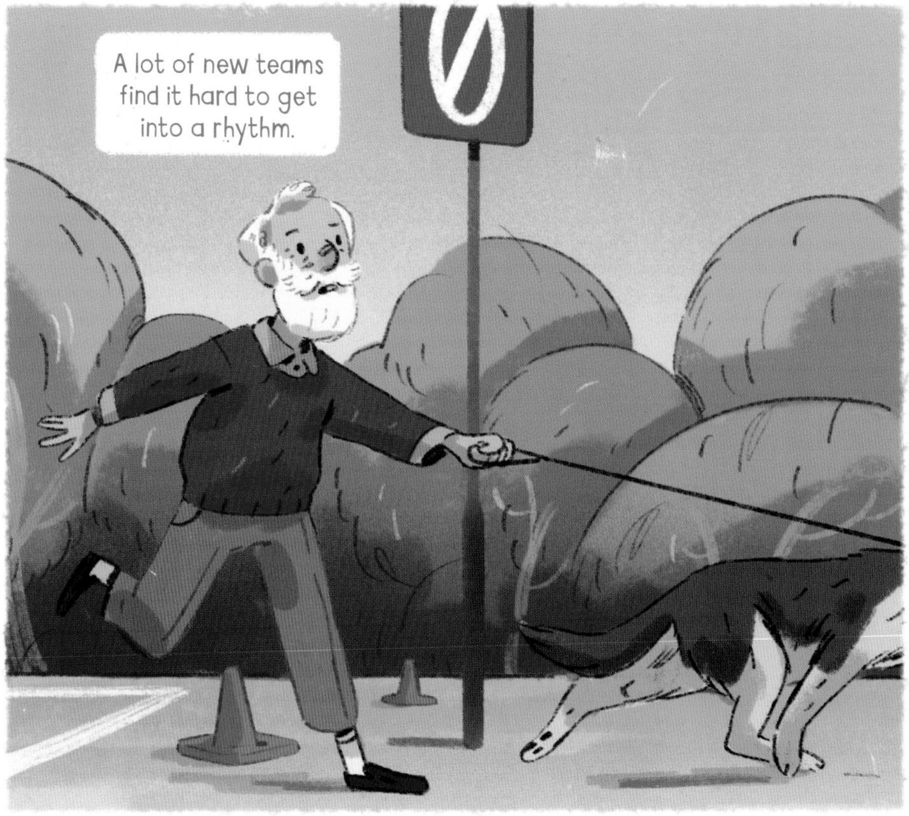
A lot of new teams find it hard to get into a rhythm.

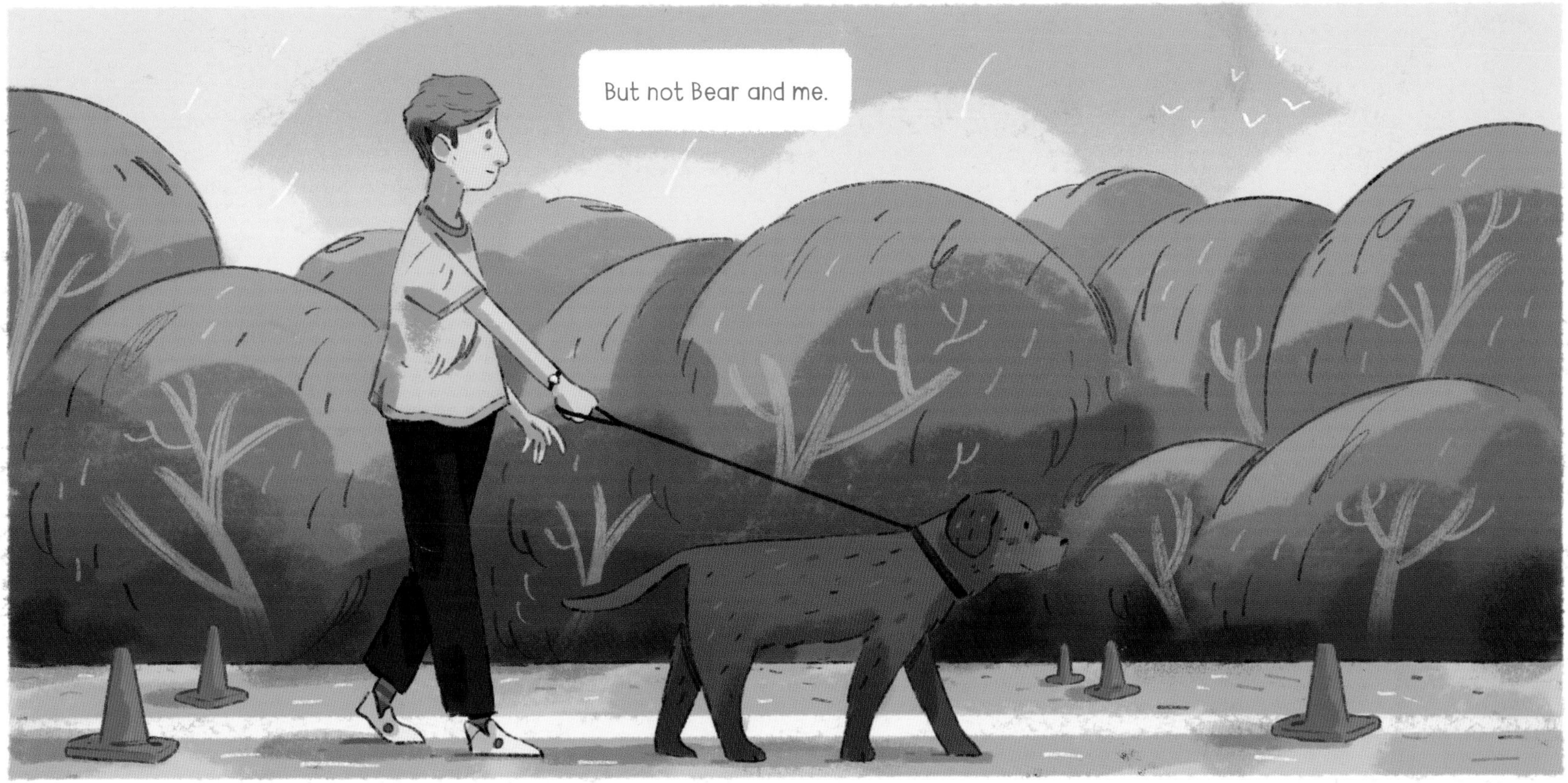
But not Bear and me.

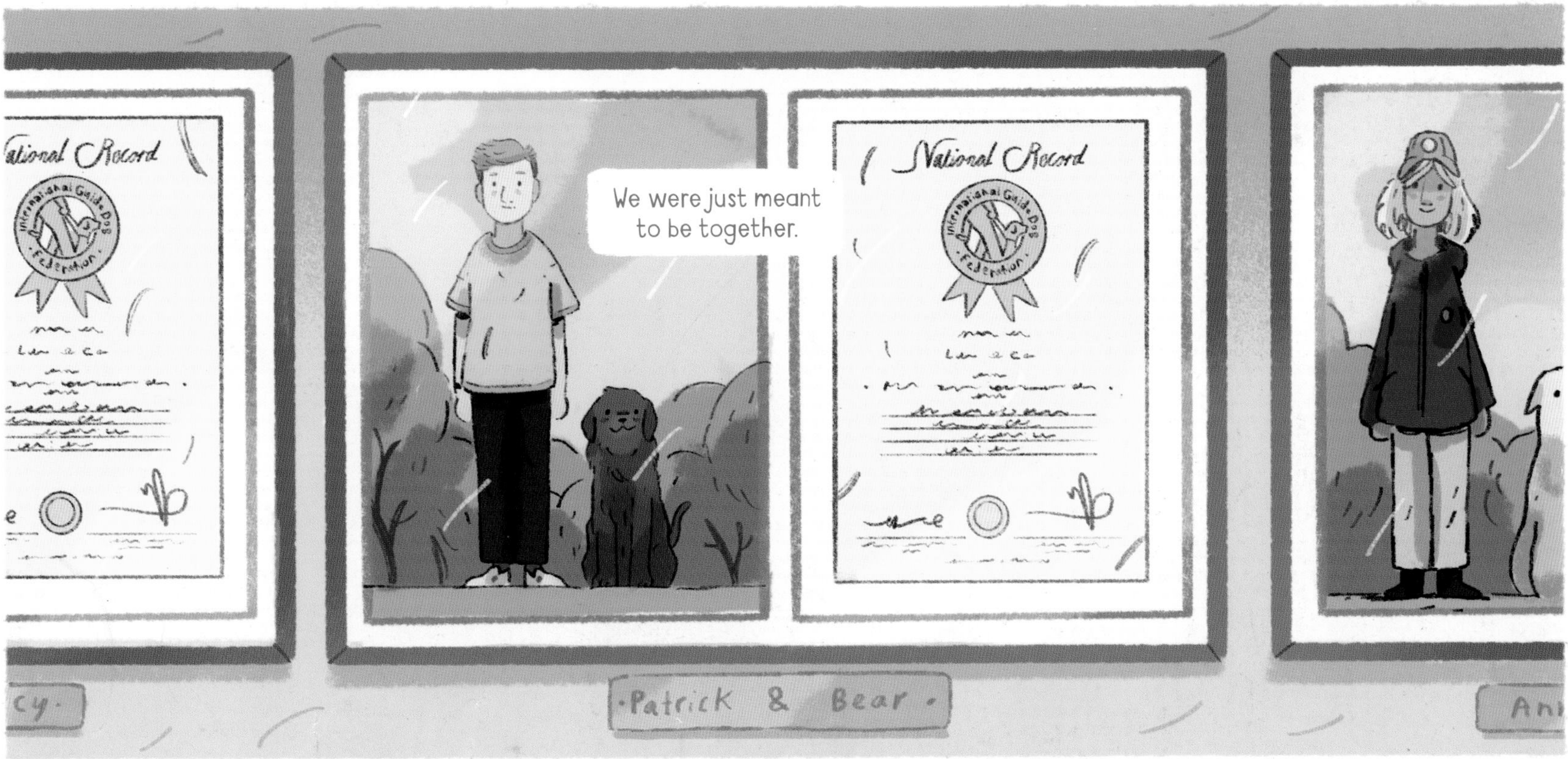
National Record
We were just meant to be together.
National Record
Patrick & Bear

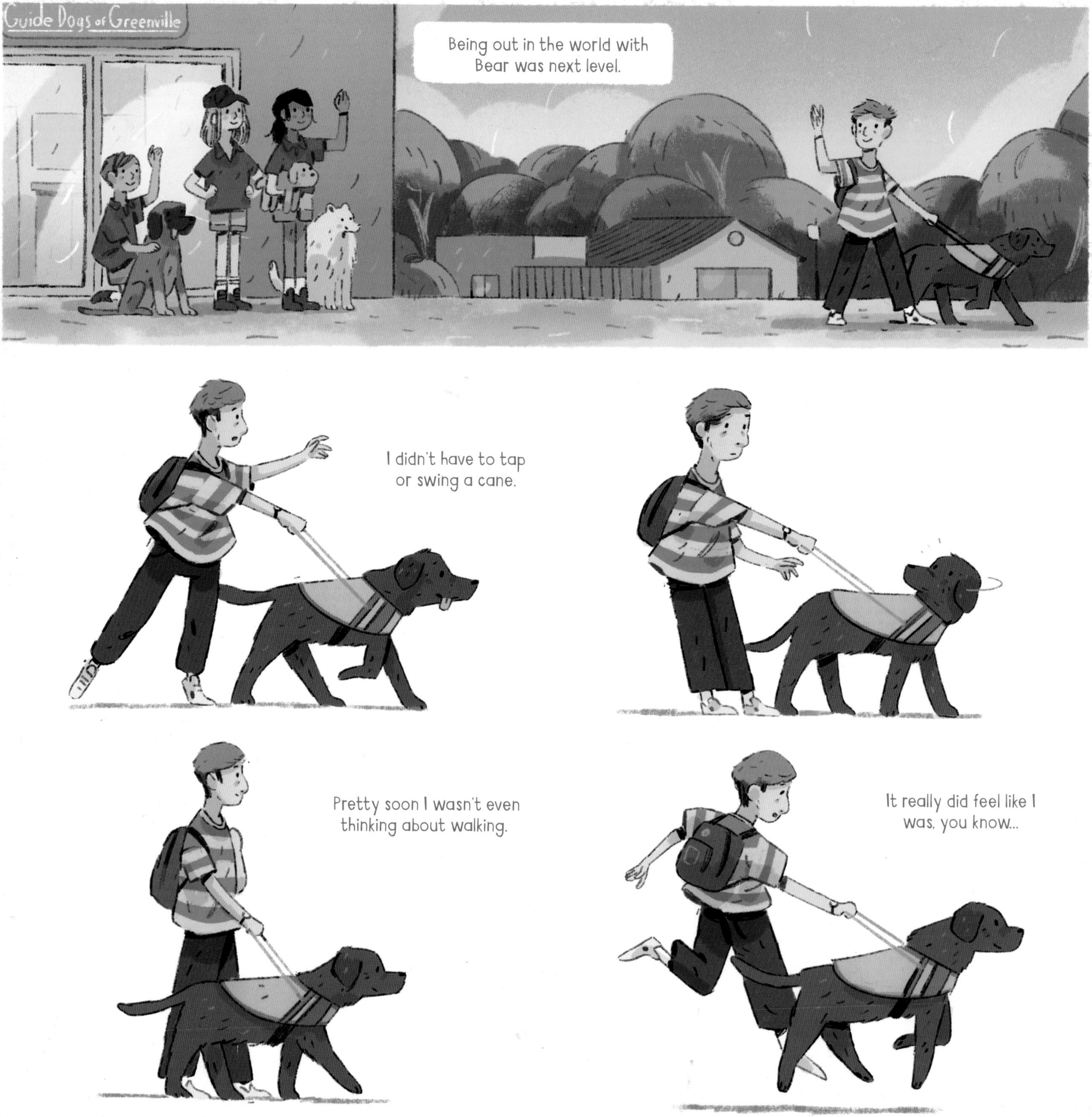
Guide Dogs of Greenville
Being out in the world with Bear was next level.
I didn't have to tap or swing a cane.
Pretty soon I wasn't even thinking about walking.
It really did feel like I was, you know...

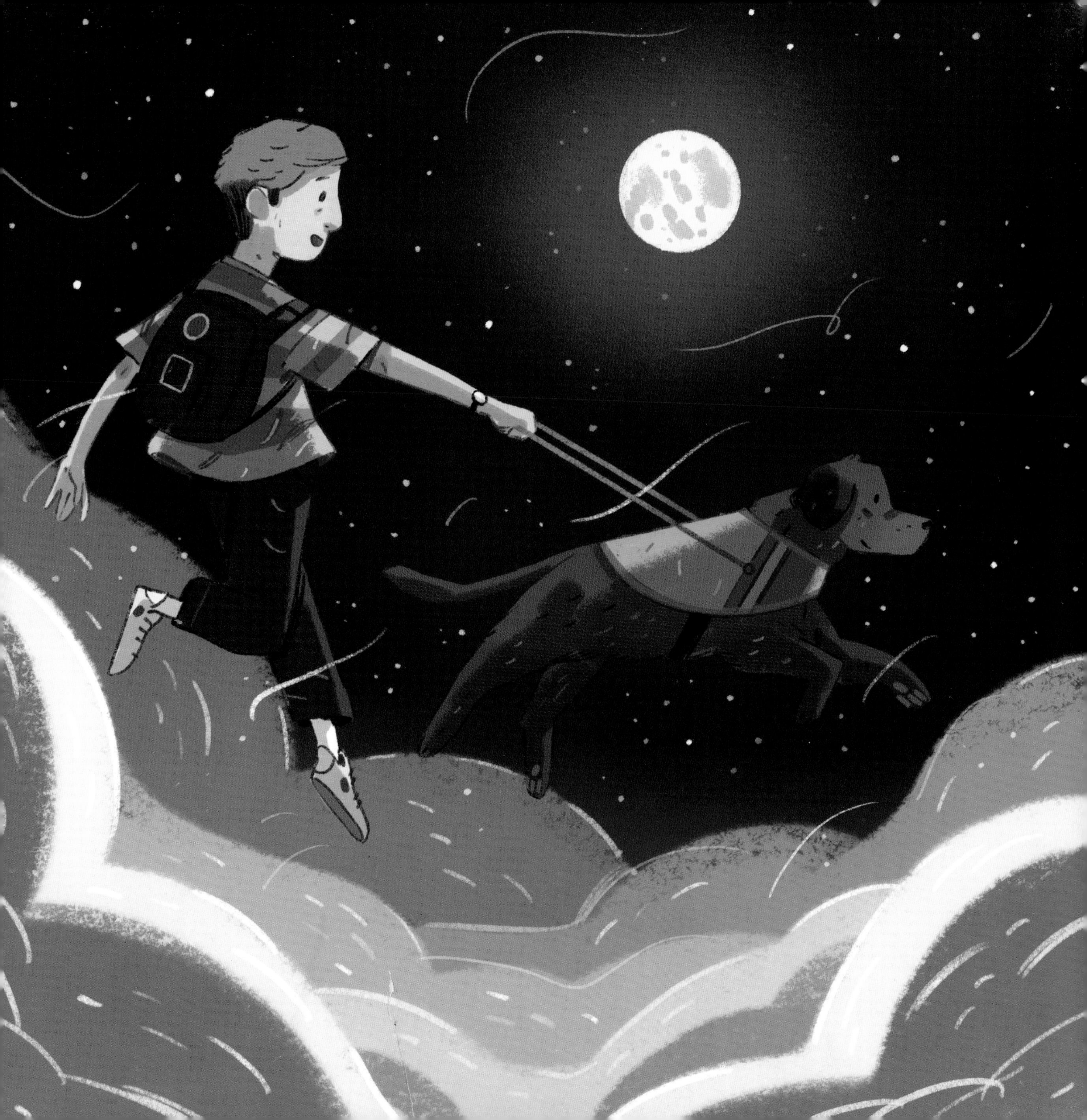

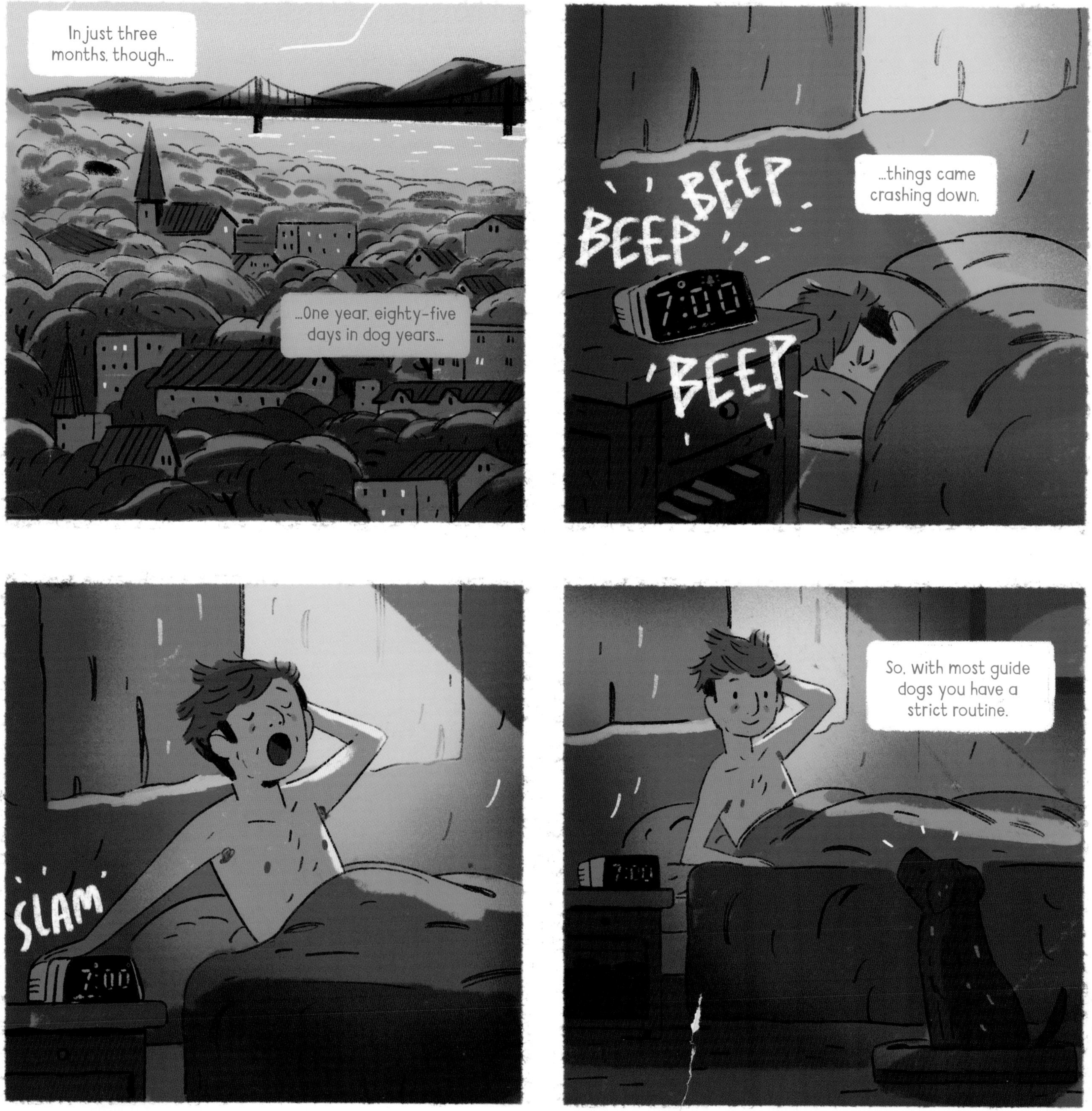
In just three months, though...
...One year, eighty-five days in dog years...
BEEP BEEP
BEEP
...things came crashing down.
7:00
SLAM
7:00
So, with most guide dogs you have a strict routine.
7:00

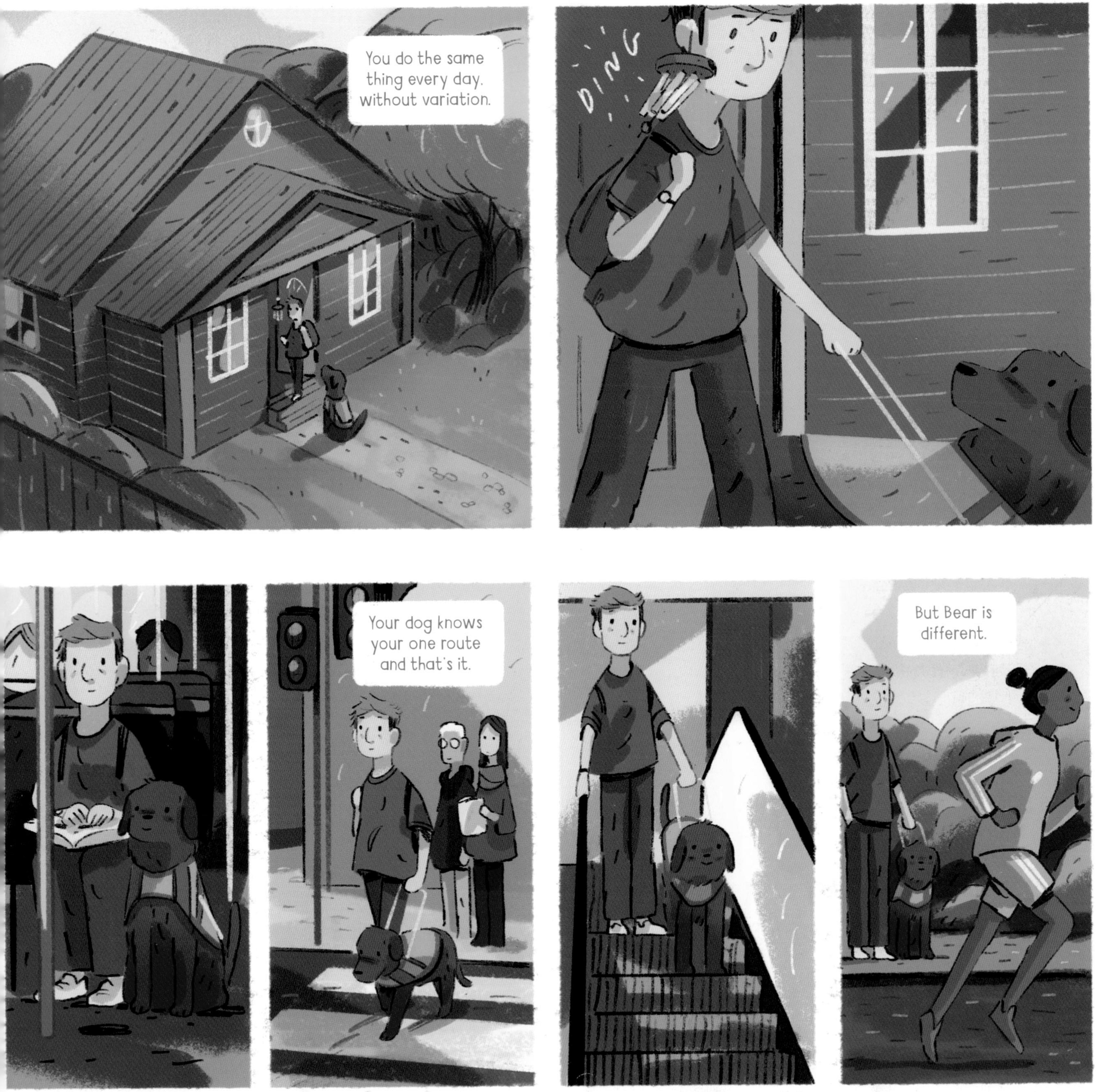
You do the same thing every day, without variation.
DING
Your dog knows your one route and that's it.
But Bear is different.

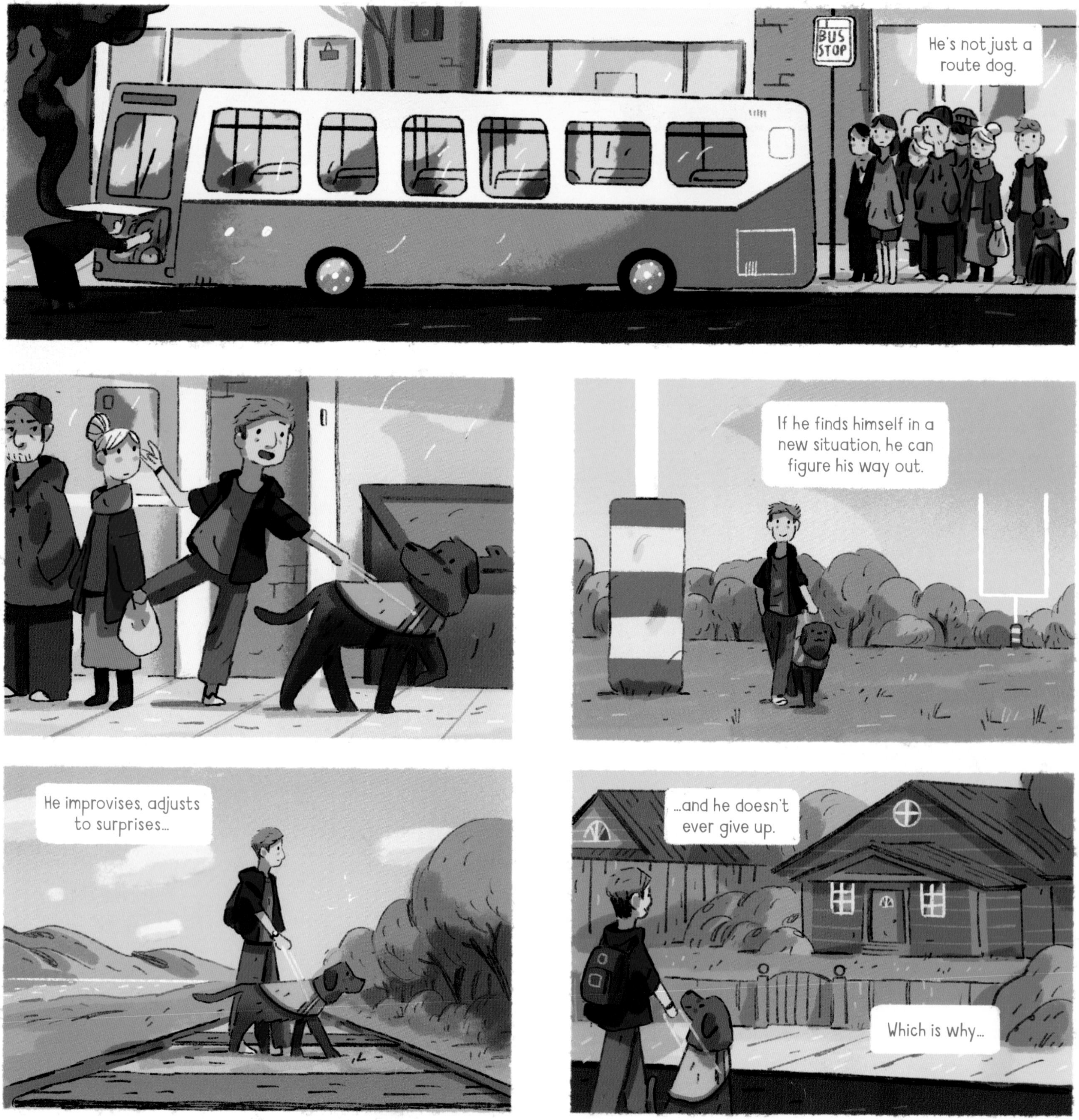
BUS STOP
He's not just a route dog.
If he finds himself in a new situation, he can figure his way out.
He improvises, adjusts to surprises...
...and he doesn't ever give up.
Which is why...

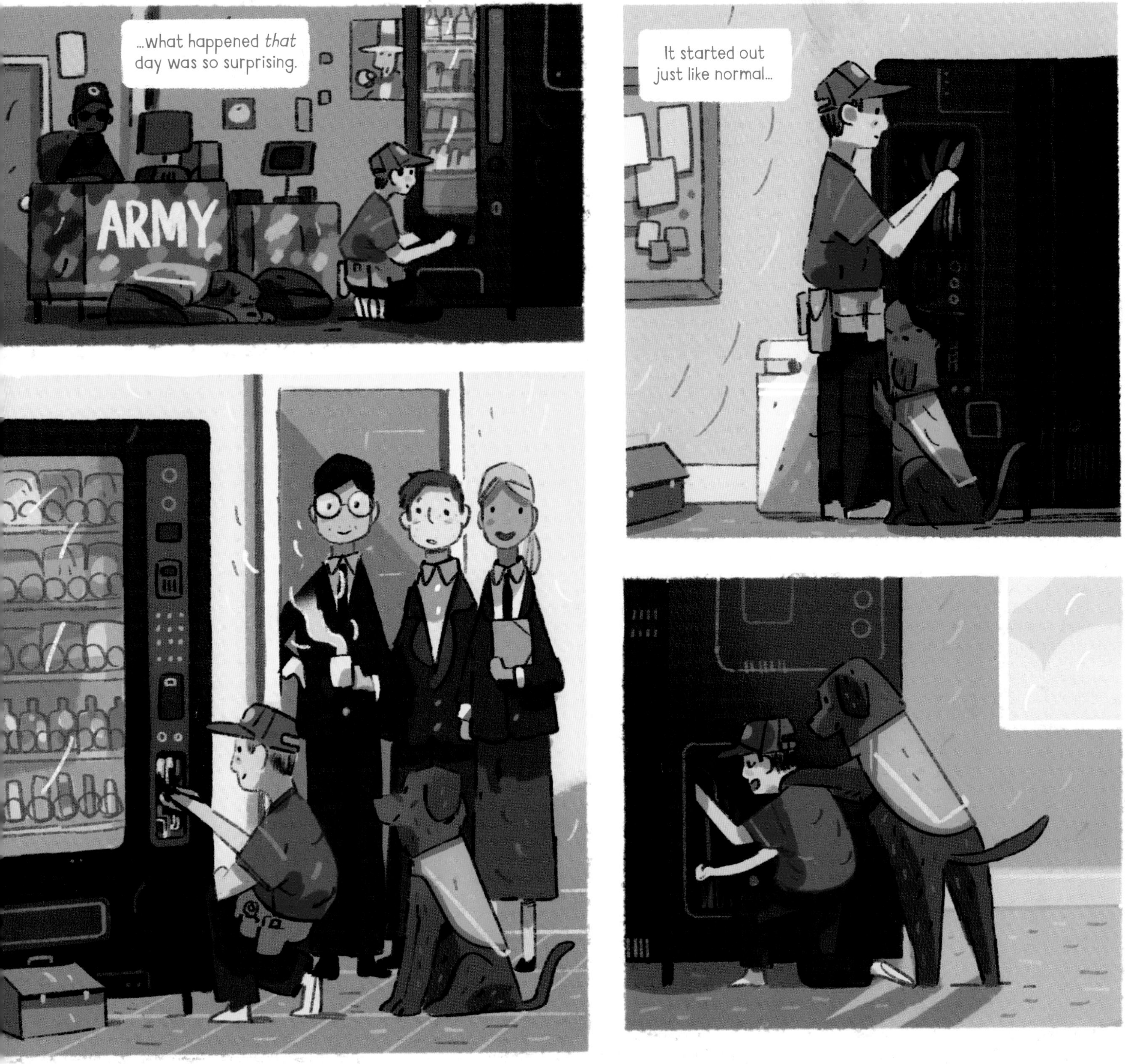
...what happened *that* day was so surprising.
ARMY
It started out just like normal...

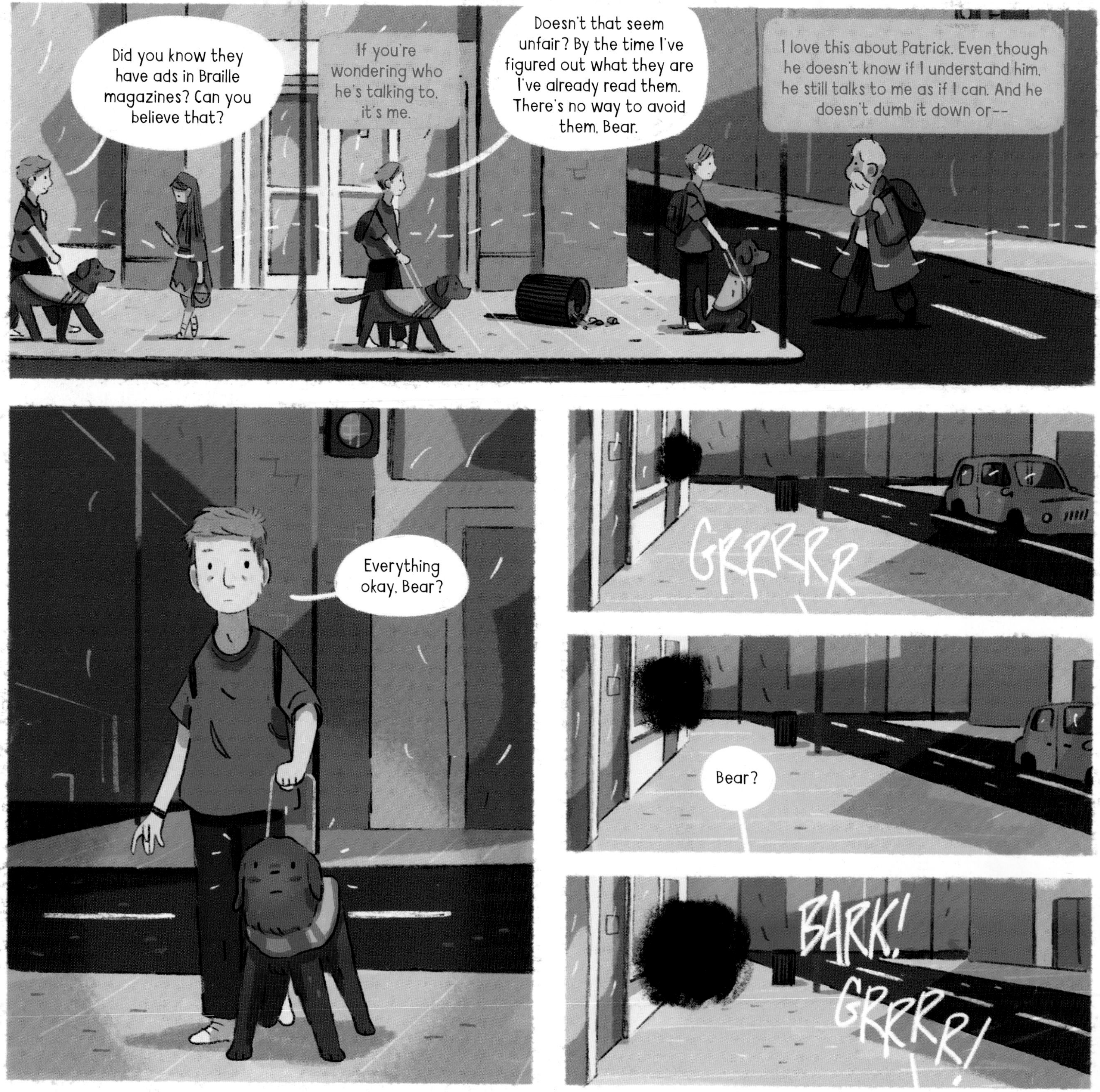
Did you know they have ads in Braille magazines? Can you believe that?
If you're wondering who he's talking to, it's me.
Doesn't that seem unfair? By the time I've figured out what they are I've already read them. There's no way to avoid them, Bear.
I love this about Patrick. Even though he doesn't know if I understand him, he still talks to me as if I can. And he doesn't dumb it down or--
Everything okay, Bear?
GRRRRR
Bear?
BARK!
GRRRR!

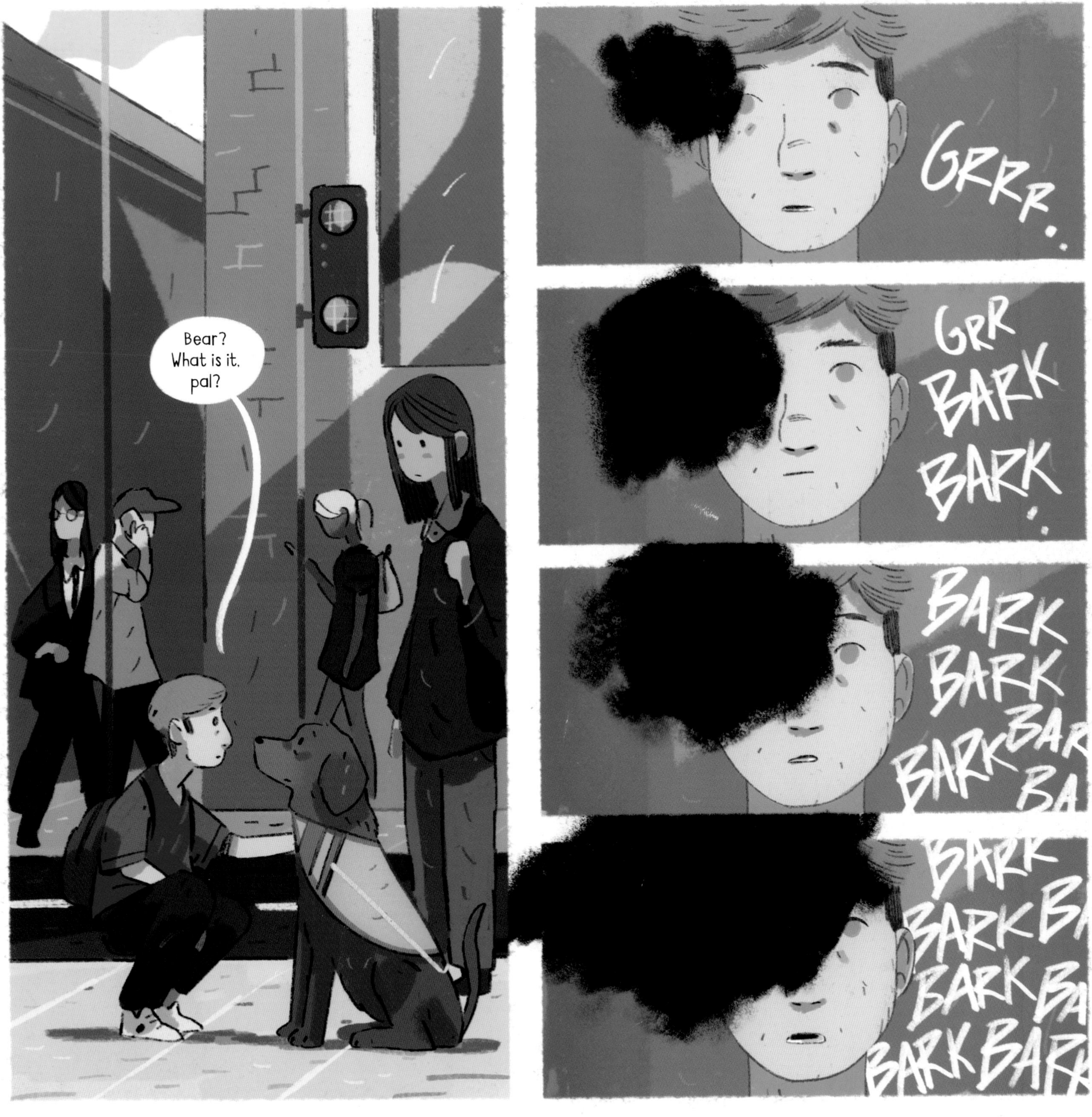
Bear? What is it, pal?
GRRR..
GRR
BARK
BARK..
BARK
BARK
BARK
BARK
BARK
BARK
BARK

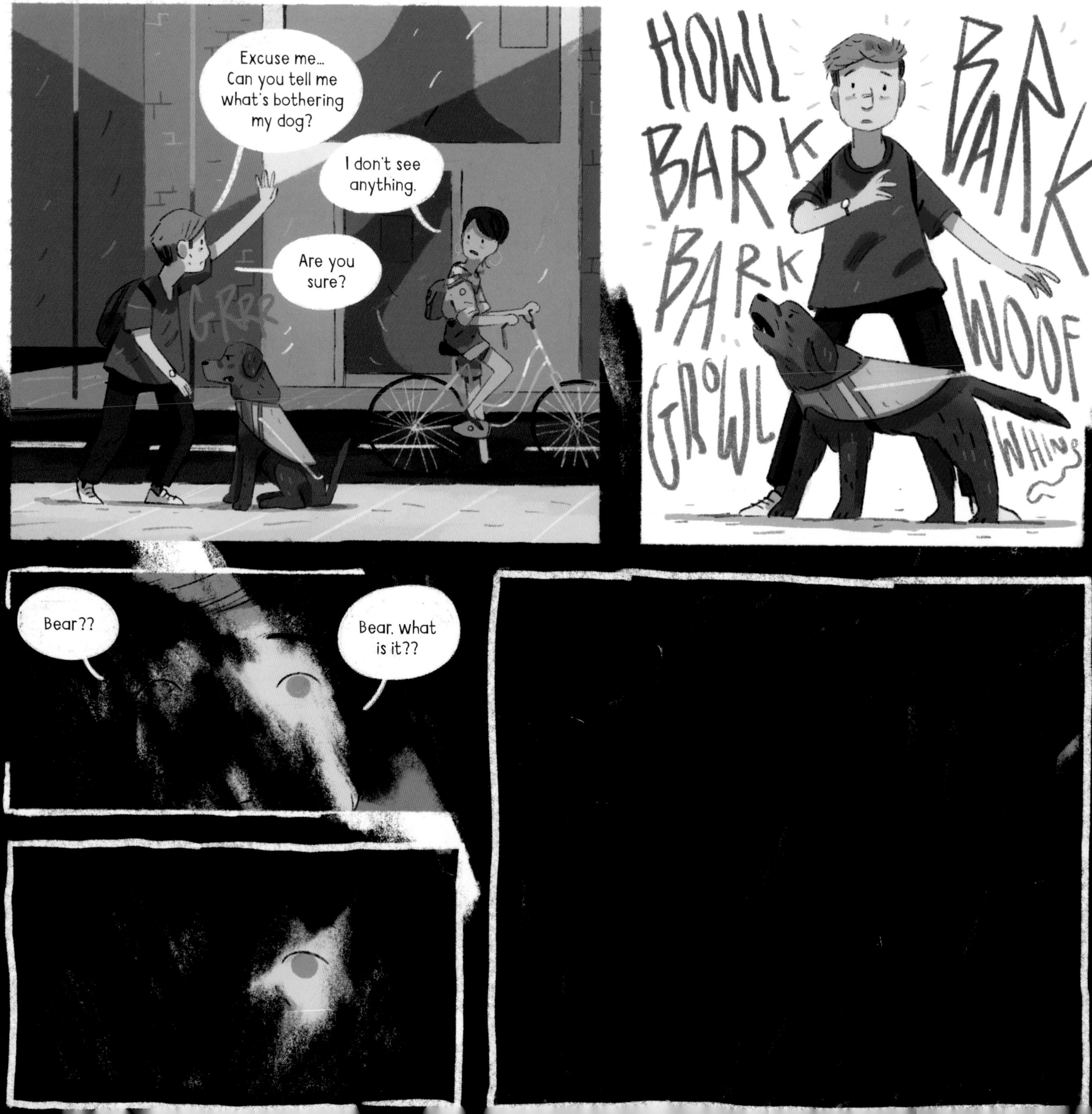

Excuse me... Can you tell me what's bothering my dog?
I don't see anything.
Are you sure?
GRRR
HOWL
BARK
BARK
GROWL
BARK
WOOF
WHINE
Bear??
Bear, what is it??

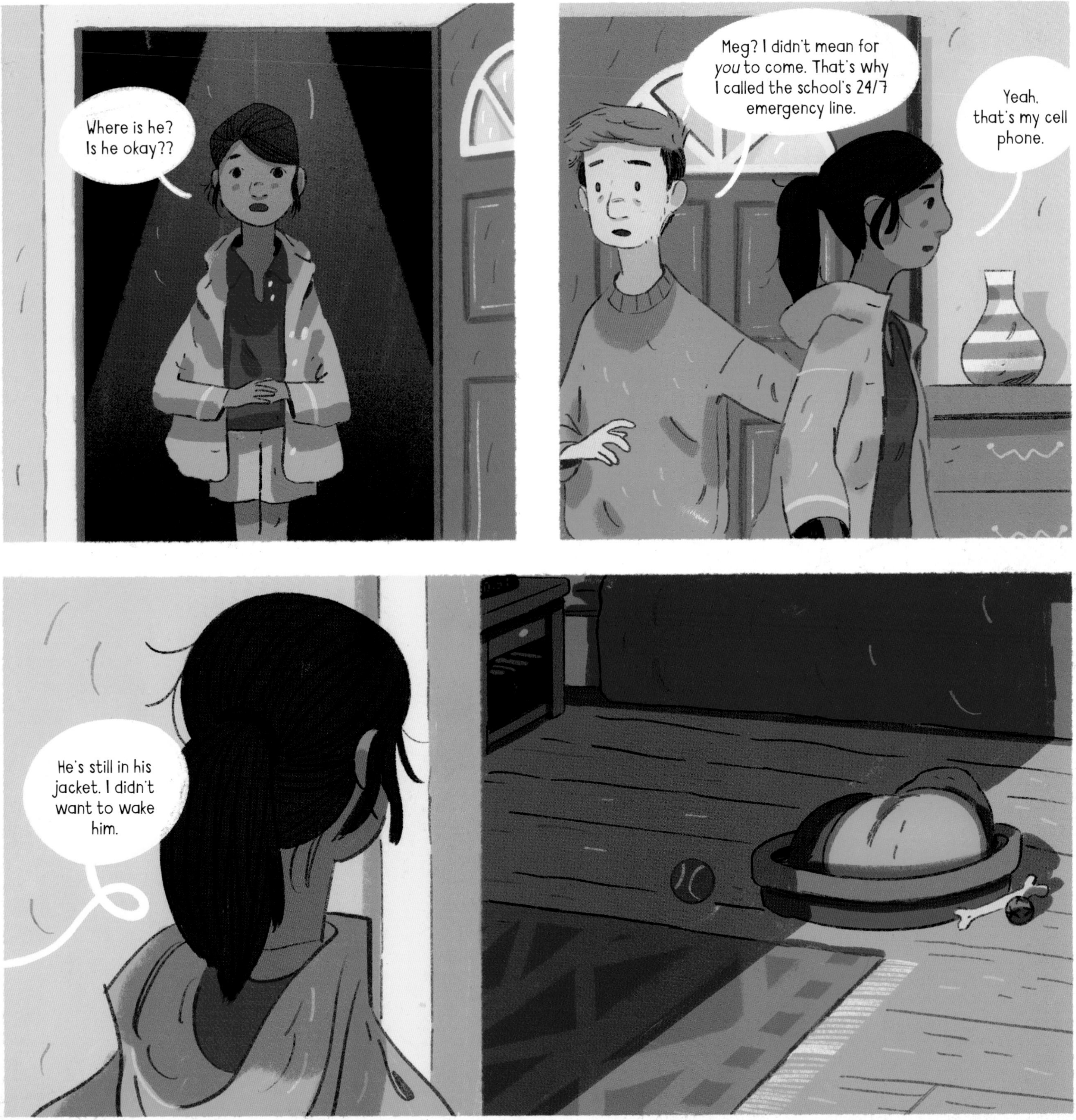
Where is he? Is he okay??
Meg? I didn't mean for *you* to come. That's why I called the school's 24/7 emergency line.
Yeah, that's my cell phone.
He's still in his jacket. I didn't want to wake him.

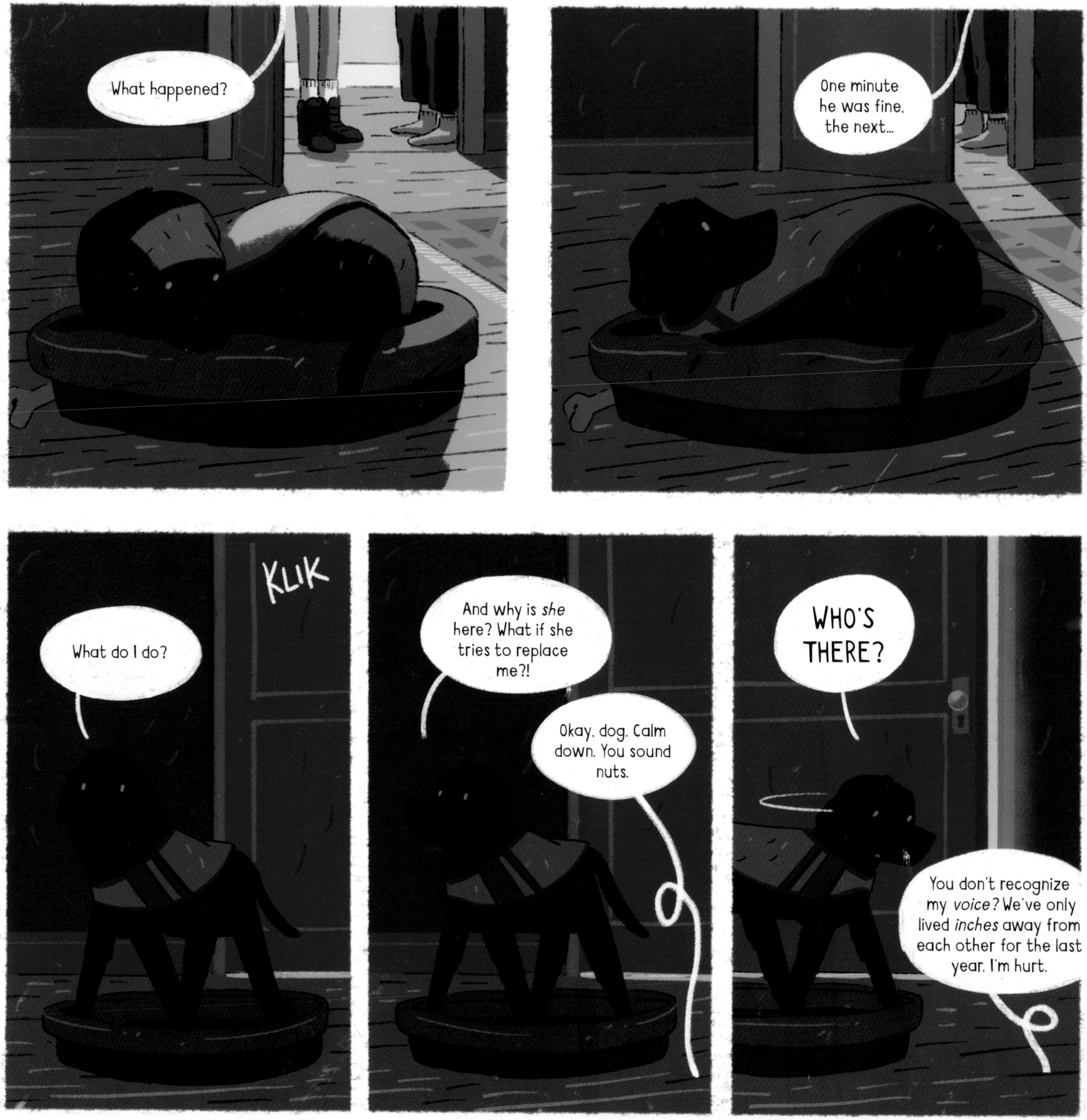
What happened?
One minute he was fine, the next...
KLIK
What do I do?
And why is *she* here? What if she tries to replace me?!
Okay, dog. Calm down. You sound nuts.
WHO'S THERE?
You don't recognize my *voice*? We've only lived *inches* away from each other for the last year. I'm hurt.

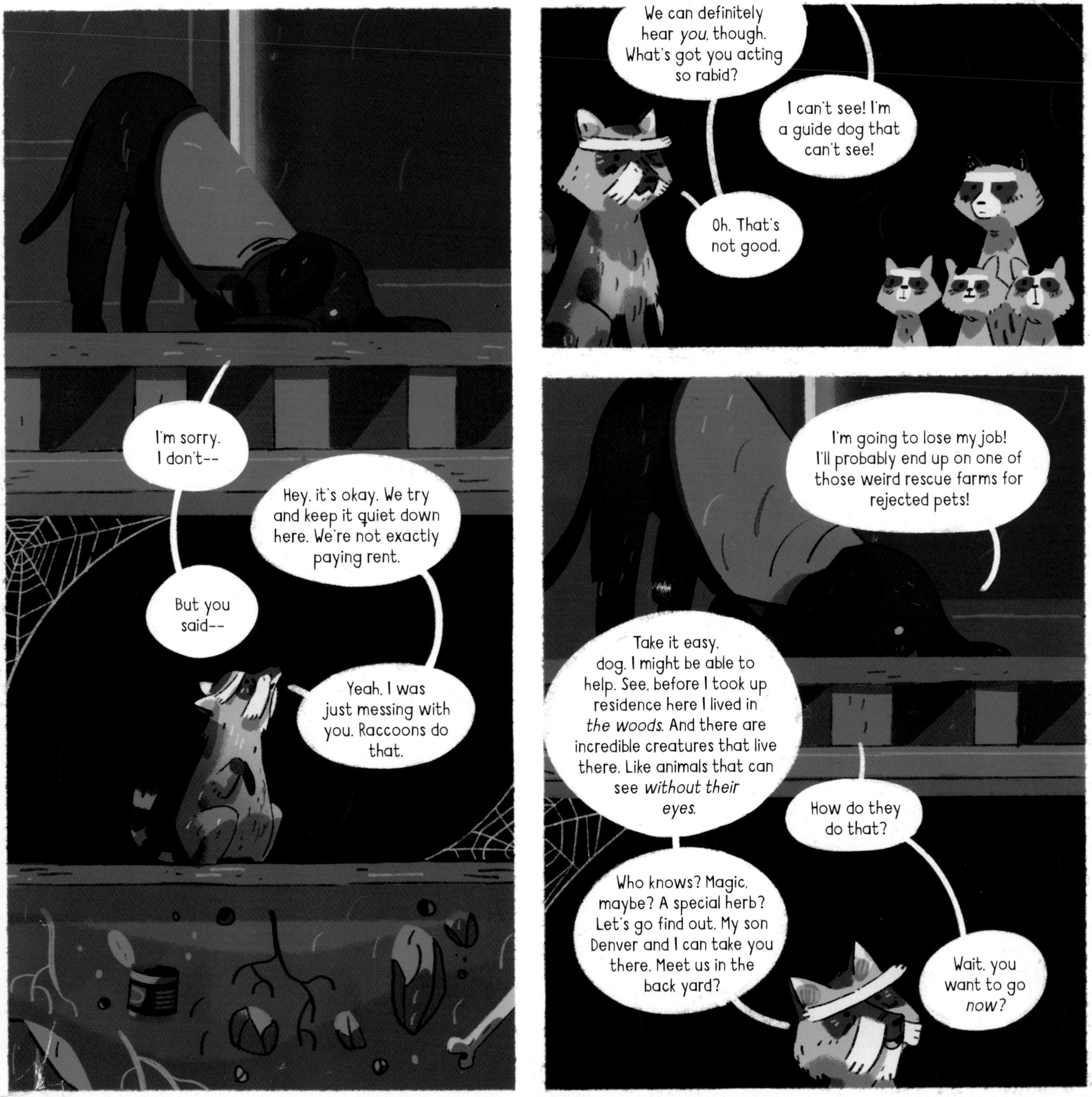
I'm sorry. I don't--
Hey, it's okay. We try and keep it quiet down here. We're not exactly paying rent.
But you said--
Yeah, I was just messing with you. Raccoons do that.
We can definitely hear *you*, though. What's got you acting so rabid?
I can't see! I'm a guide dog that can't see!
Oh. That's not good.
I'm going to lose my job! I'll probably end up on one of those weird rescue farms for rejected pets!
Take it easy, dog. I might be able to help. See, before I took up residence here I lived in *the woods*. And there are incredible creatures that live there. Like animals that can see *without their eyes*.
How do they do that?
Who knows? Magic, maybe? A special herb? Let's go find out. My son Denver and I can take you there. Meet us in the back yard?
Wait, you want to go *now*?

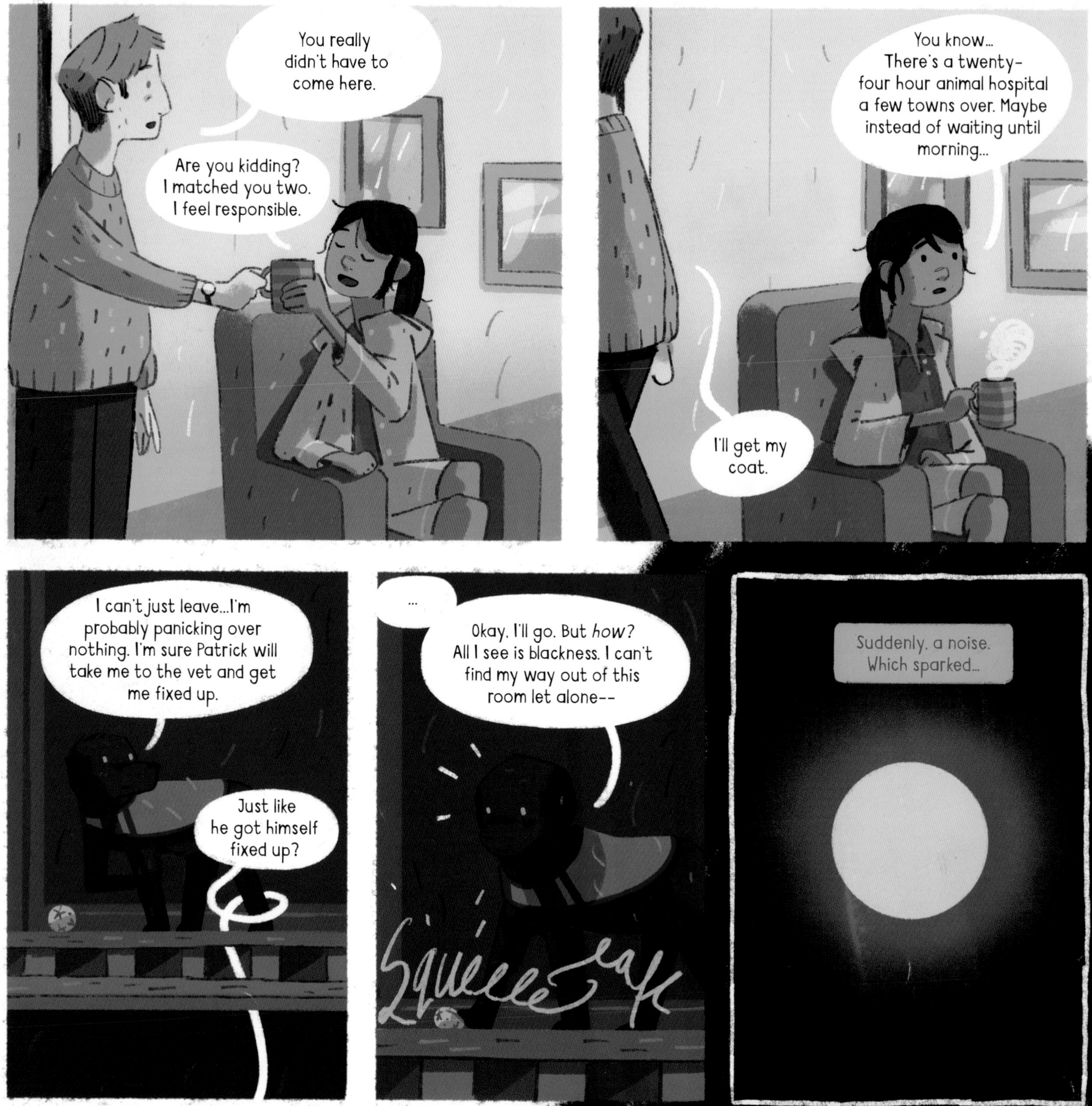
You really didn't have to come here.
Are you kidding? I matched you two. I feel responsible.
You know... There's a twenty-four hour animal hospital a few towns over. Maybe instead of waiting until morning...
I'll get my coat.
I can't just leave...I'm probably panicking over nothing. I'm sure Patrick will take me to the vet and get me fixed up.
Just like he got himself fixed up?
...
Okay. I'll go. But *how?* All I see is blackness. I can't find my way out of this room let alone--
Suddenly, a noise. Which sparked...

a MEMORY

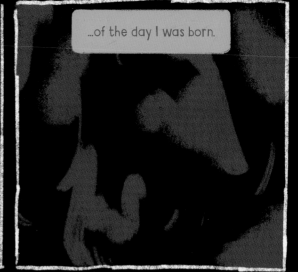

...of the day I was born.

I couldn't see then either.

But that's not unusual.

All dogs are blind for the first couple weeks.

My mom told me it was nature's way of protecting puppies.

Idea was, if we could see, we might wander off.

And wandering can be dangerous, Bear.

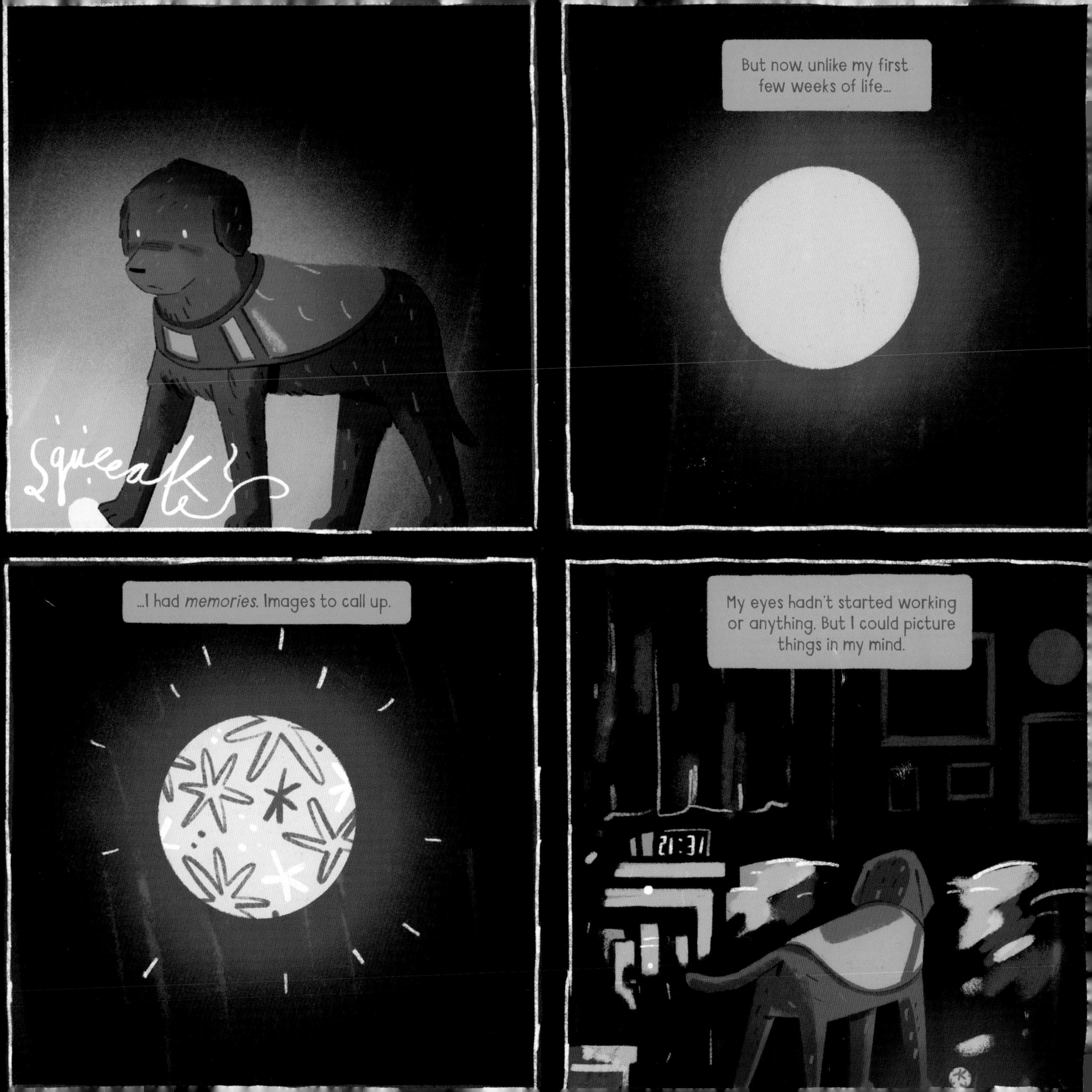
squeak
But now, unlike my first few weeks of life...
...I had *memories*. Images to call up.
My eyes hadn't started working or anything. But I could picture things in my mind.
21:31

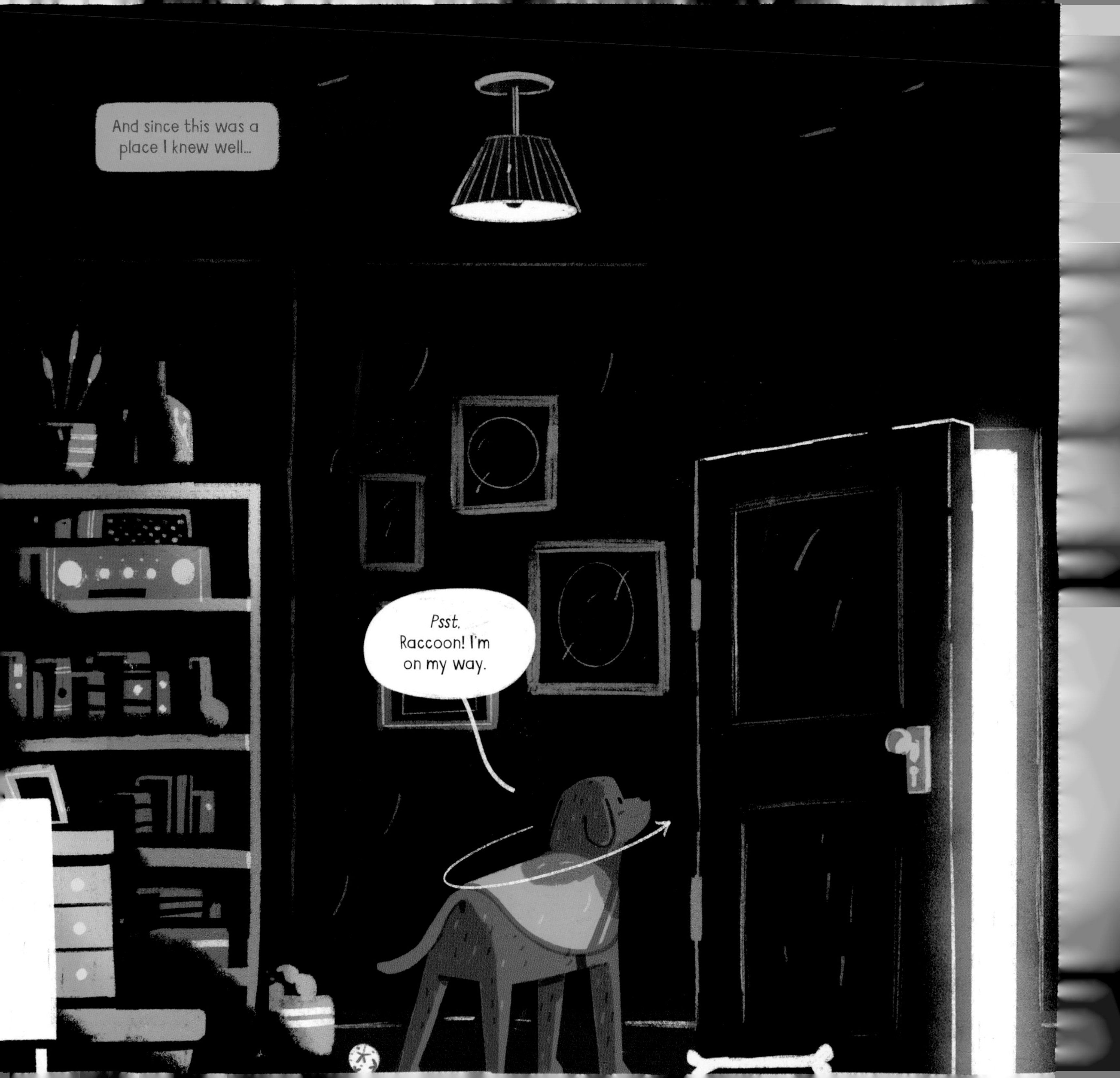
And since this was a place I knew well...
Psst. Raccoon! I'm on my way.

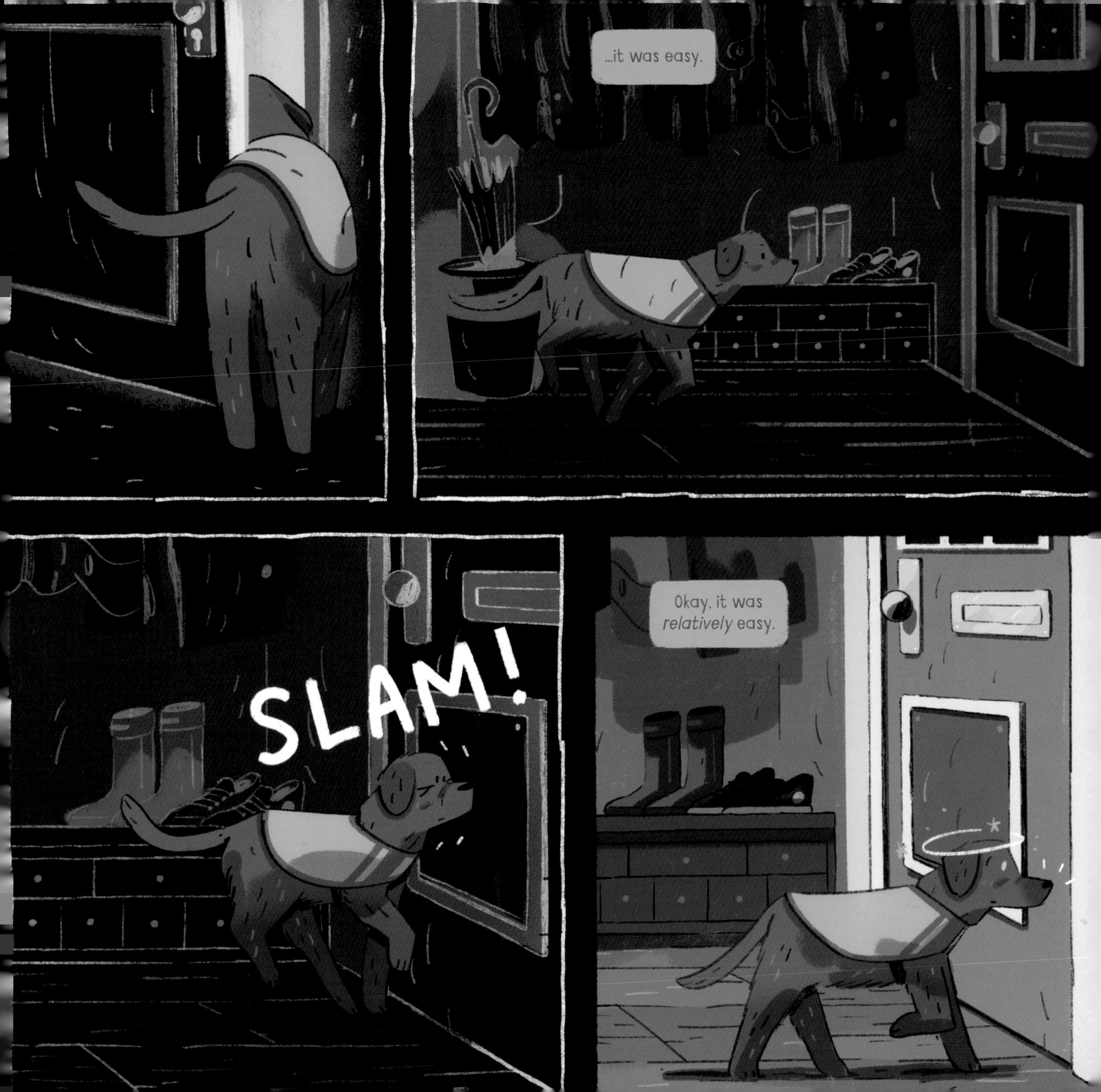
...it was easy.
SLAM!
Okay, it was *relatively* easy.

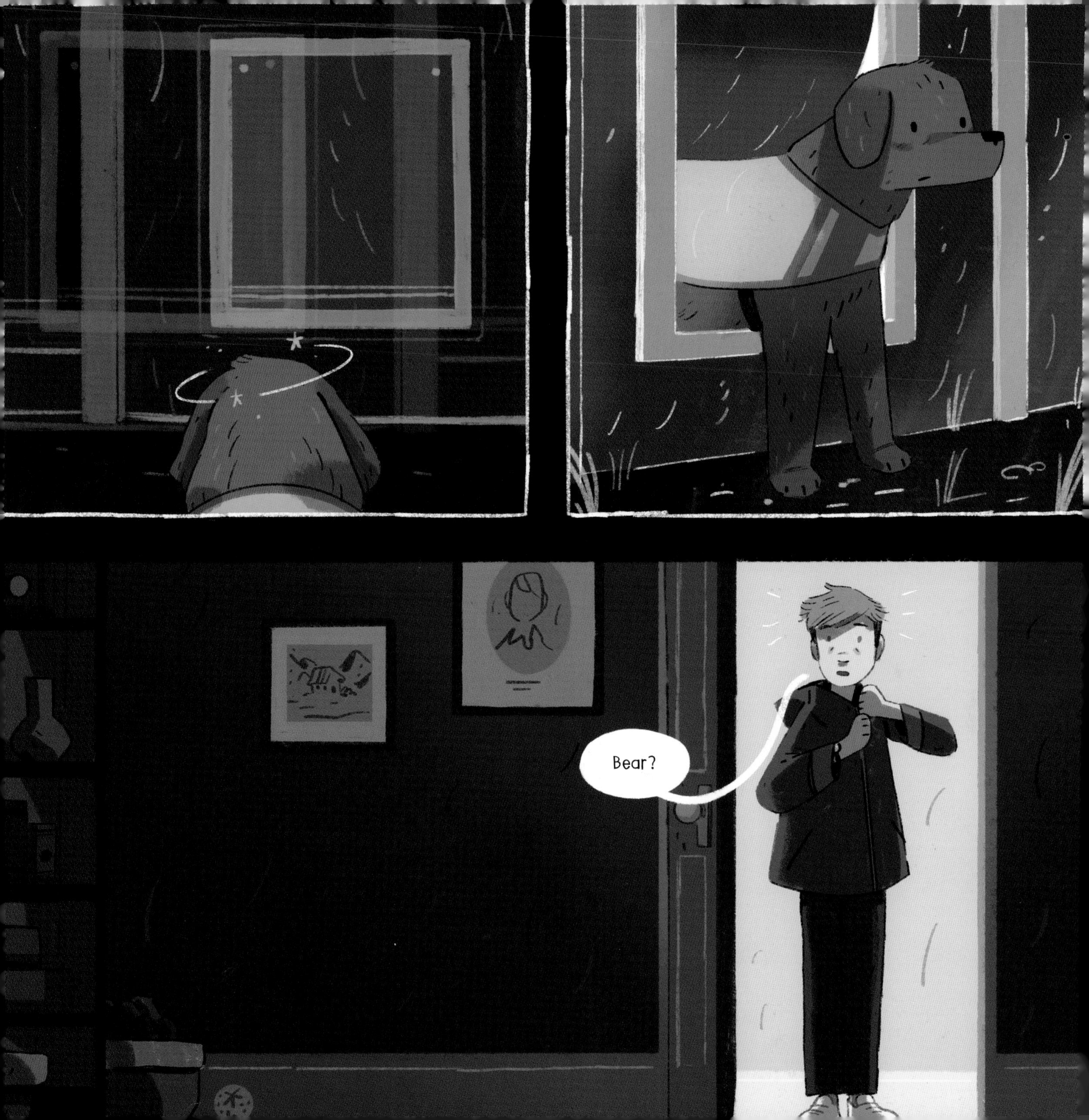
Bear?

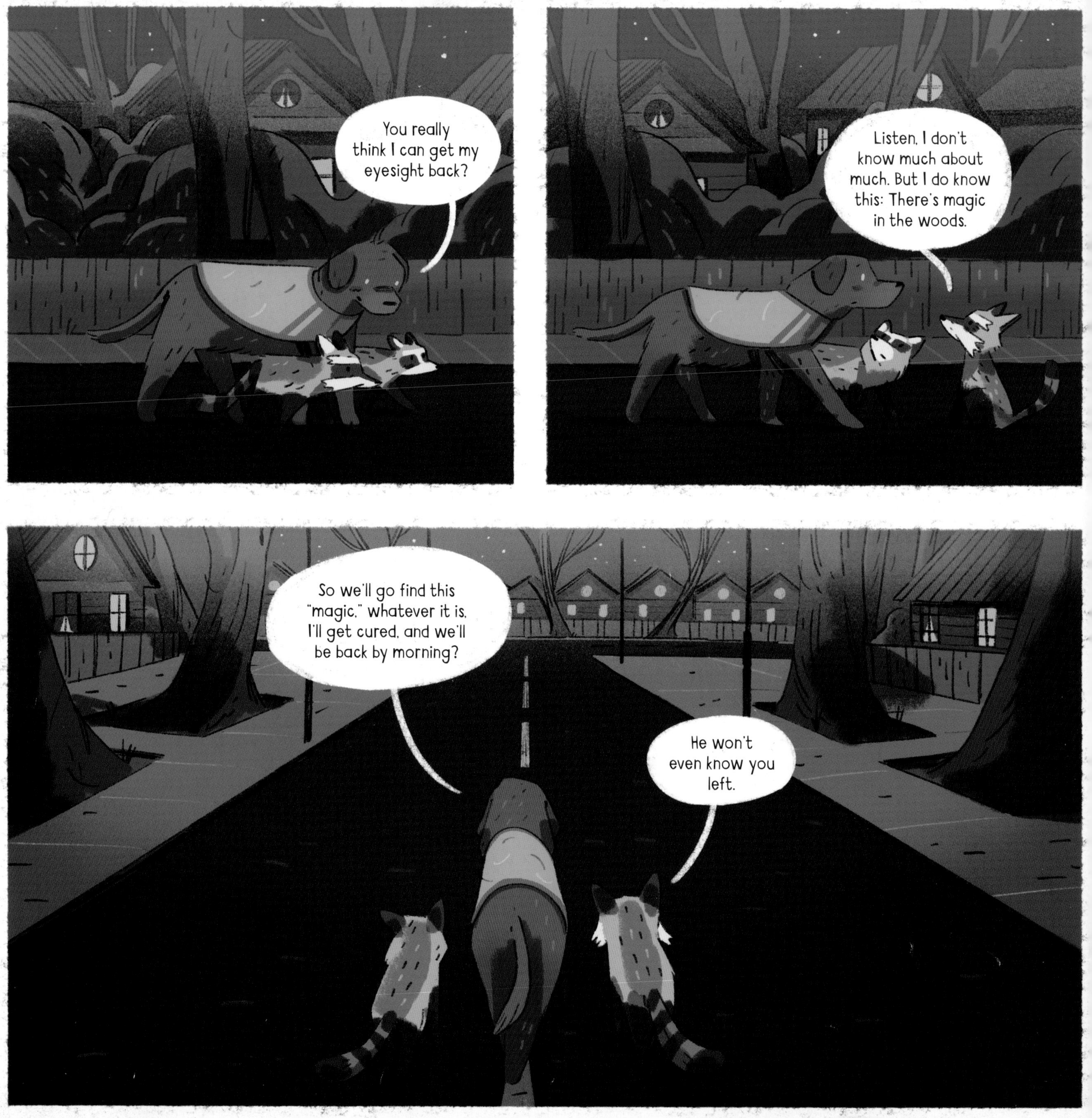
You really think I can get my eyesight back?
Listen. I don't know much about much. But I do know this: There's magic in the woods.
So we'll go find this "magic," whatever it is. I'll get cured, and we'll be back by morning?
He won't even know you left.

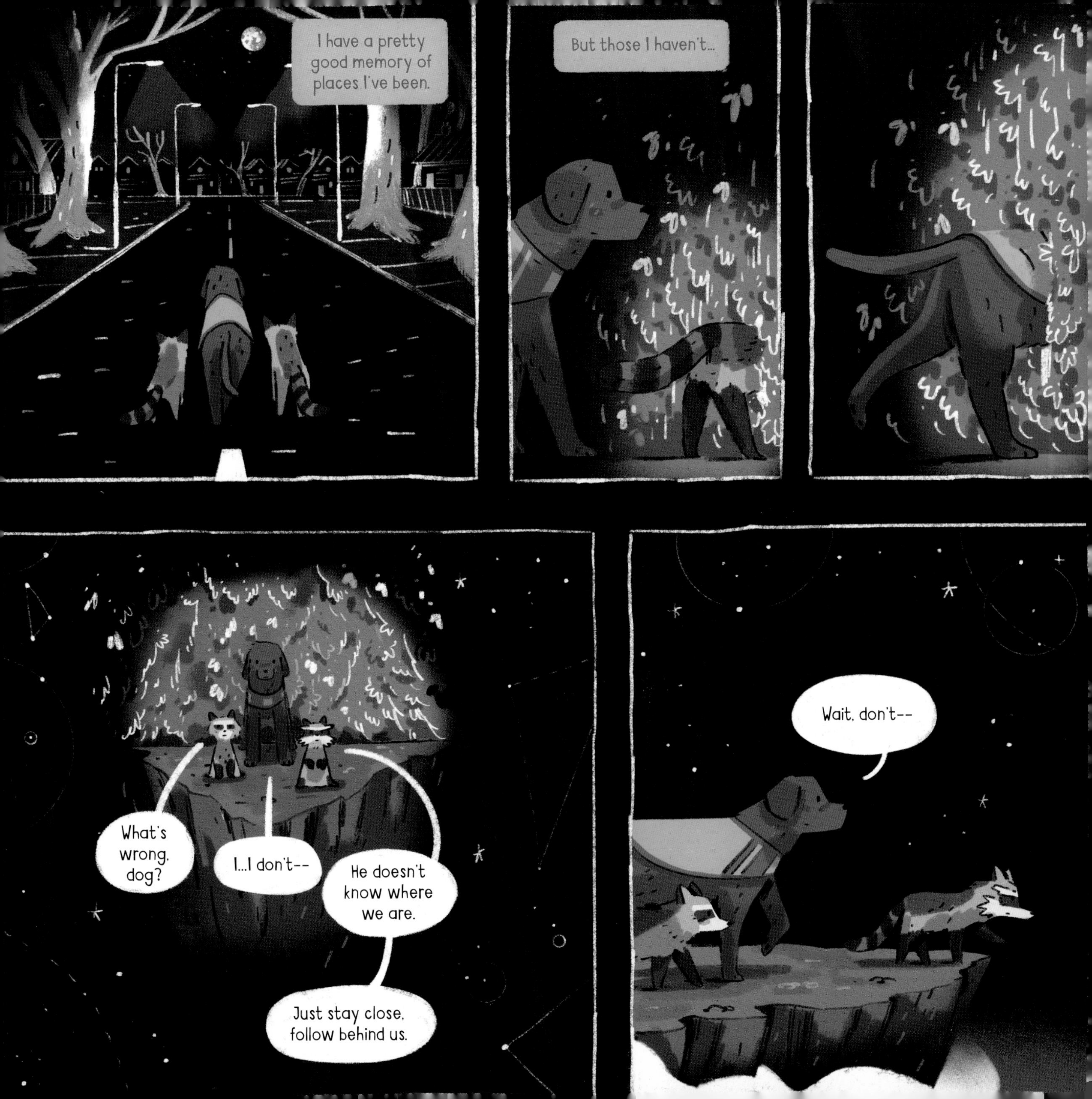
I have a pretty good memory of places I've been.
But those I haven't...
What's wrong, dog?
I...I don't--
He doesn't know where we are.
Just stay close, follow behind us.
Wait, don't--

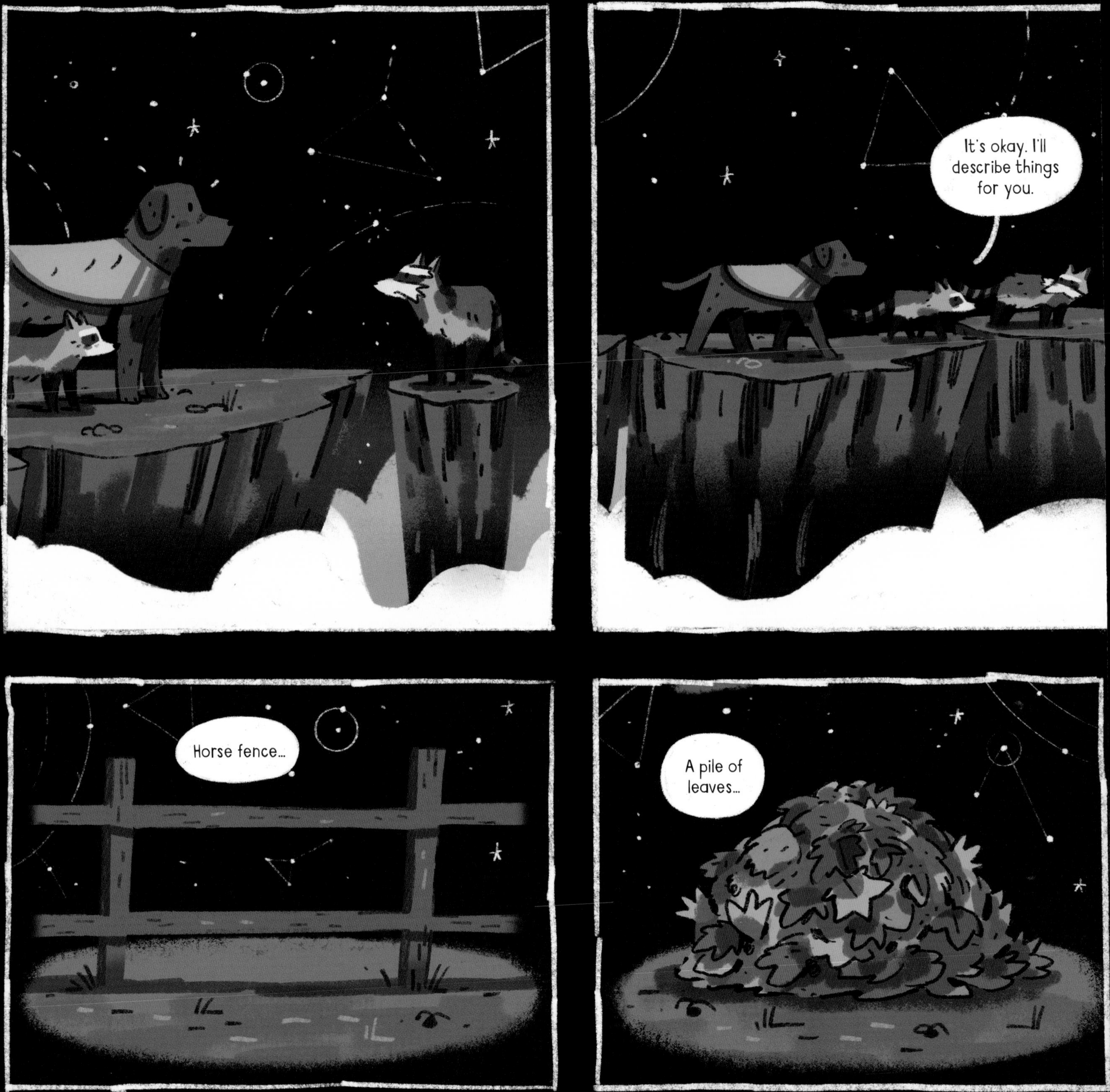
It's okay. I'll describe things for you.
Horse fence...
A pile of leaves...

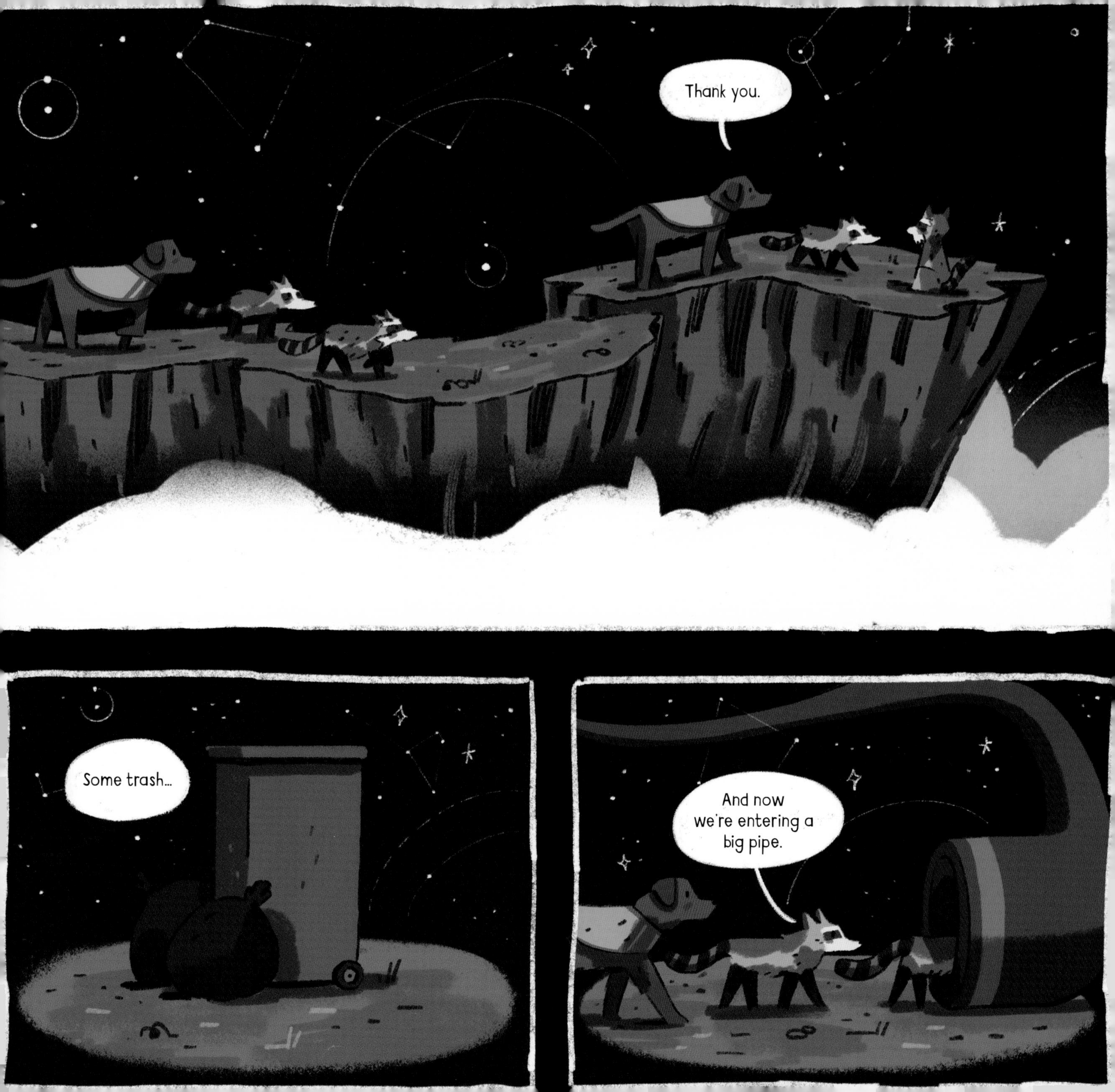
Thank you.
Some trash...
And now we're entering a big pipe.

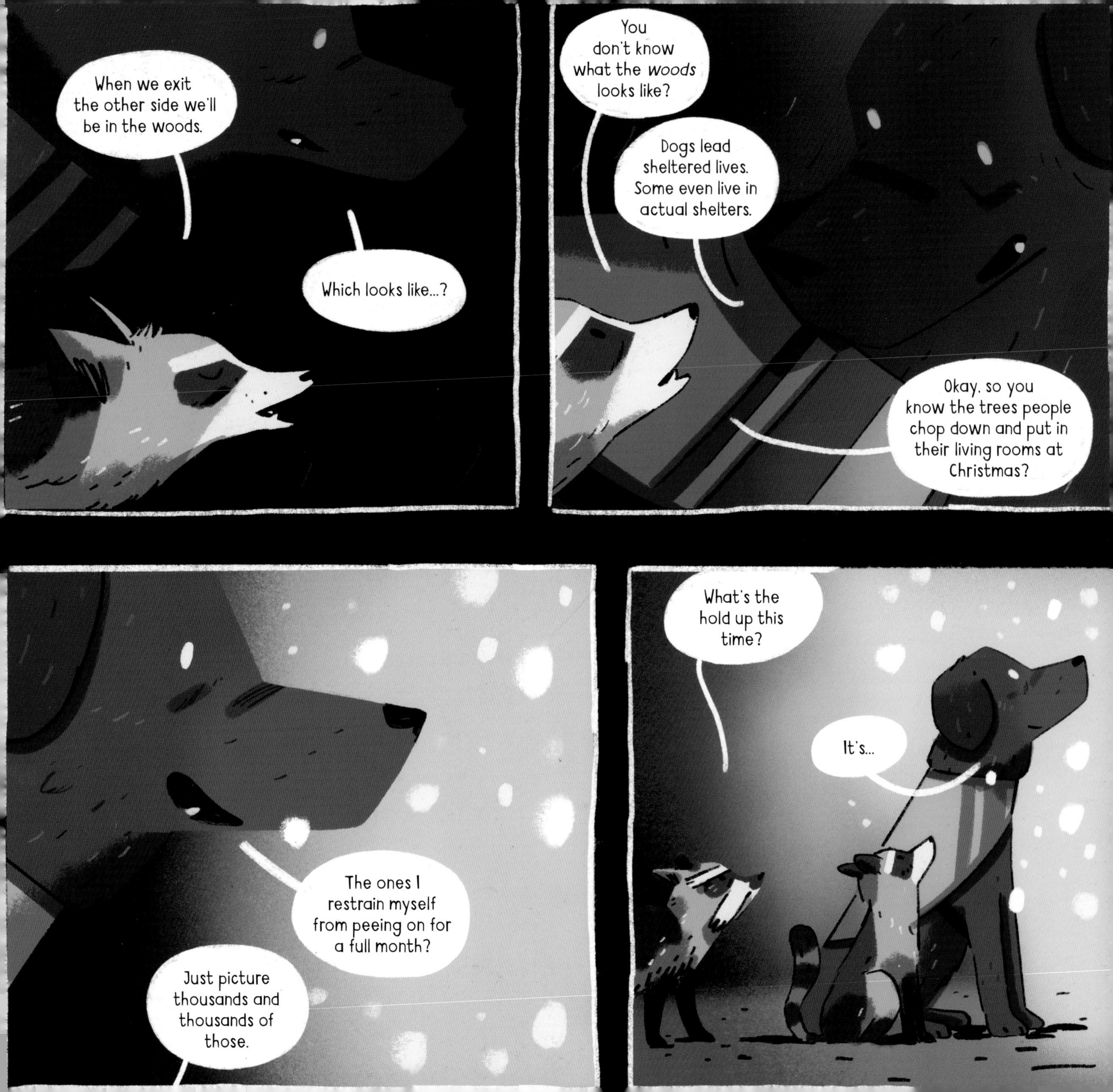
When we exit the other side we'll be in the woods.
Which looks like...?
You don't know what the *woods* looks like?
Dogs lead sheltered lives. Some even live in actual shelters.
Okay, so you know the trees people chop down and put in their living rooms at Christmas?
The ones I restrain myself from peeing on for a full month?
Just picture thousands and thousands of those.
What's the hold up this time?
It's...

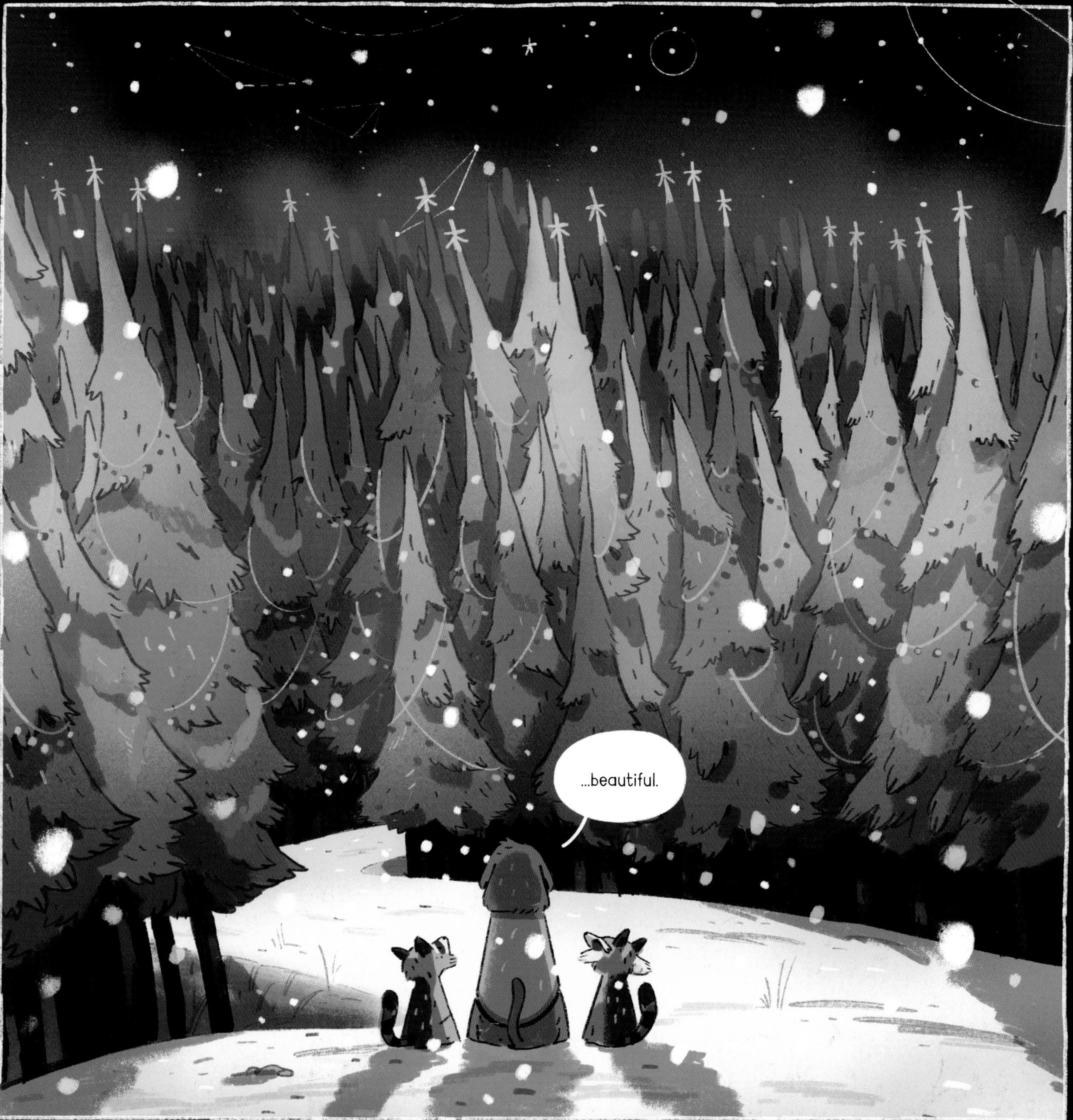
...beautiful.

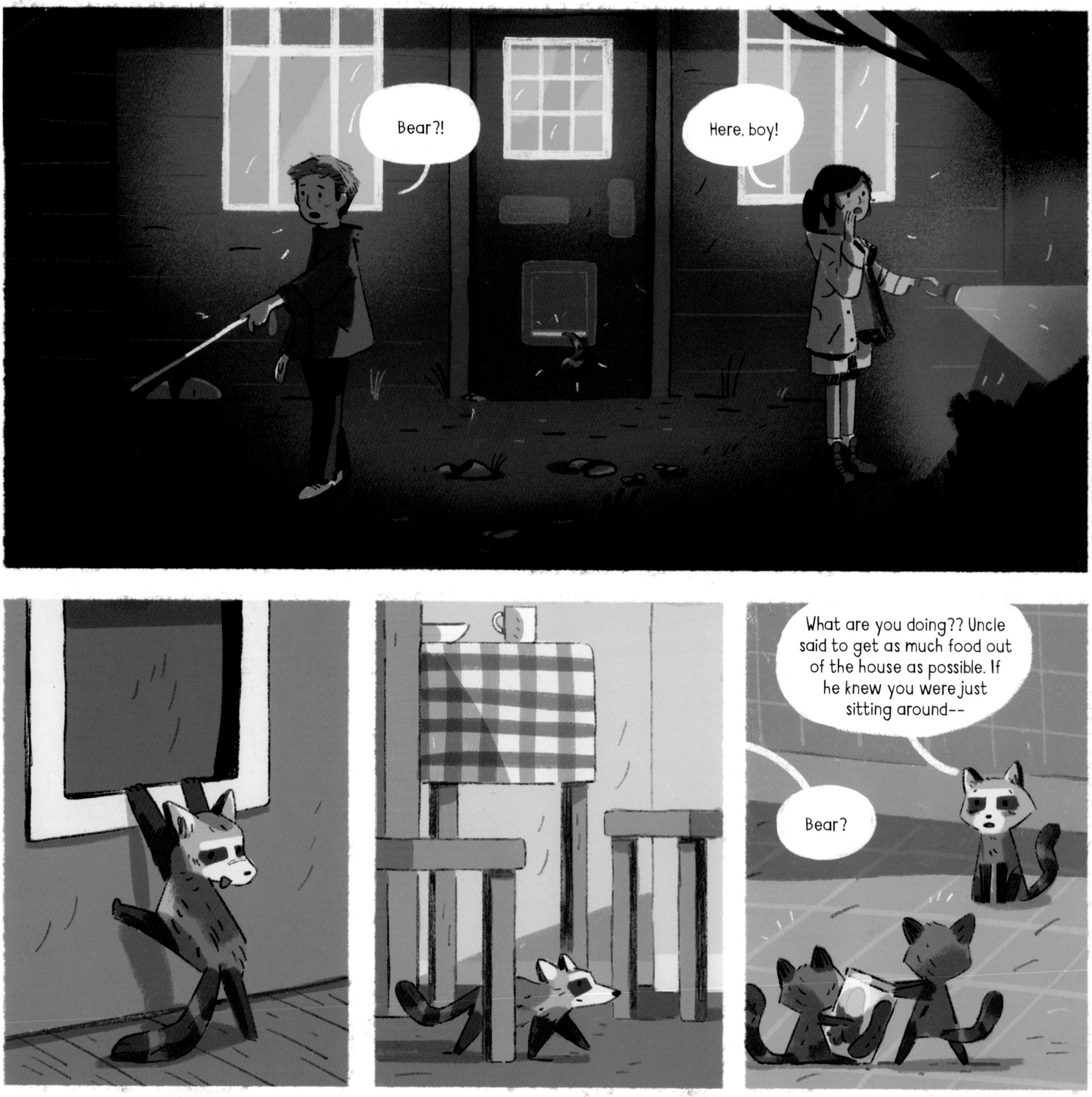
Bear?!
Here, boy!
What are you doing?? Uncle said to get as much food out of the house as possible. If he knew you were just sitting around--
Bear?

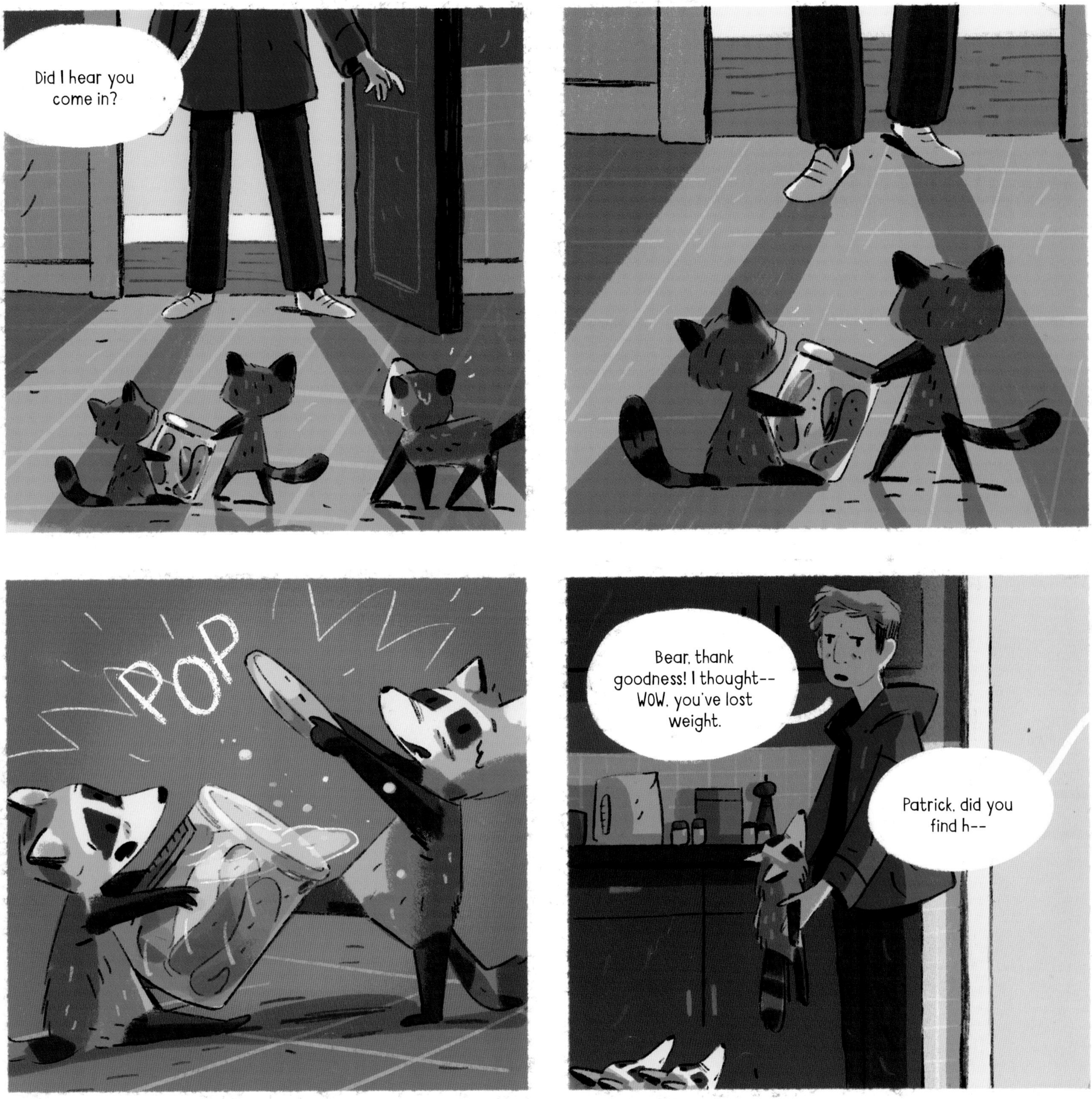
Did I hear you come in?
POP
Bear, thank goodness! I thought-- WOW, you've lost weight.
Patrick, did you find h--

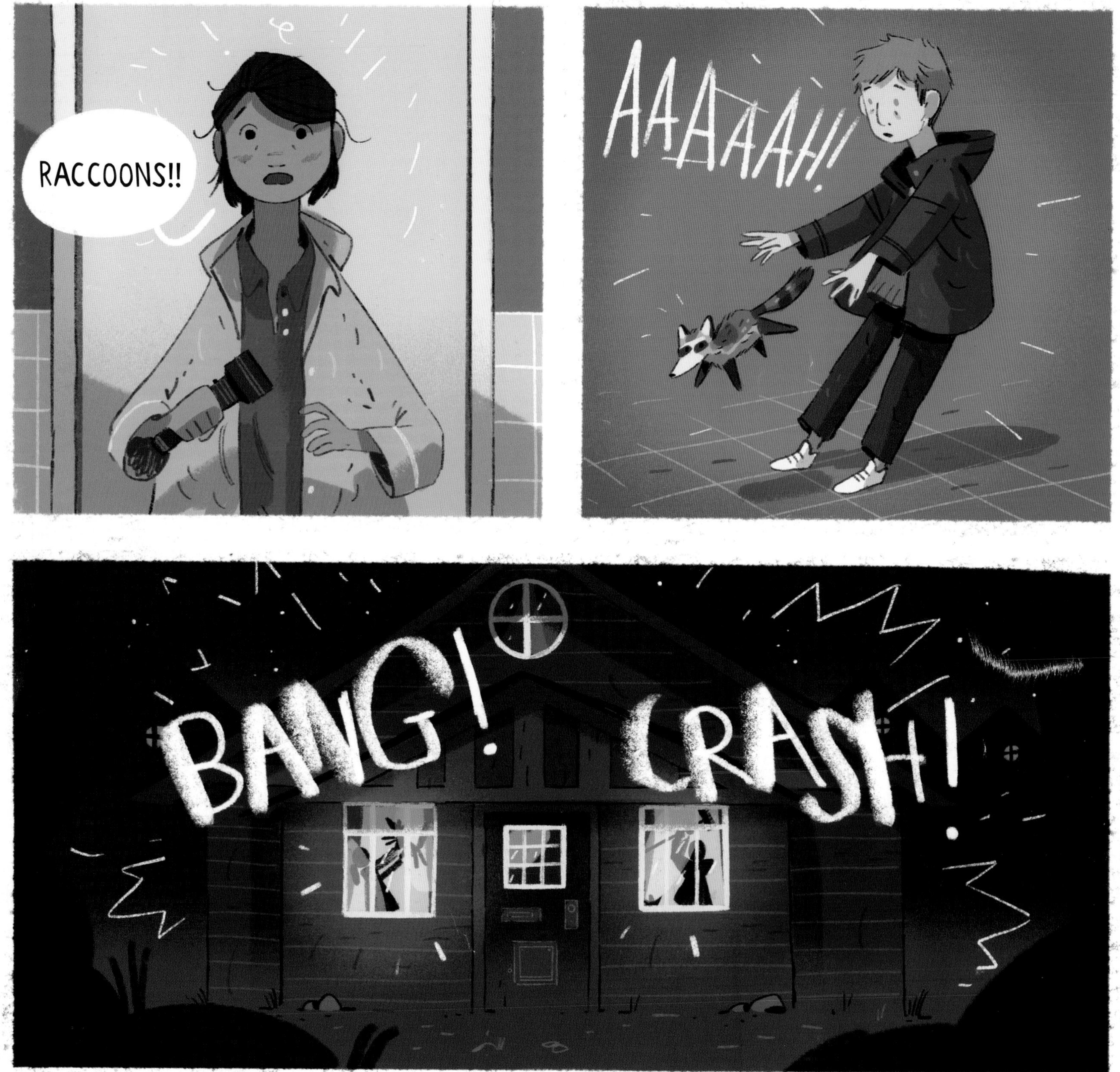
RACCOONS!!
AAAAAH!!
BANG!
CRASH!

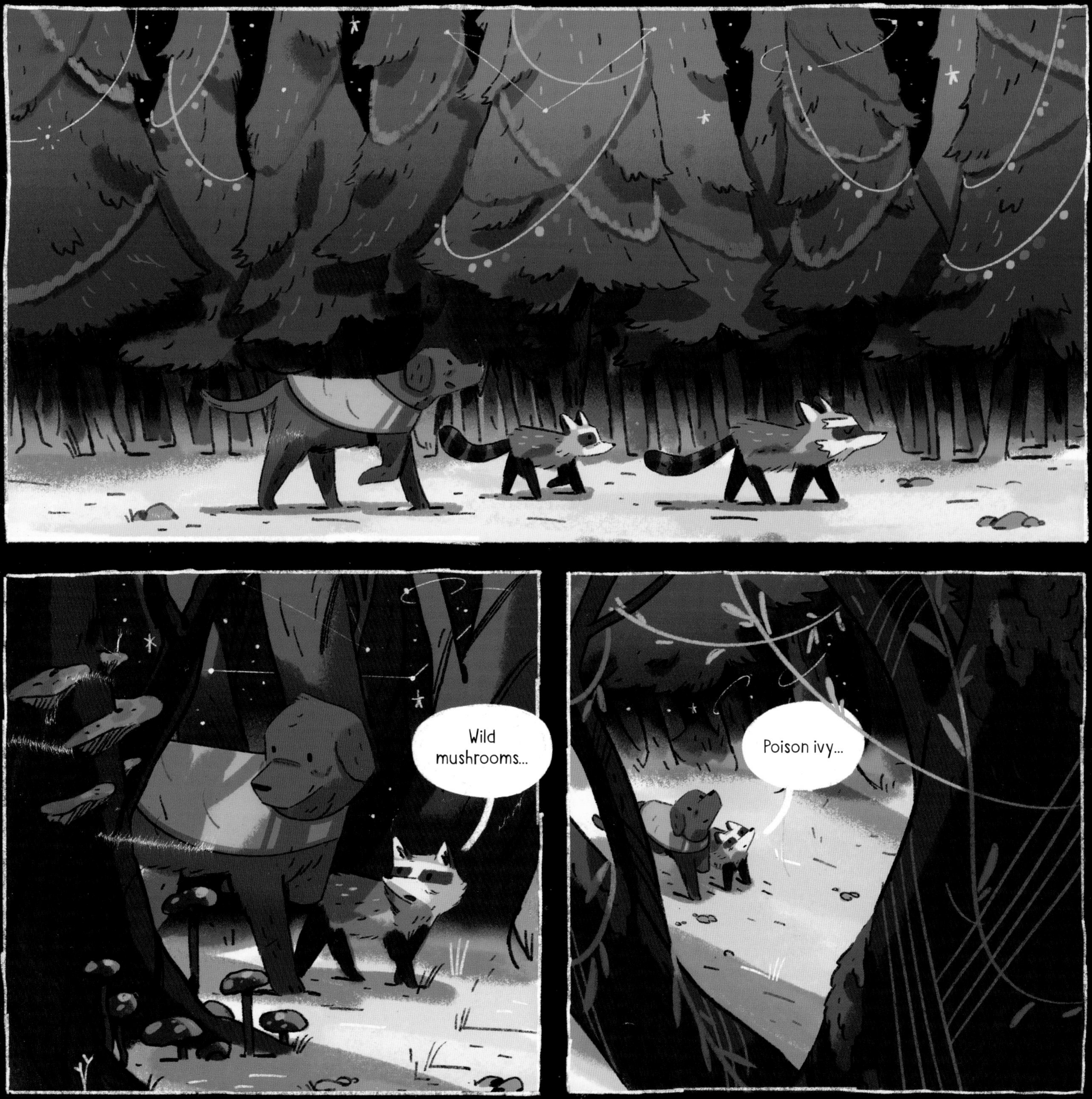
Wild mushrooms...
Poison ivy...

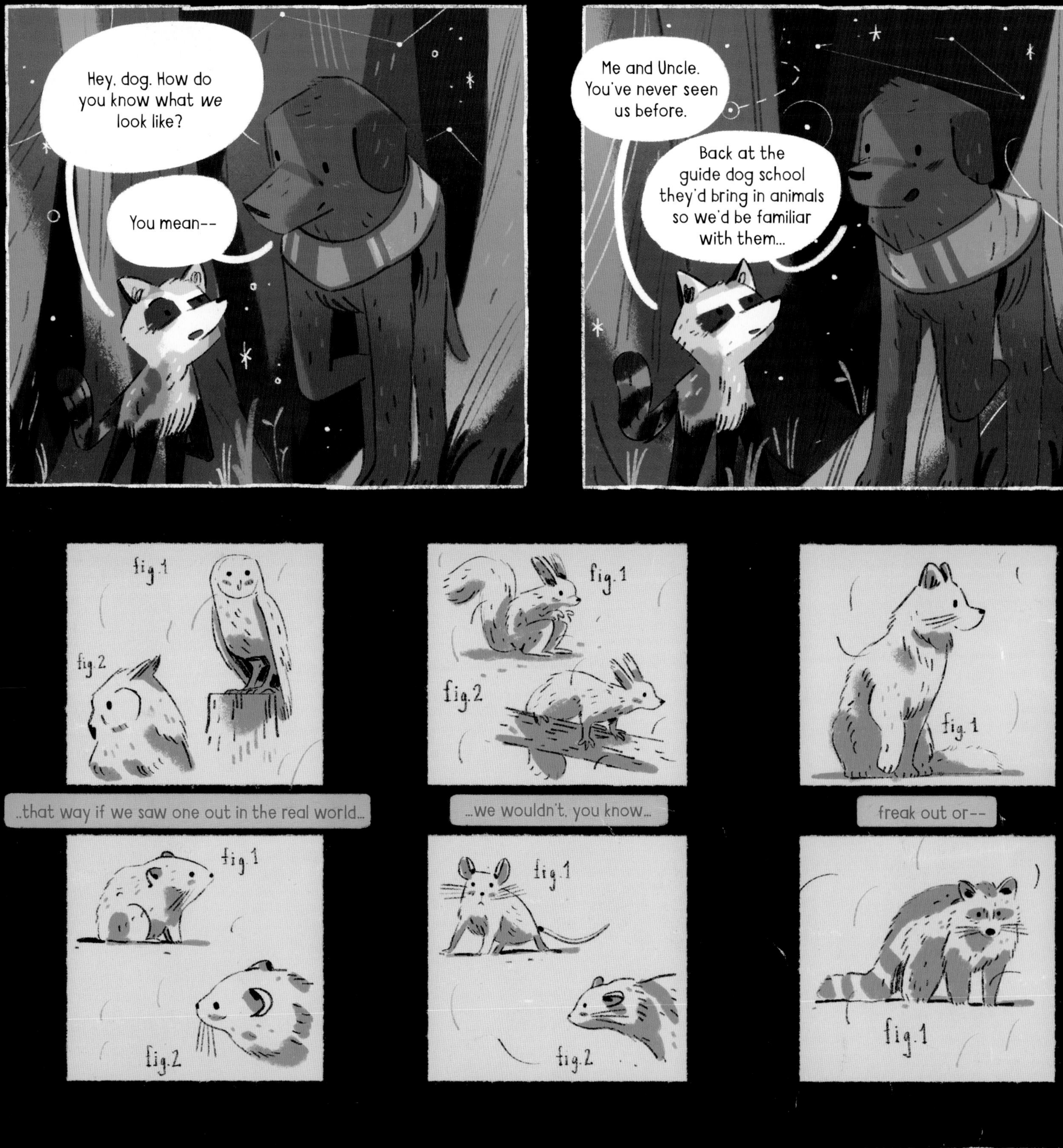
Hey, dog. How do you know what *we* look like?
You mean--
Me and Uncle. You've never seen us before.
Back at the guide dog school they'd bring in animals so we'd be familiar with them...
fig.1
fig.2
fig.1
fig.2
fig.1
..that way if we saw one out in the real world...
...we wouldn't, you know...
freak out or--
fig.1
fig.2
fig.1
fig.2
fig.1

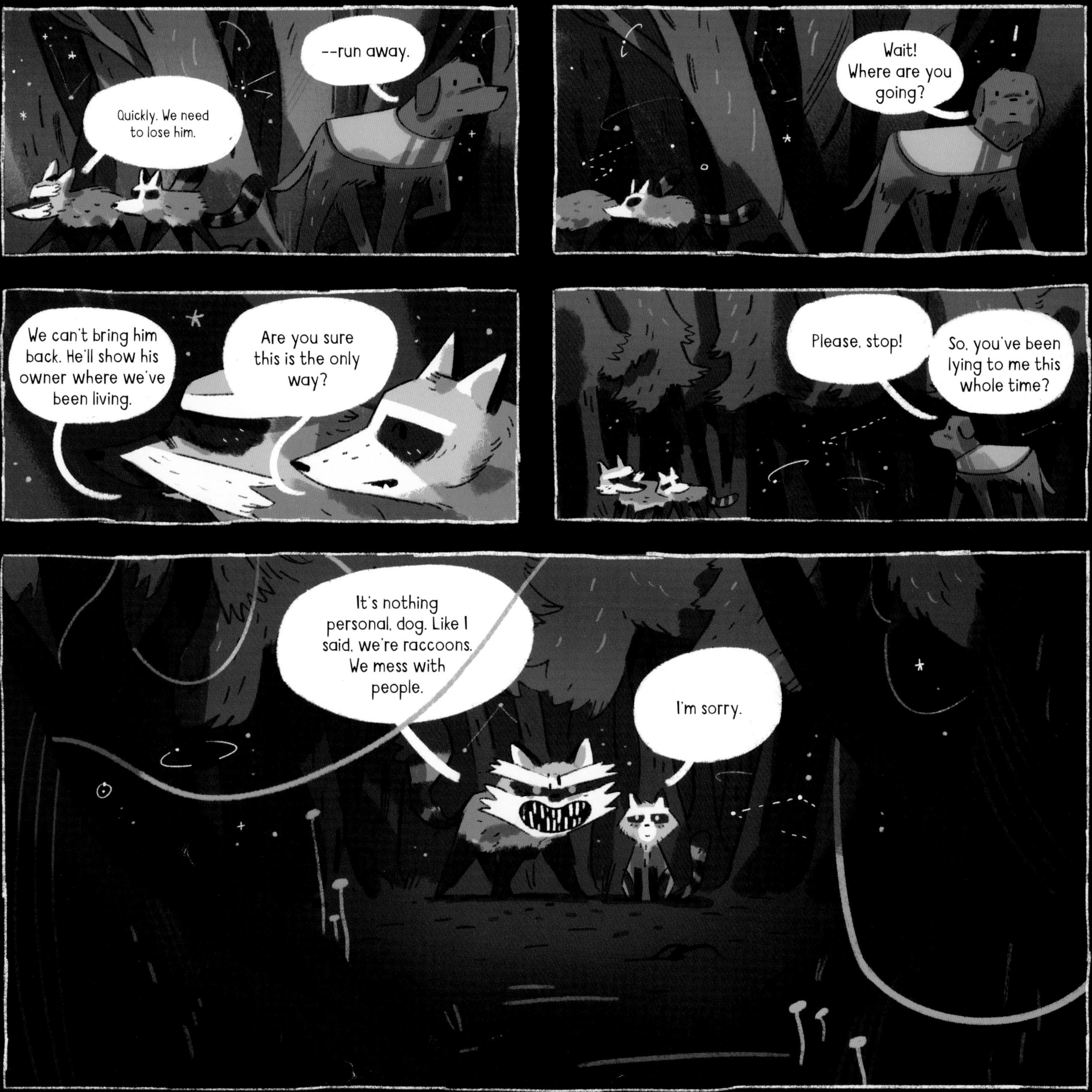
Quickly. We need to lose him.
--run away.
Wait! Where are you going?
We can't bring him back. He'll show his owner where we've been living.
Are you sure this is the only way?
Please, stop!
So, you've been lying to me this whole time?
It's nothing personal, dog. Like I said, we're raccoons. We mess with people.
I'm sorry.

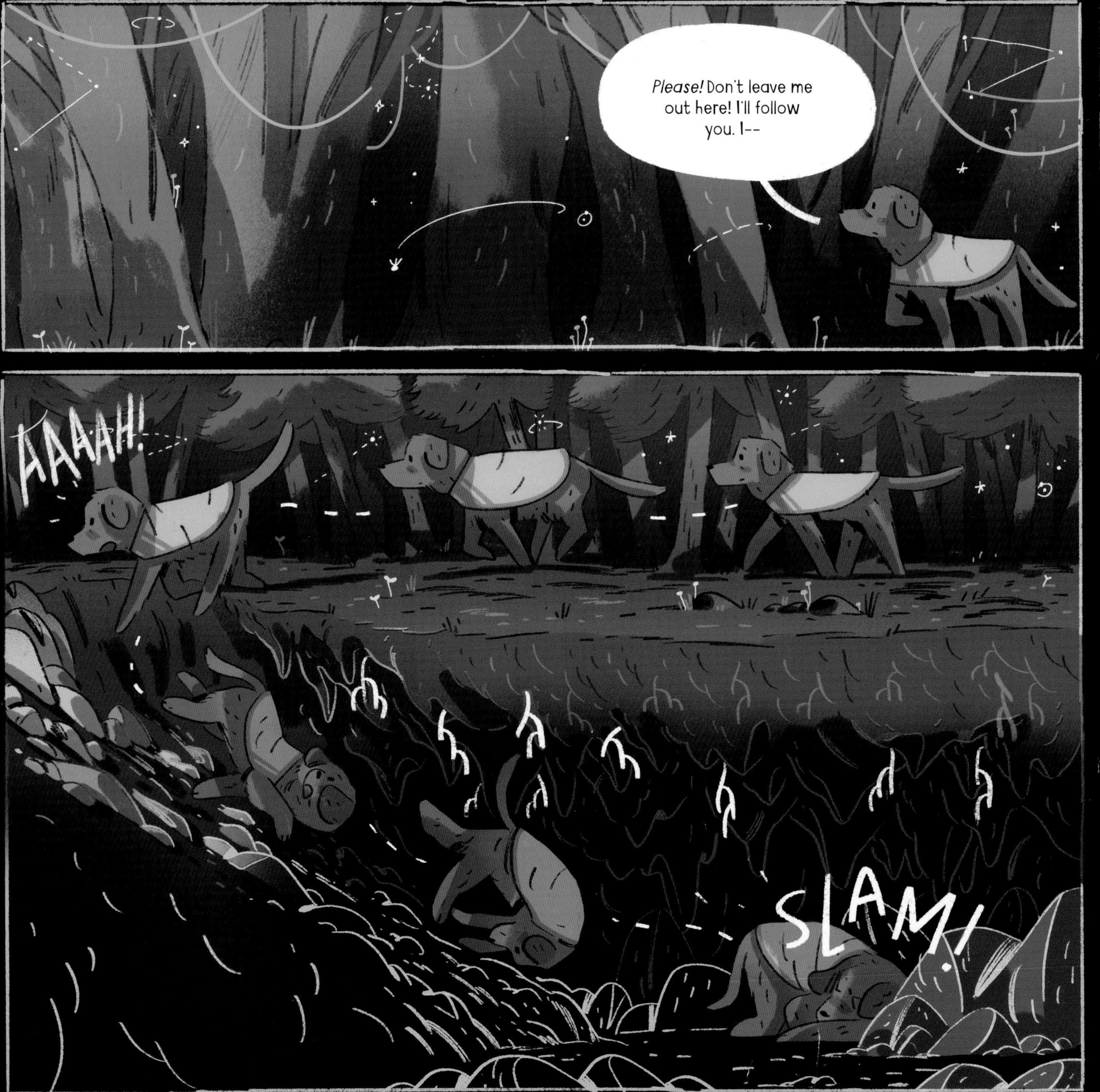
Please! Don't leave me out here! I'll follow you. I--
AAAAH!
SLAM!

Son, what did I tell you about wandering?

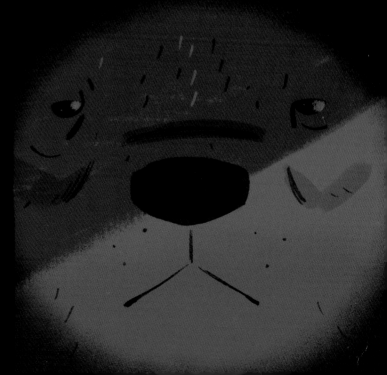

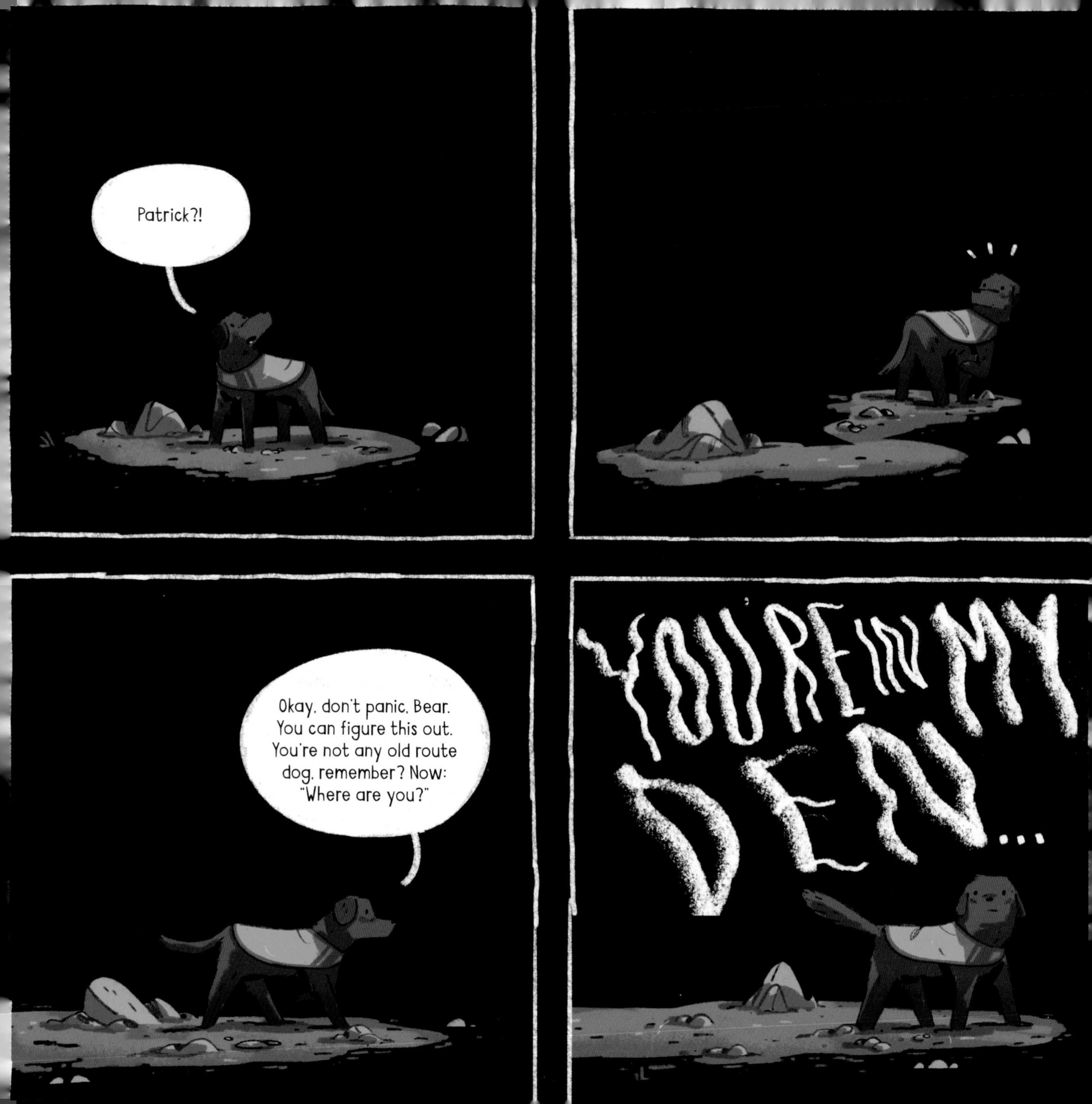
Patrick?!
Okay, don't panic, Bear. You can figure this out. You're not any old route dog, remember? Now: "Where are you?"
YOU'RE IN MY DEN...

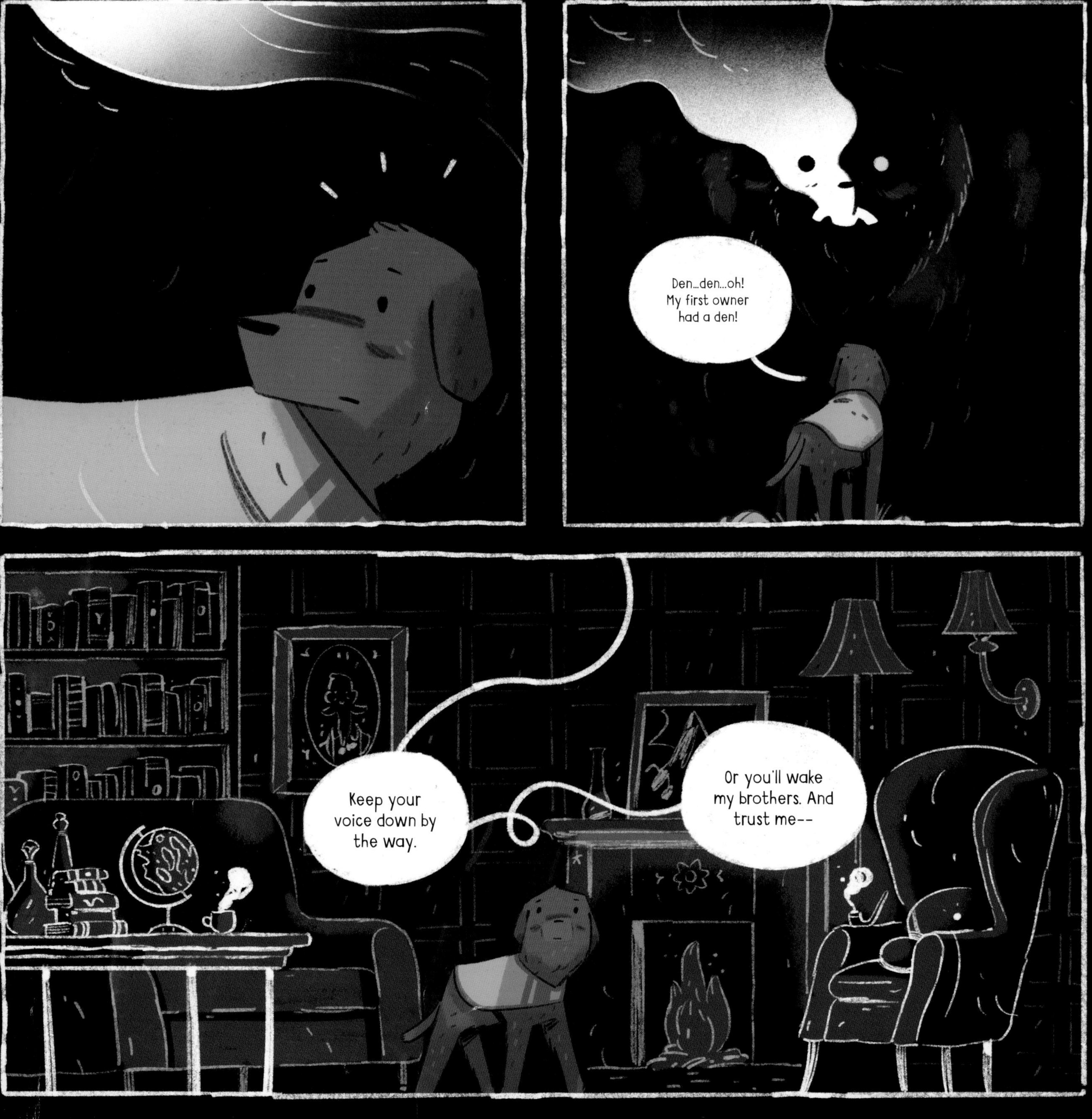
Den...den...oh! My first owner had a den!
Keep your voice down by the way.
Or you'll wake my brothers. And trust me--

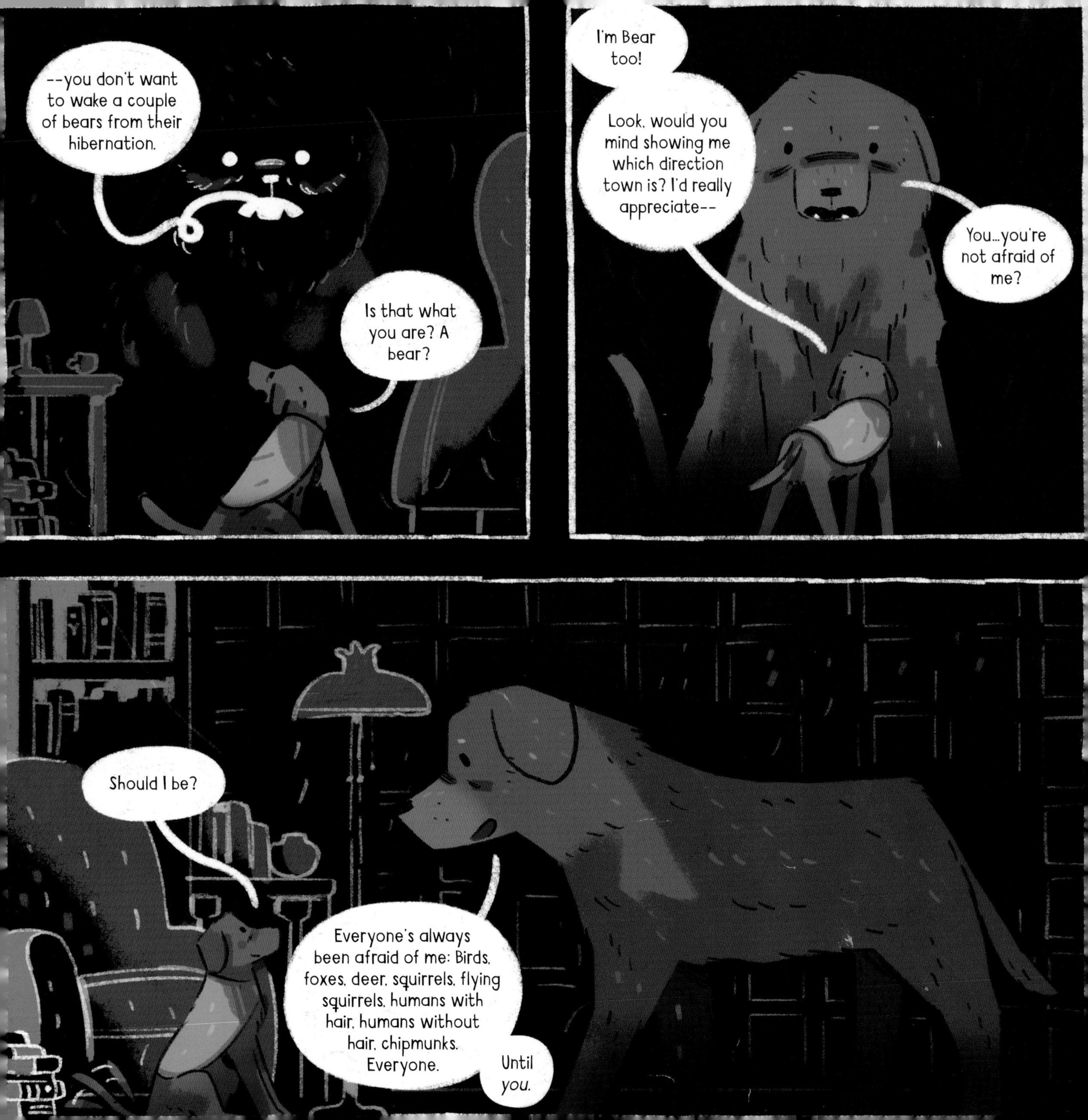
--you don't want to wake a couple of bears from their hibernation.
Is that what you are? A bear?
I'm Bear too!
Look, would you mind showing me which direction town is? I'd really appreciate--
You...you're not afraid of me?
Should I be?
Everyone's always been afraid of me: Birds, foxes, deer, squirrels, flying squirrels, humans with hair, humans without hair, chipmunks. Everyone.
Until *you.*

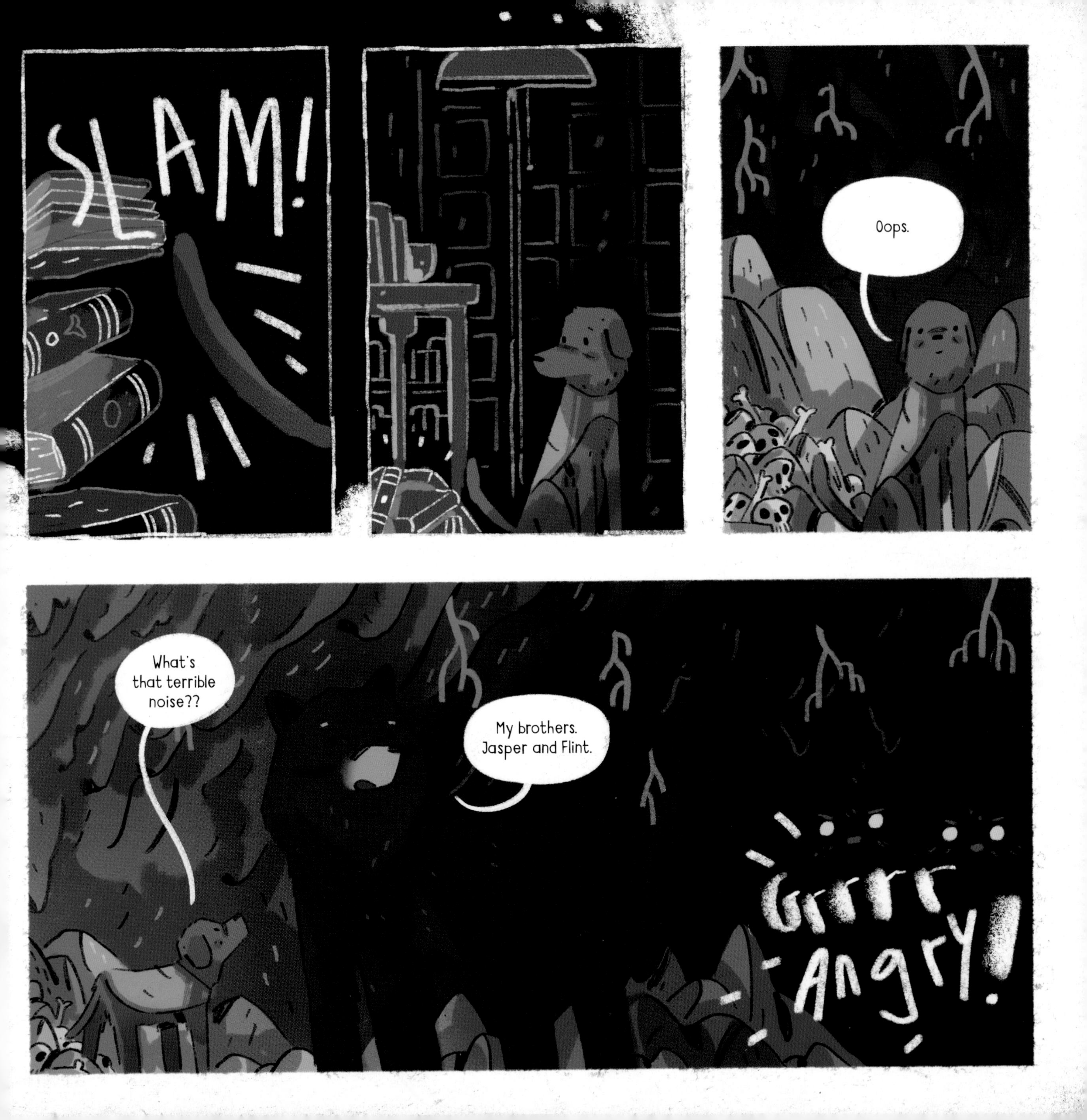
SLAM!
Oops.
What's that terrible noise??
My brothers. Jasper and Flint.
Grrrr
Angry!

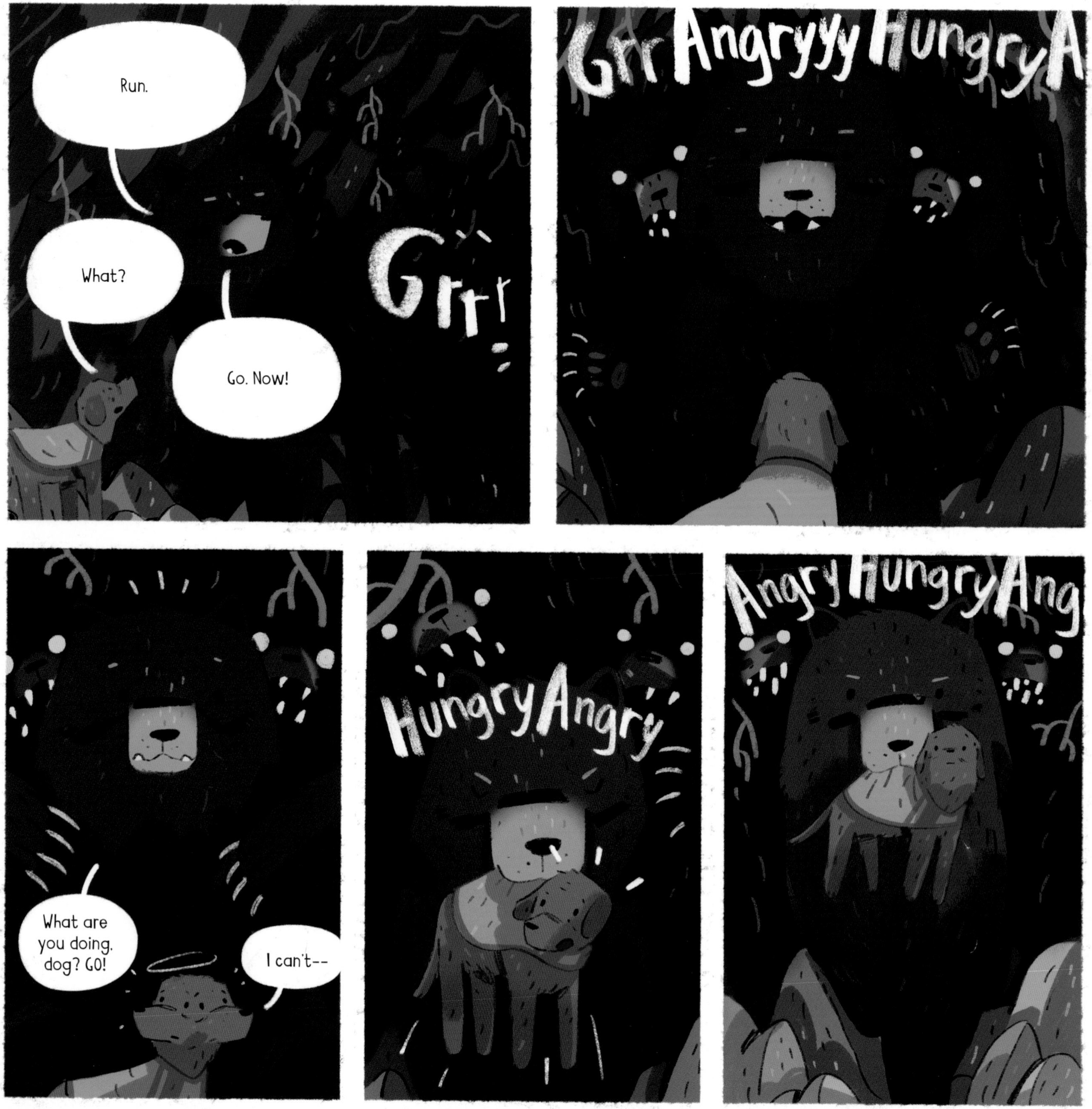
Run.
What?
Go. Now!
Grrr!
GrrAngryyyHungryA
What are you doing, dog? GO!
I can't--
HungryAngry
AngryHungryAng

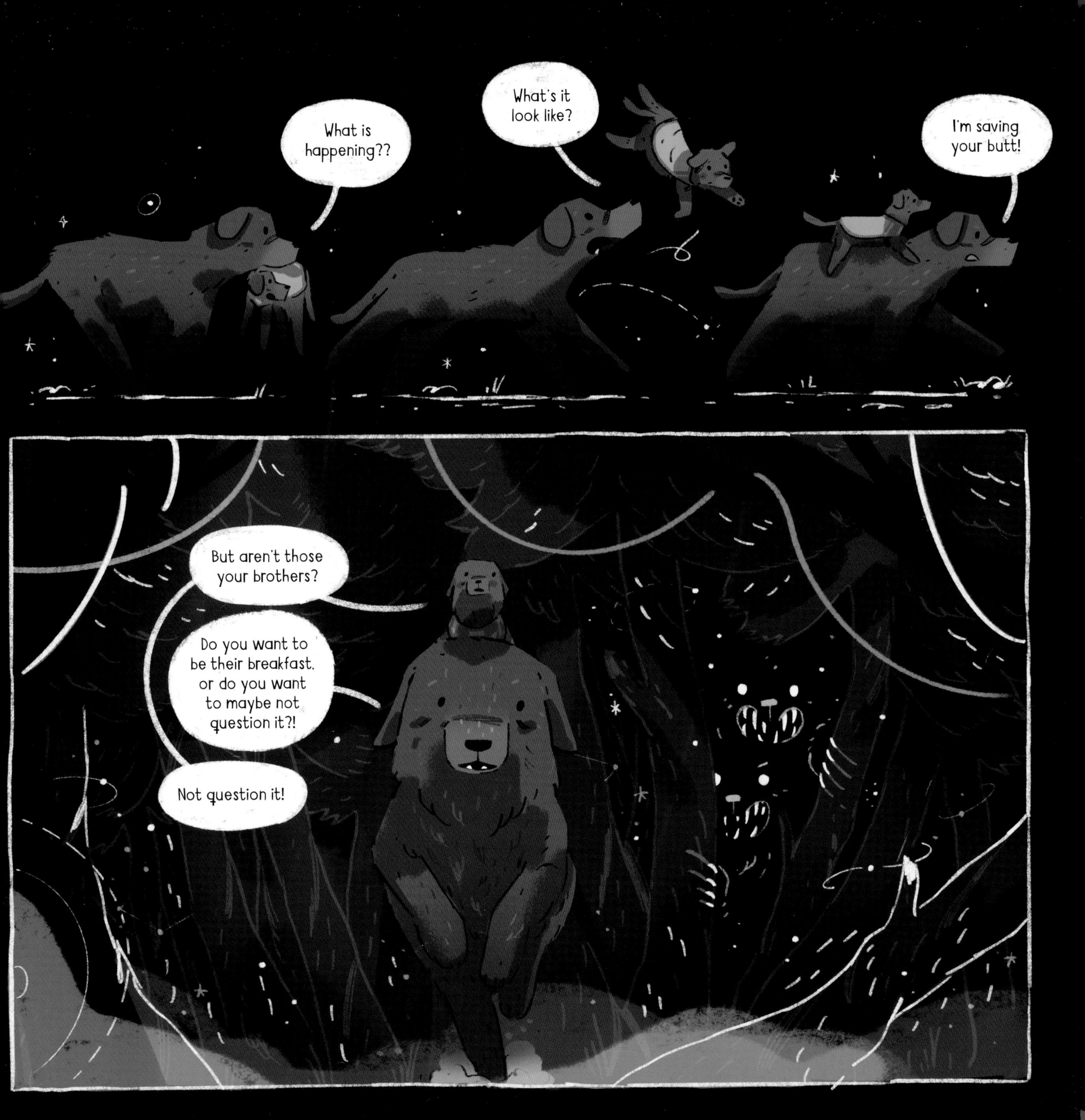
What is happening??
What's it look like?
I'm saving your butt!
But aren't those your brothers?
Do you want to be their breakfast, or do you want to maybe not question it?!
Not question it!

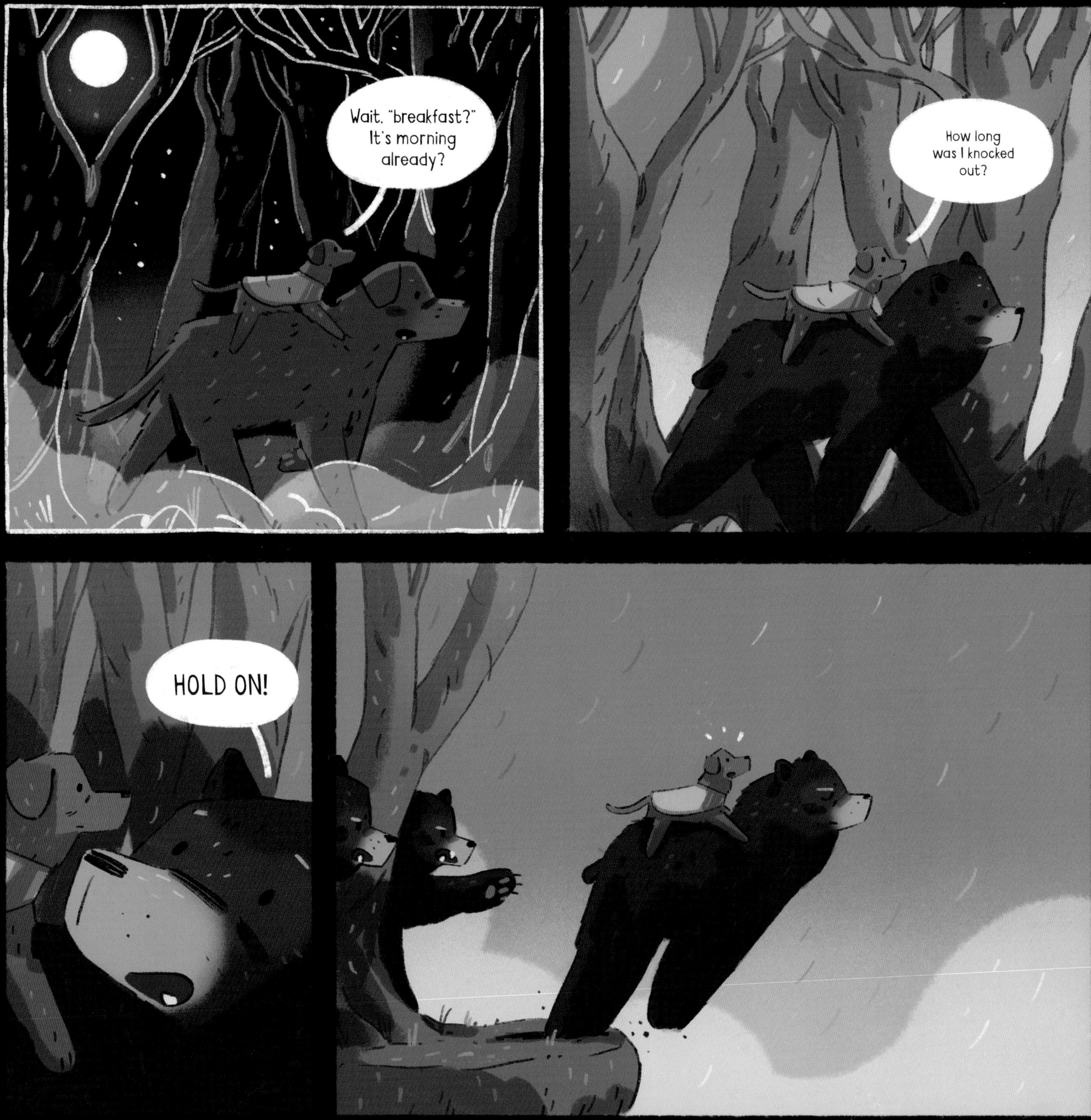
Wait, "breakfast?" It's morning already?
How long was I knocked out?
HOLD ON!

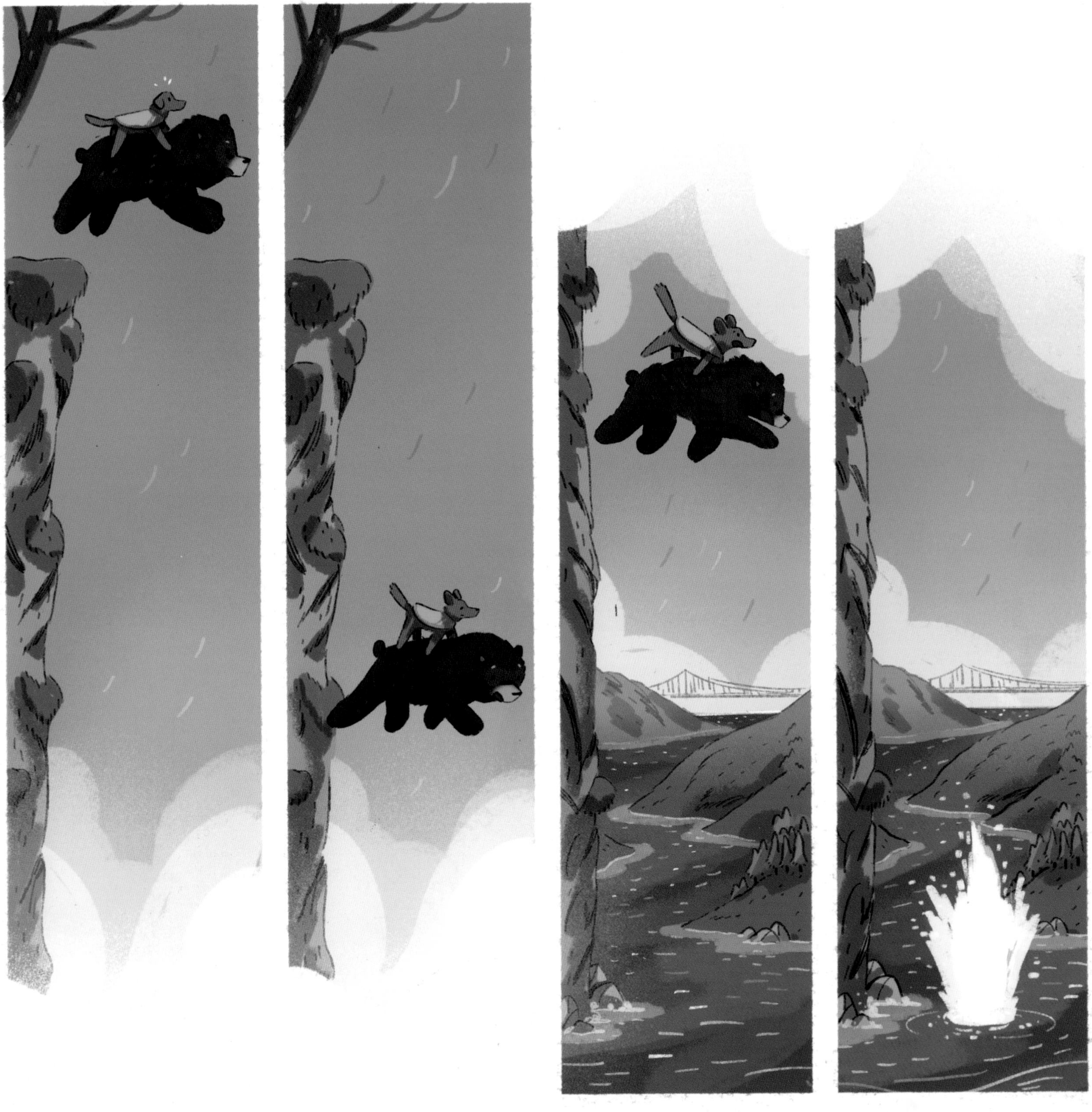

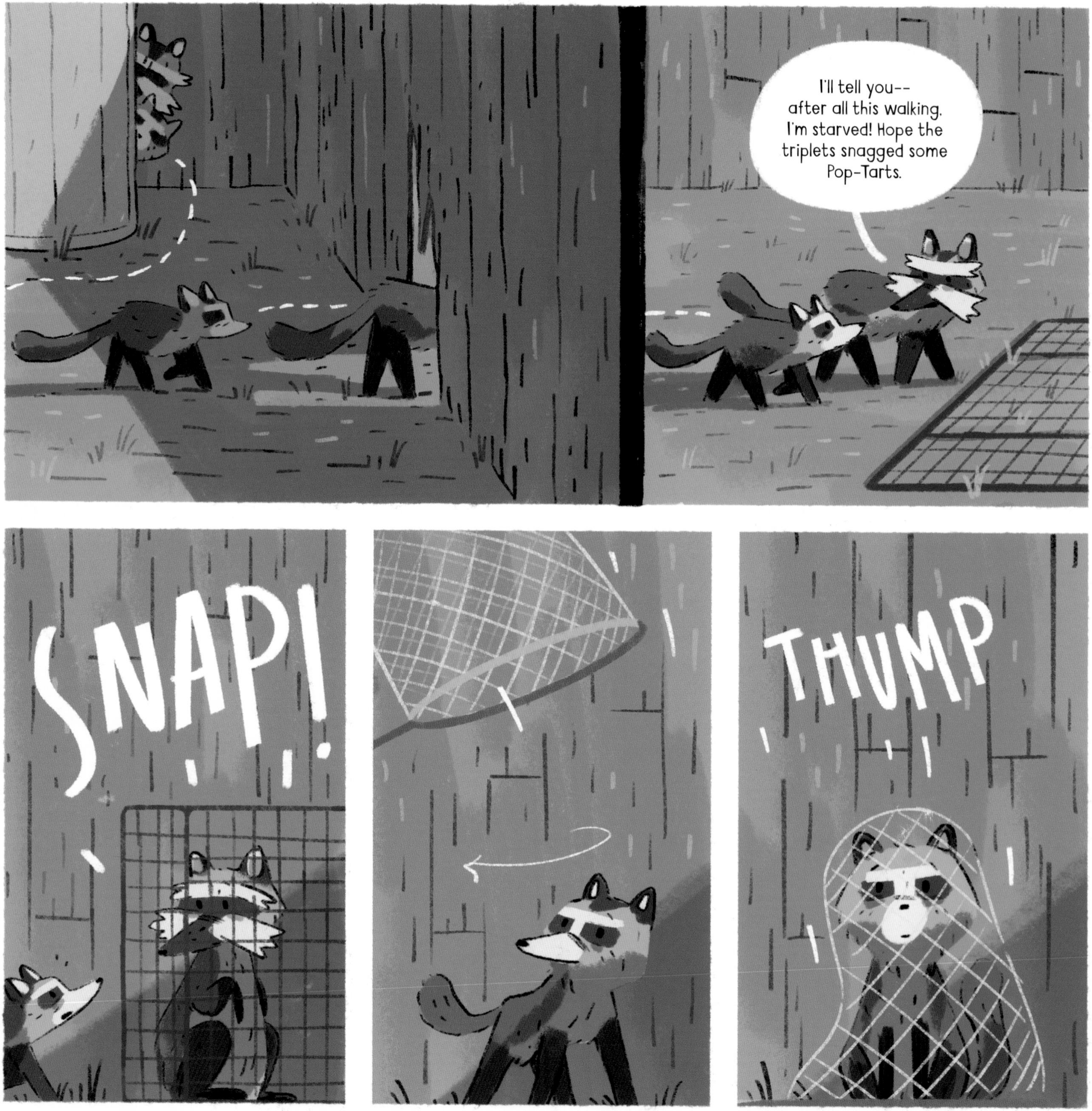
I'll tell you-- after all this walking. I'm starved! Hope the triplets snagged some Pop-Tarts.
SNAP!
THUMP

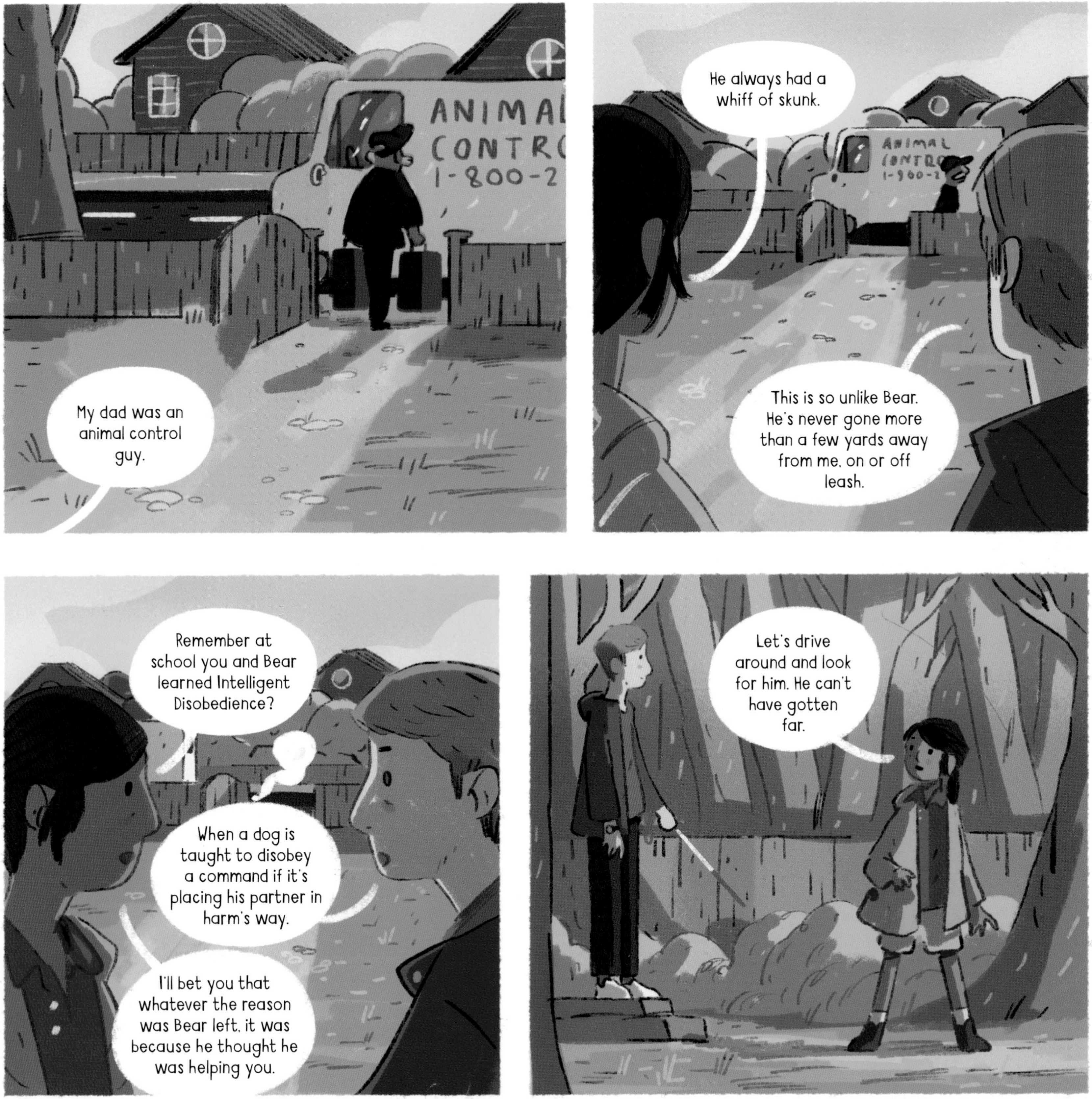
ANIMAL CONTRO 1-800-2
My dad was an animal control guy.
He always had a whiff of skunk.
This is so unlike Bear. He's never gone more than a few yards away from me, on or off leash.
Remember at school you and Bear learned Intelligent Disobedience?
When a dog is taught to disobey a command if it's placing his partner in harm's way.
I'll bet you that whatever the reason was Bear left, it was because he thought he was helping you.
Let's drive around and look for him. He can't have gotten far.

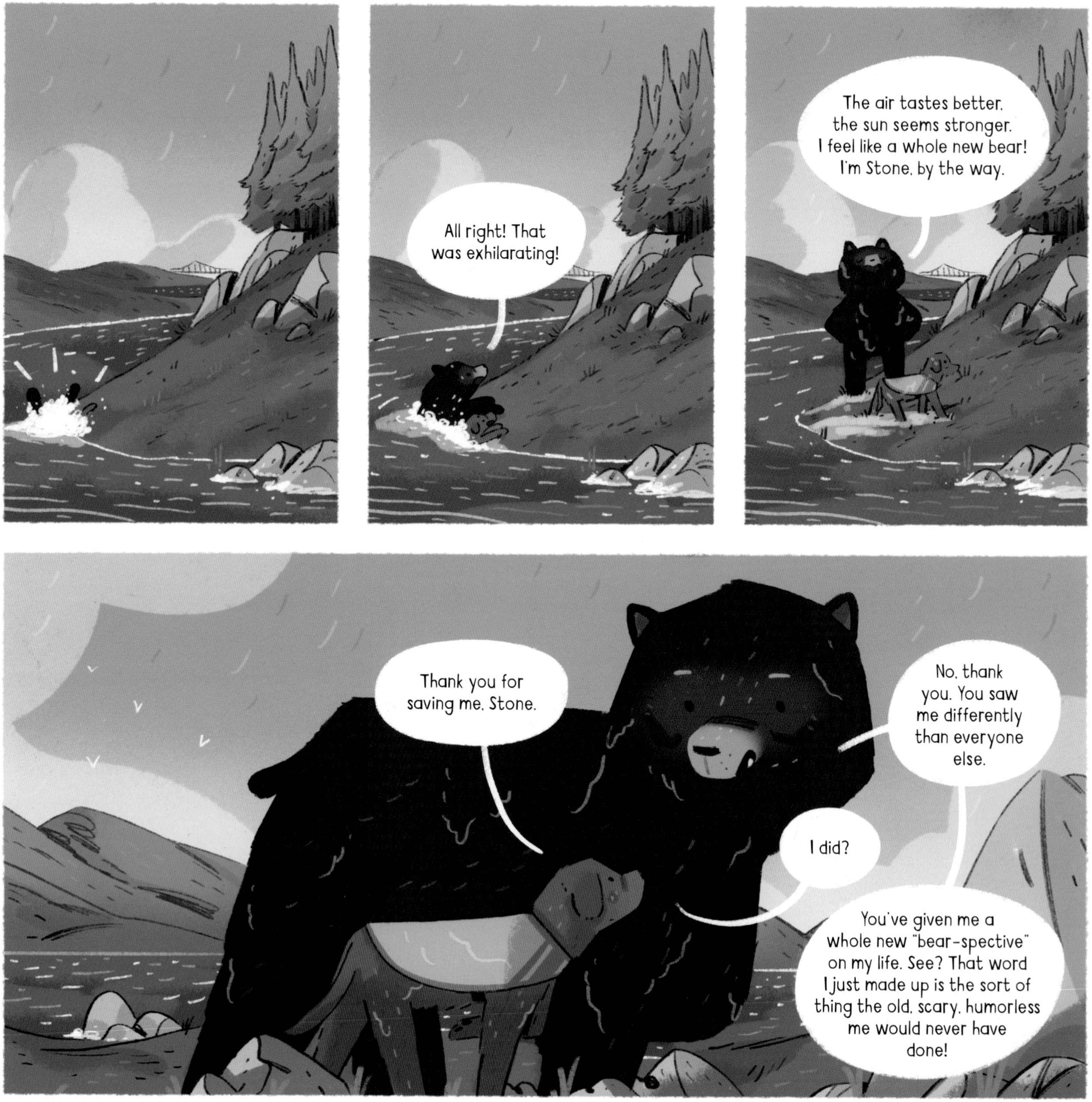
All right! That was exhilarating!
The air tastes better, the sun seems stronger. I feel like a whole new bear! I'm Stone, by the way.
Thank you for saving me, Stone.
No, thank you. You saw me differently than everyone else.
I did?
You've given me a whole new "bear-spective" on my life. See? That word I just made up is the sort of thing the old, scary, humorless me would never have done!

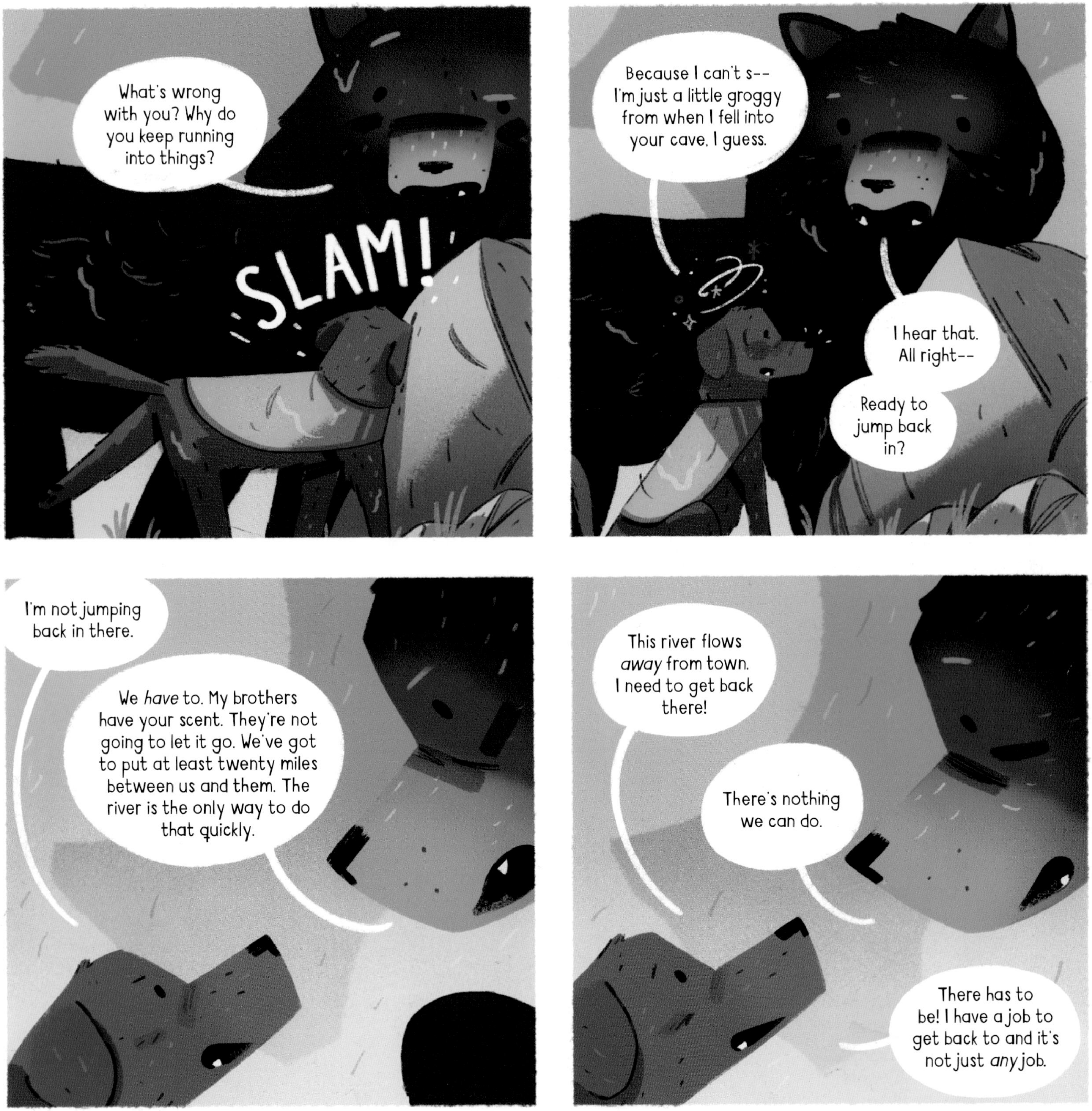
What's wrong with you? Why do you keep running into things?
SLAM!
Because I can't s-- I'm just a little groggy from when I fell into your cave, I guess.
I hear that. All right--
Ready to jump back in?
I'm not jumping back in there.
We *have* to. My brothers have your scent. They're not going to let it go. We've got to put at least twenty miles between us and them. The river is the only way to do that quickly.
This river flows *away* from town. I need to get back there!
There's nothing we can do.
There has to be! I have a job to get back to and it's not just *any* job.

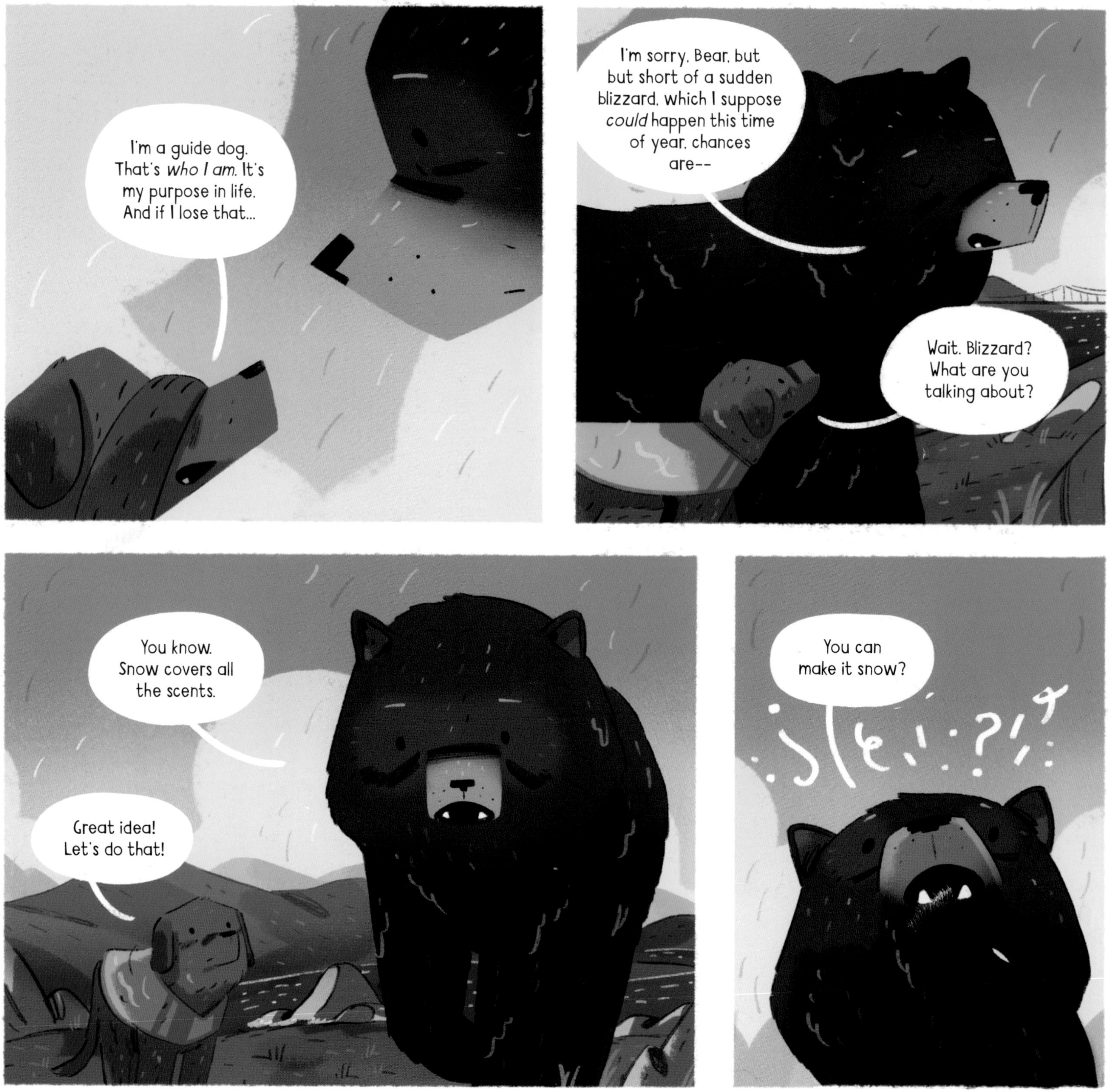
I'm a guide dog. That's *who I am.* It's my purpose in life. And if I lose that...
I'm sorry, Bear, but but short of a sudden blizzard, which I suppose *could* happen this time of year, chances are--
Wait. Blizzard? What are you talking about?
You know. Snow covers all the scents.
Great idea! Let's do that!
You can make it snow?

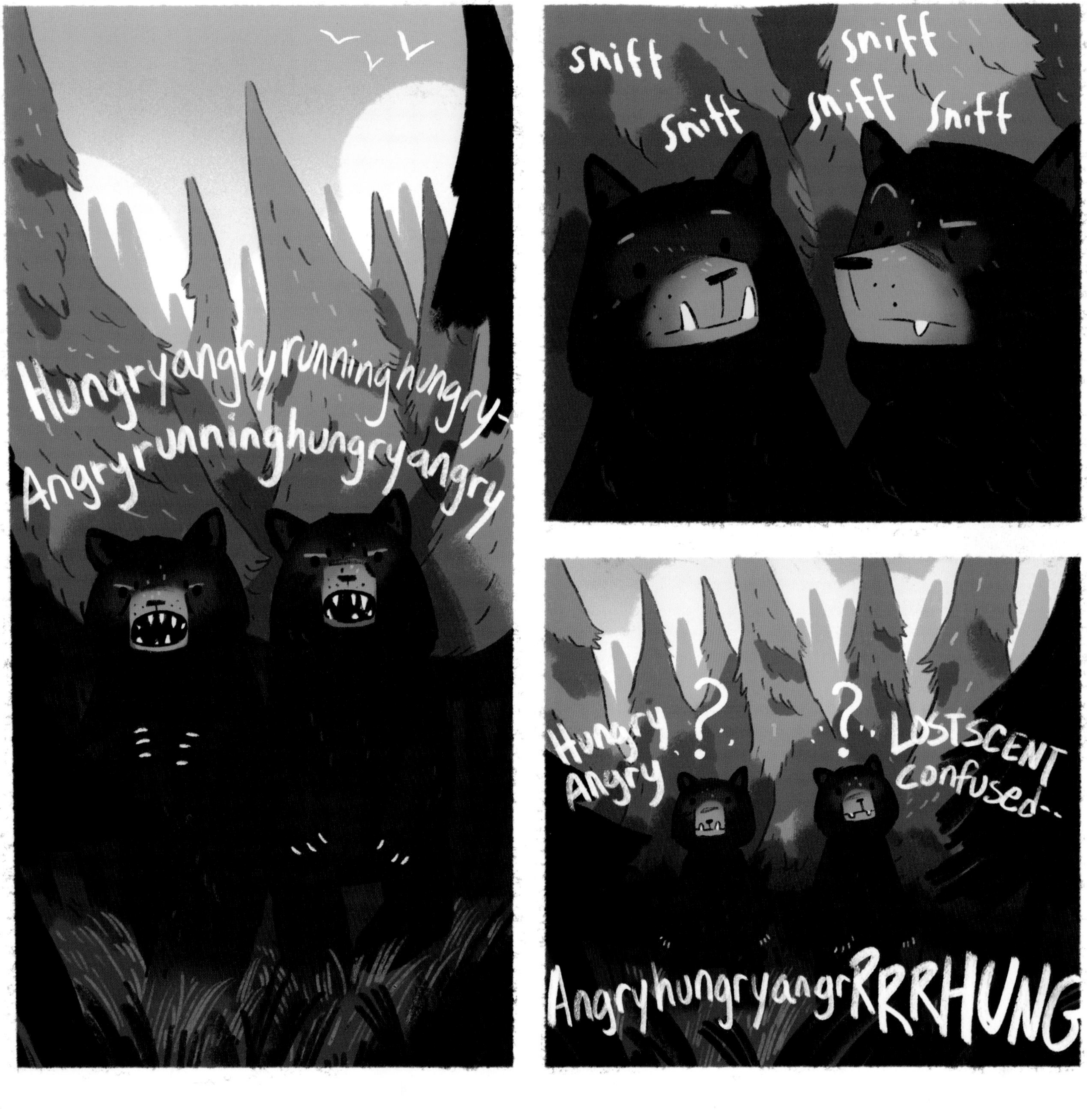
Hungryangryrunninghungry-
Angryrunninghungryangry
sniff
sniff
sniff
sniff
sniff
Hungry
Angry
?
?
LOSTSCENT
confused--
AngryhungryangrRRRHUNG

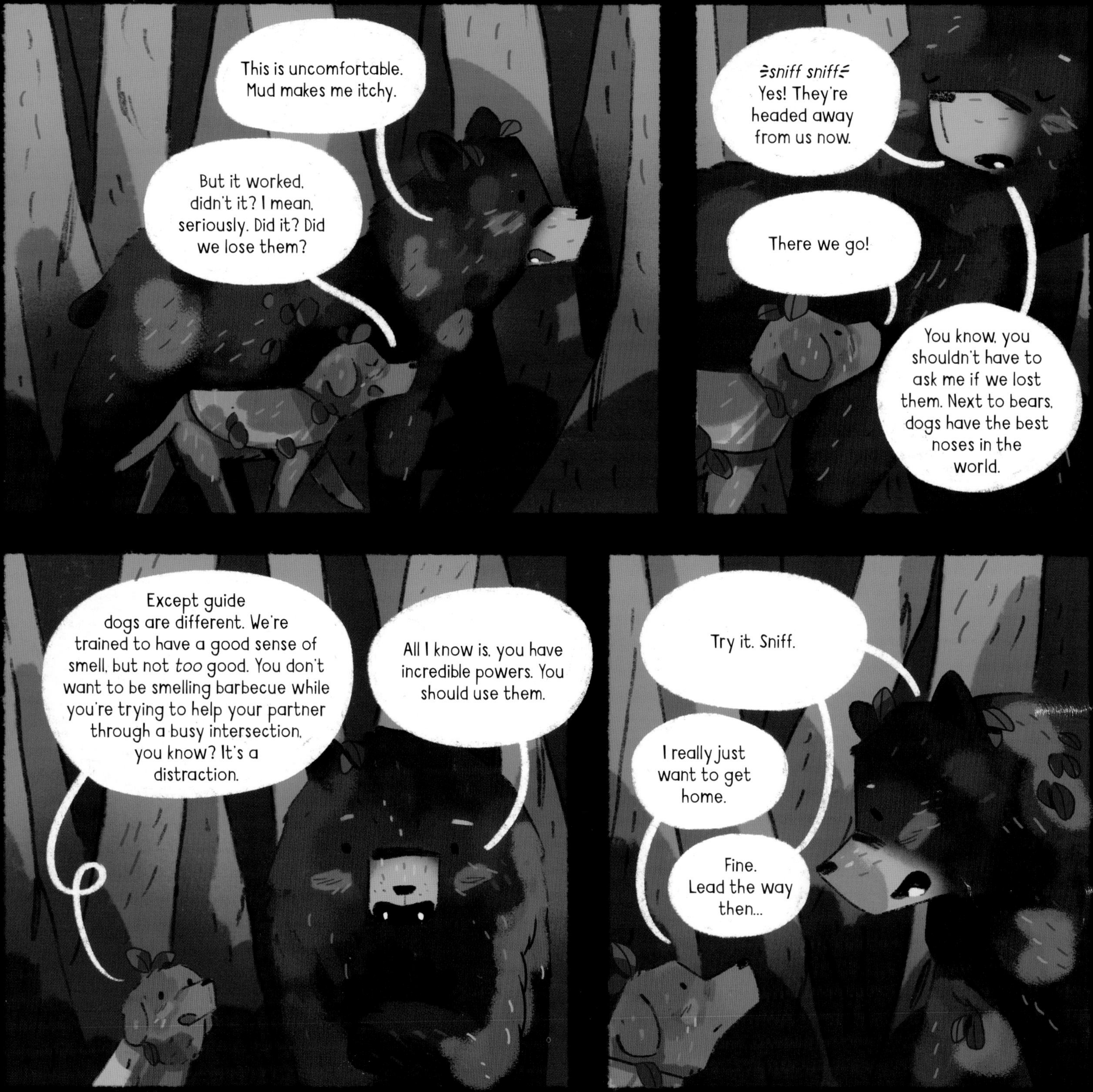
This is uncomfortable. Mud makes me itchy.
But it worked, didn't it? I mean, seriously. Did it? Did we lose them?
sniff sniff Yes! They're headed away from us now.
There we go!
You know, you shouldn't have to ask me if we lost them. Next to bears, dogs have the best noses in the world.
Except guide dogs are different. We're trained to have a good sense of smell, but not *too* good. You don't want to be smelling barbecue while you're trying to help your partner through a busy intersection, you know? It's a distraction.
All I know is, you have incredible powers. You should use them.
Try it. Sniff.
I really just want to get home.
Fine. Lead the way then...

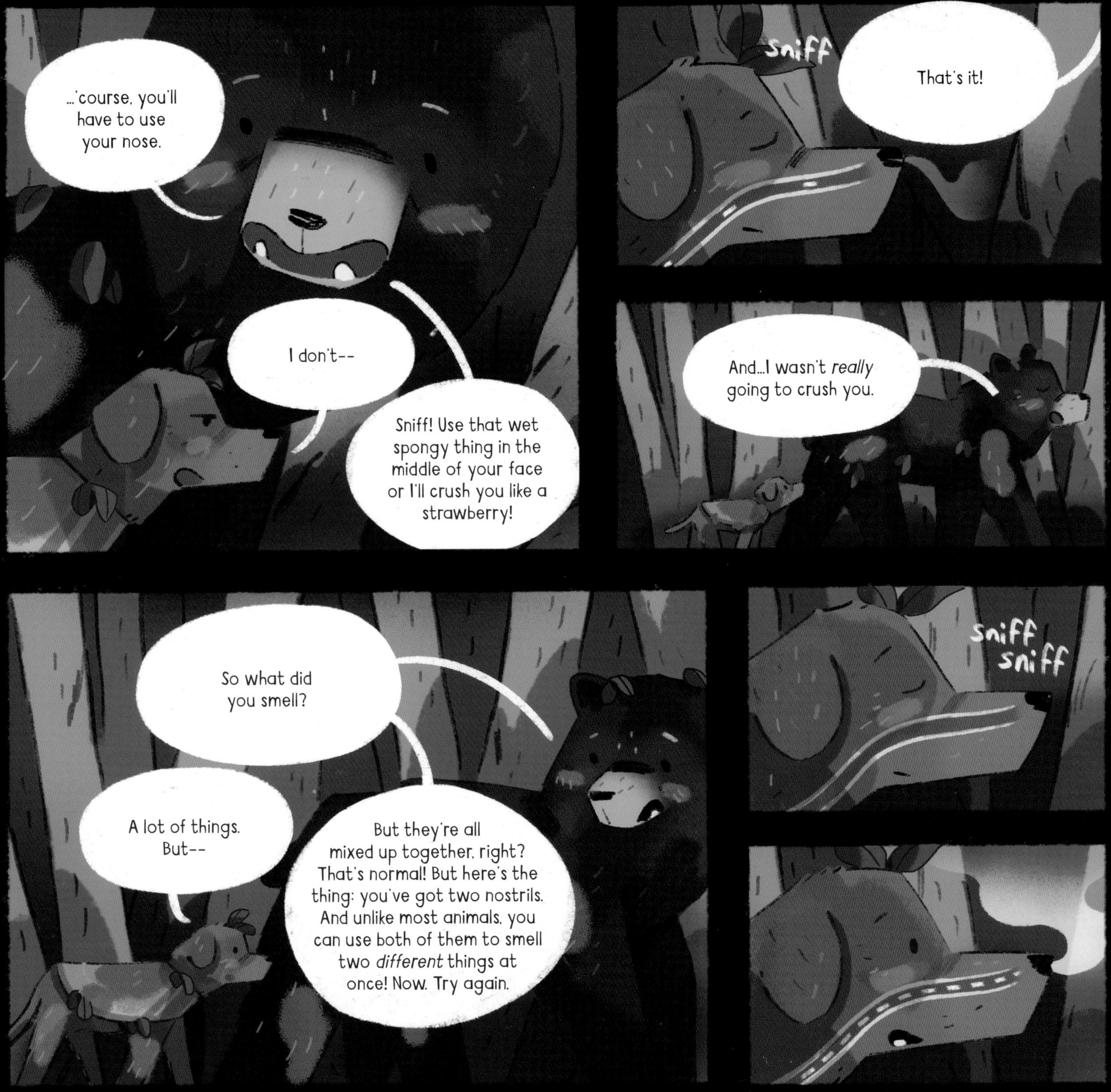
...'course, you'll have to use your nose.
I don't--
Sniff! Use that wet spongy thing in the middle of your face or I'll crush you like a strawberry!
sniff
That's it!
And...I wasn't *really* going to crush you.
So what did you smell?
A lot of things. But--
But they're all mixed up together, right? That's normal! But here's the thing: you've got two nostrils. And unlike most animals, you can use both of them to smell two *different* things at once! Now. Try again.
sniff sniff

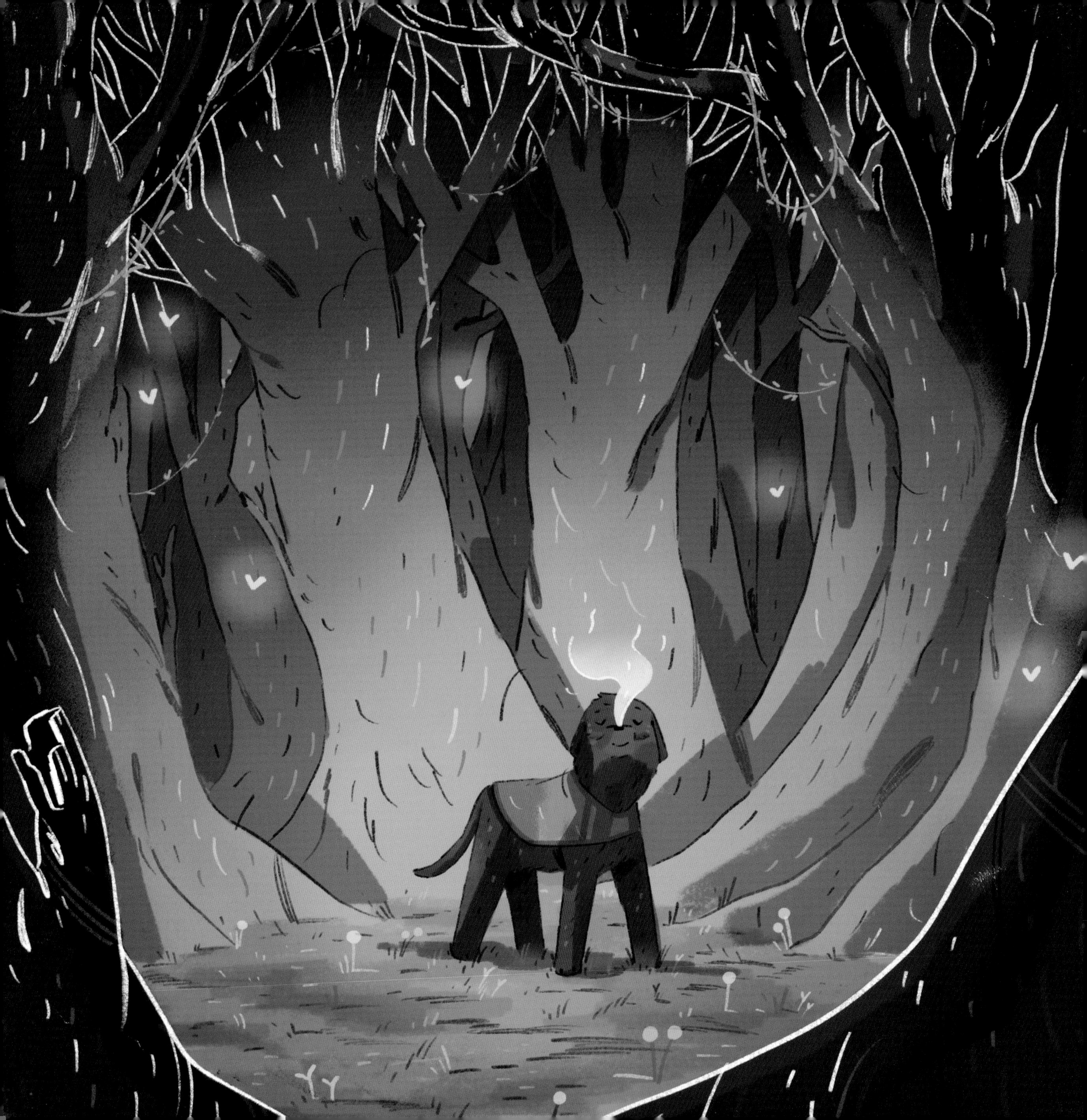

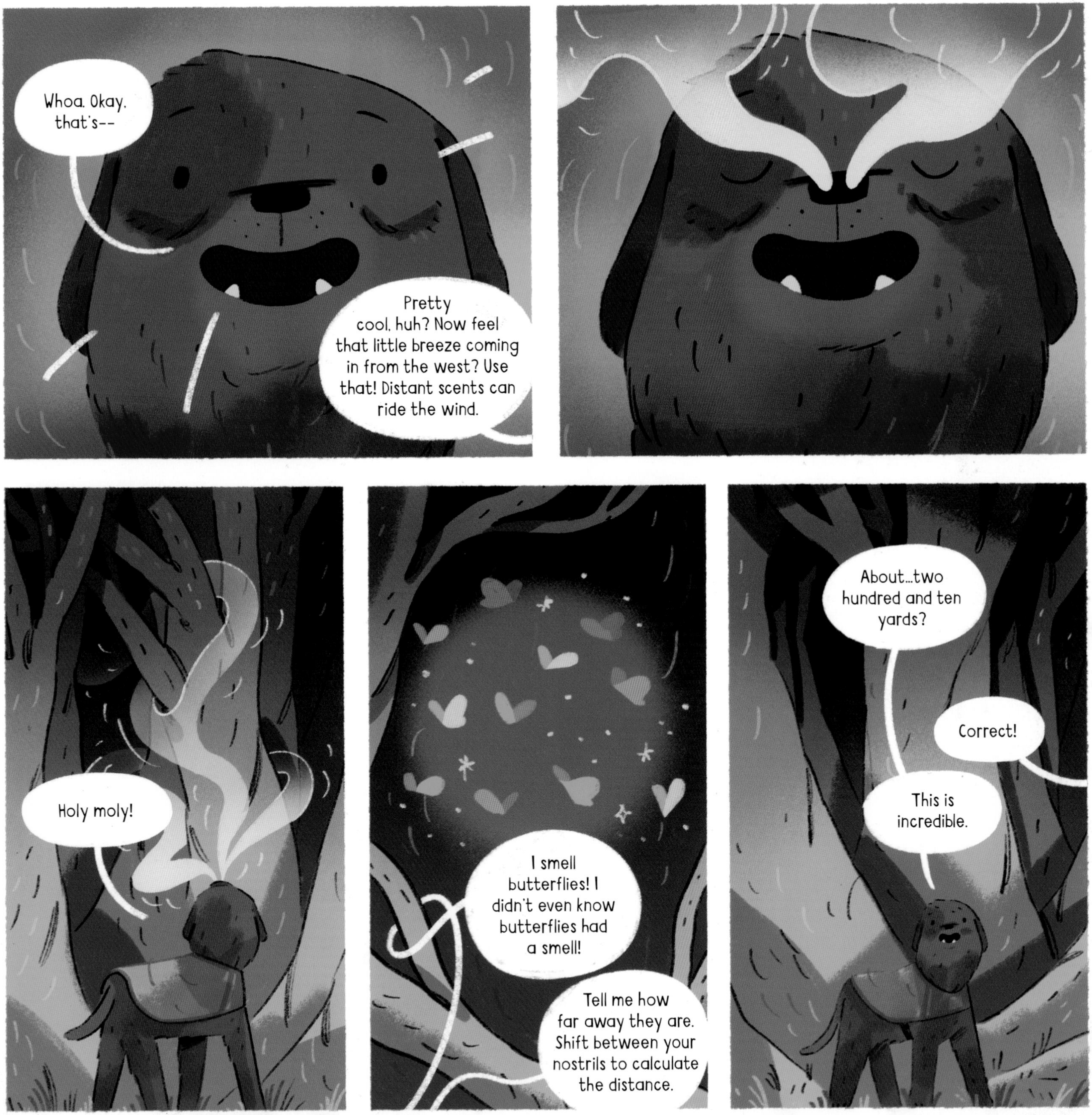

Whoa. Okay, that's--
Pretty cool, huh? Now feel that little breeze coming in from the west? Use that! Distant scents can ride the wind.
Holy moly!
I smell butterflies! I didn't even know butterflies had a smell!
Tell me how far away they are. Shift between your nostrils to calculate the distance.
About...two hundred and ten yards?
Correct!
This is incredible.

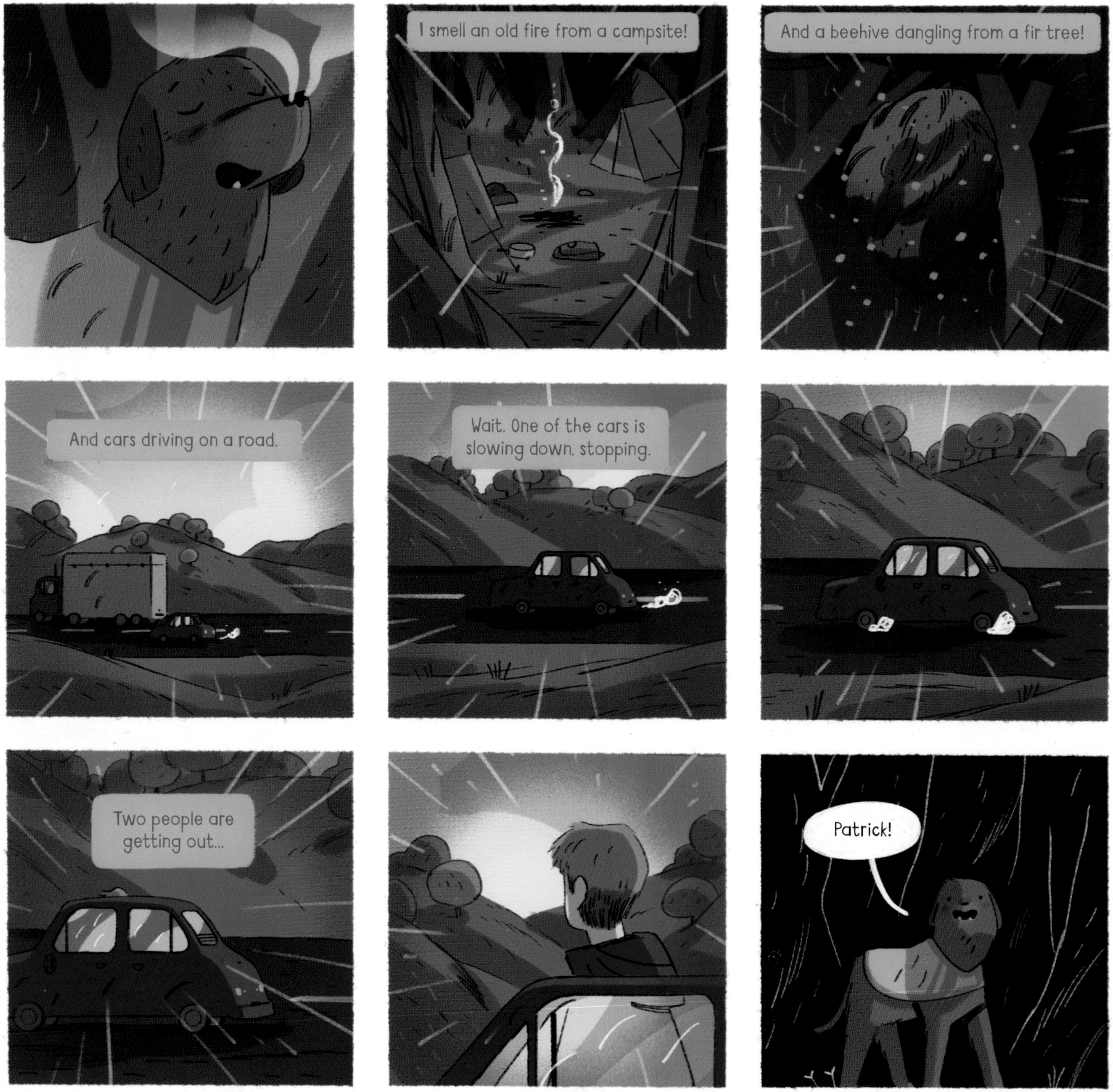
I smell an old fire from a campsite!
And a beehive dangling from a fir tree!
And cars driving on a road.
Wait. One of the cars is slowing down, stopping.
Two people are getting out...
Patrick!

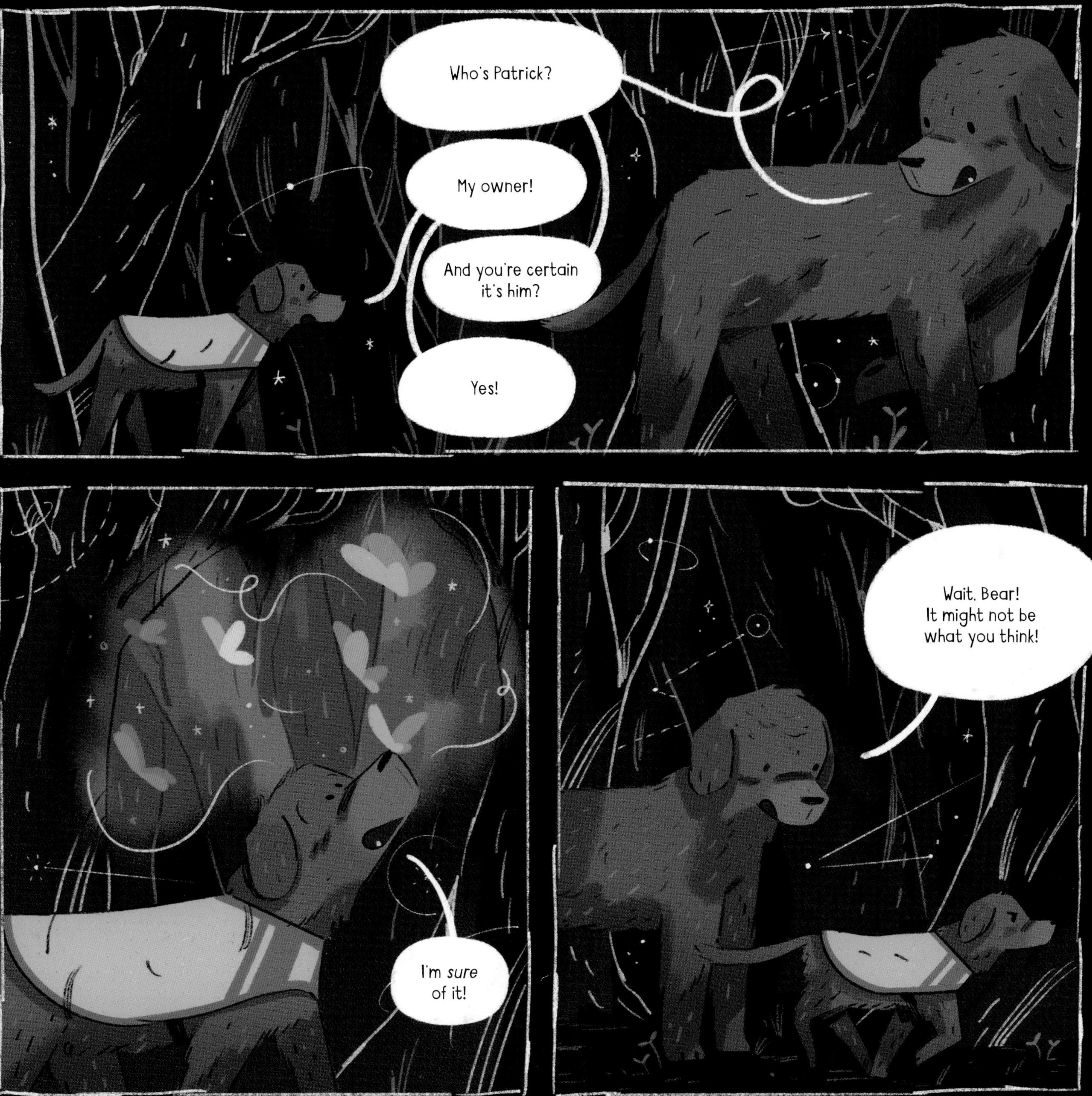
Who's Patrick?
My owner!
And you're certain it's him?
Yes!
I'm *sure* of it!
Wait, Bear! It might not be what you think!

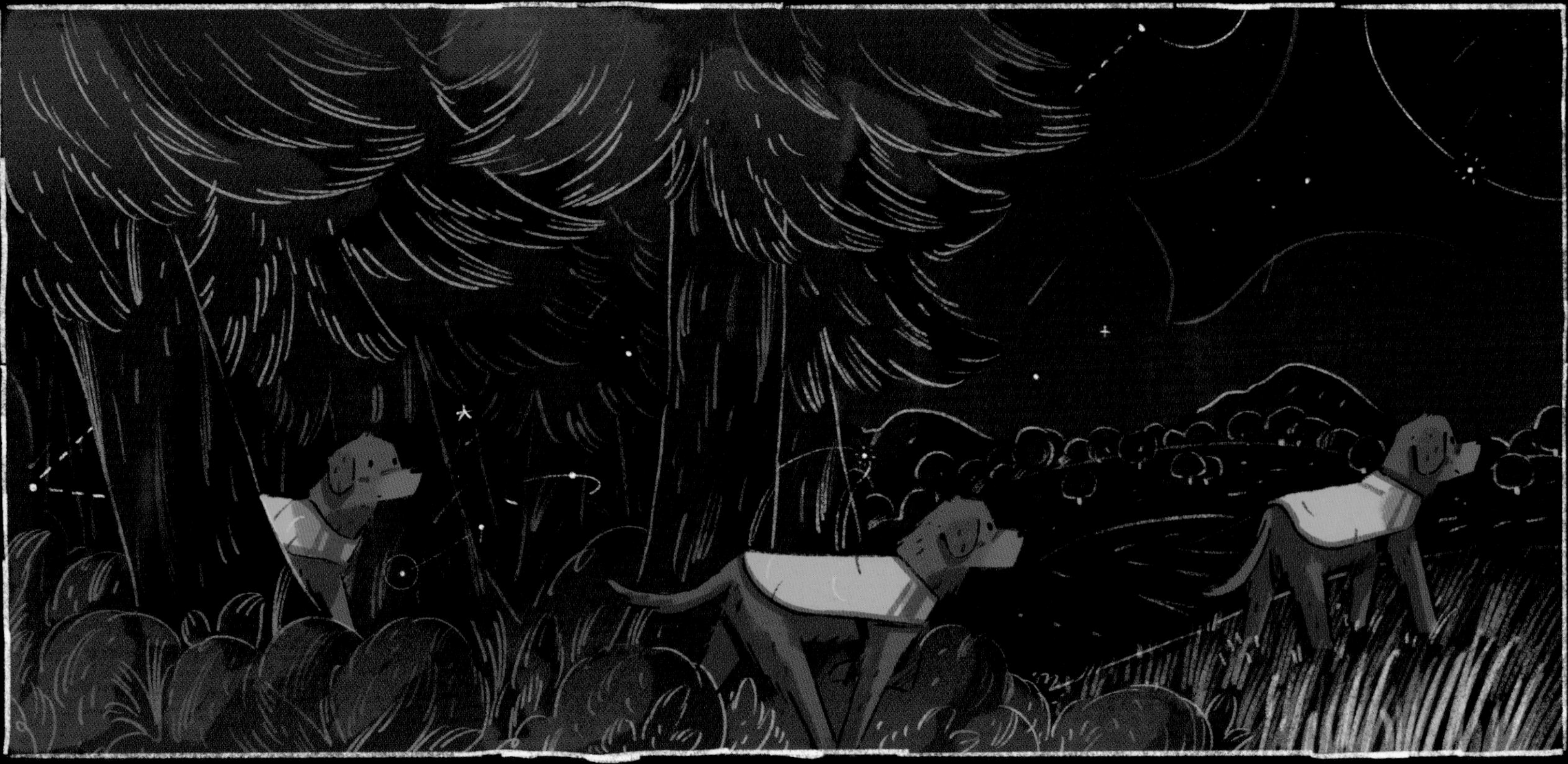

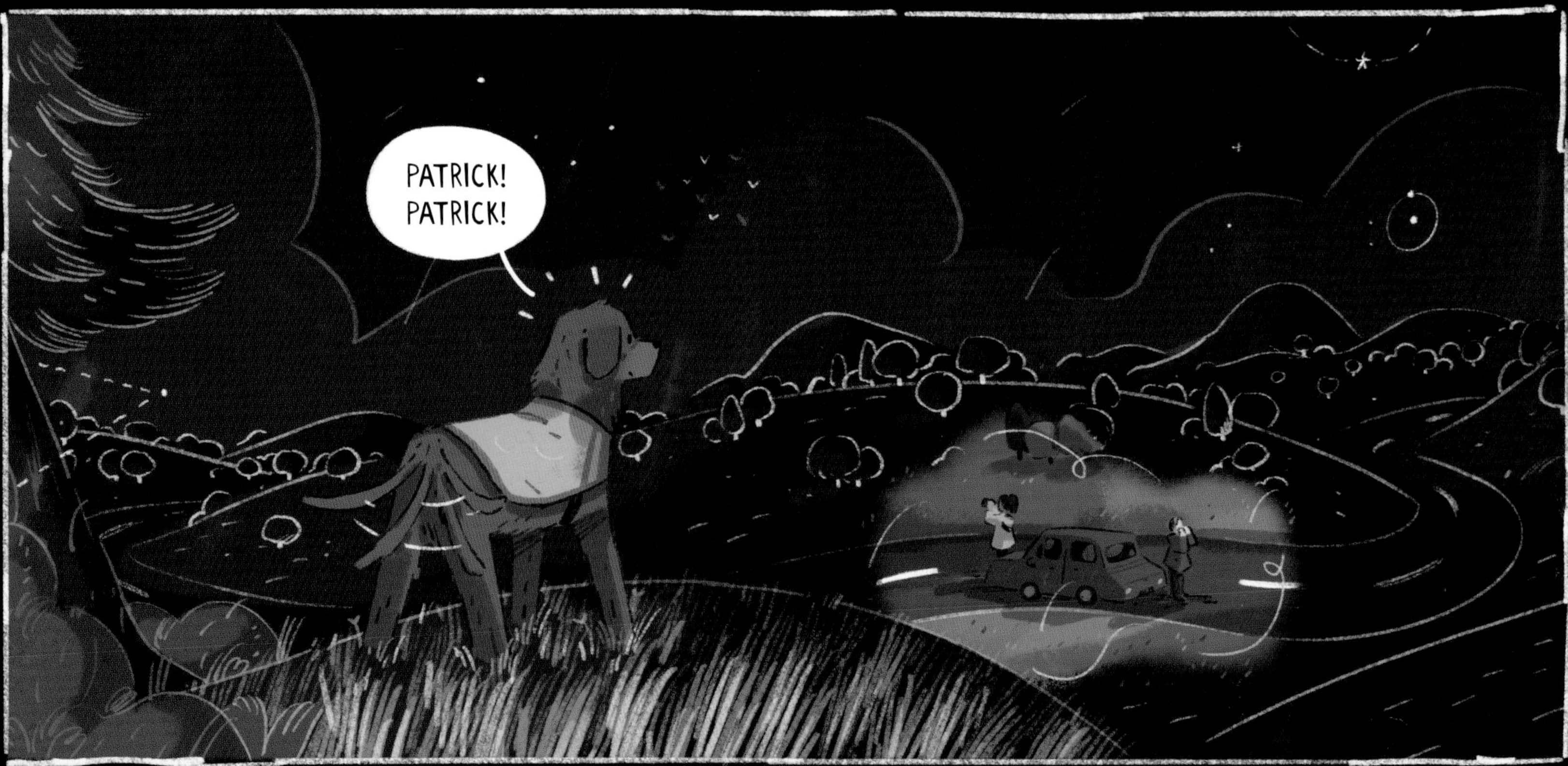
PATRICK!
PATRICK!

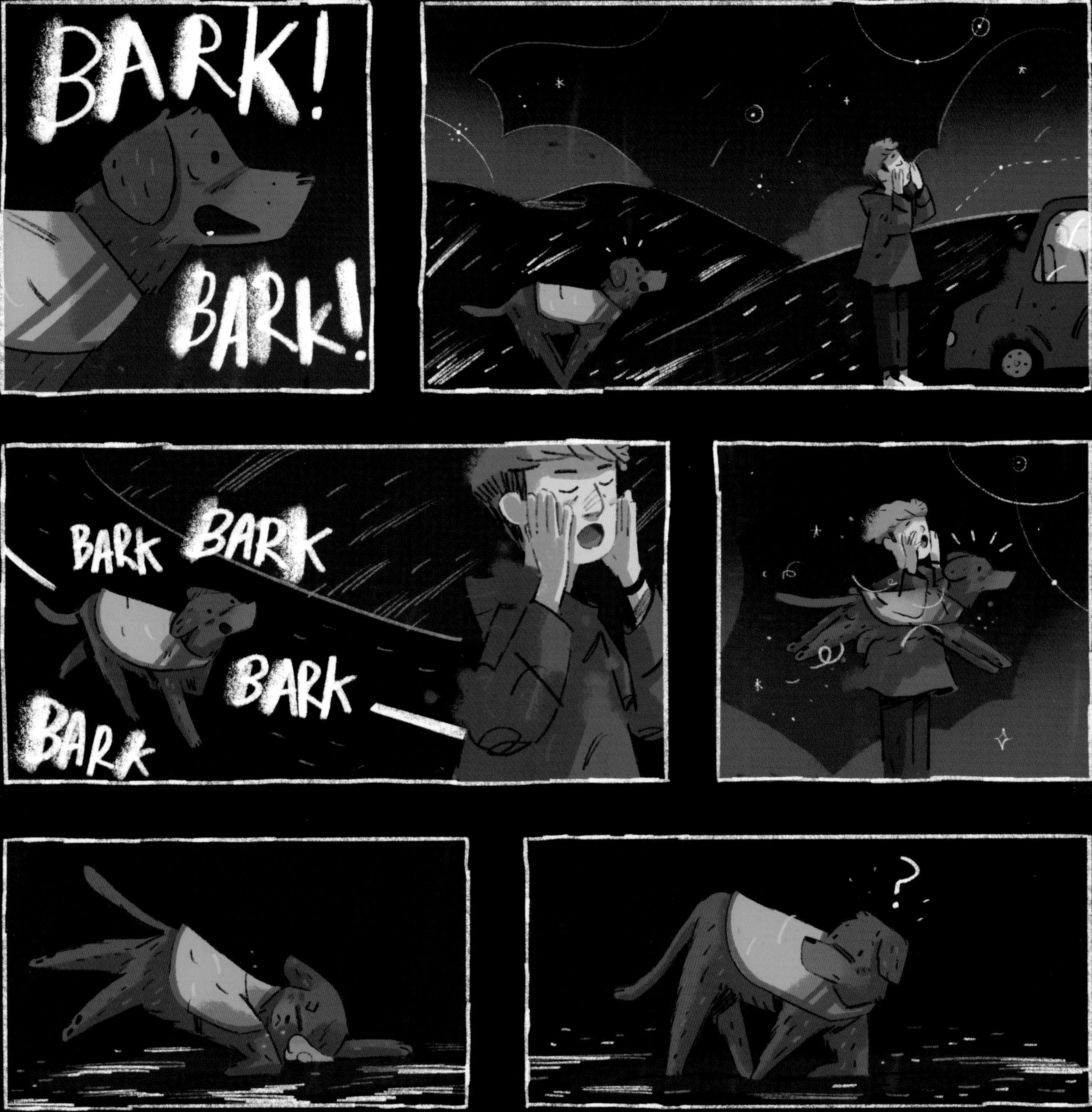
BARK!
BARK!
BARK
BARK
BARK
BARK
?

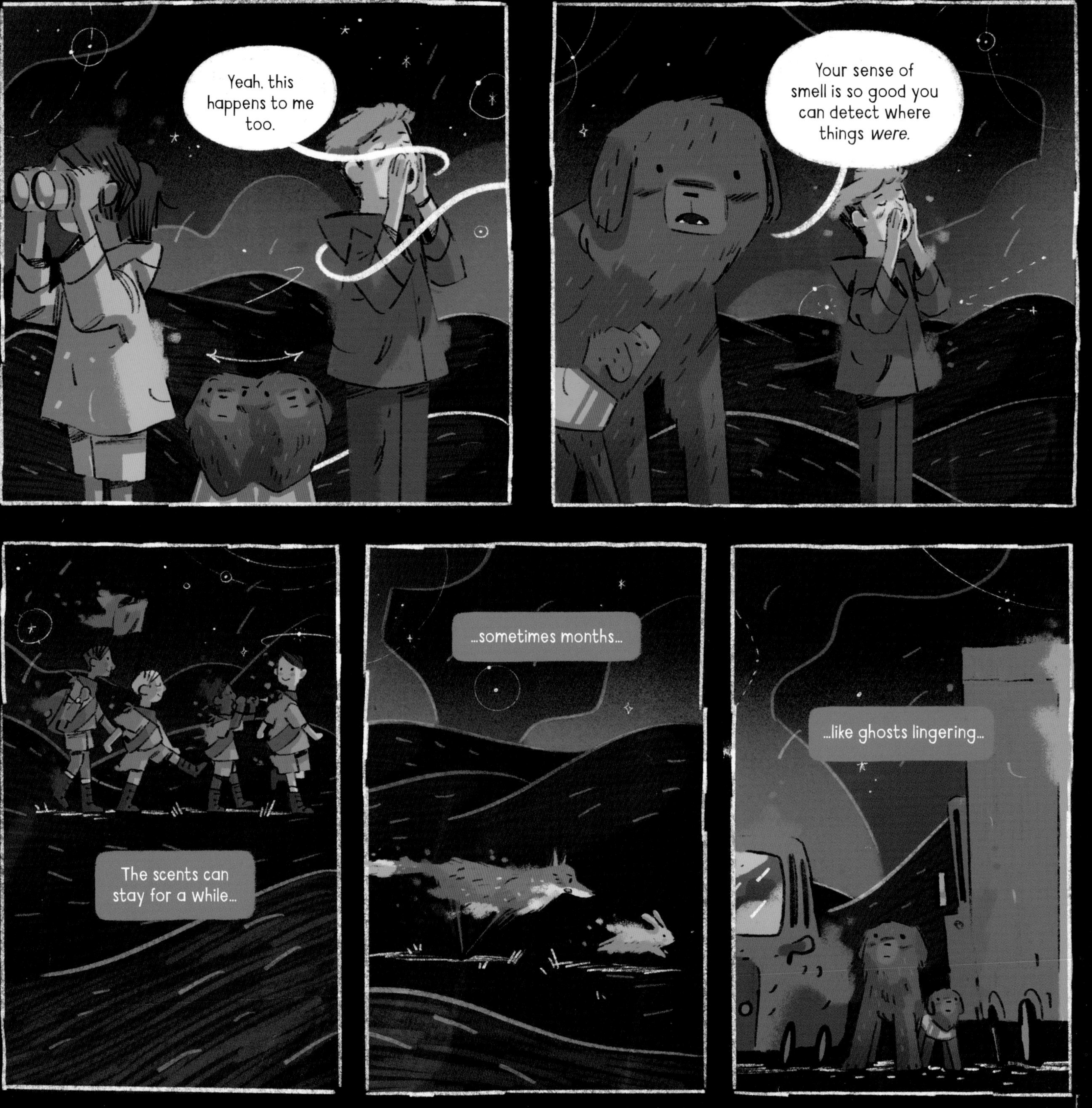
Yeah, this happens to me too.
Your sense of smell is so good you can detect where things *were*.
The scents can stay for a while...
...sometimes months...
...like ghosts lingering...

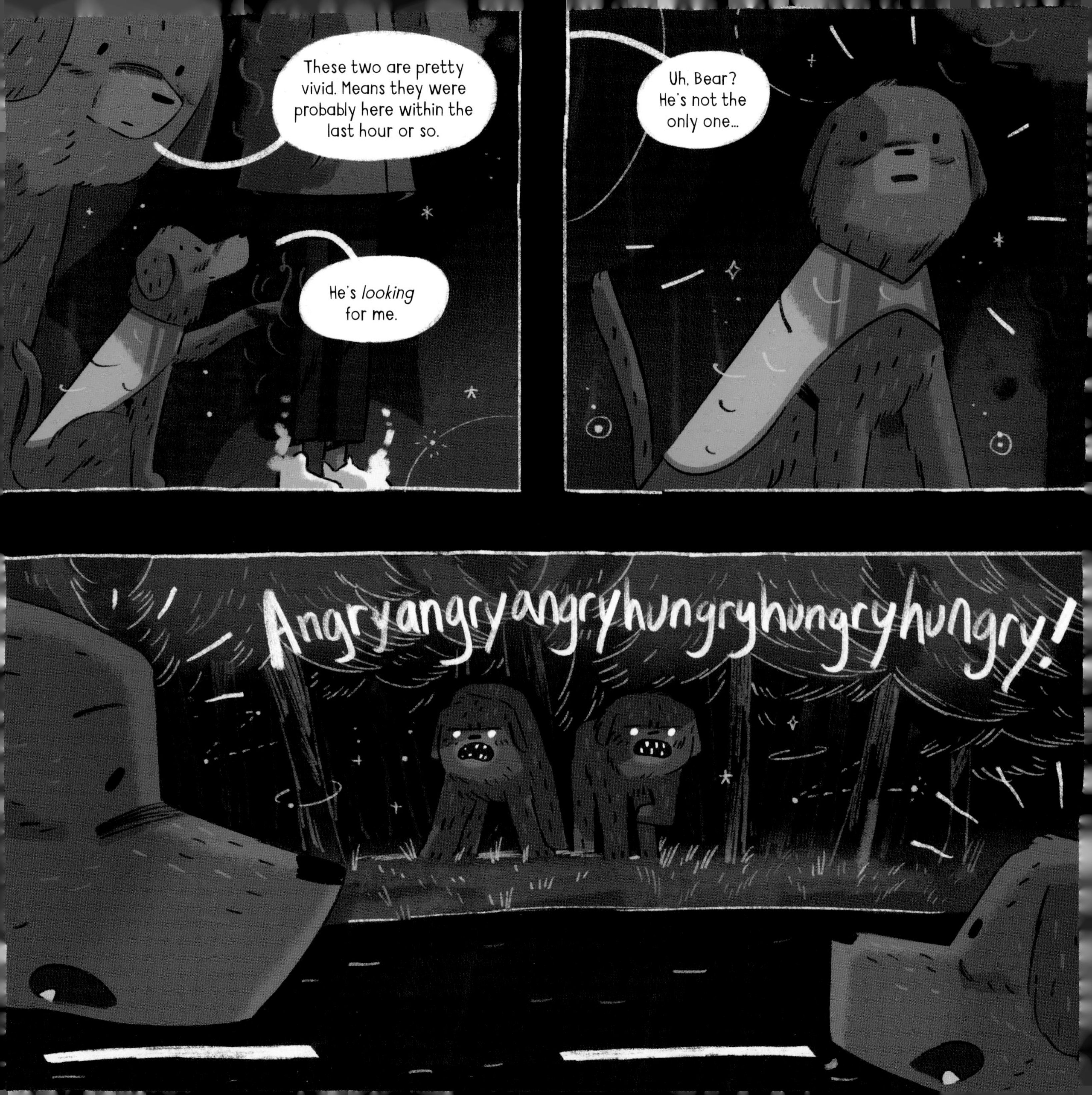
These two are pretty vivid. Means they were probably here within the last hour or so.
He's *looking* for me.
Uh, Bear? He's not the only one...
Angryangryangryhungryhungryhungry!

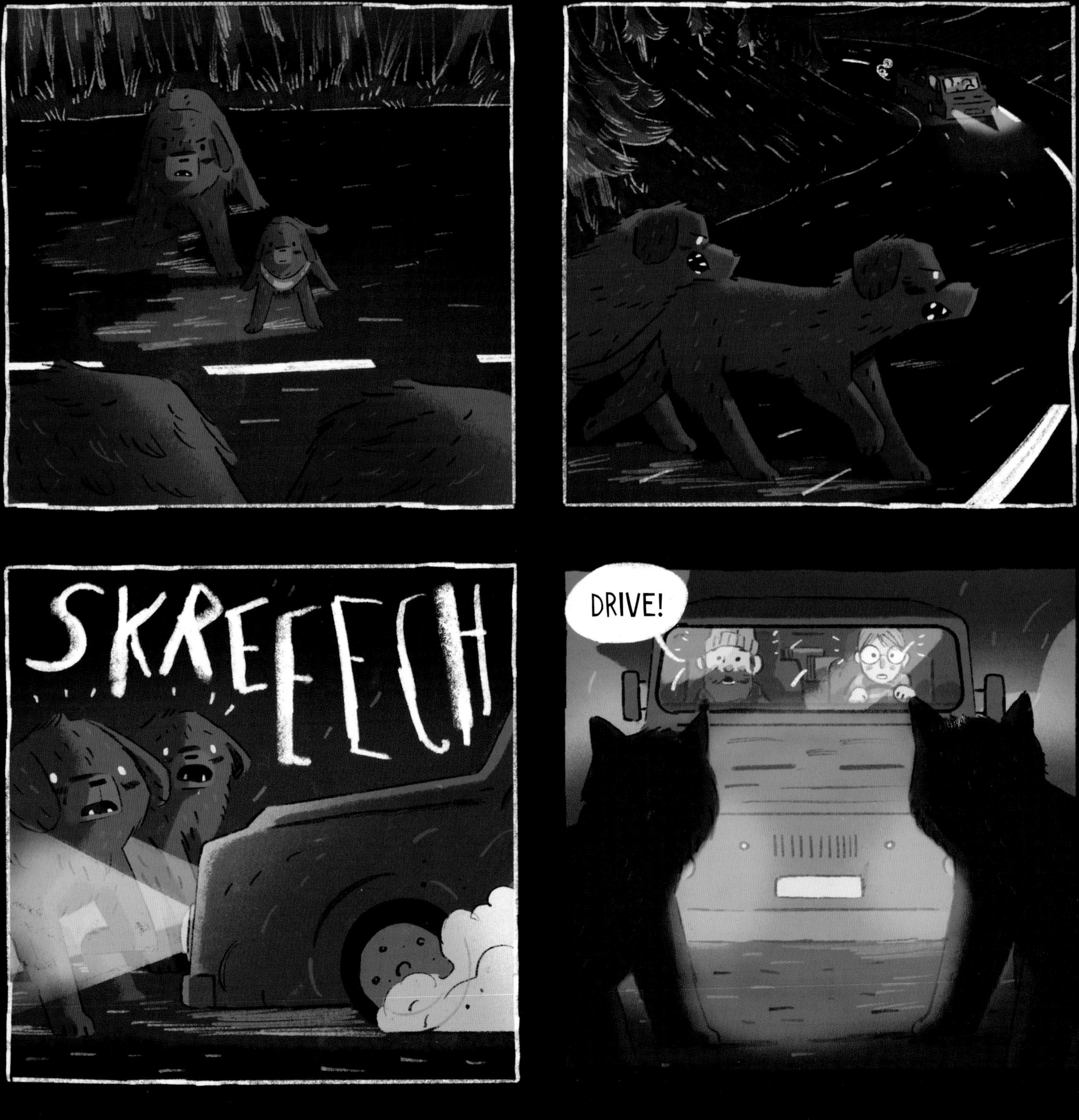
SKREEECH
DRIVE!

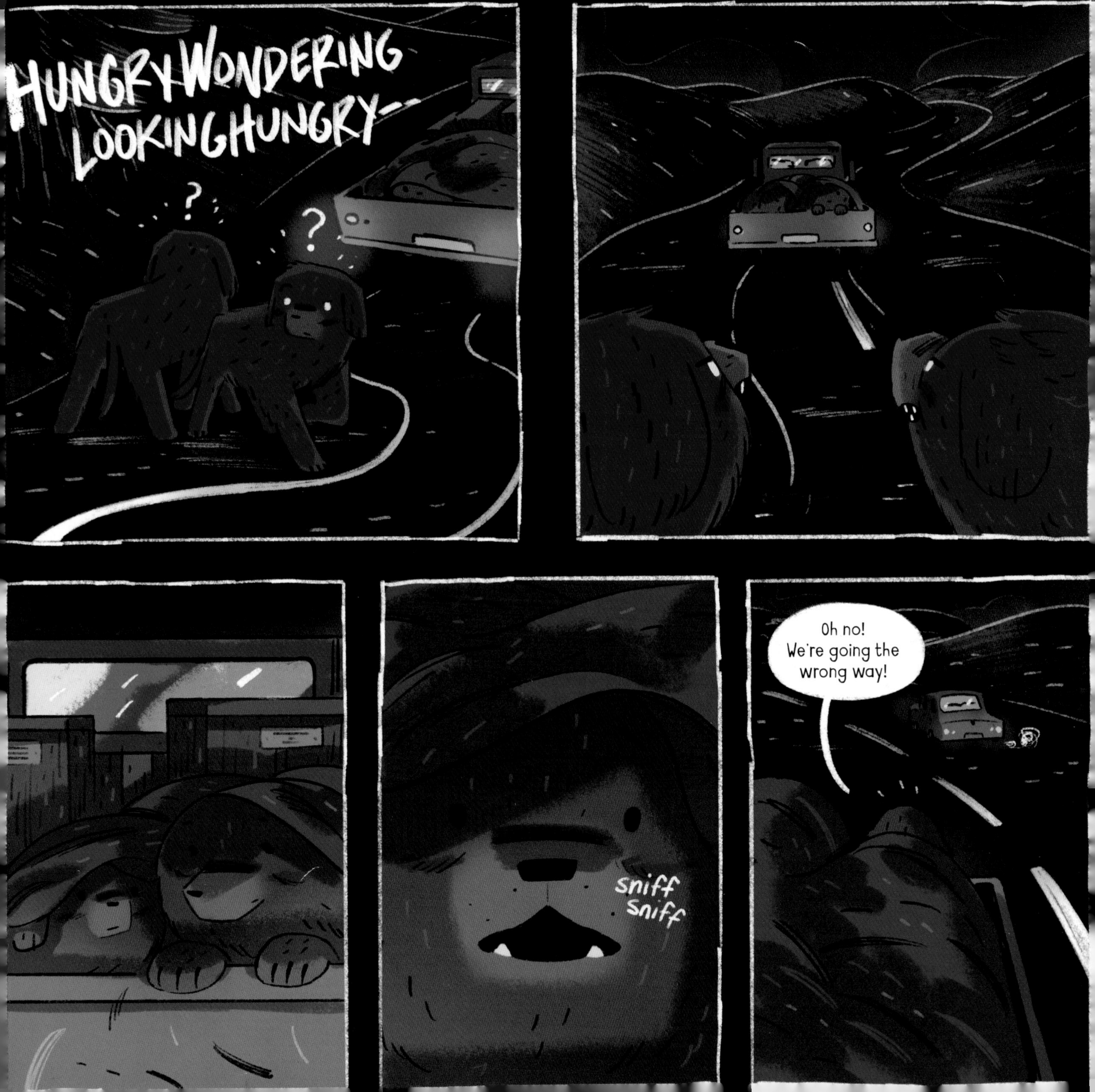
HUNGRY WONDERING LOOKING HUNGRY--
sniff sniff
Oh no! We're going the wrong way!

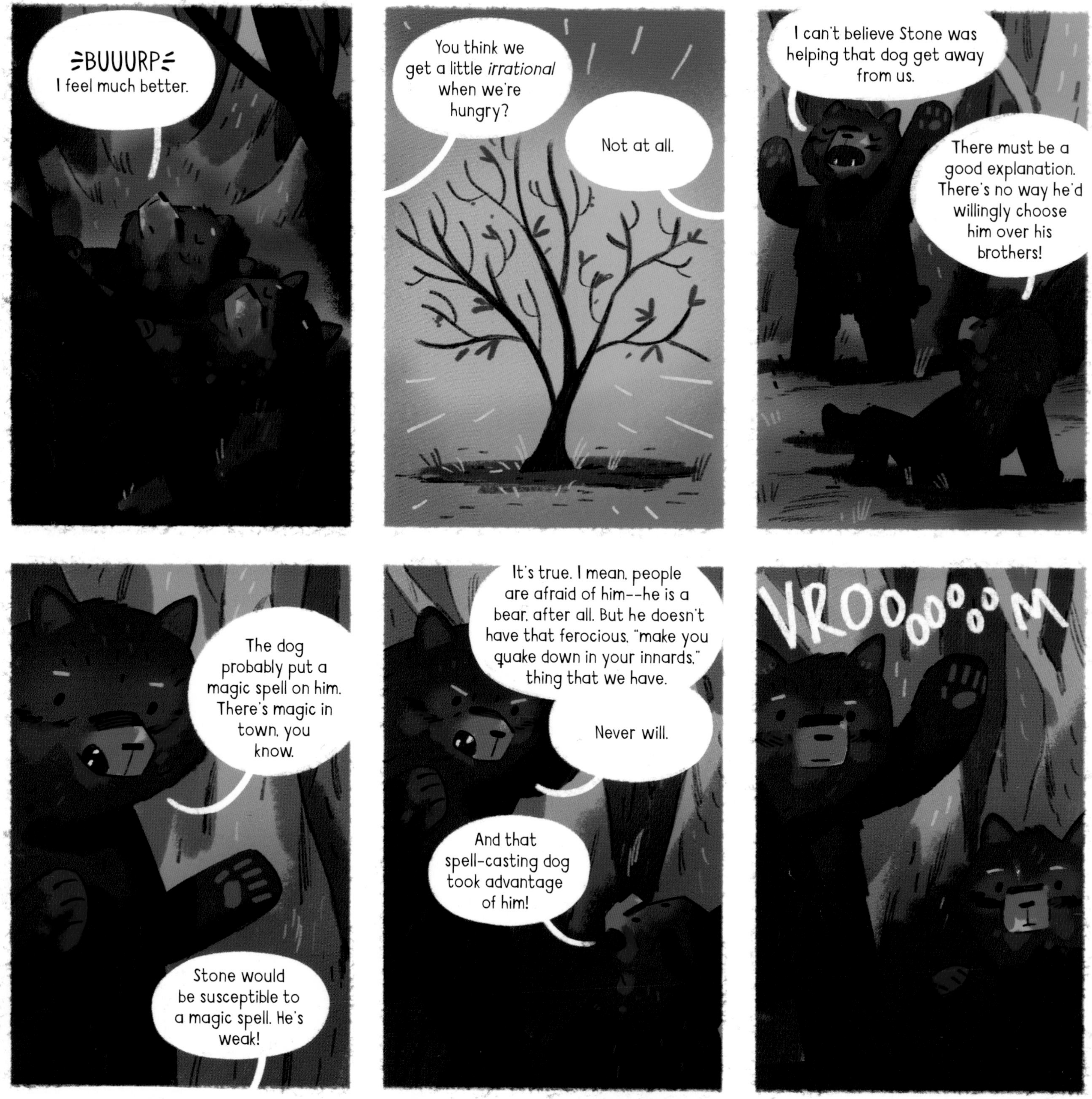

BUUURP
I feel much better.
You think we get a little *irrational* when we're hungry?
Not at all.
I can't believe Stone was helping that dog get away from us.
There must be a good explanation. There's no way he'd willingly choose him over his brothers!
The dog probably put a magic spell on him. There's magic in town, you know.
Stone would be susceptible to a magic spell. He's weak!
It's true. I mean, people are afraid of him--he is a bear, after all. But he doesn't have that ferocious, "make you quake down in your innards," thing that we have.
Never will.
And that spell-casting dog took advantage of him!
VROOooooM

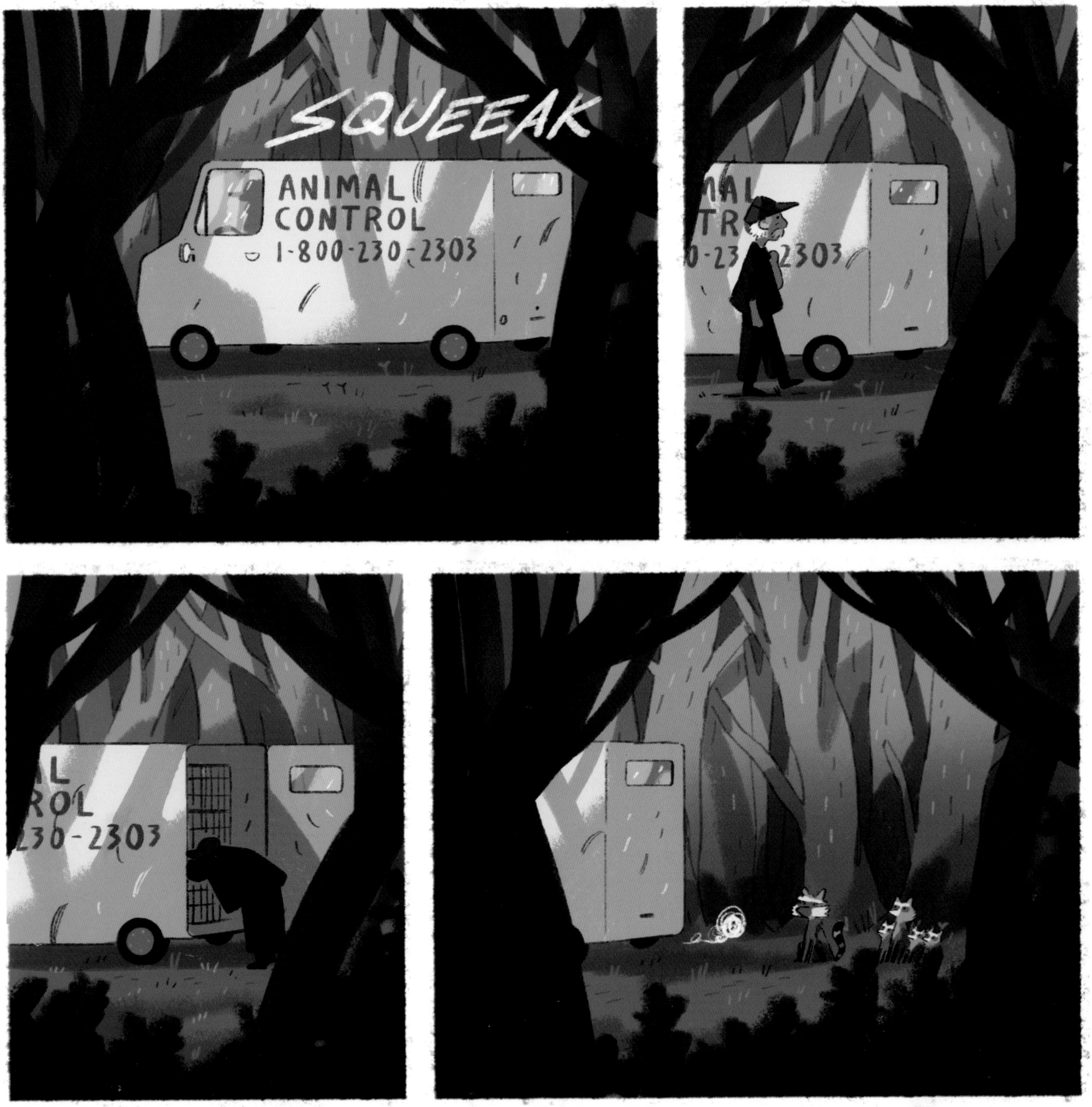
SQUEEAK
ANIMAL
CONTROL
1-800-230-2303

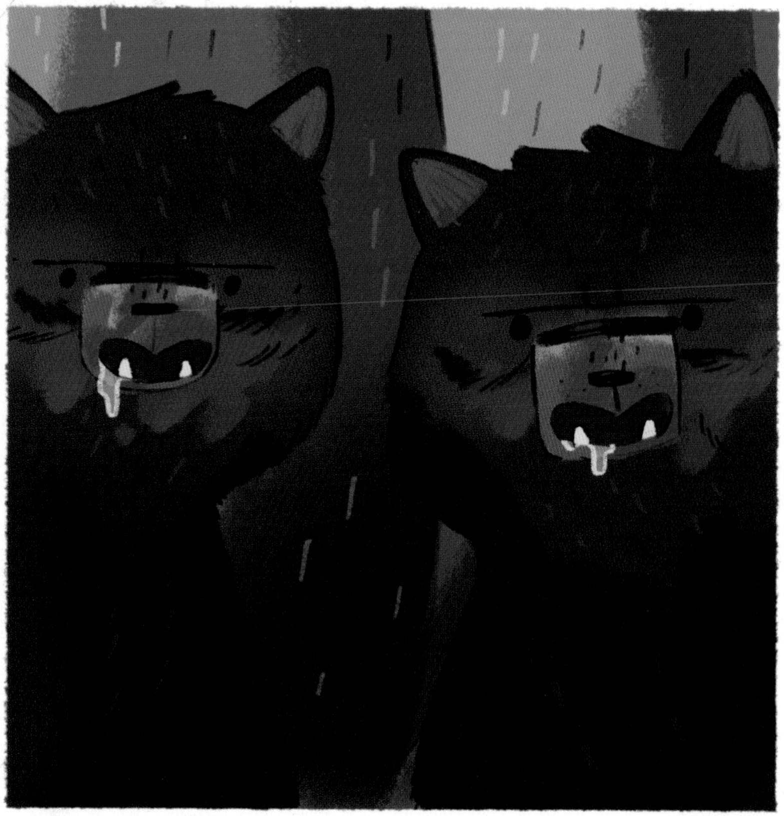

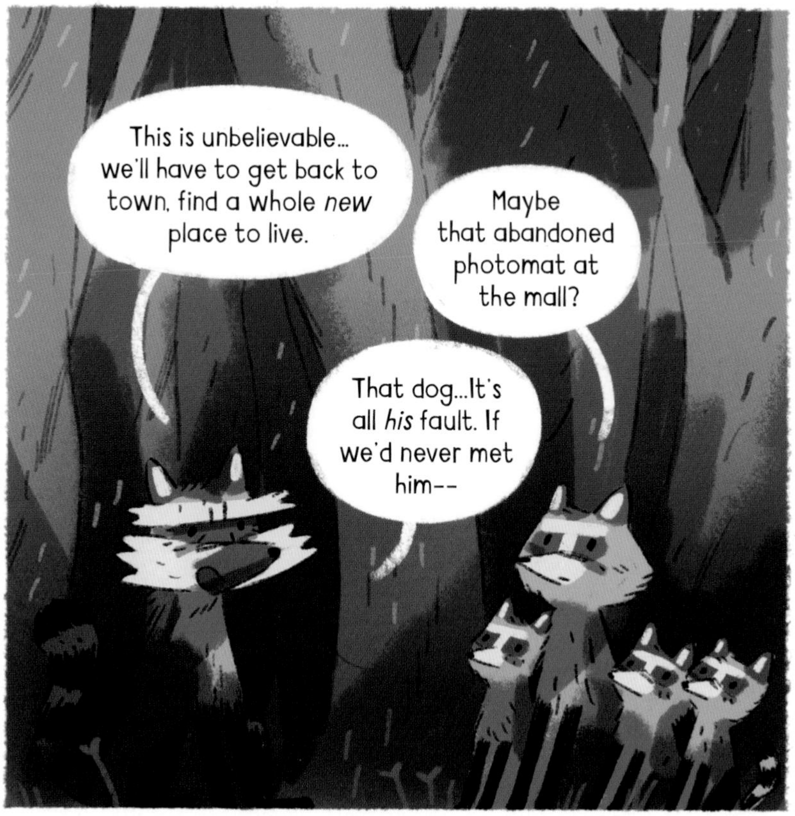
This is unbelievable... we'll have to get back to town, find a whole *new* place to live.
Maybe that abandoned photomat at the mall?
That dog...It's all *his* fault. If we'd never met him--

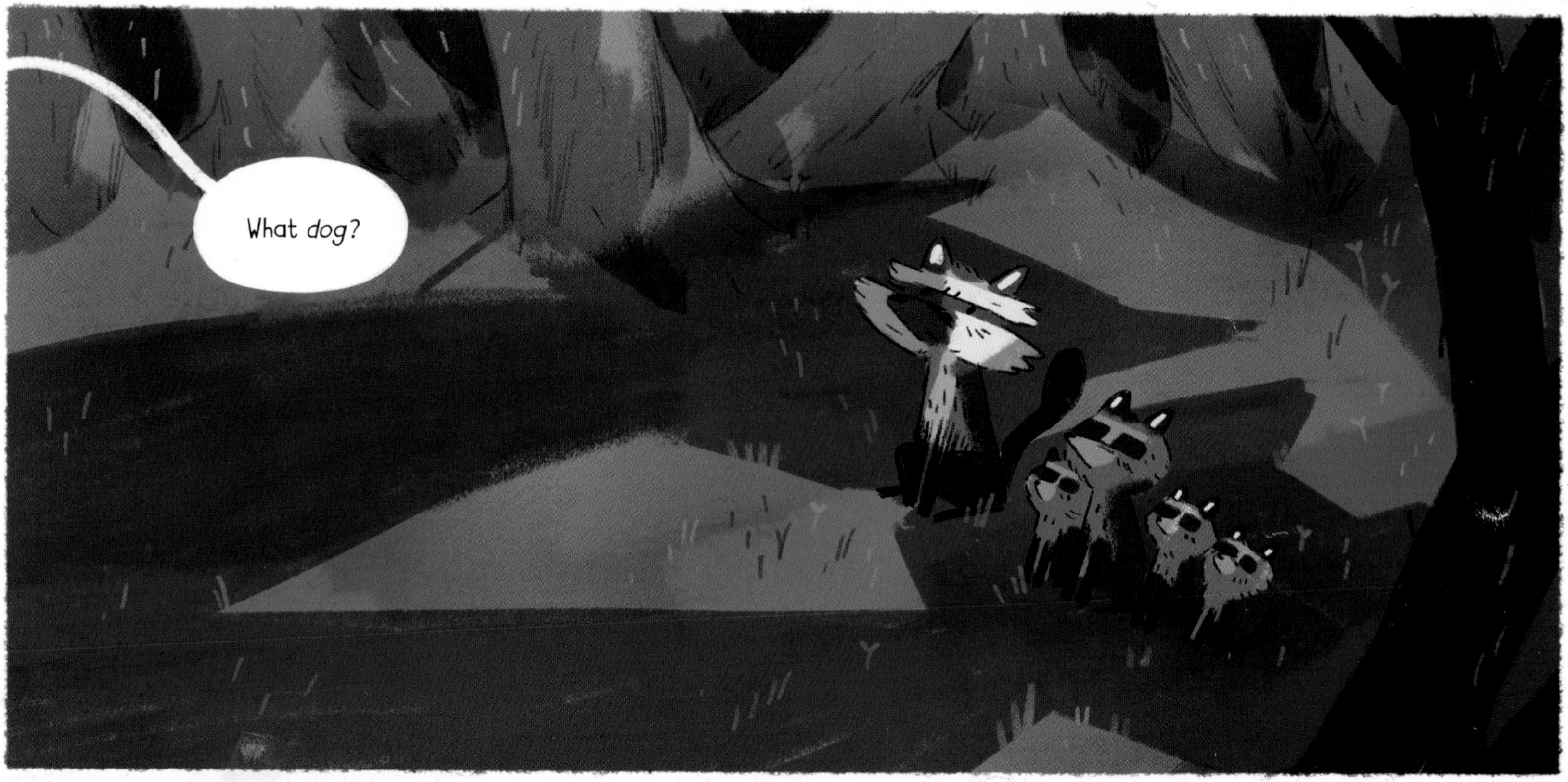
What *dog*?

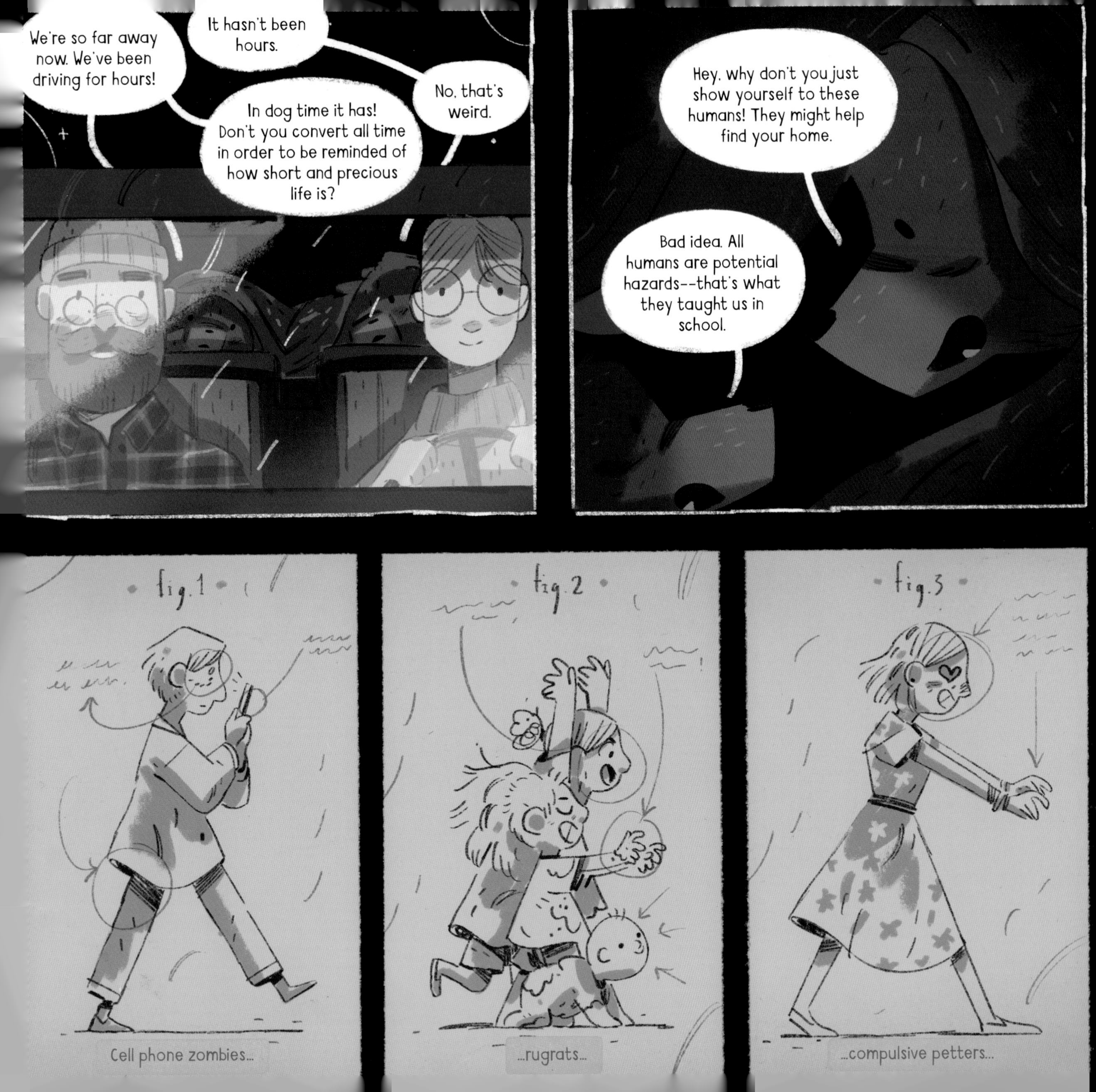
We're so far away now. We've been driving for hours!
It hasn't been hours.
In dog time it has! Don't you convert all time in order to be reminded of how short and precious life is?
No, that's weird.
Hey, why don't you just show yourself to these humans! They might help find your home.
Bad idea. All humans are potential hazards--that's what they taught us in school.
fig. 1
Cell phone zombies...
fig. 2
...rugrats...
fig. 3
...compulsive petters...

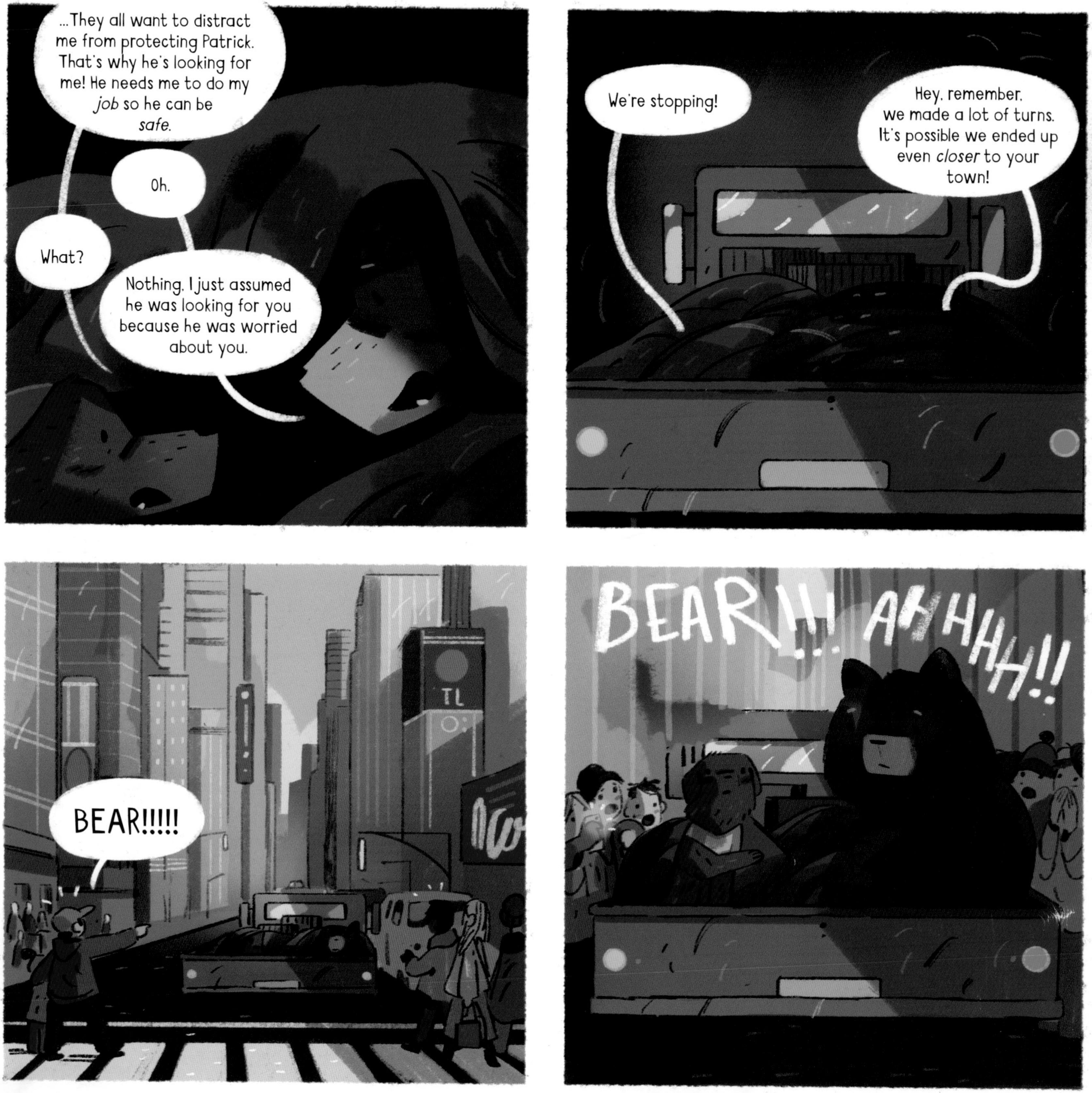
...They all want to distract me from protecting Patrick. That's why he's looking for me! He needs me to do my *job* so he can be *safe*.
Oh.
What?
Nothing. I just assumed he was looking for you because he was worried about you.
We're stopping!
Hey, remember, we made a lot of turns. It's possible we ended up even *closer* to your town!
BEAR!!!!!
BEAR!!!
AHHHH!!

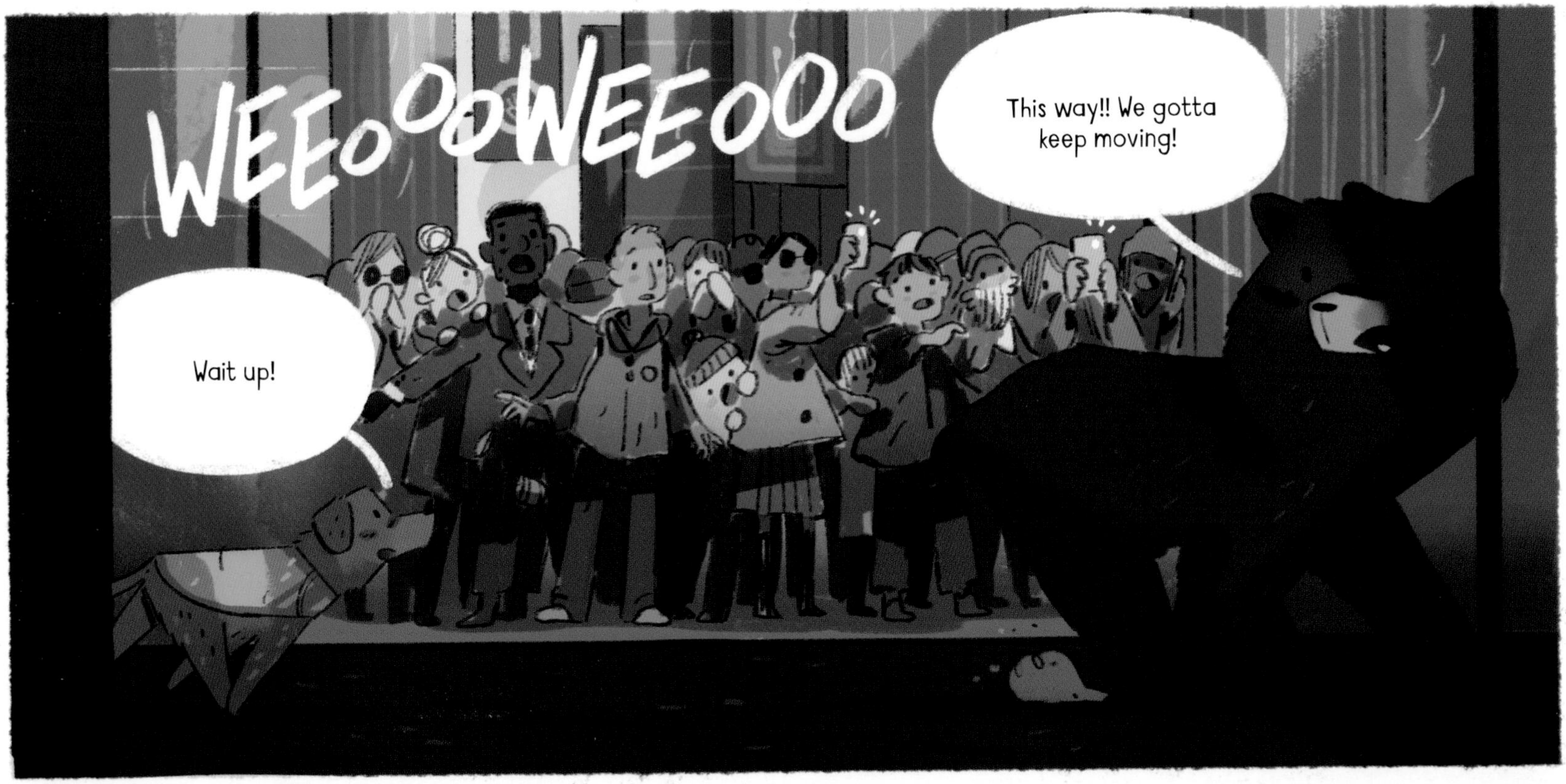
WEEoOoWEEooo
This way!! We gotta keep moving!
Wait up!

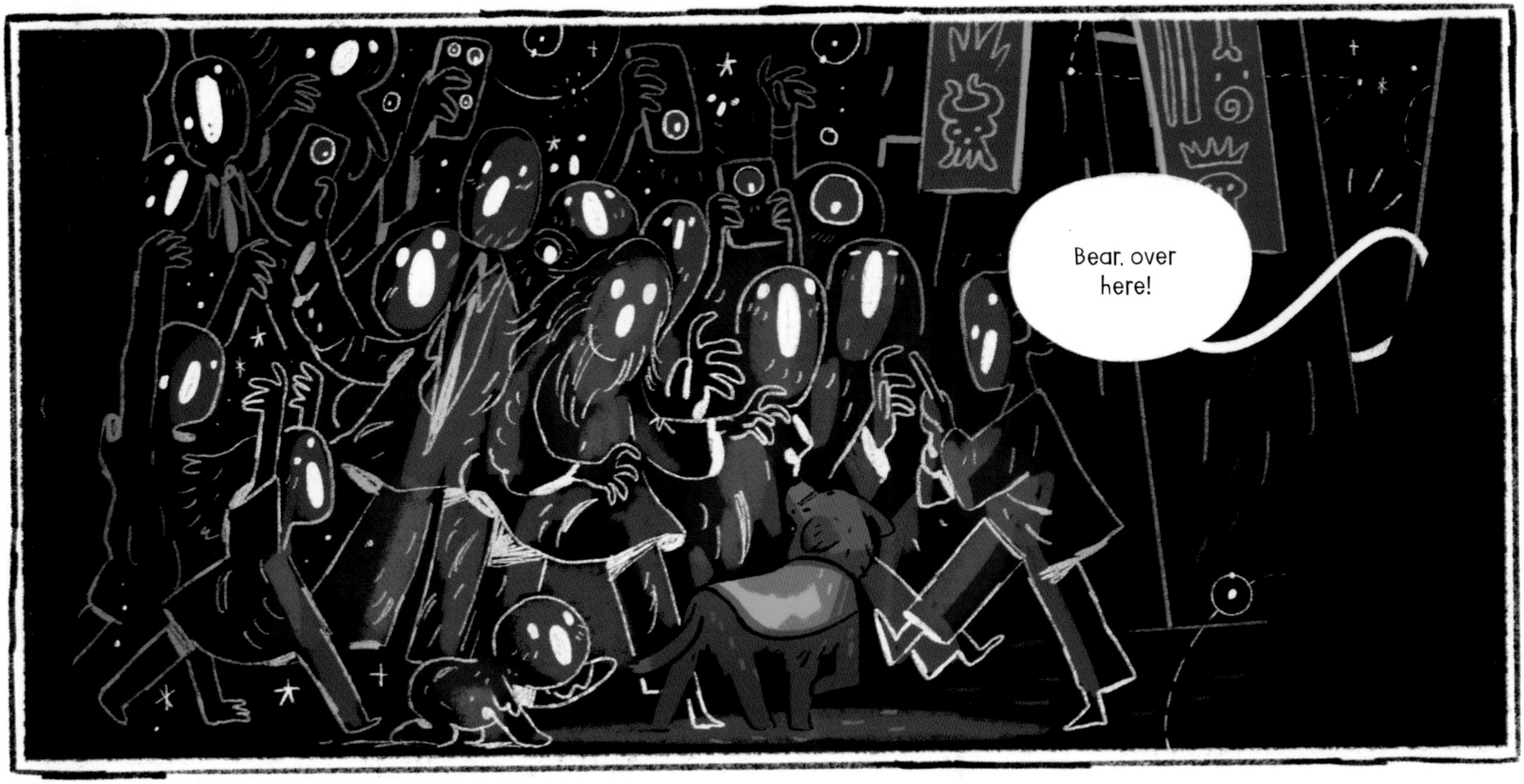
Bear, over here!

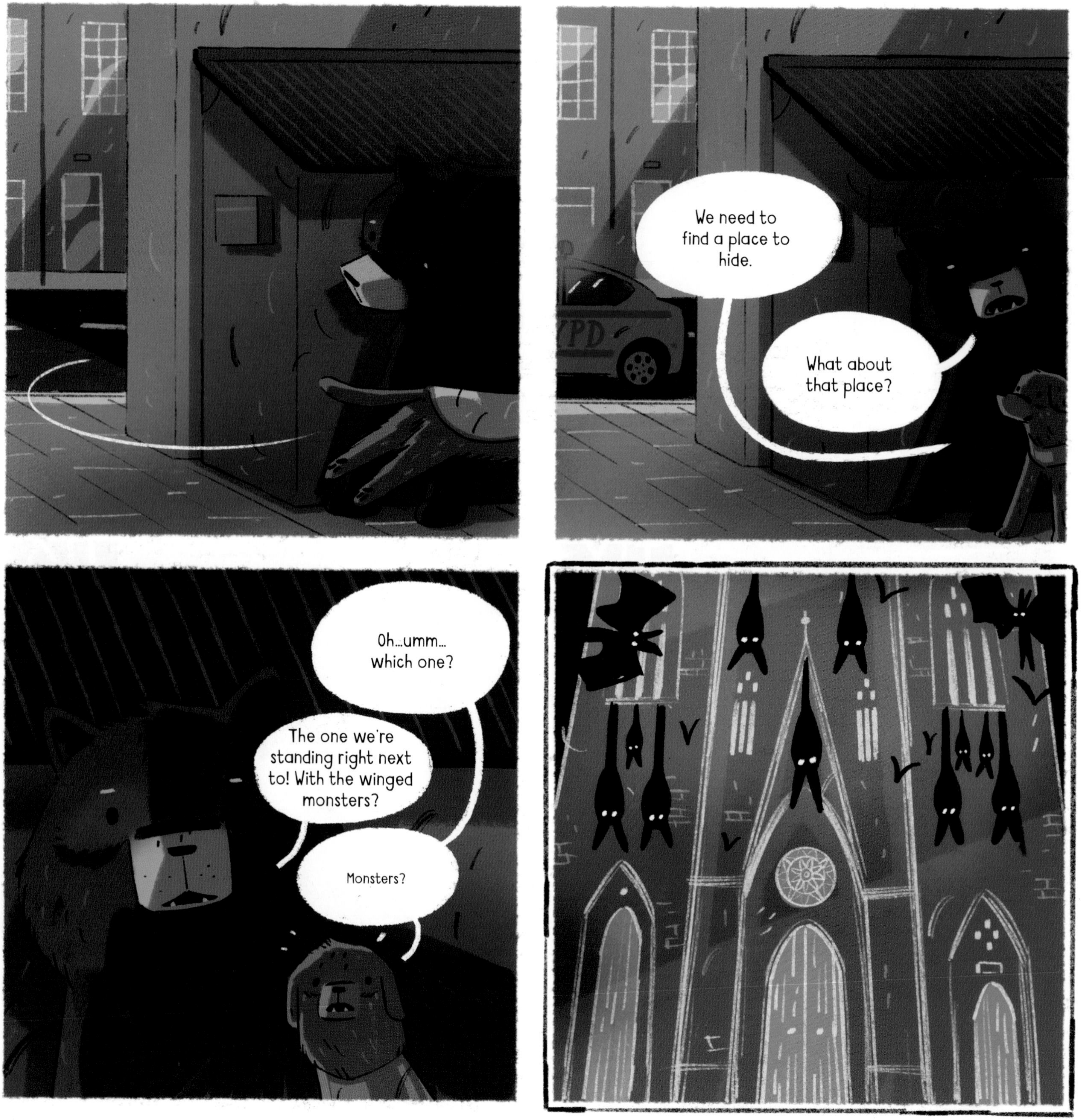
We need to find a place to hide.
What about that place?
Oh...umm... which one?
The one we're standing right next to! With the winged monsters?
Monsters?

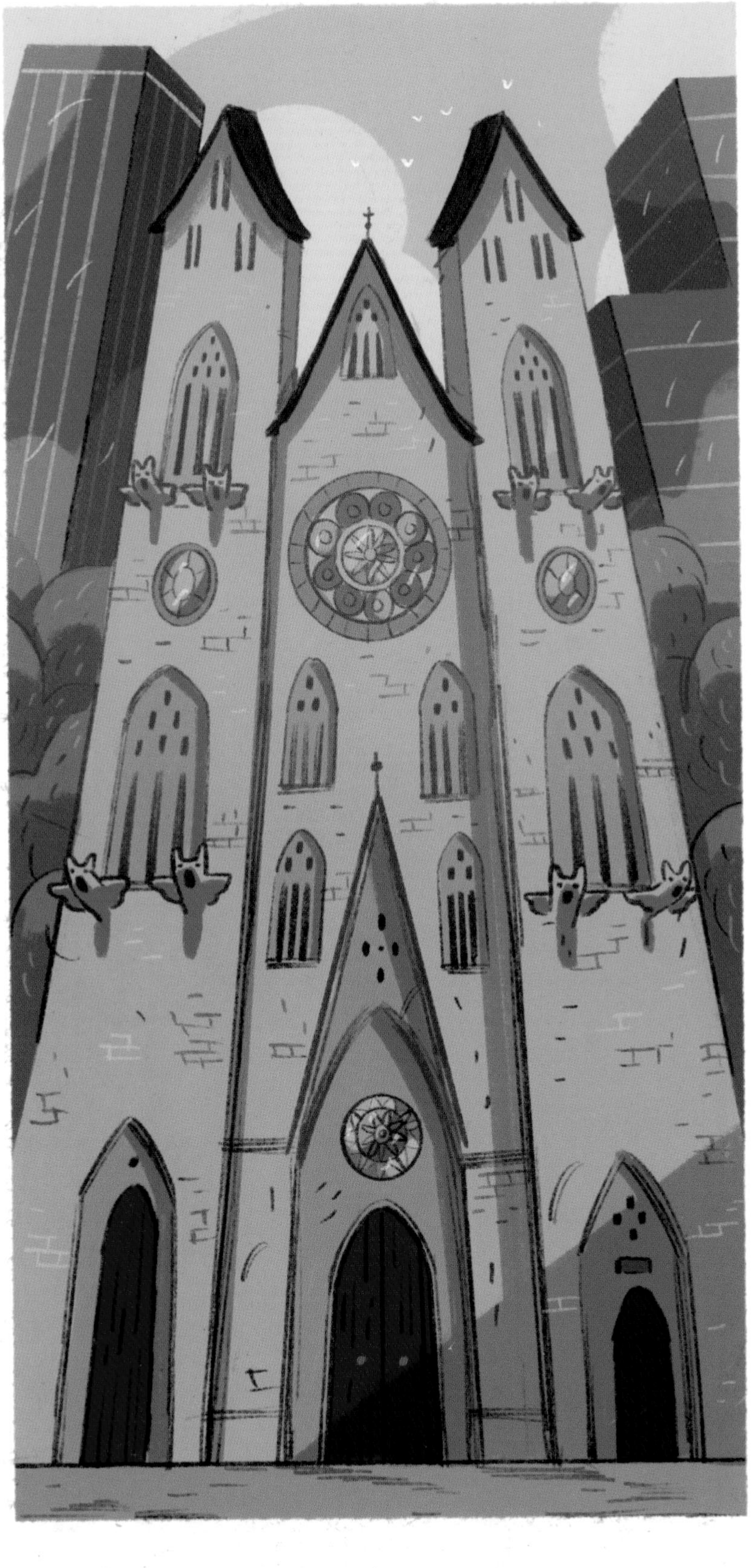

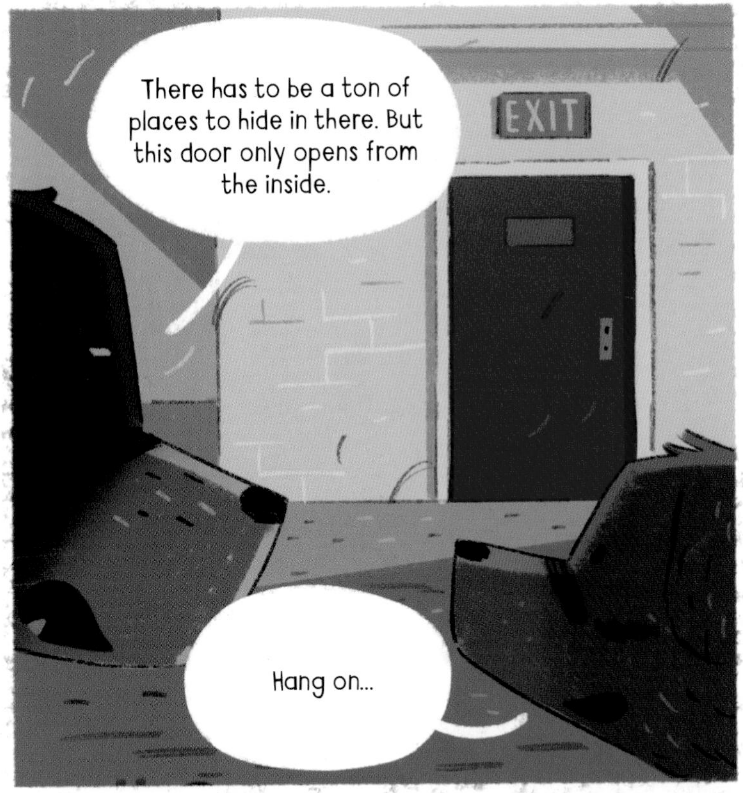
There has to be a ton of places to hide in there. But this door only opens from the inside.
EXIT
Hang on...

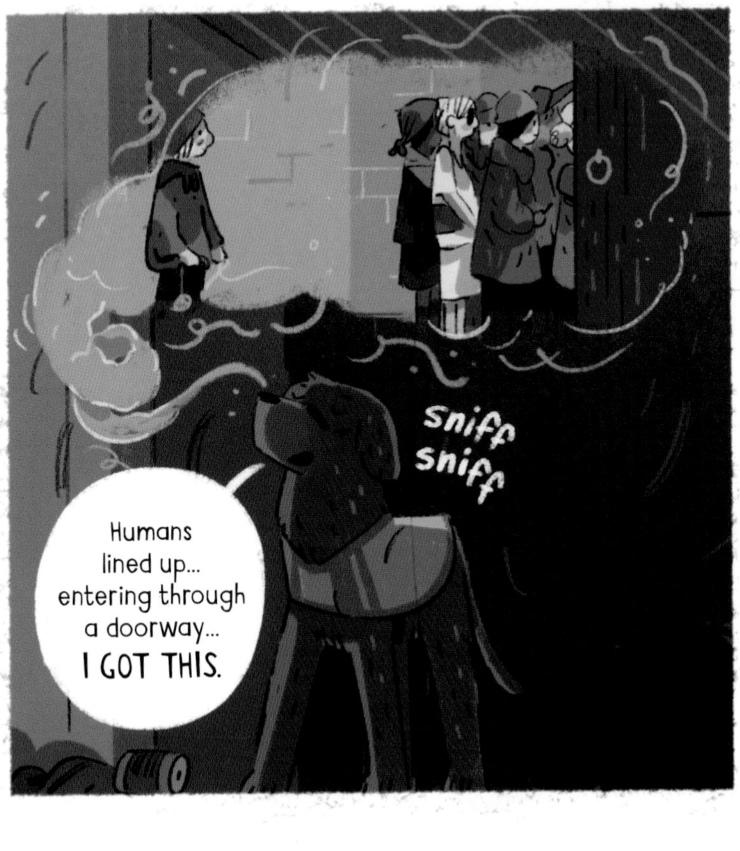
sniff sniff
Humans lined up... entering through a doorway... I GOT THIS.

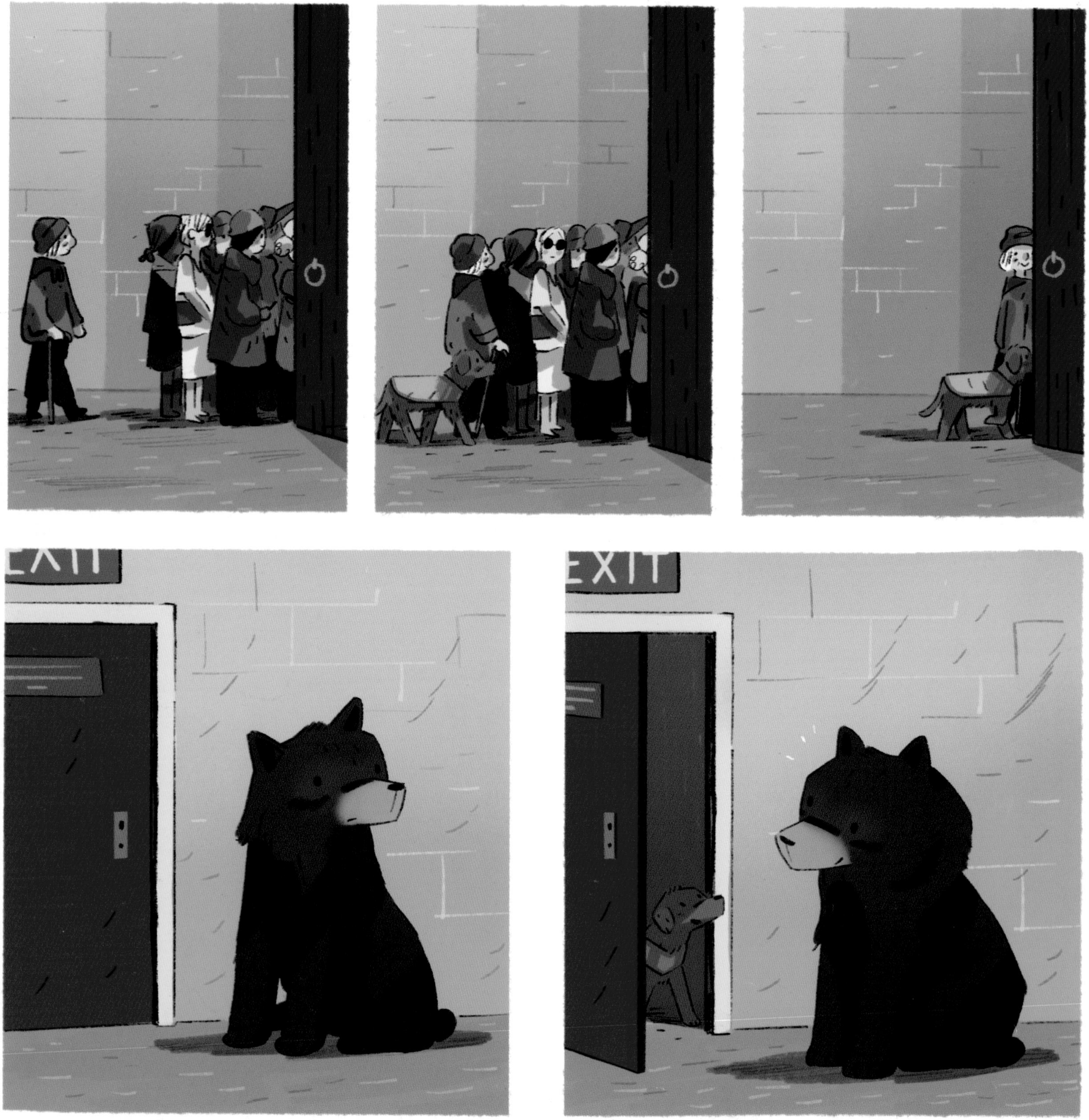
EXIT
EXIT

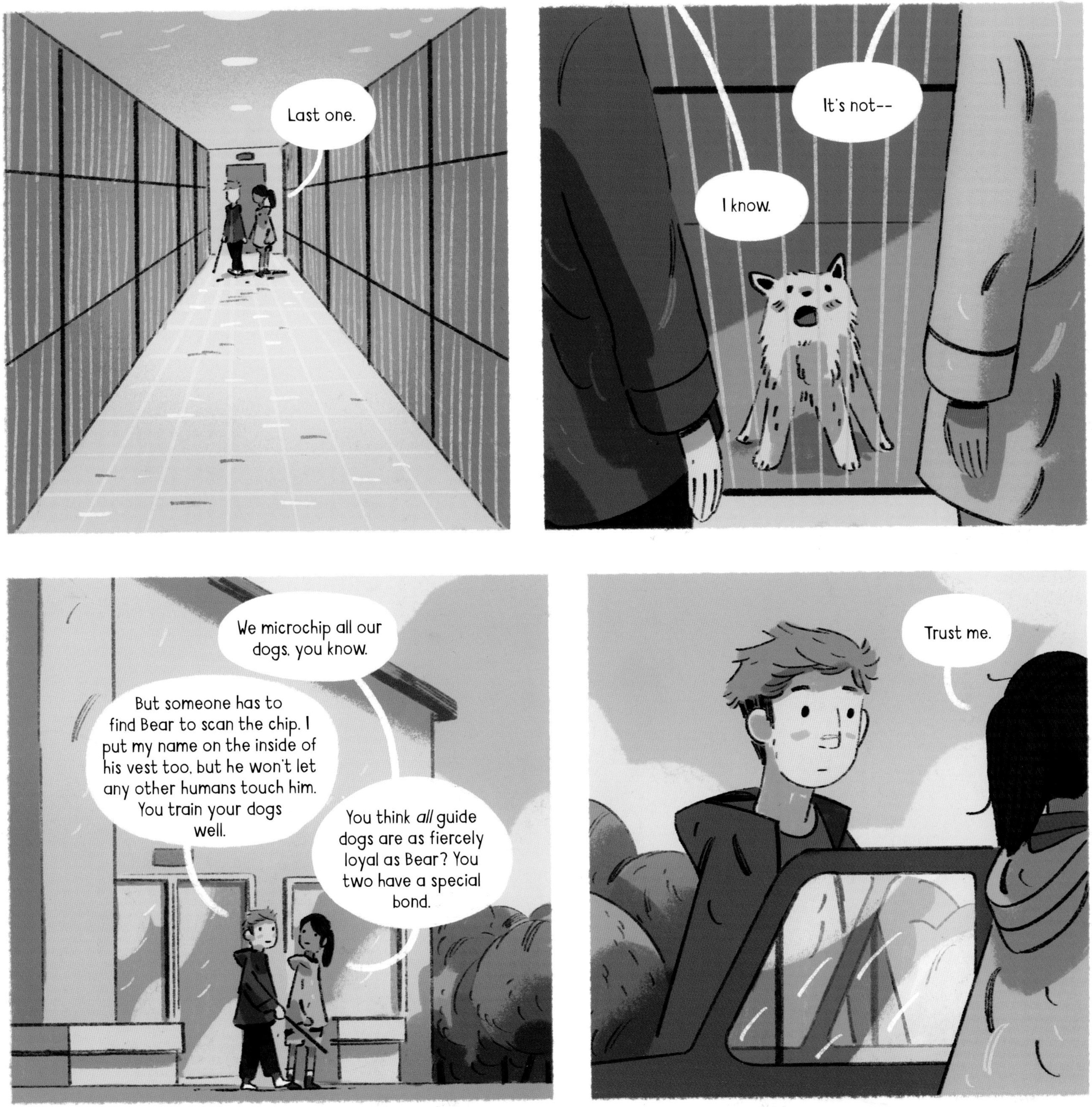

Last one.
It's not--
I know.
We microchip all our dogs, you know.
But someone has to find Bear to scan the chip. I put my name on the inside of his vest too, but he won't let any other humans touch him. You train your dogs well.
You think *all* guide dogs are as fiercely loyal as Bear? You two have a special bond.
Trust me.

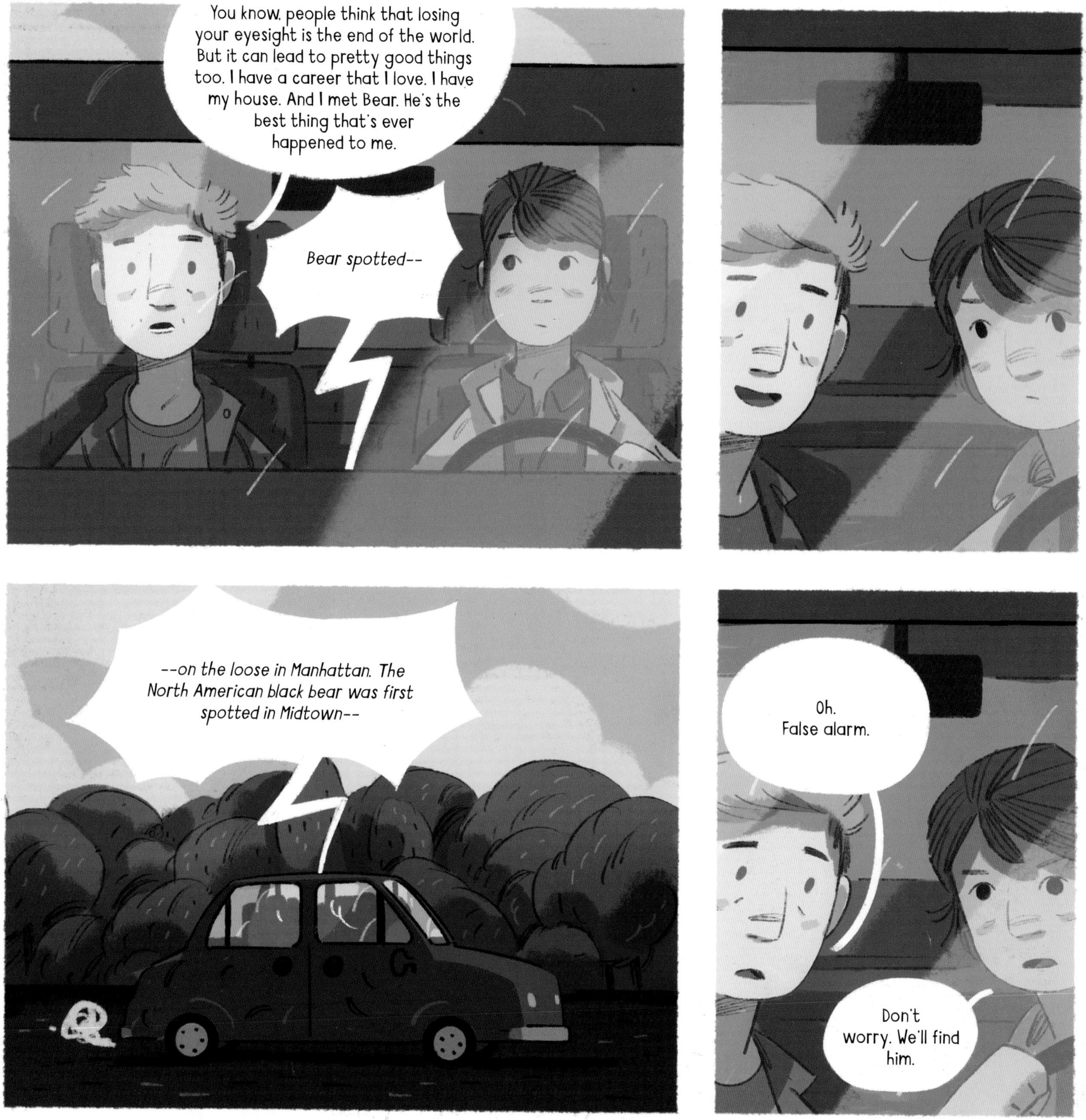

You know, people think that losing your eyesight is the end of the world. But it can lead to pretty good things too. I have a career that I love. I have my house. And I met Bear. He's the best thing that's ever happened to me.
Bear spotted--
--on the loose in Manhattan. The North American black bear was first spotted in Midtown--
Oh. False alarm.
Don't worry. We'll find him.

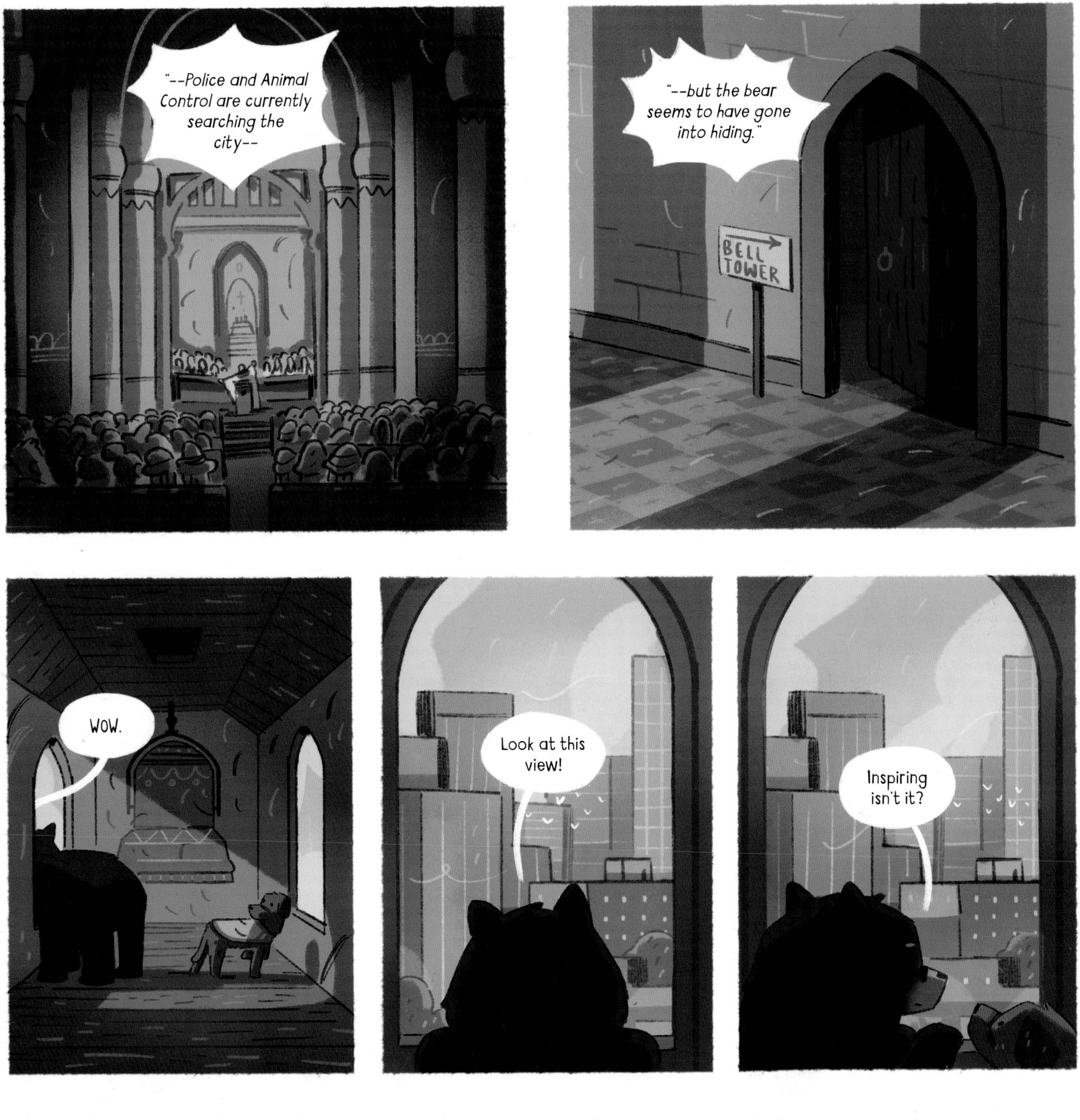
"--Police and Animal Control are currently searching the city--
"--but the bear seems to have gone into hiding."
BELL TOWER
WOW.
Look at this view!
Inspiring isn't it?

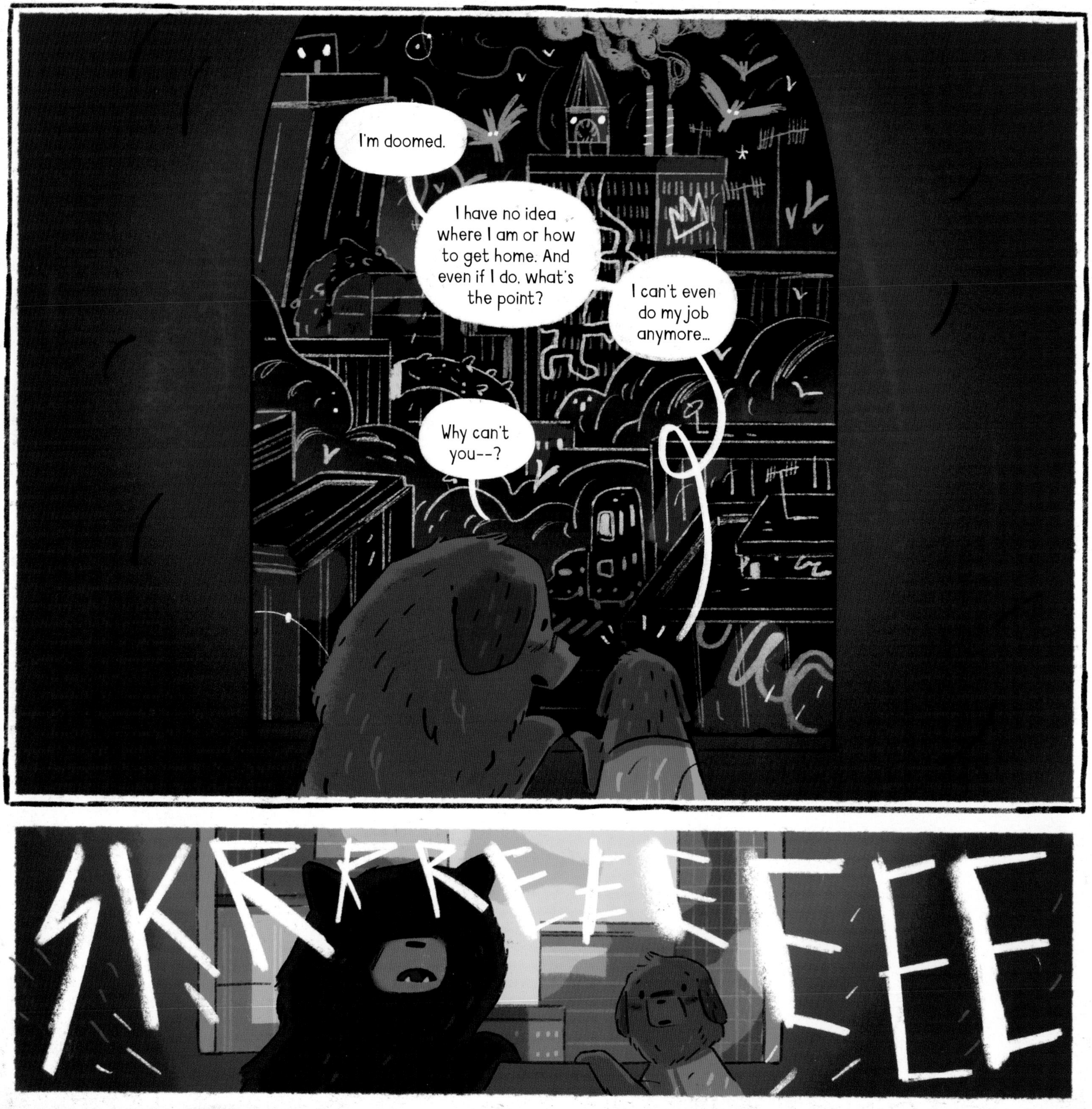
I'm doomed.
I have no idea where I am or how to get home. And even if I do, what's the point?
I can't even do my job anymore...
Why can't you--?
SKRRPREEEEEEE

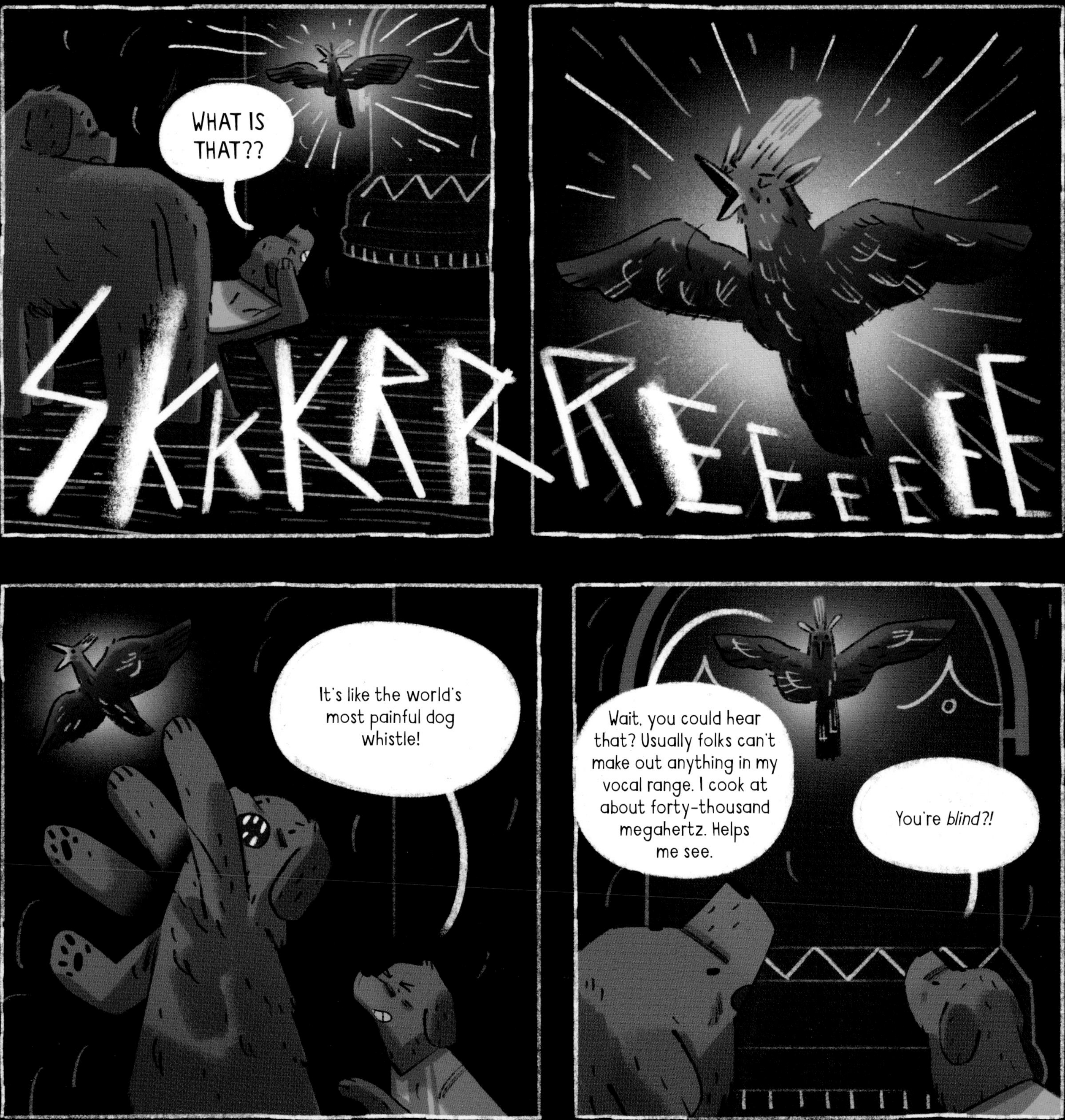
WHAT IS THAT??
SKKKRRRREEEEEEE
It's like the world's most painful dog whistle!
Wait, you could hear that? Usually folks can't make out anything in my vocal range. I cook at about forty-thousand megahertz. Helps me see.
You're *blind?!*

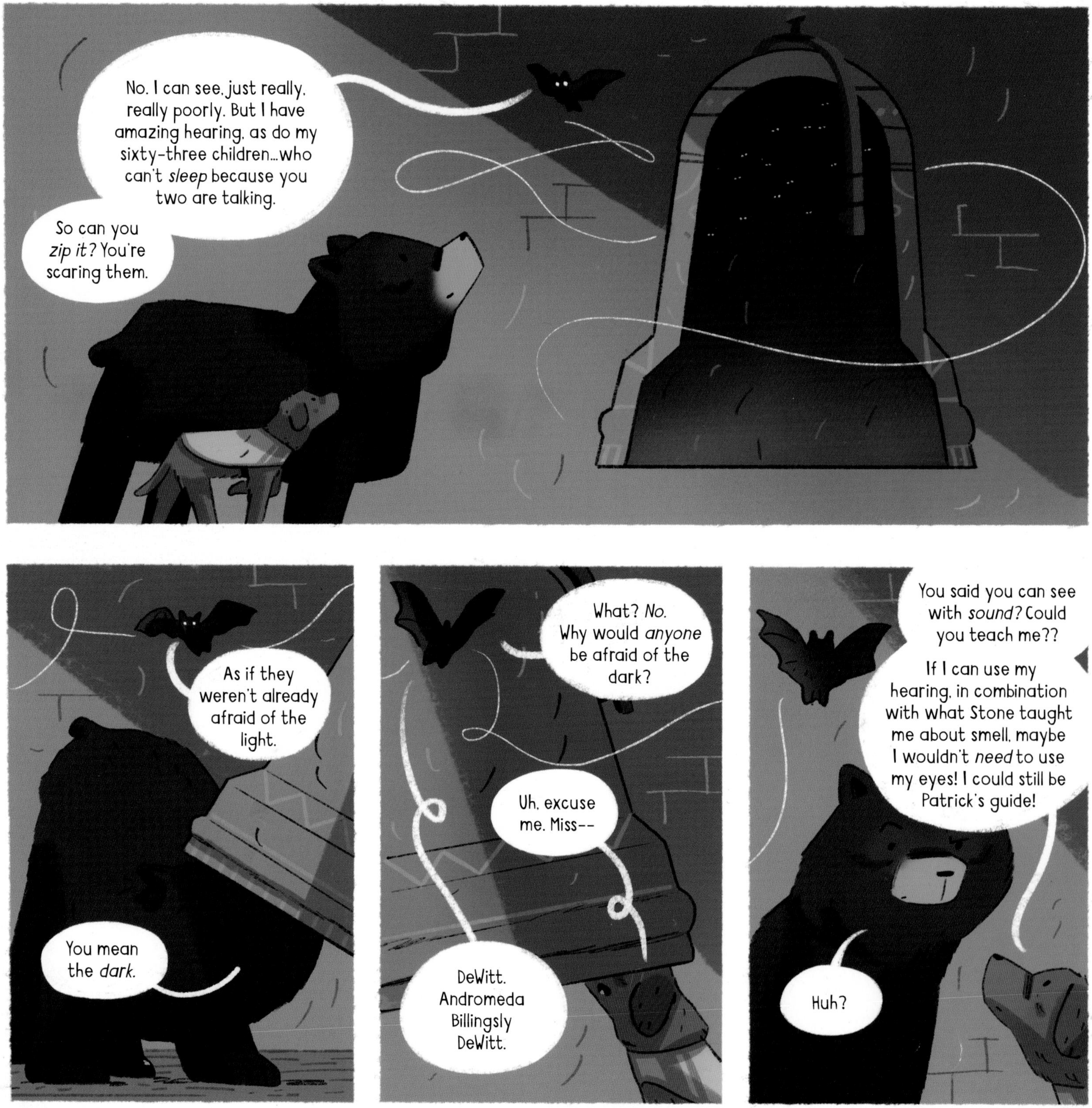
No. I can see, just really, really poorly. But I have amazing hearing, as do my sixty-three children...who can't *sleep* because you two are talking.
So can you *zip it*? You're scaring them.
As if they weren't already afraid of the light.
You mean the *dark*.
What? *No.* Why would *anyone* be afraid of the dark?
Uh, excuse me, Miss--
DeWitt. Andromeda Billingsly DeWitt.
You said you can see with *sound*? Could you teach me??
If I can use my hearing, in combination with what Stone taught me about smell, maybe I wouldn't *need* to use my eyes! I could still be Patrick's guide!
Huh?

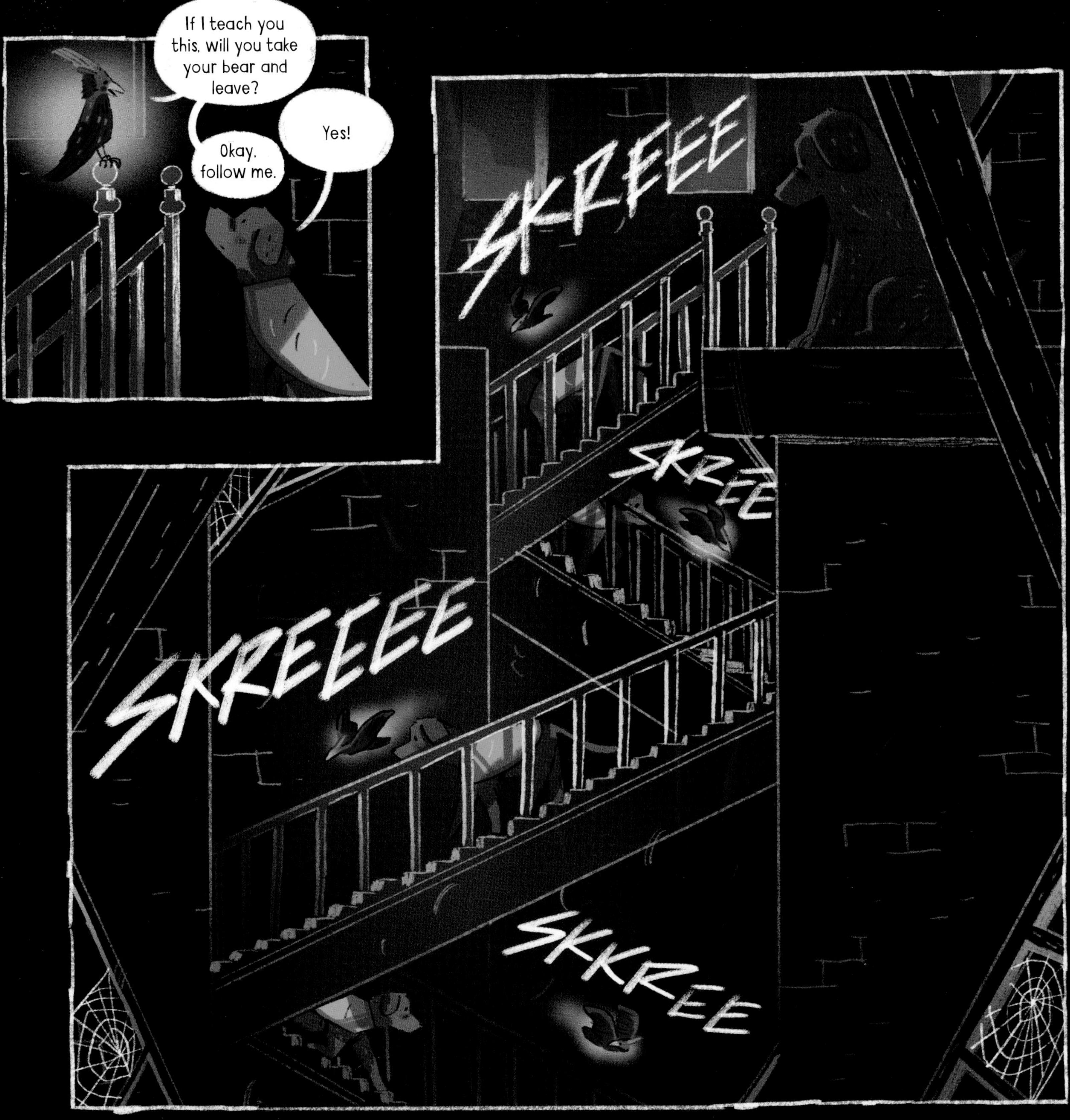

If I teach you this, will you take your bear and leave?
Yes!
Okay, follow me.
SKREEE
SKREE
SKREEEE
SKKREE

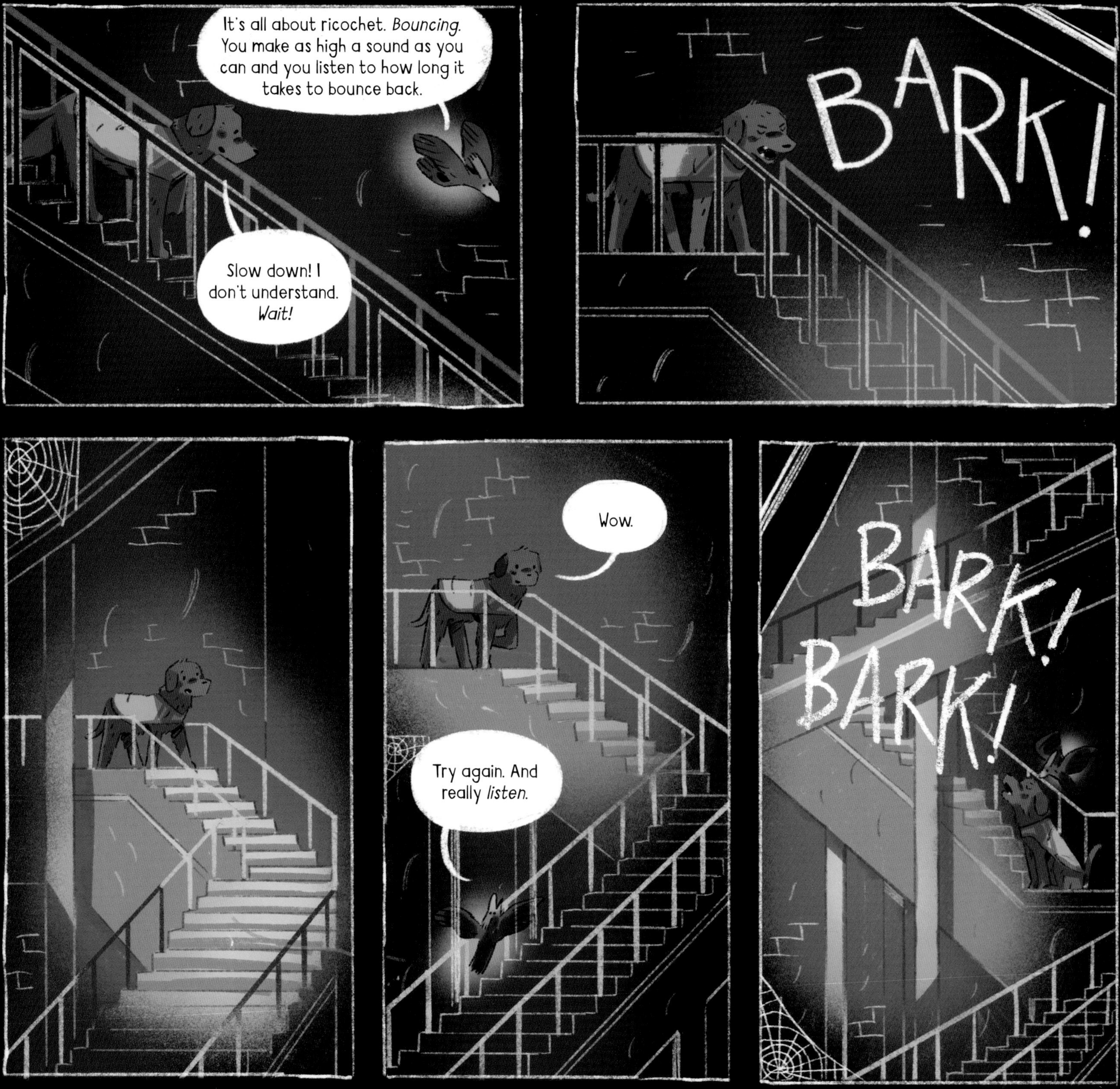

It's all about ricochet. *Bouncing.* You make as high a sound as you can and you listen to how long it takes to bounce back.
Slow down! I don't understand. *Wait!*
BARK!
Wow.
Try again. And really *listen.*
BARK! BARK!

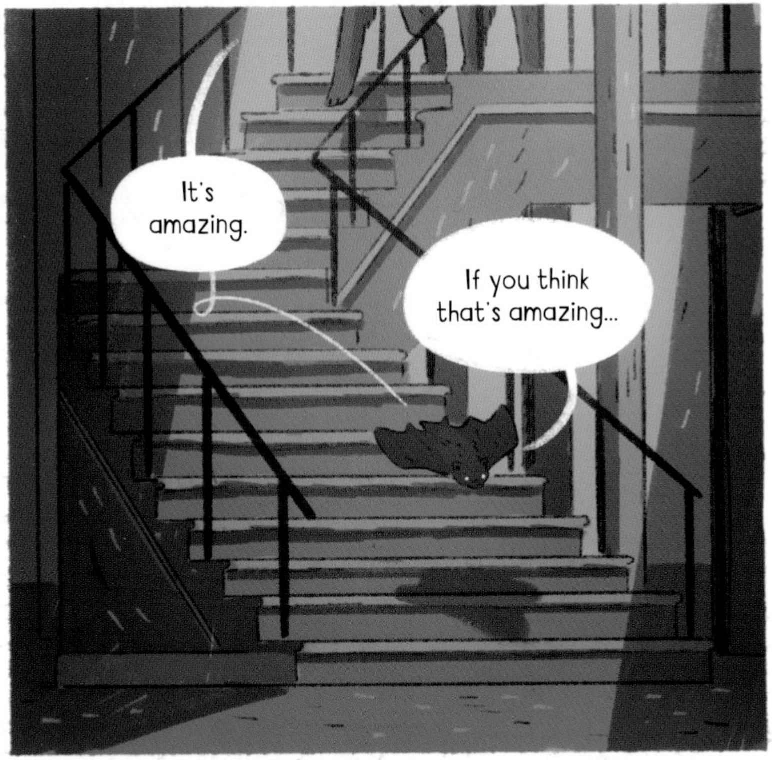
It's amazing.
If you think that's amazing...

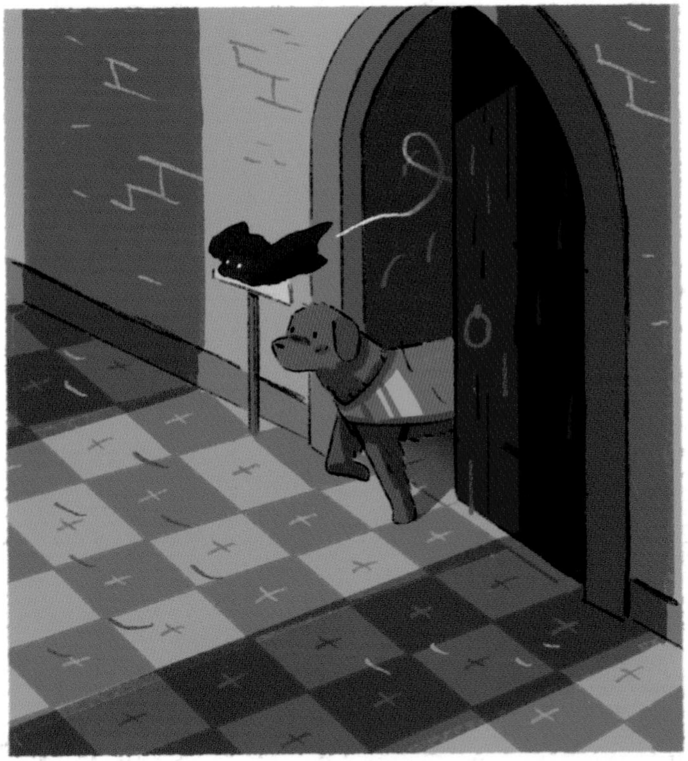

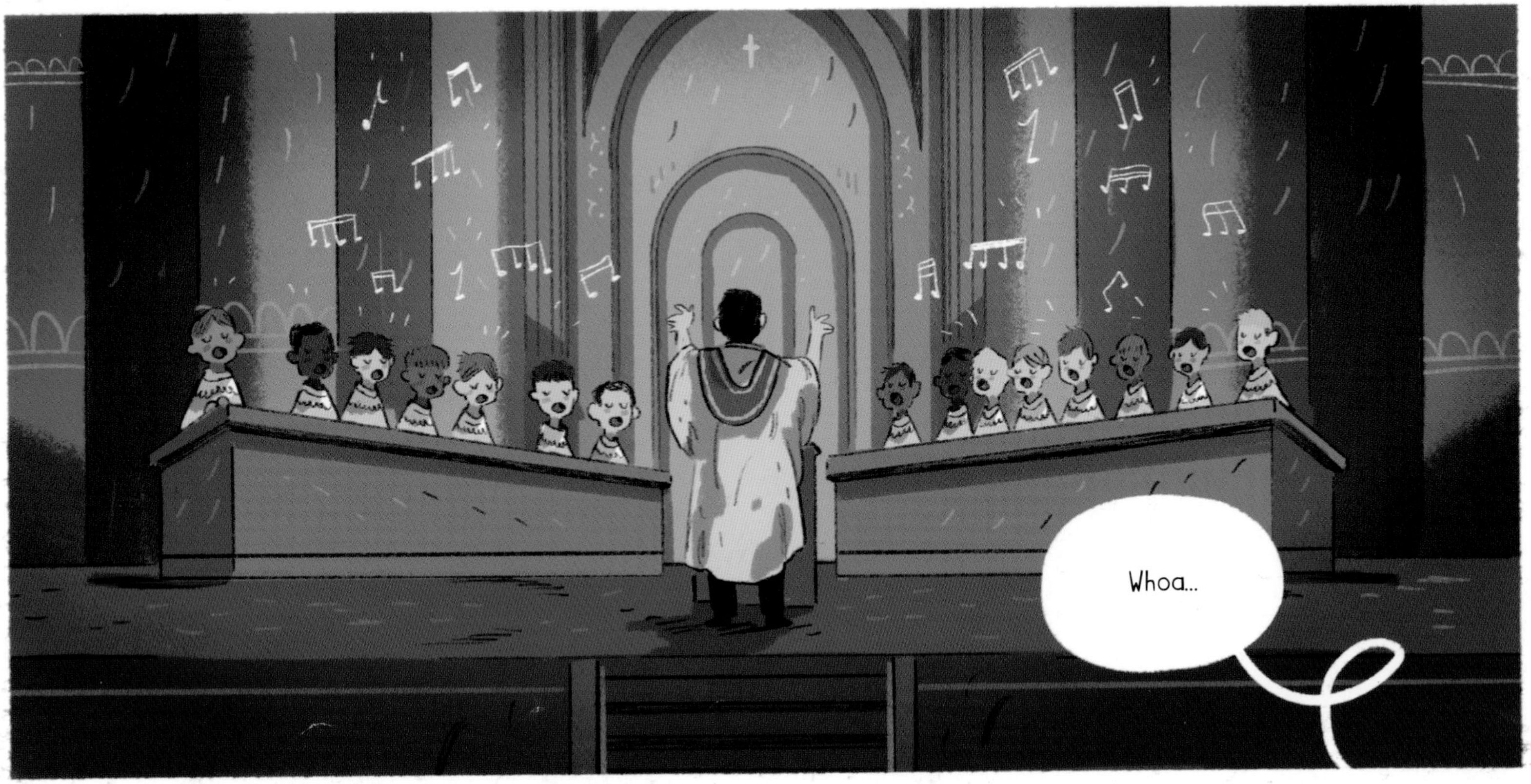
Whoa...

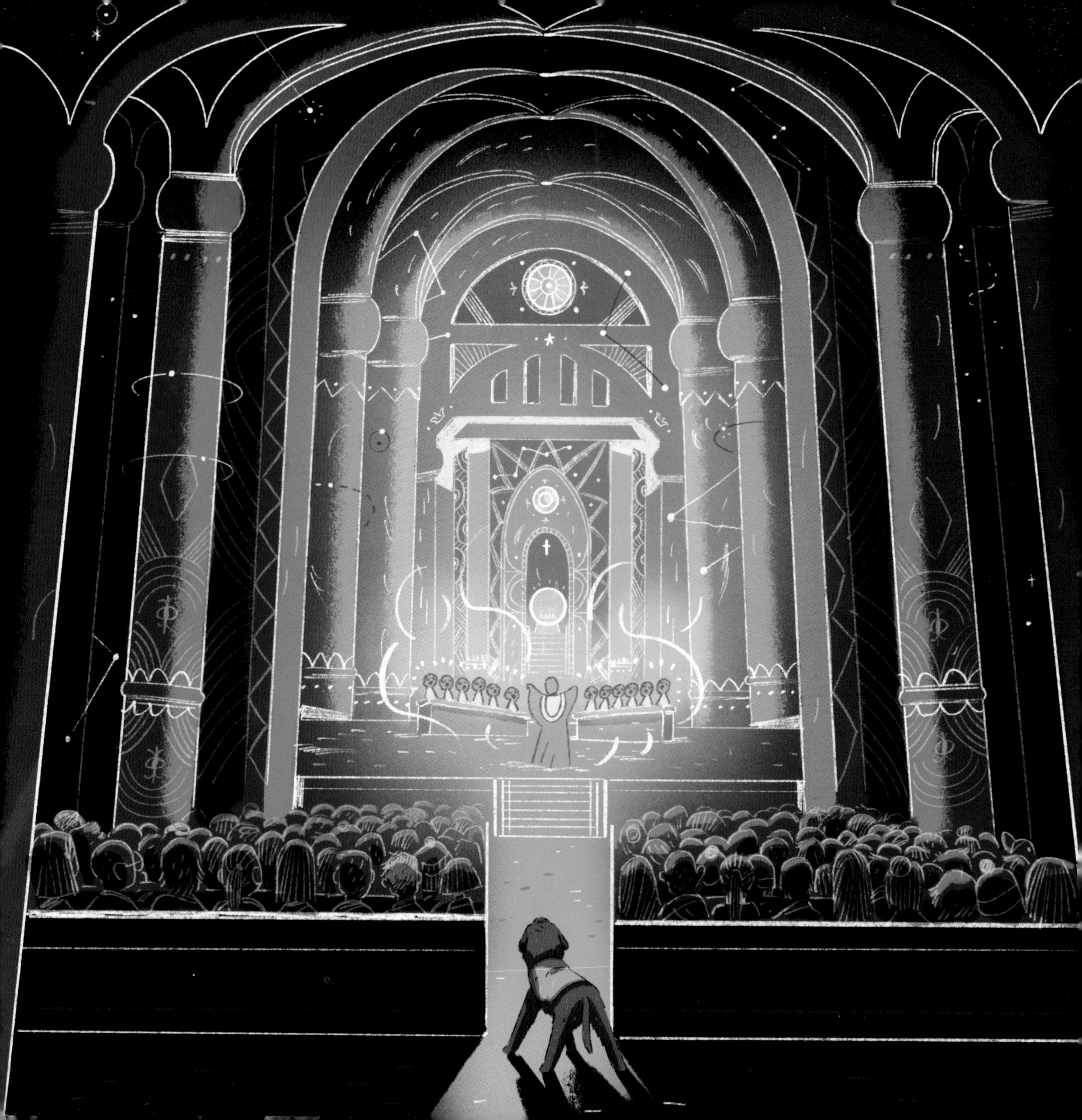

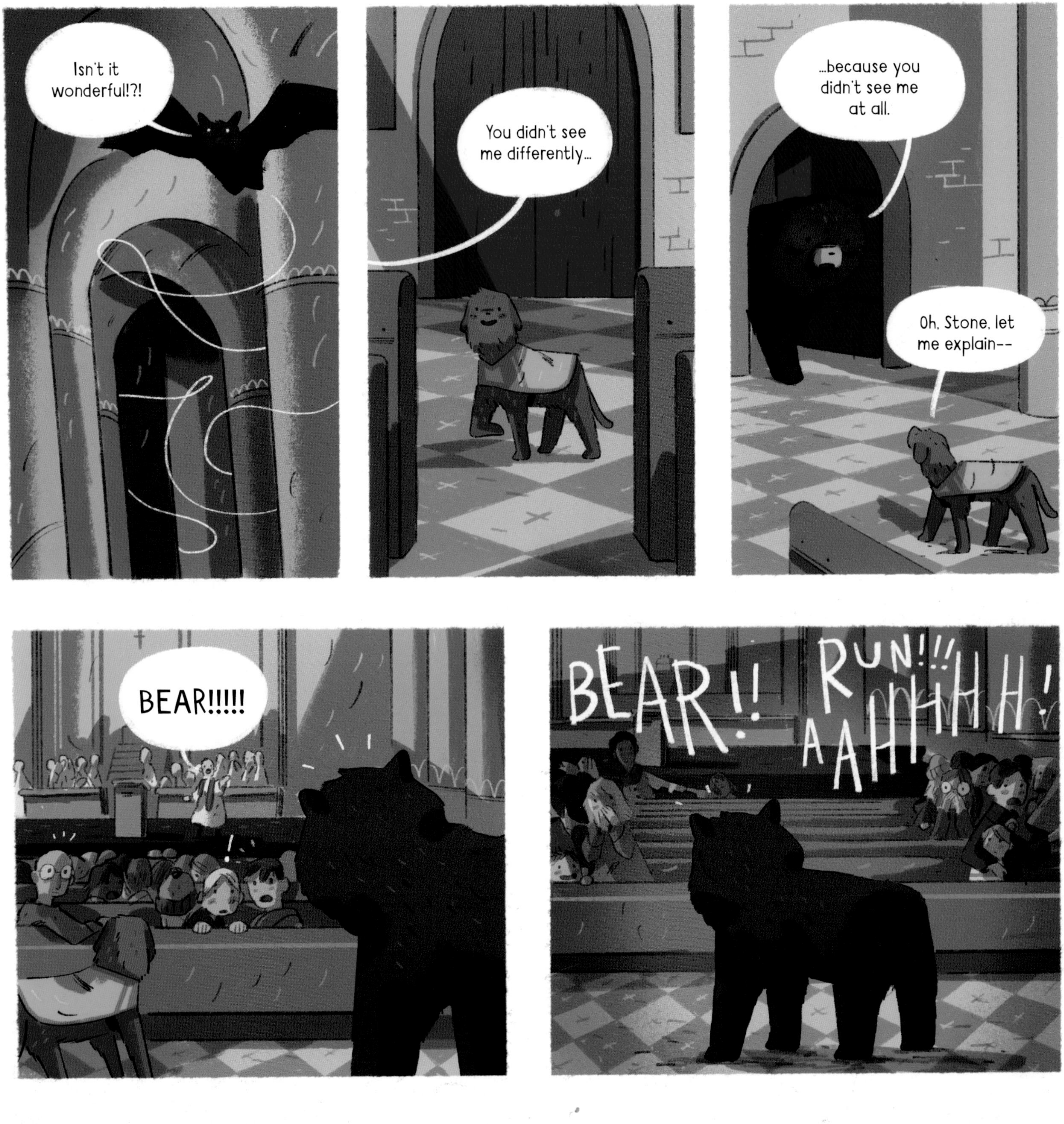
Isn't it wonderful!?!
You didn't see me differently...
...because you didn't see me at all.
Oh, Stone, let me explain--
BEAR!!!!!
BEAR!!
RUN!!!
AAHHHHH!

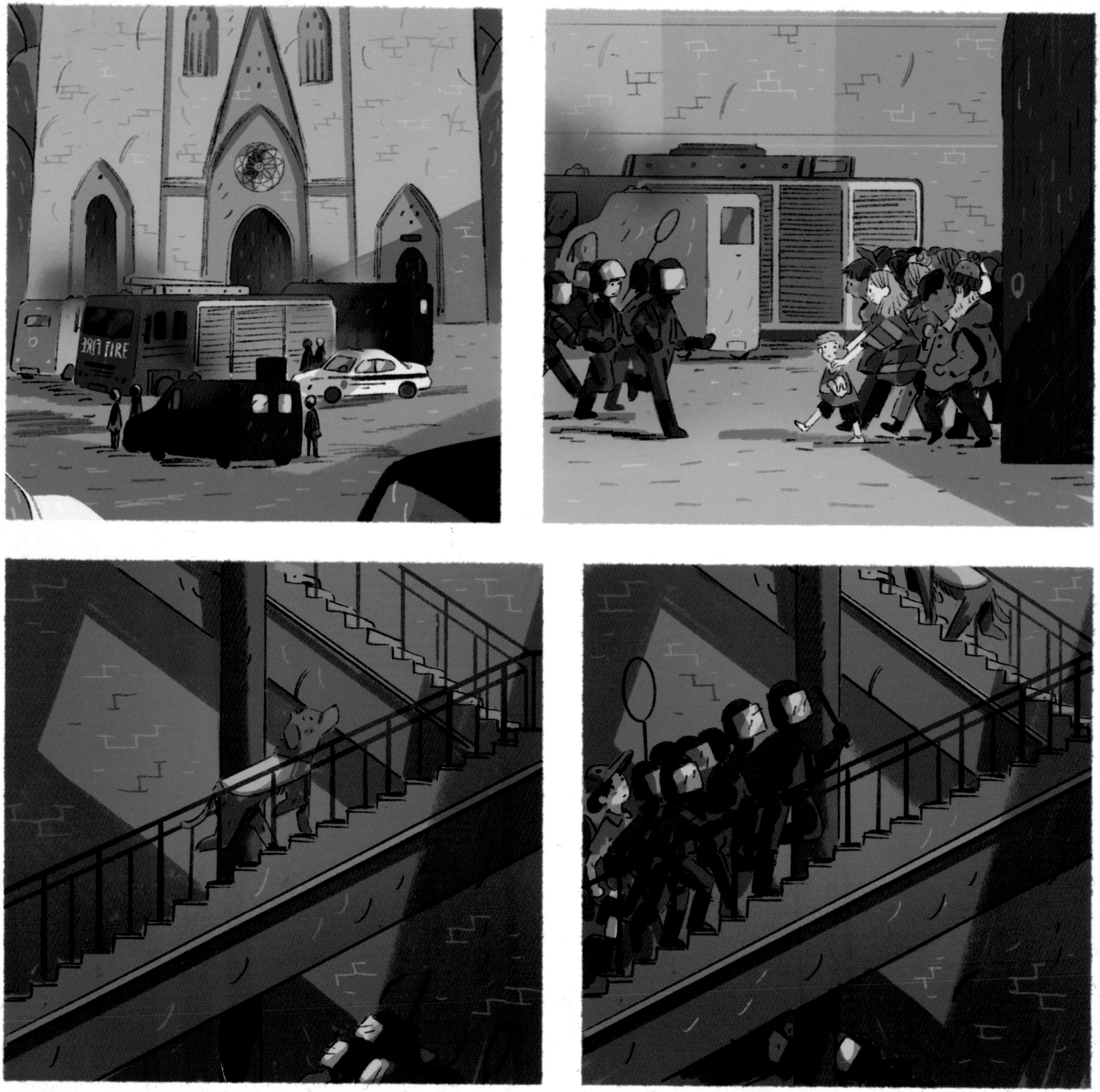
FIRE

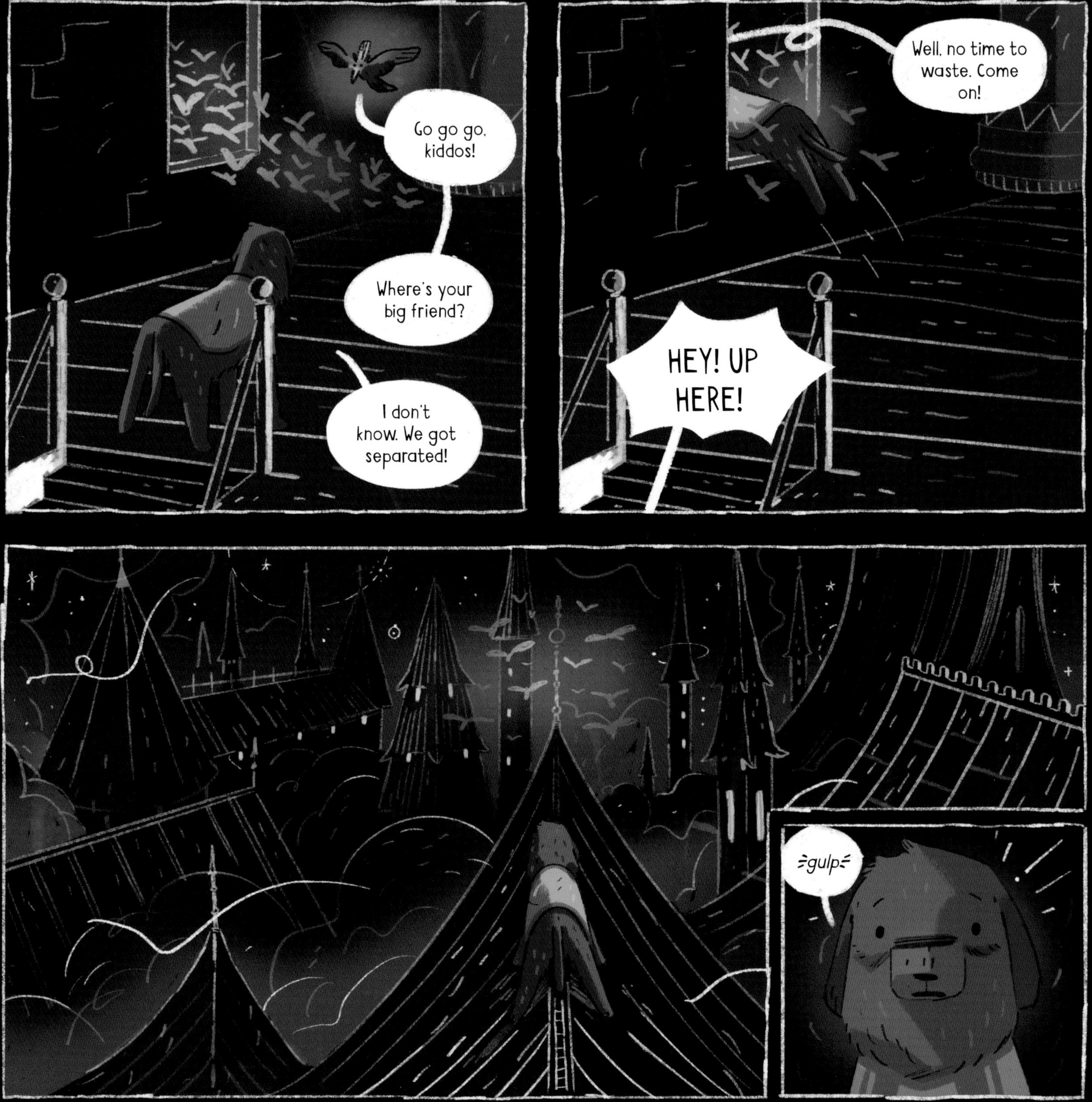
Go go go, kiddos!
Where's your big friend?
I don't know. We got separated!
Well, no time to waste. Come on!
HEY! UP HERE!
gulp

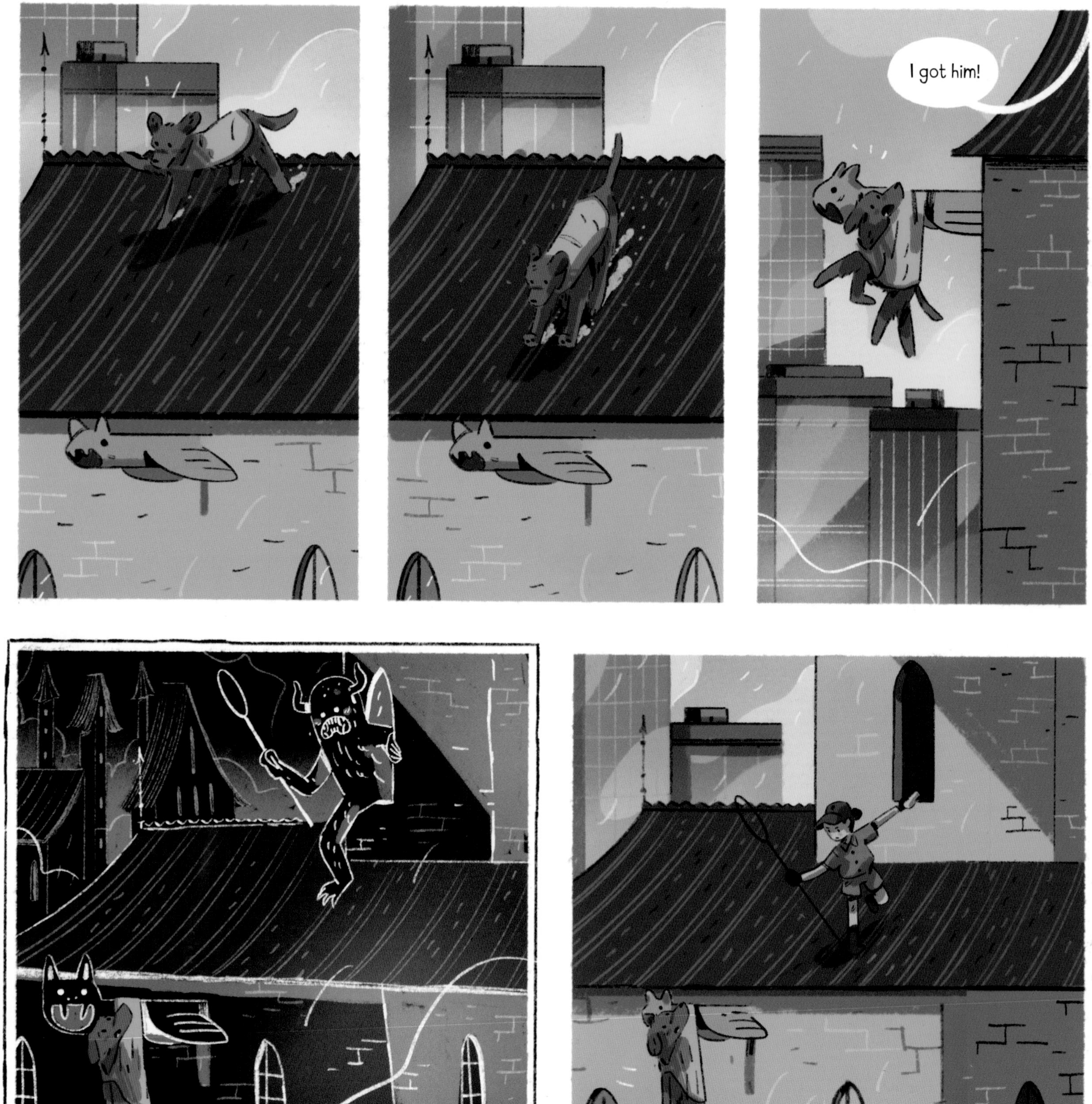
I got him!

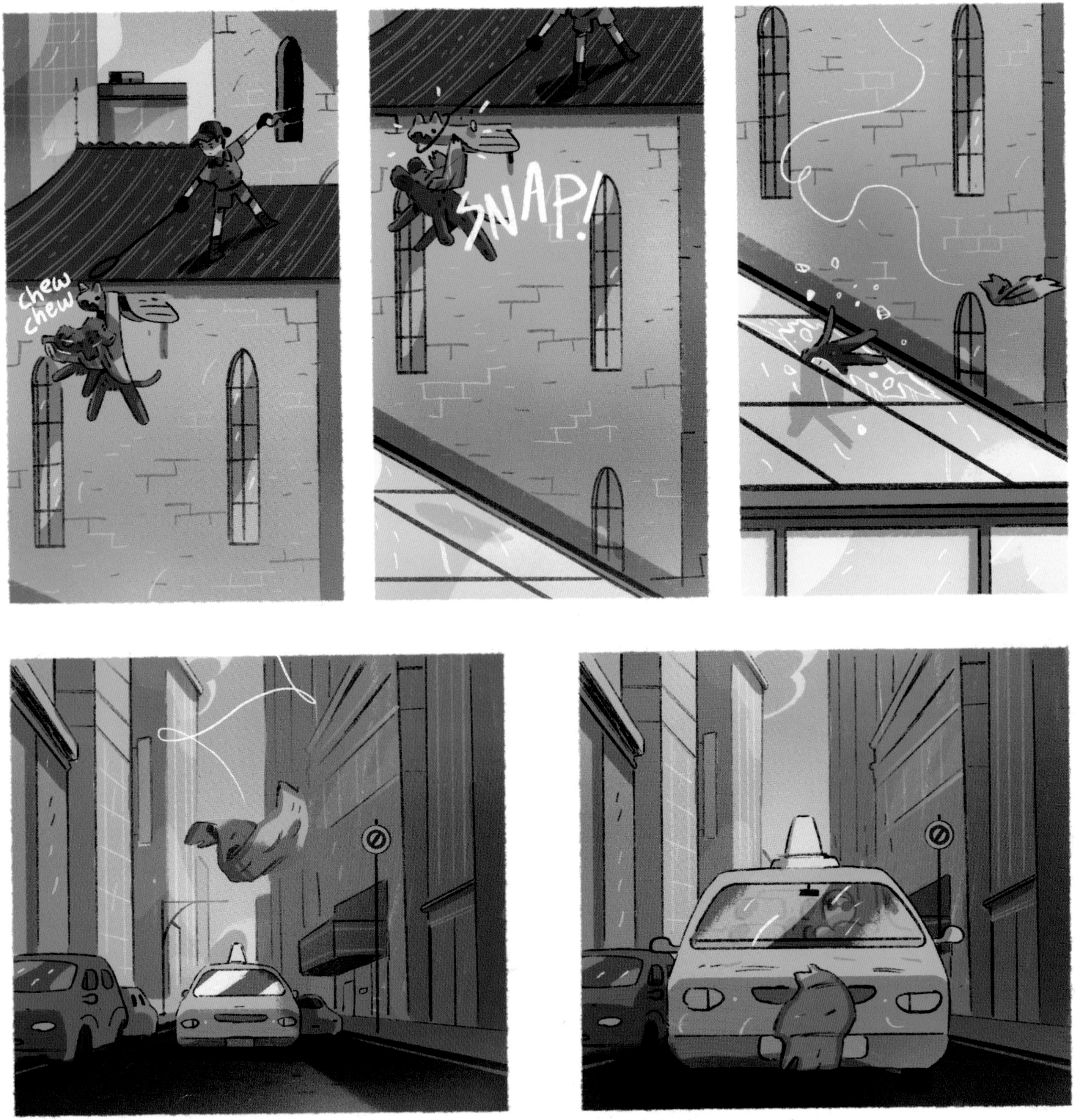
chew
chew
SNAP!

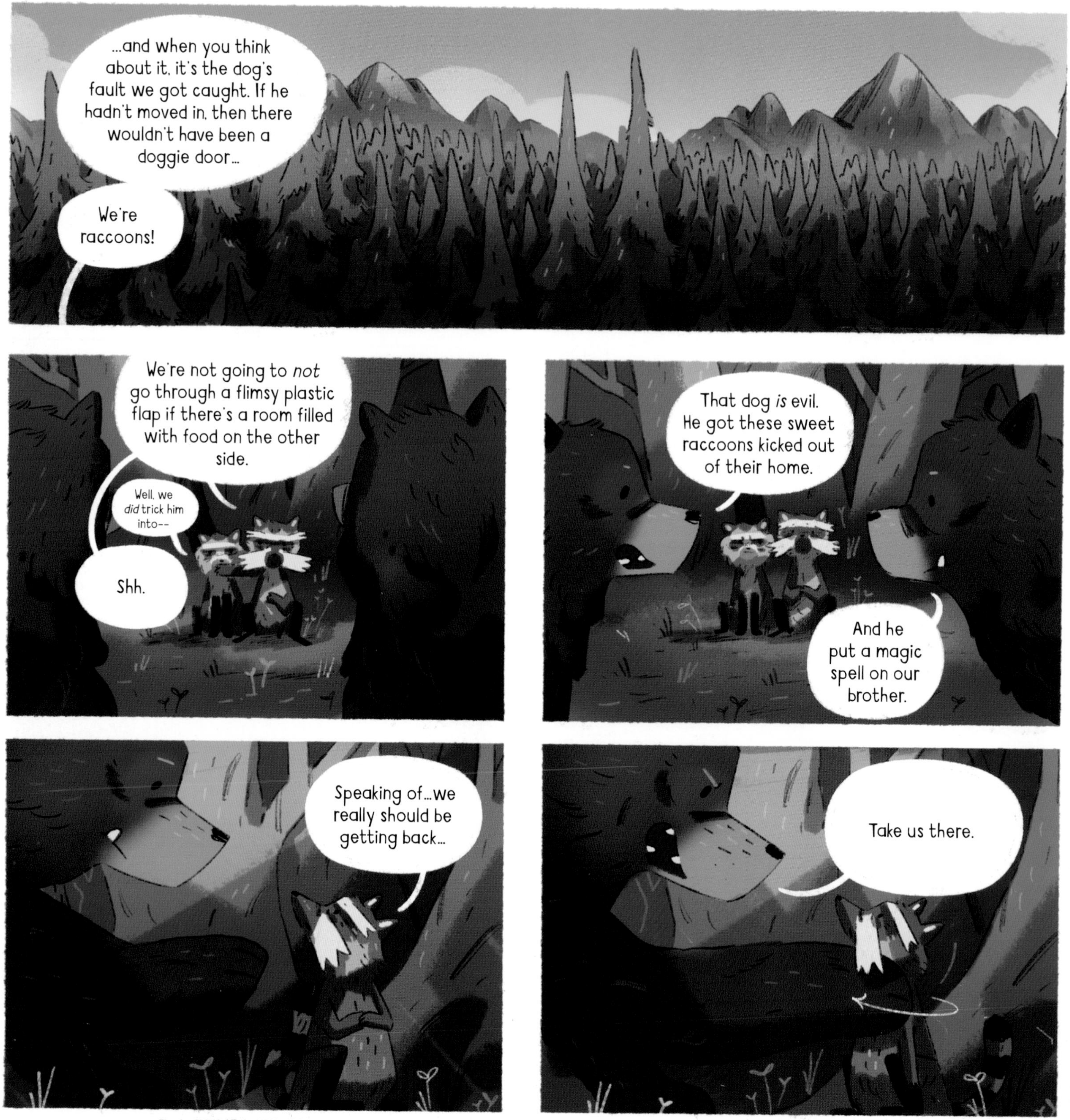
...and when you think about it, it's the dog's fault we got caught. If he hadn't moved in, then there wouldn't have been a doggie door...
We're raccoons!
We're not going to *not* go through a flimsy plastic flap if there's a room filled with food on the other side.
Well, we *did* trick him into--
Shh.
That dog *is* evil. He got these sweet raccoons kicked out of their home.
And he put a magic spell on our brother.
Speaking of...we really should be getting back...
Take us there.

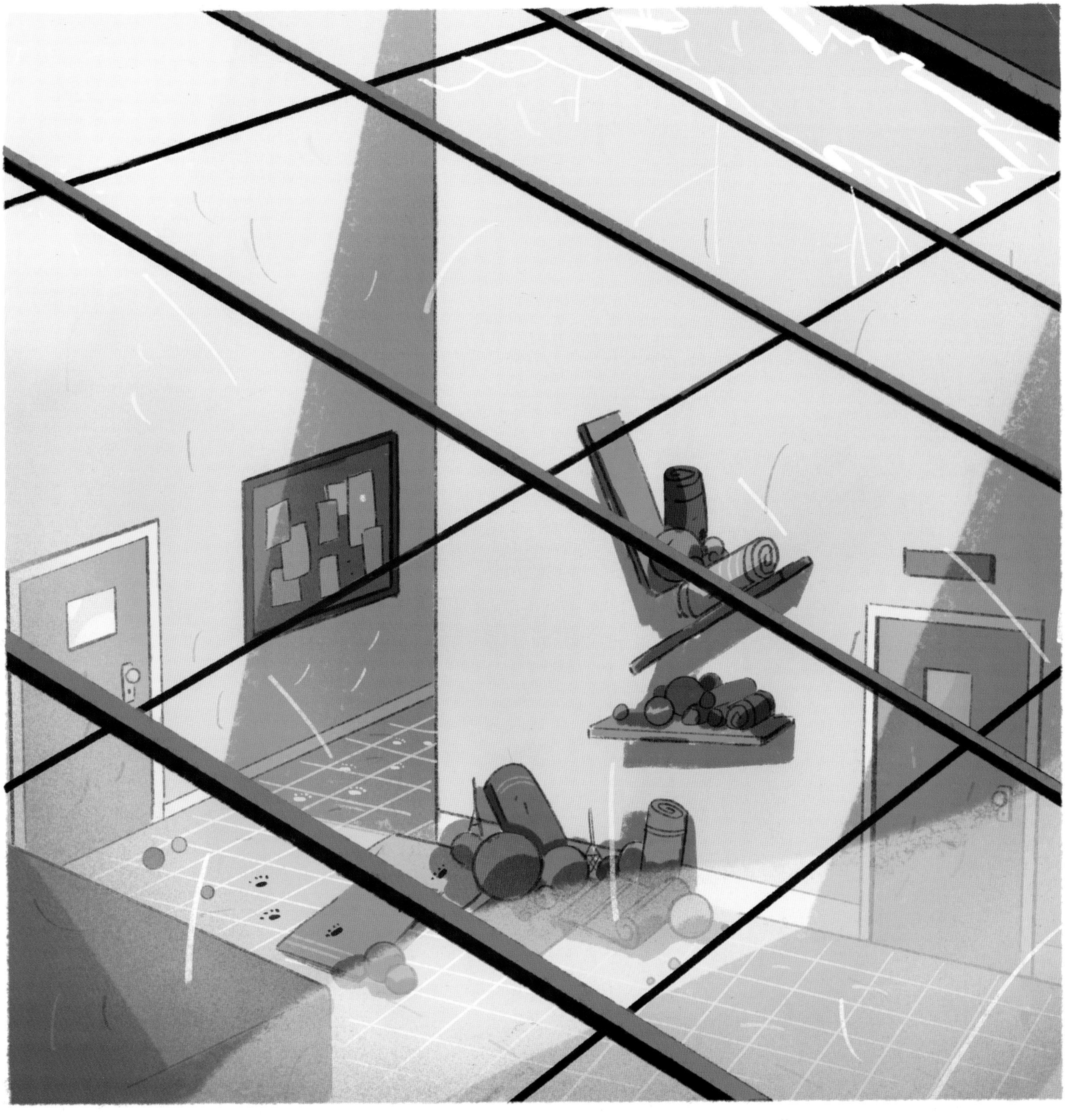

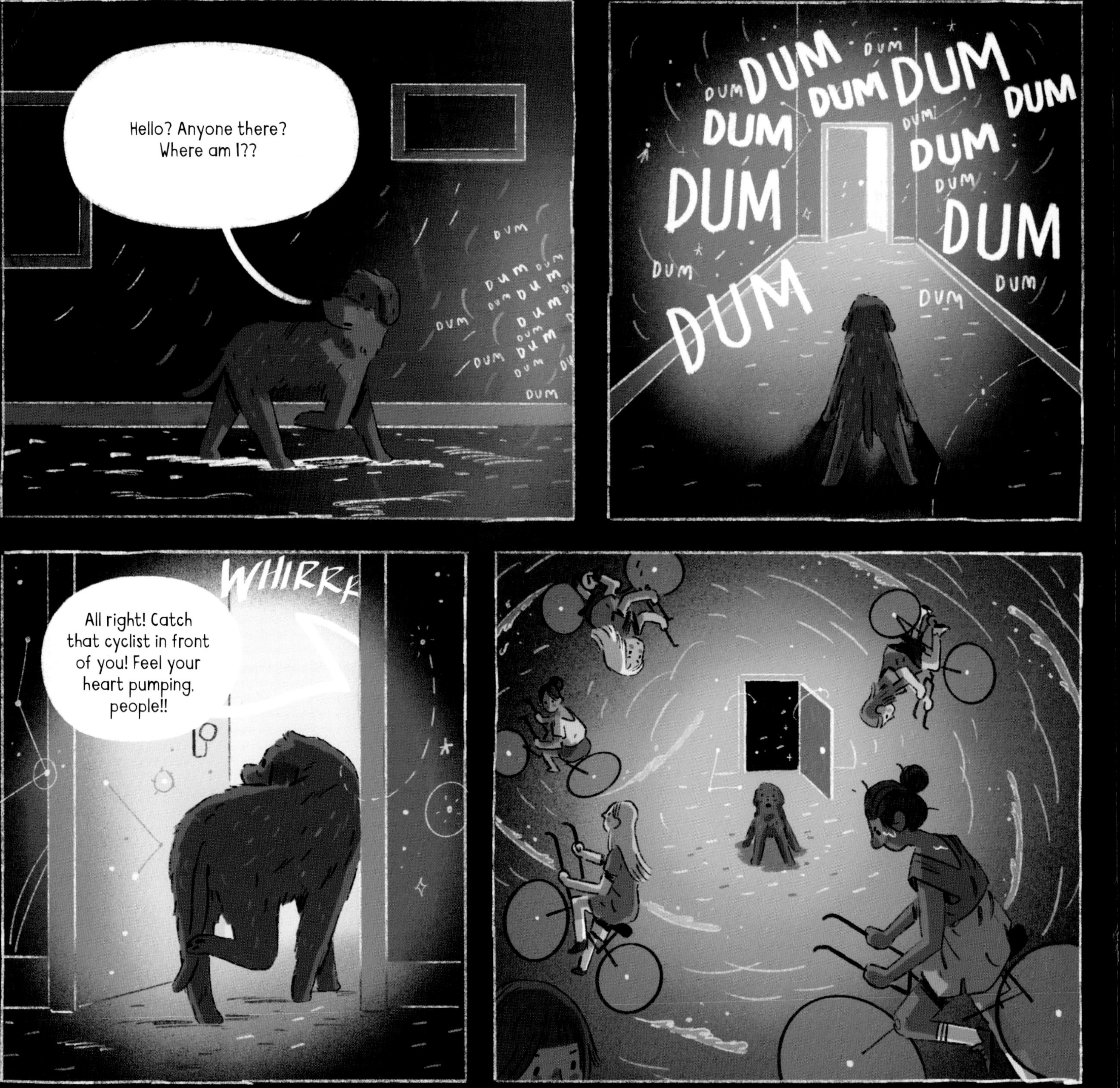
Hello? Anyone there? Where am I??
DUM
DUM DUM DUM
DUM DUM DUM DUM DUM
DUM
DUM
DUM
DUM
DUM DUM DUM DUM DUM DUM DUM
DUM
DUM
DUM
DUM
DUM
DUM
DUM
DUM DUM
DUM
DUM DUM
WHIRRR
All right! Catch that cyclist in front of you! Feel your heart pumping, people!!

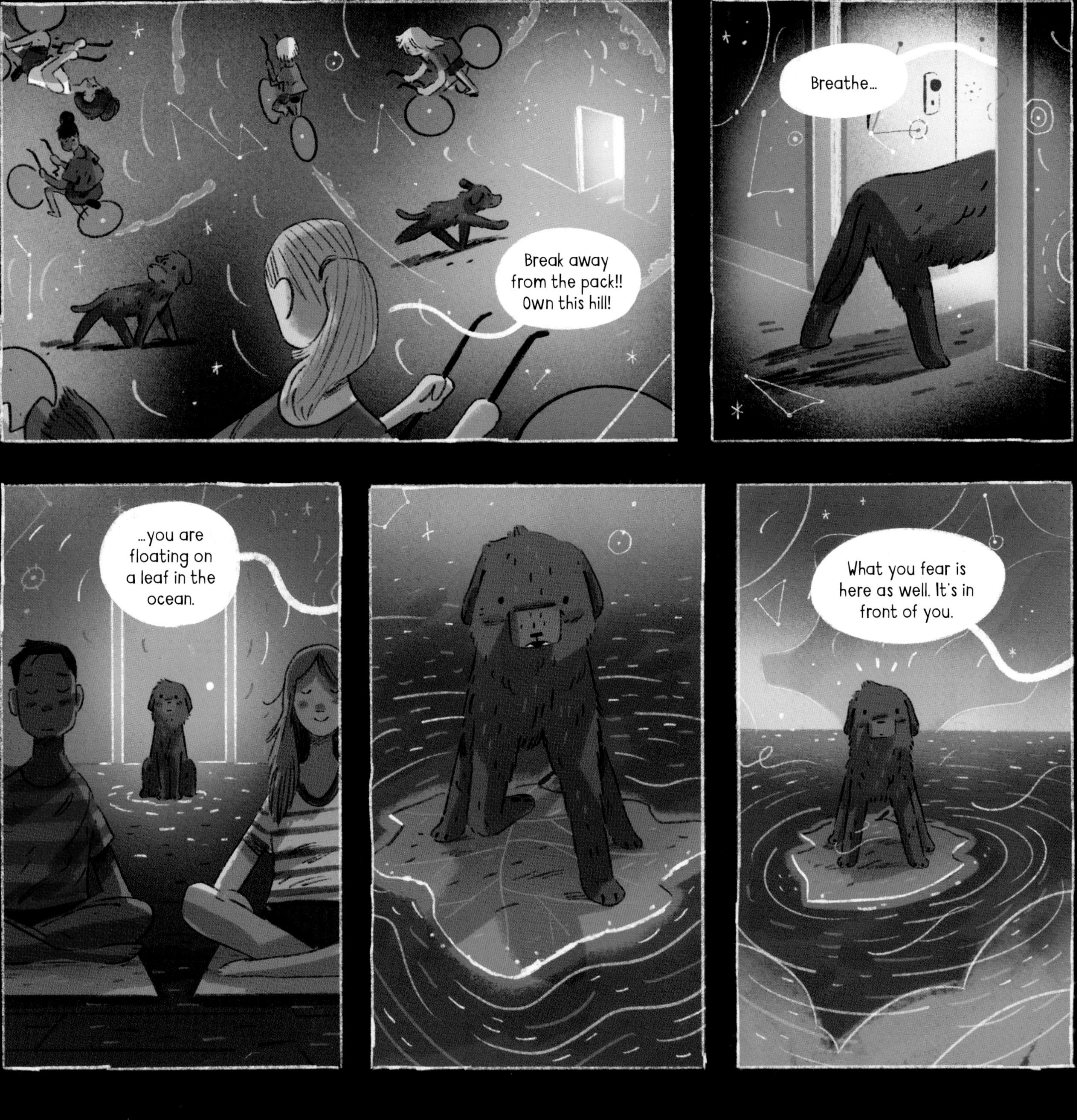
Break away from the pack!! Own this hill!
Breathe...
...you are floating on a leaf in the ocean.
What you fear is here as well. It's in front of you.

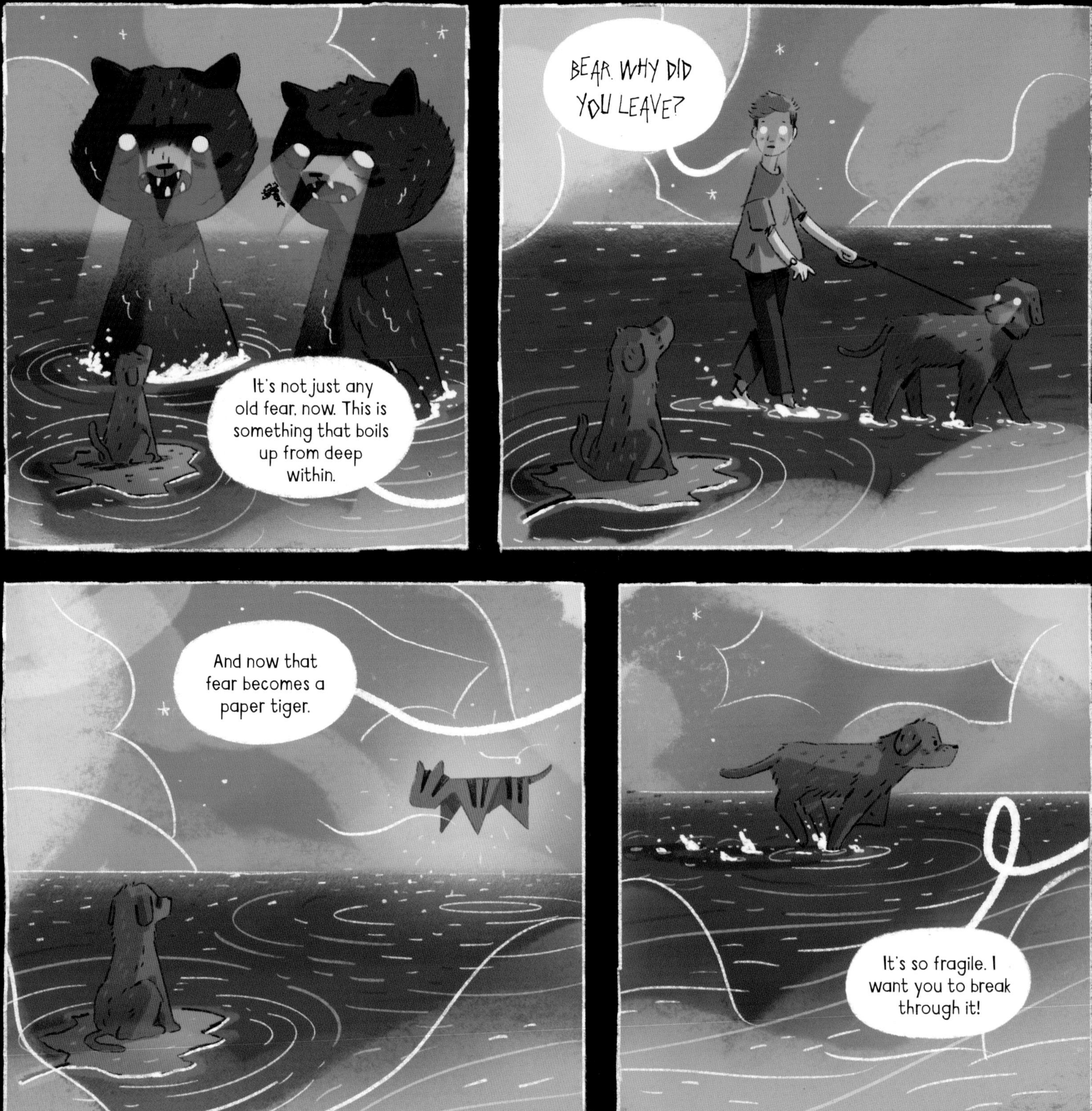
It's not just any old fear, now. This is something that boils up from deep within.
BEAR. WHY DID YOU LEAVE?
And now that fear becomes a paper tiger.
It's so fragile. I want you to break through it!

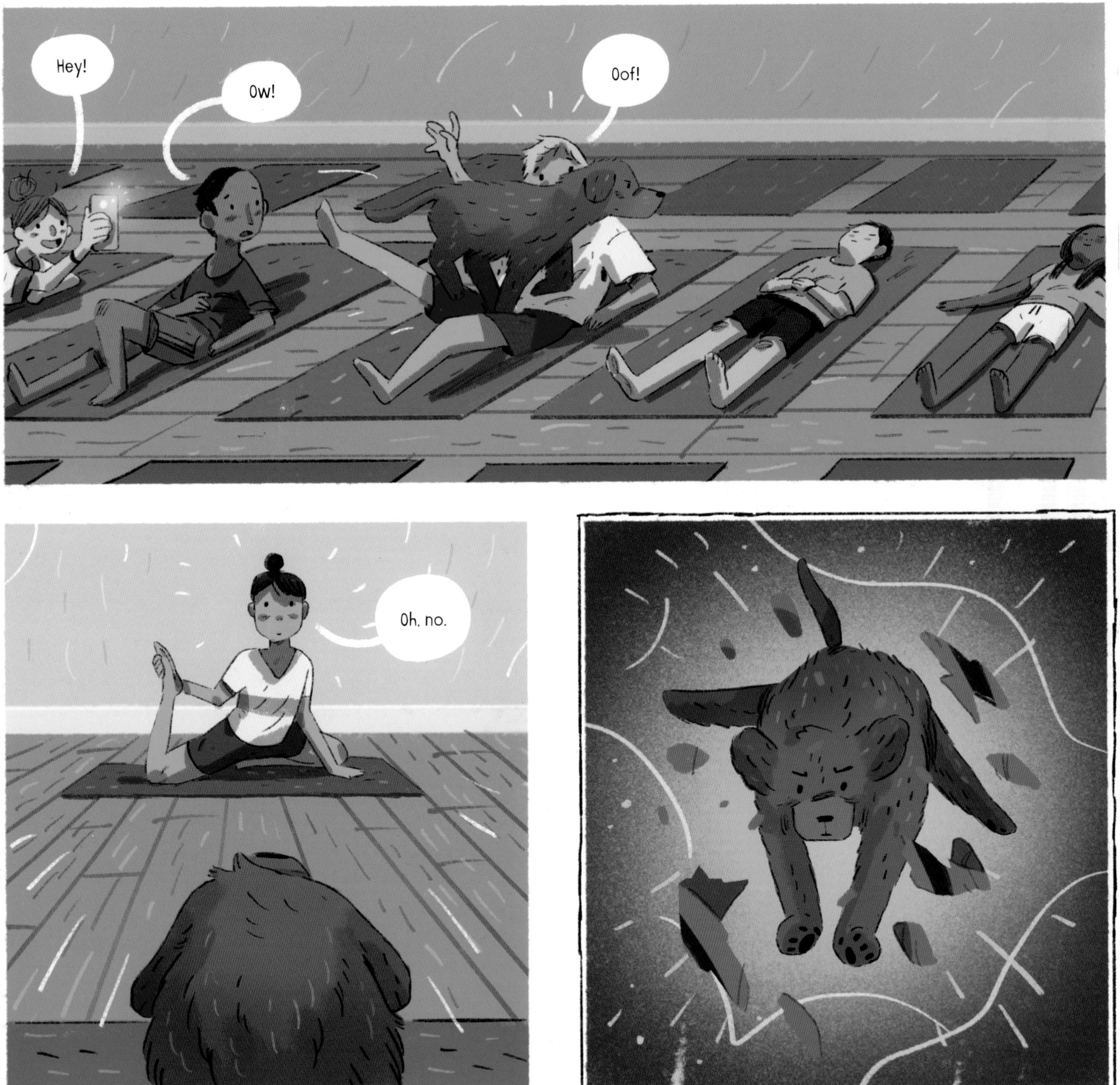
Hey!
Ow!
Oof!
Oh, no.

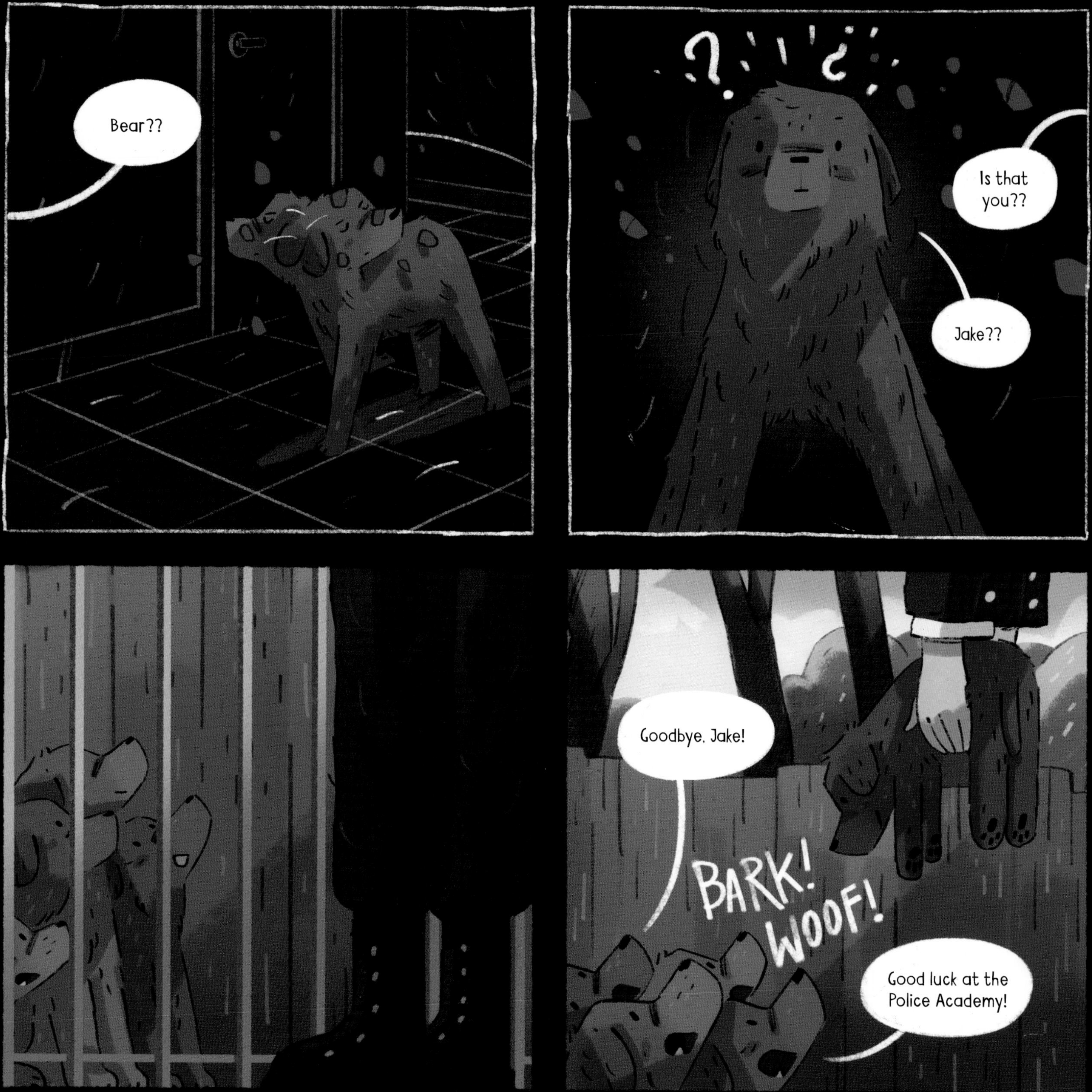
Bear??
Is that you??
Jake??
Goodbye, Jake!
BARK!
WOOF!
Good luck at the Police Academy!

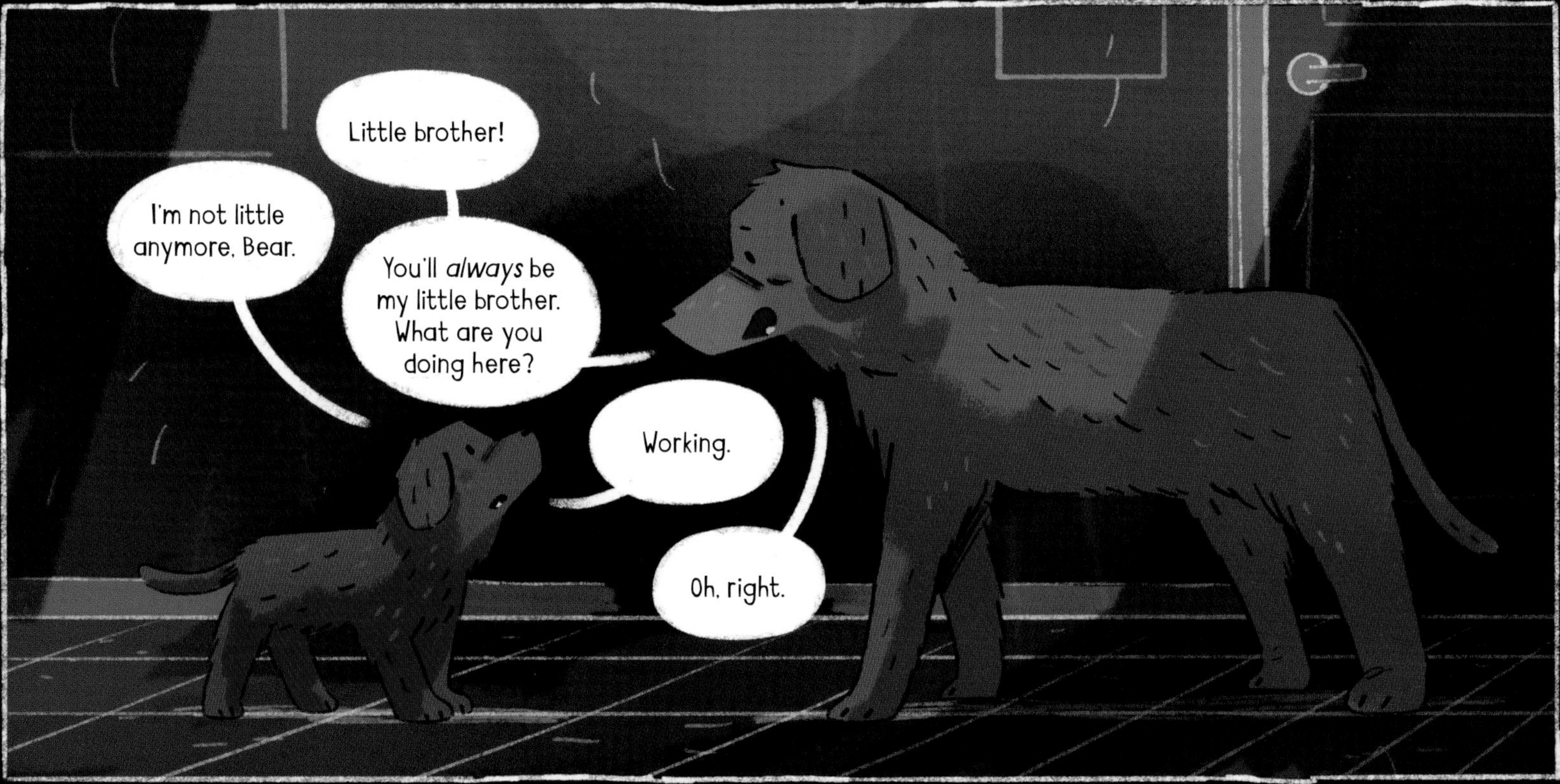
Little brother!
I'm not little anymore, Bear.
You'll *always* be my little brother. What are you doing here?
Working.
Oh, right.

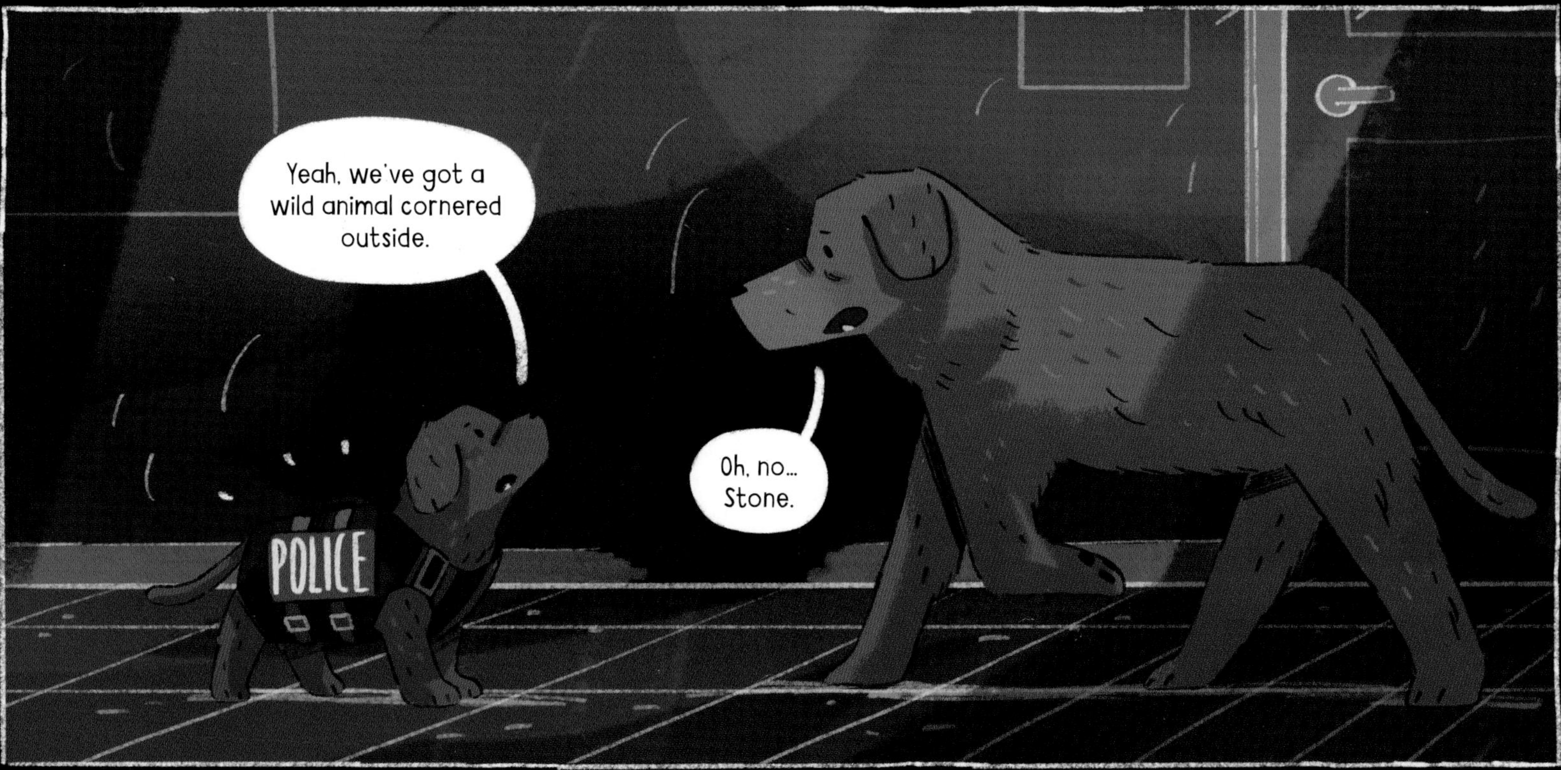
Yeah, we've got a wild animal cornered outside.
Oh, no... Stone.
POLICE

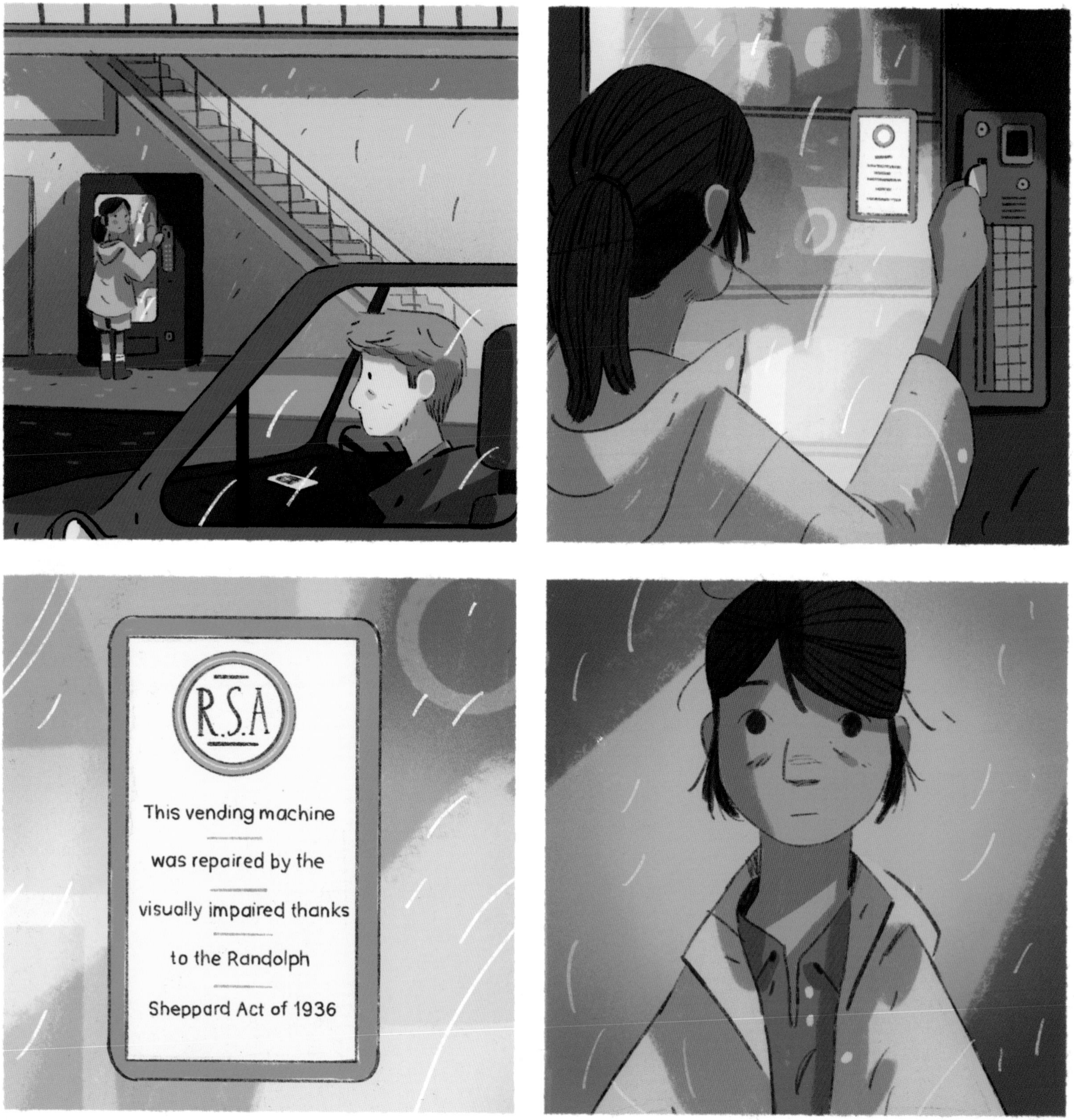
R.S.A
This vending machine
was repaired by the
visually impaired thanks
to the Randolph
Sheppard Act of 1936

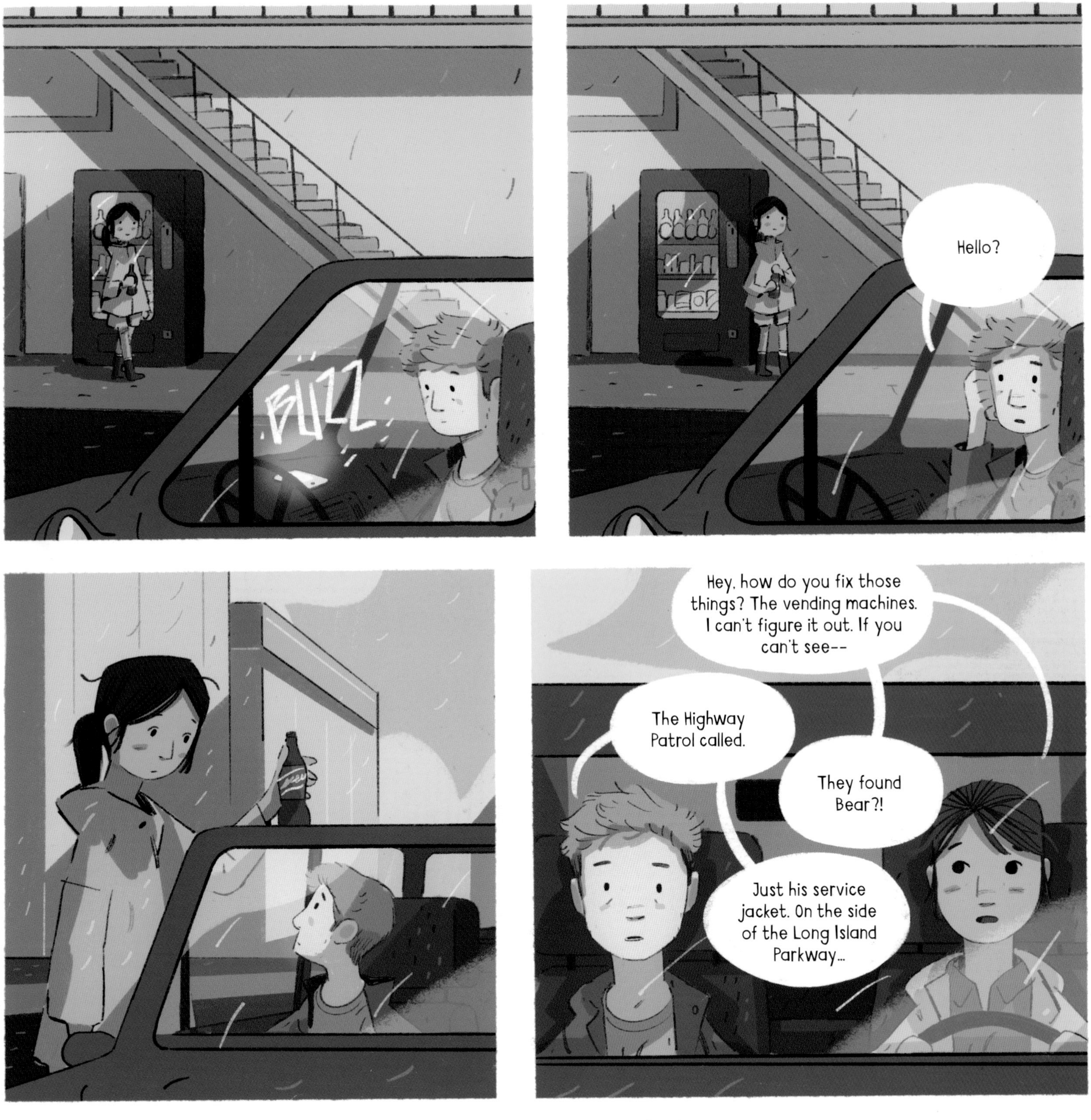
BUZZ
Hello?
Hey, how do you fix those things? The vending machines. I can't figure it out. If you can't see--
The Highway Patrol called.
They found Bear?!
Just his service jacket. On the side of the Long Island Parkway...

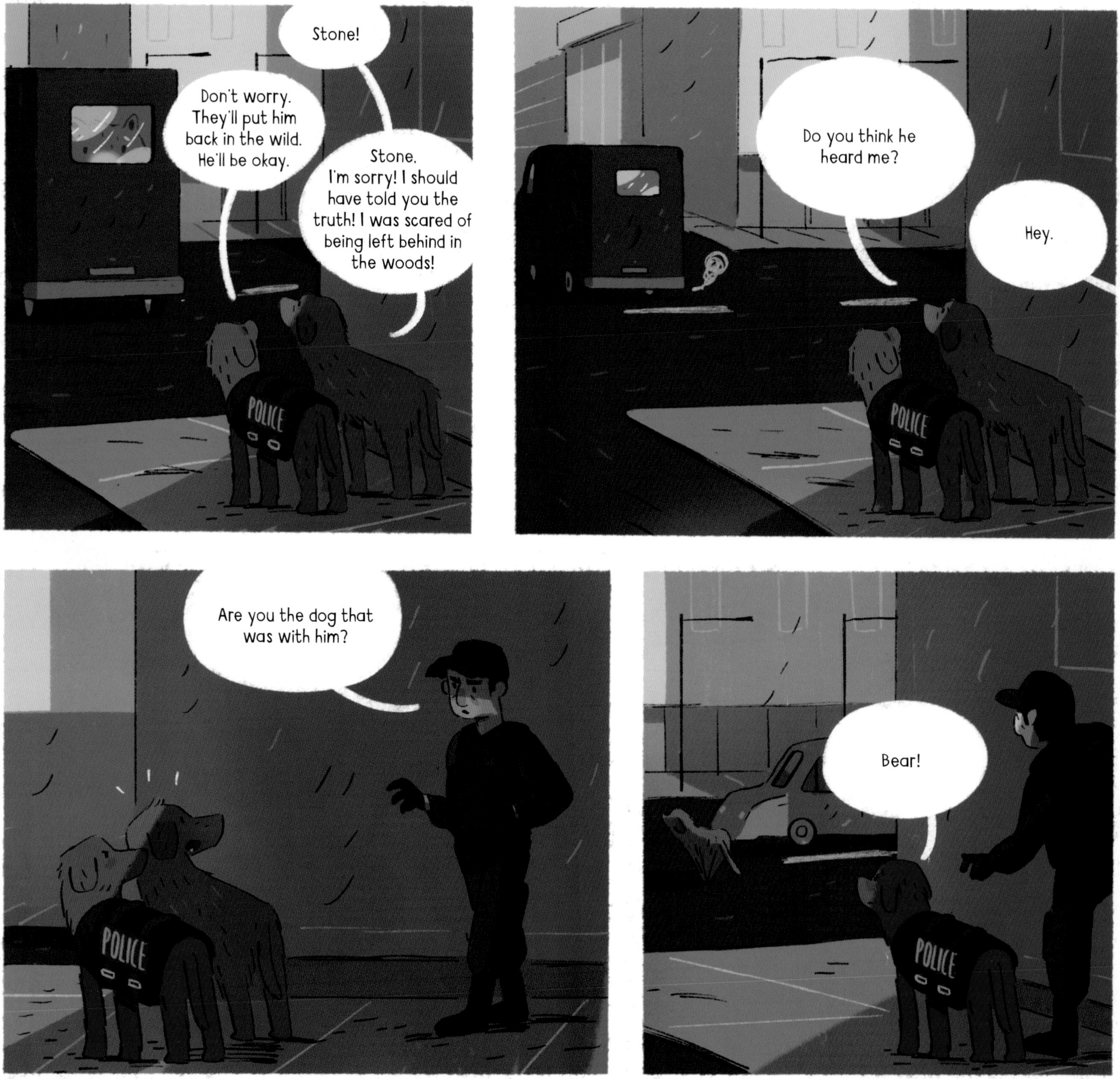
Stone!
Don't worry. They'll put him back in the wild. He'll be okay.
Stone, I'm sorry! I should have told you the truth! I was scared of being left behind in the woods!
Do you think he heard me?
Hey.
Are you the dog that was with him?
POLICE
Bear!

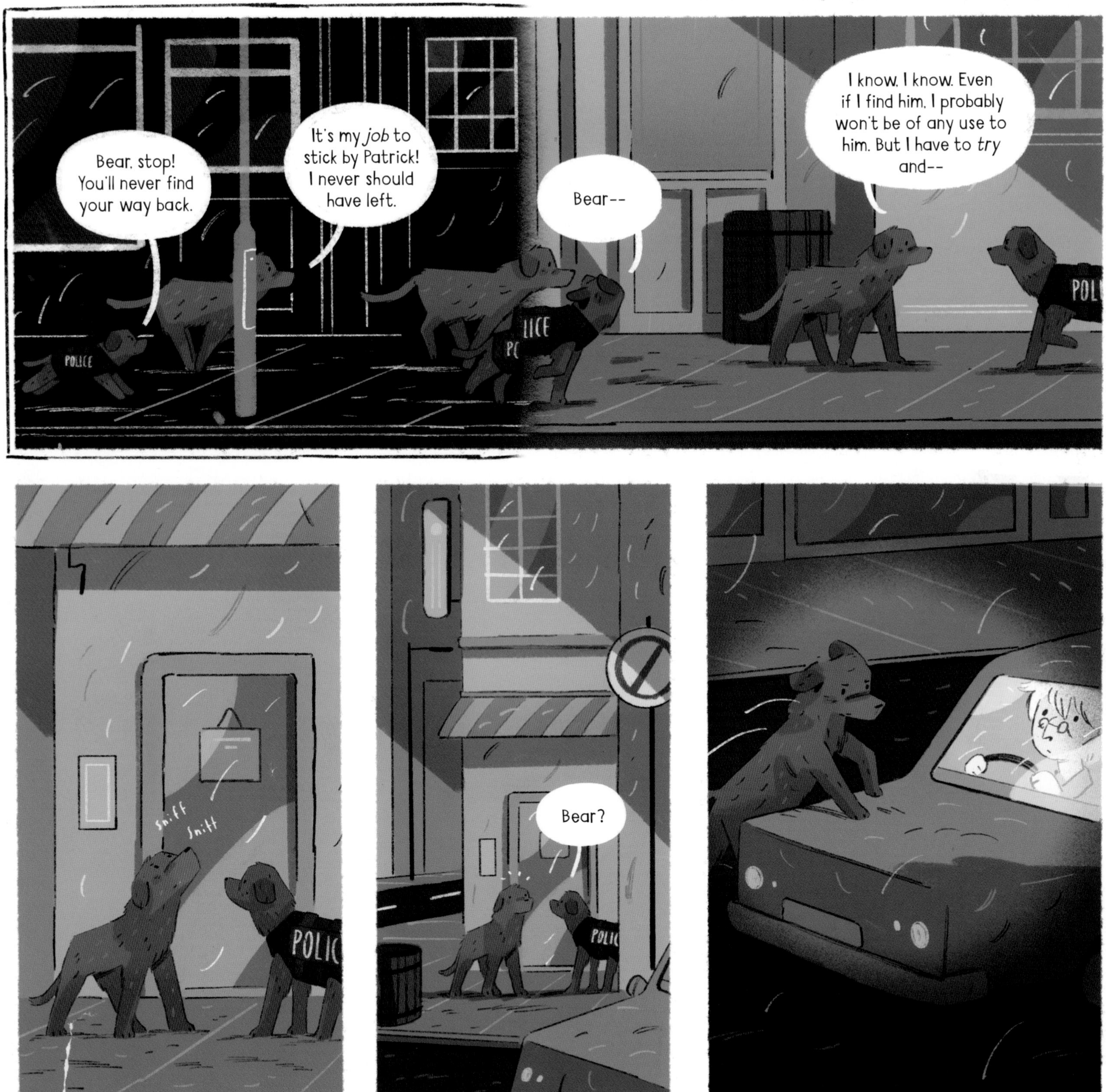
Bear, stop! You'll never find your way back.
It's my *job* to stick by Patrick! I never should have left.
Bear--
I know, I know. Even if I find him, I probably won't be of any use to him. But I have to *try* and--
sniff
sniff
Bear?

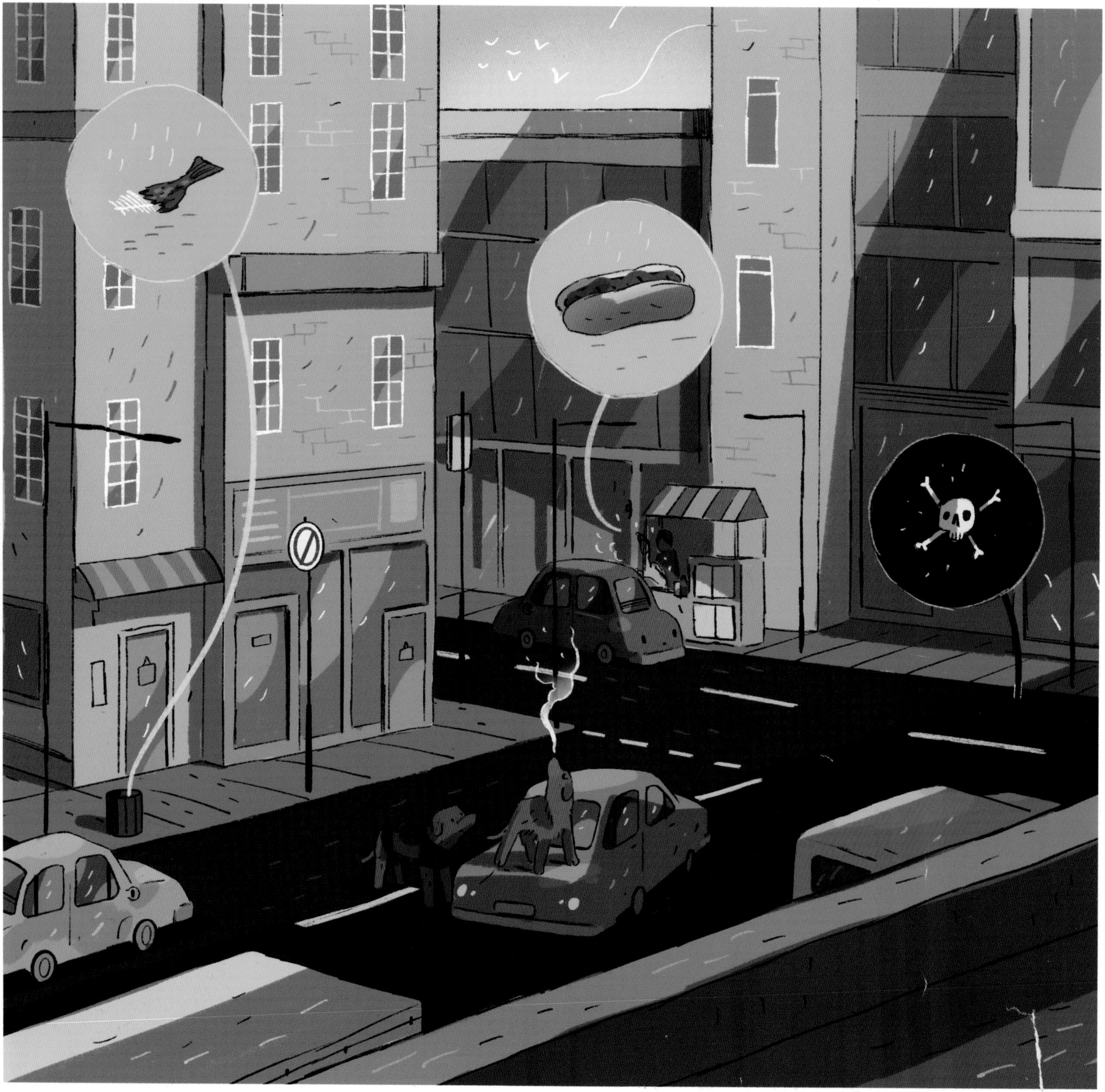

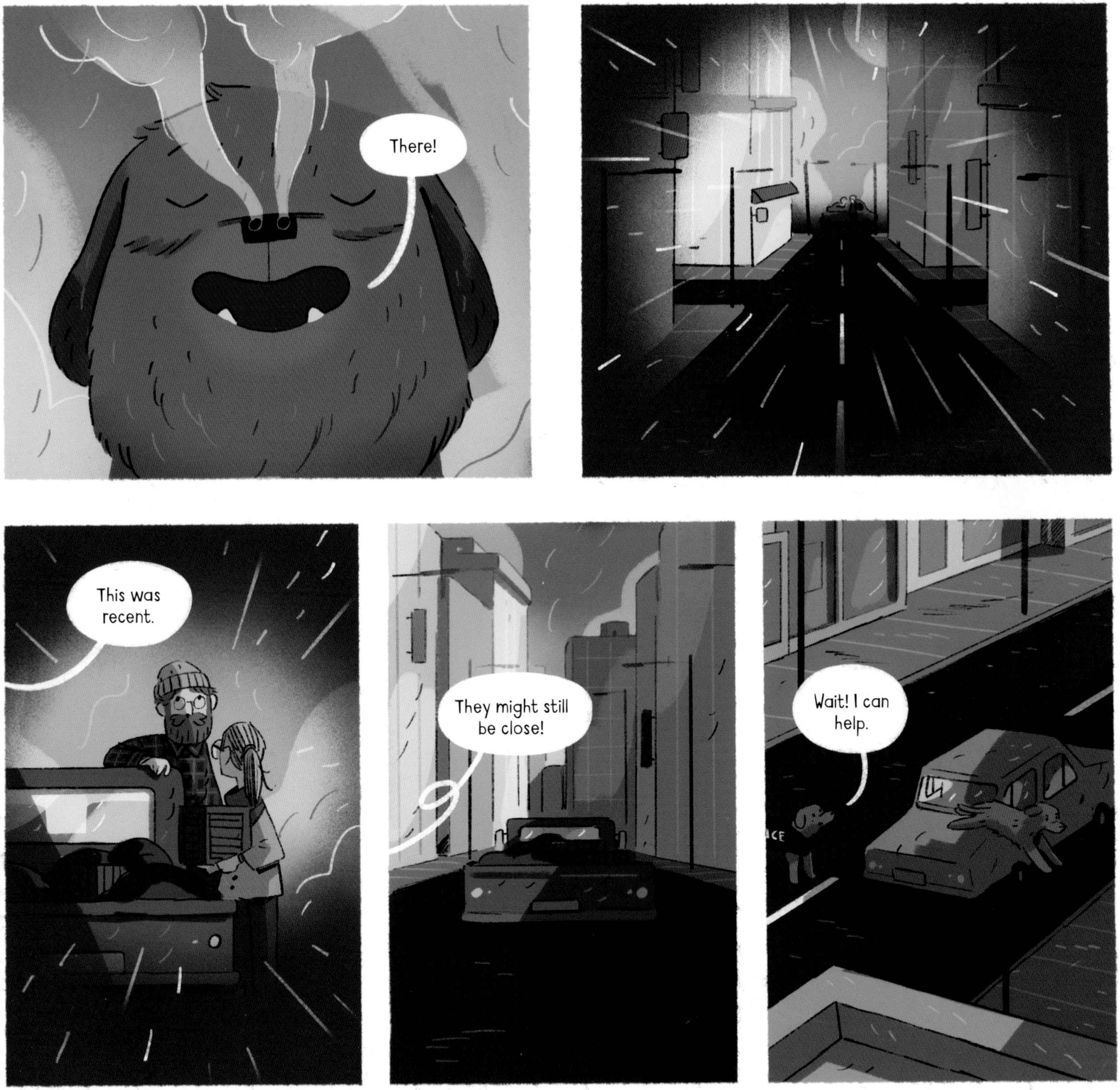
There!
This was recent.
They might still be close!
Wait! I can help.

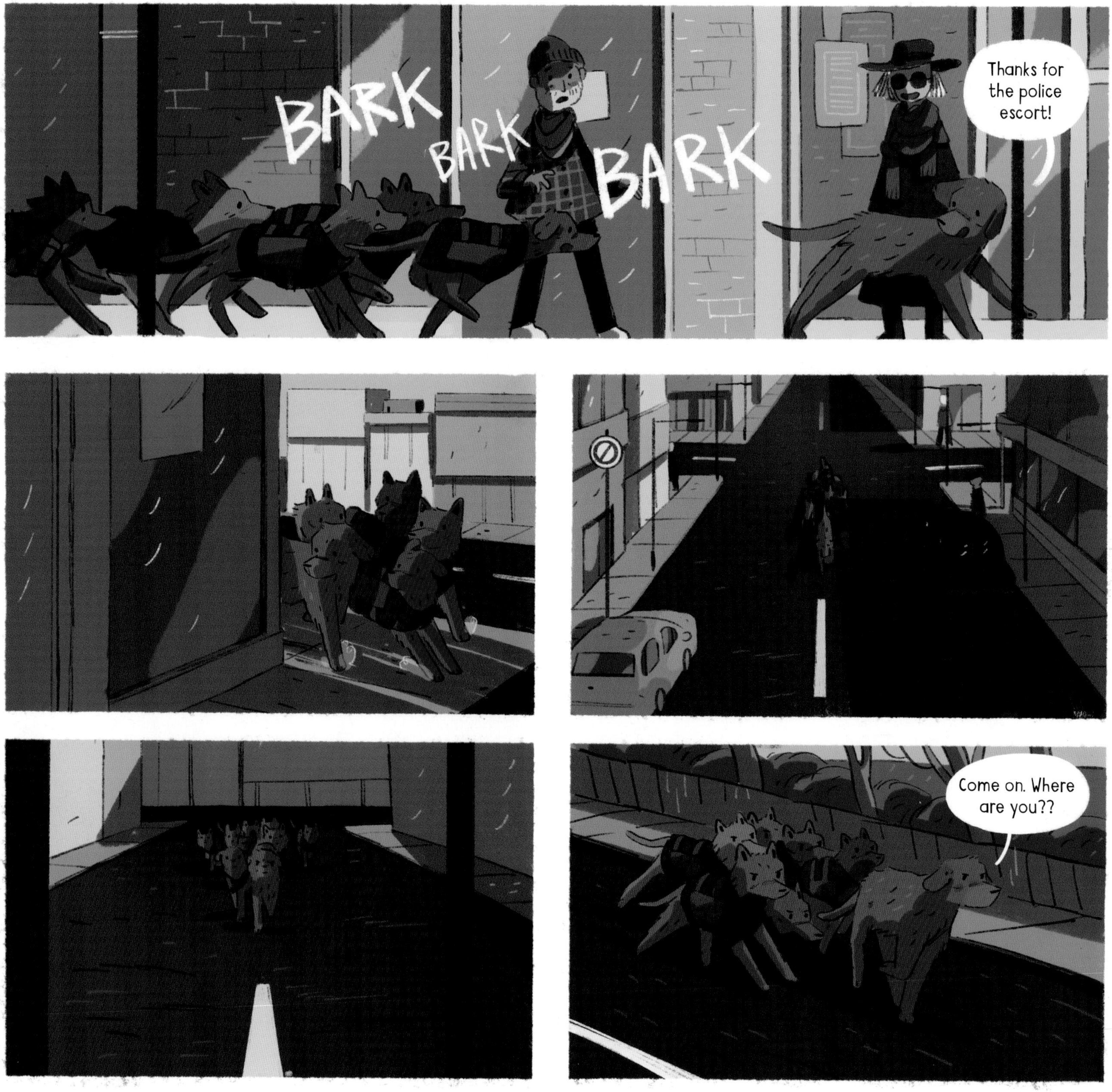
BARK
BARK
BARK
Thanks for the police escort!
Come on. Where are you??

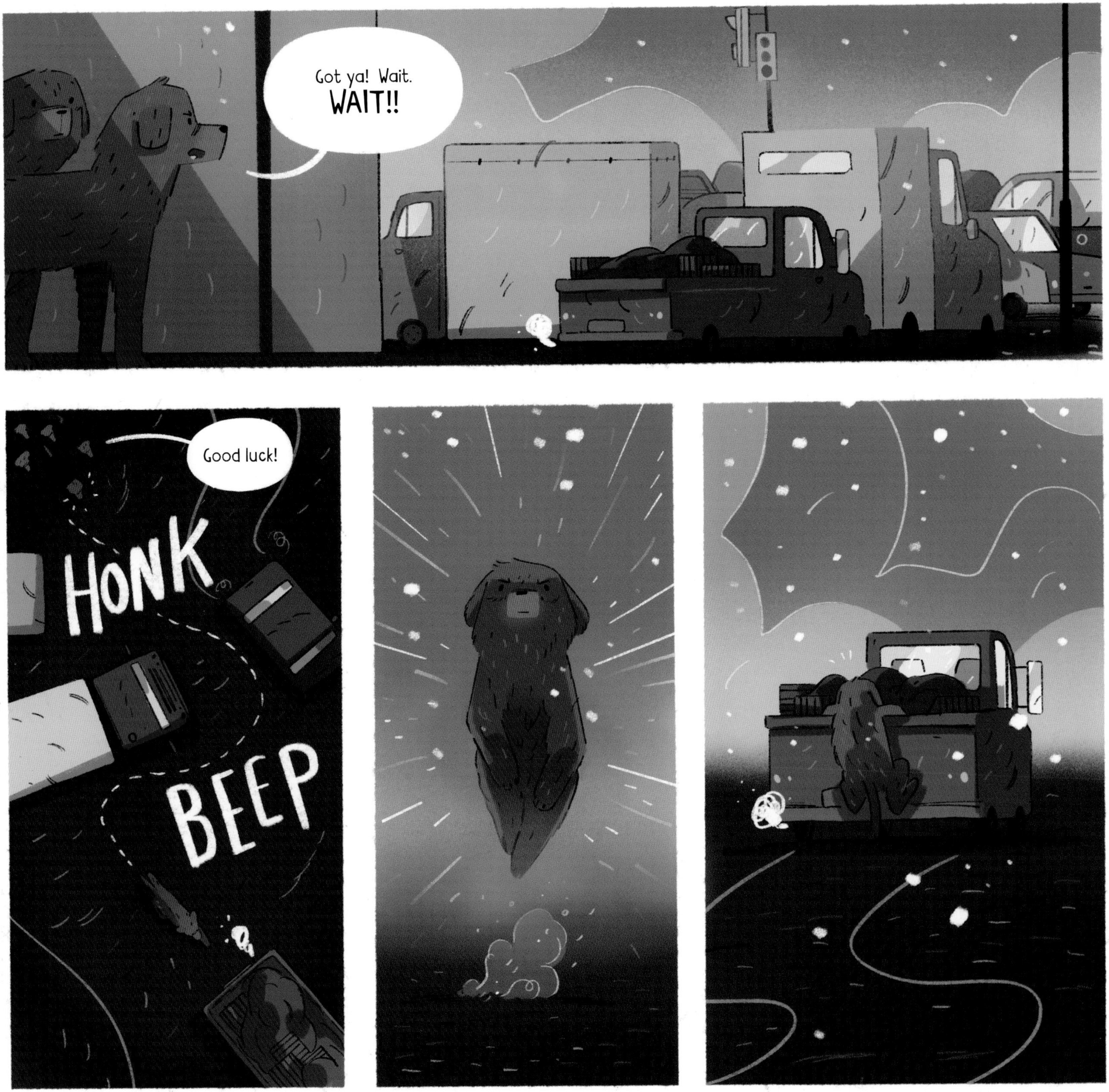

Got ya! Wait. WAIT!!
Good luck!
HONK
BEEP

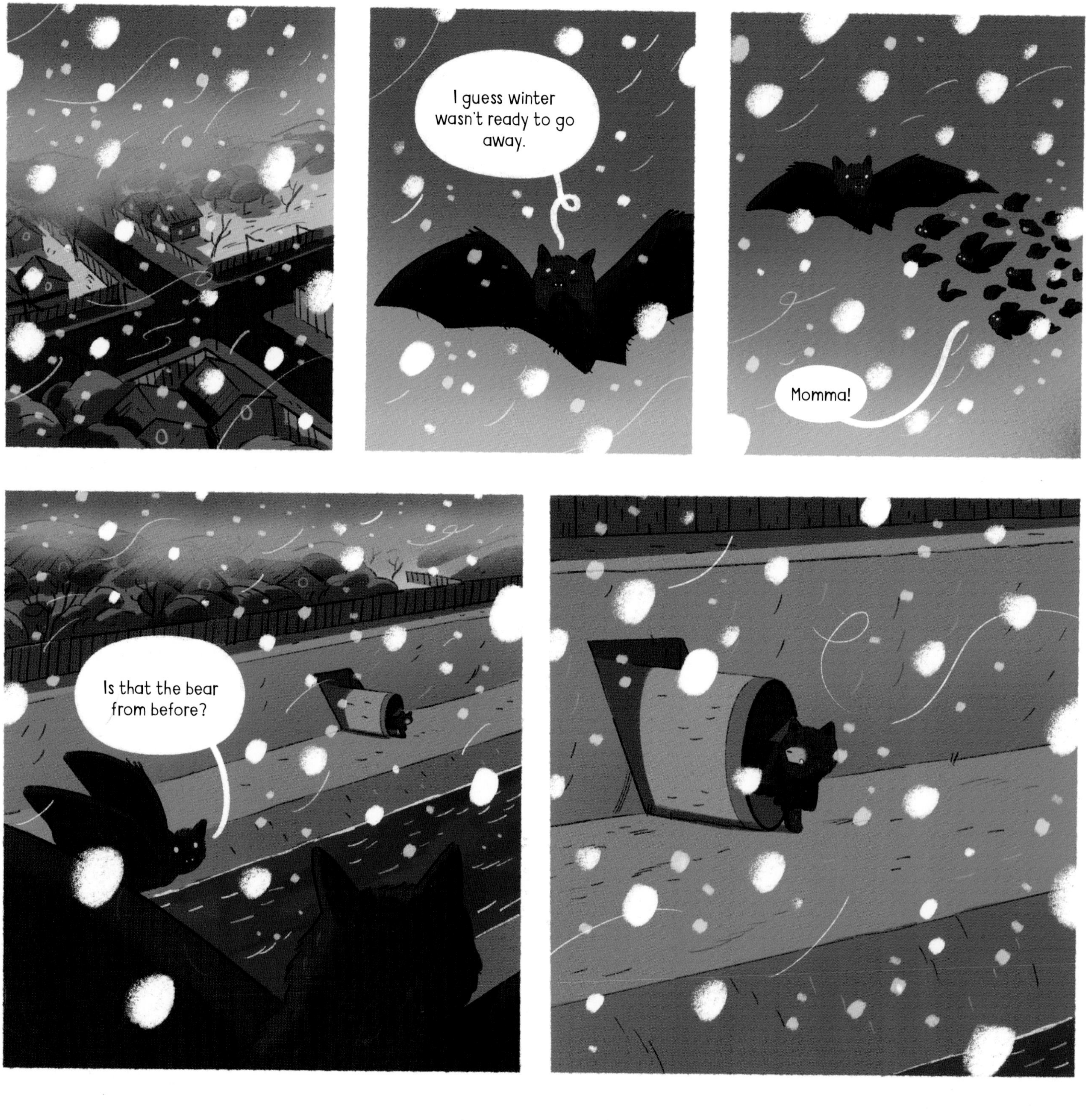
I guess winter wasn't ready to go away.
Momma!
Is that the bear from before?

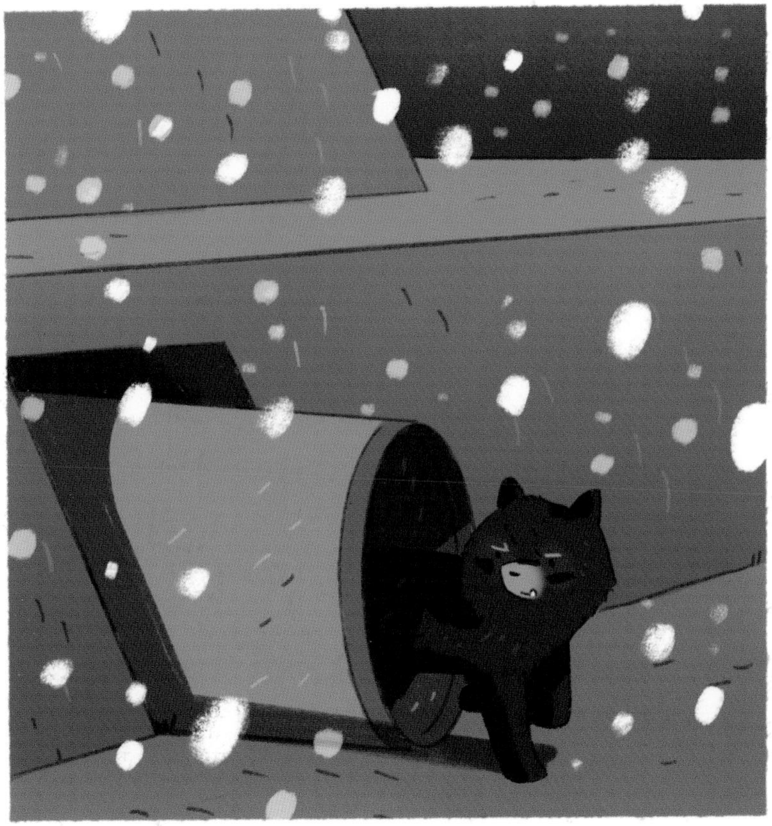

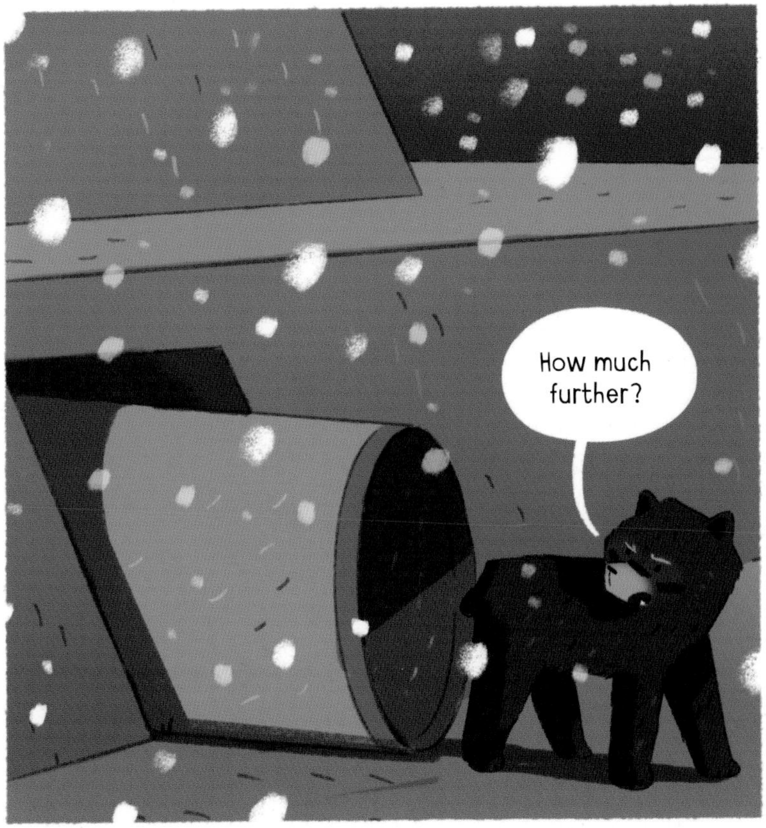
How much further?

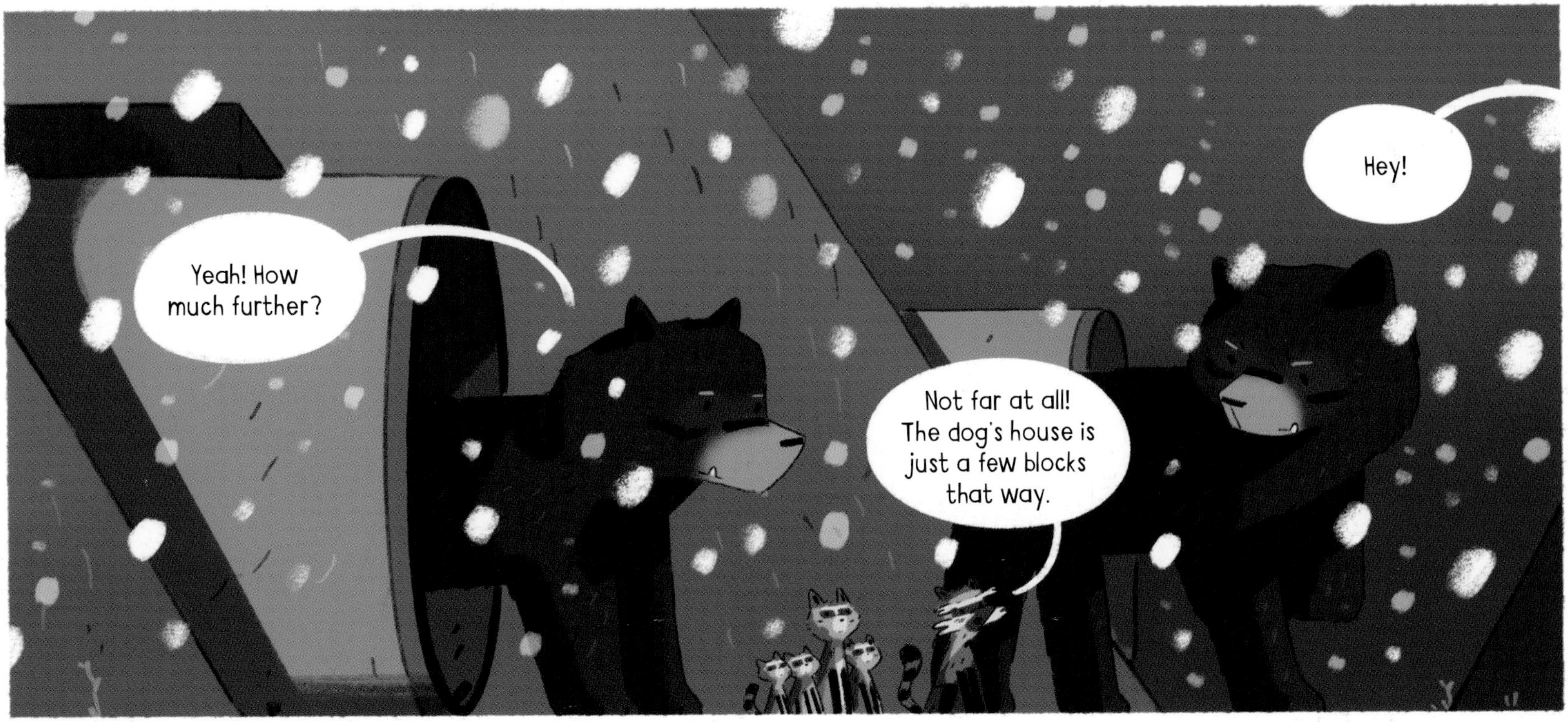
Yeah! How much further?
Hey!
Not far at all! The dog's house is just a few blocks that way.

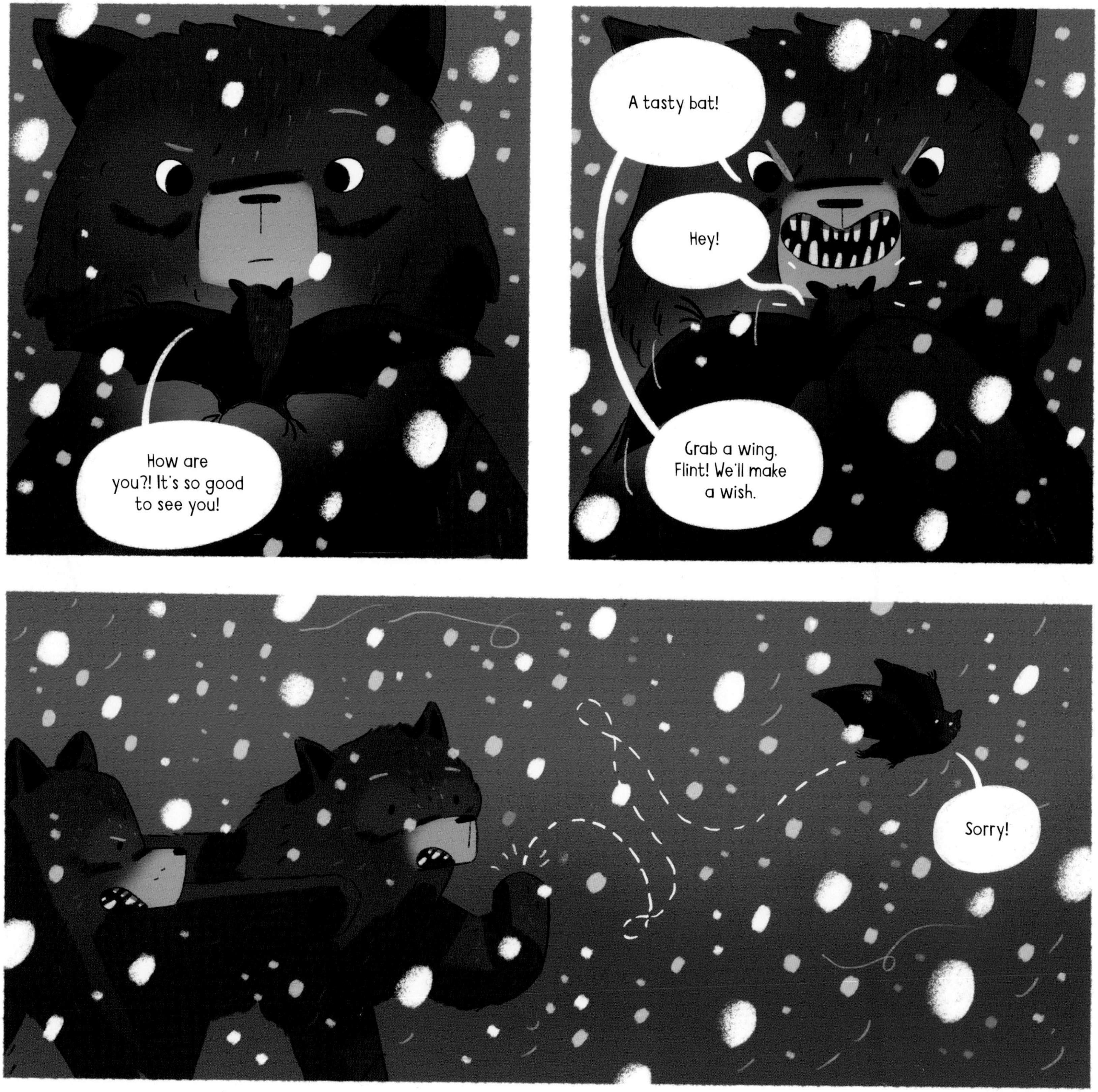
How are you?! It's so good to see you!
A tasty bat!
Hey!
Grab a wing. Flint! We'll make a wish.
Sorry!

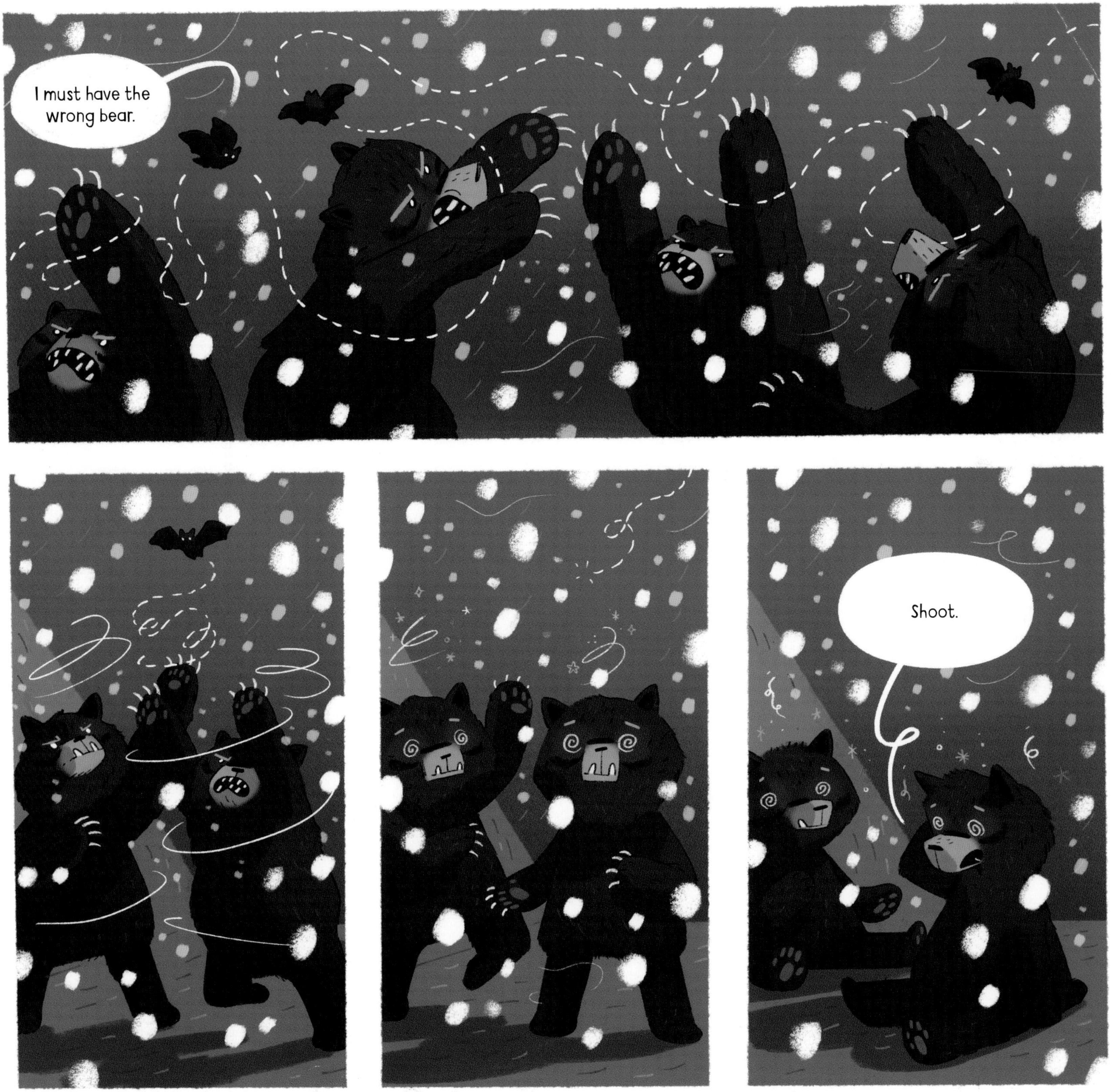
I must have the wrong bear.
Shoot.

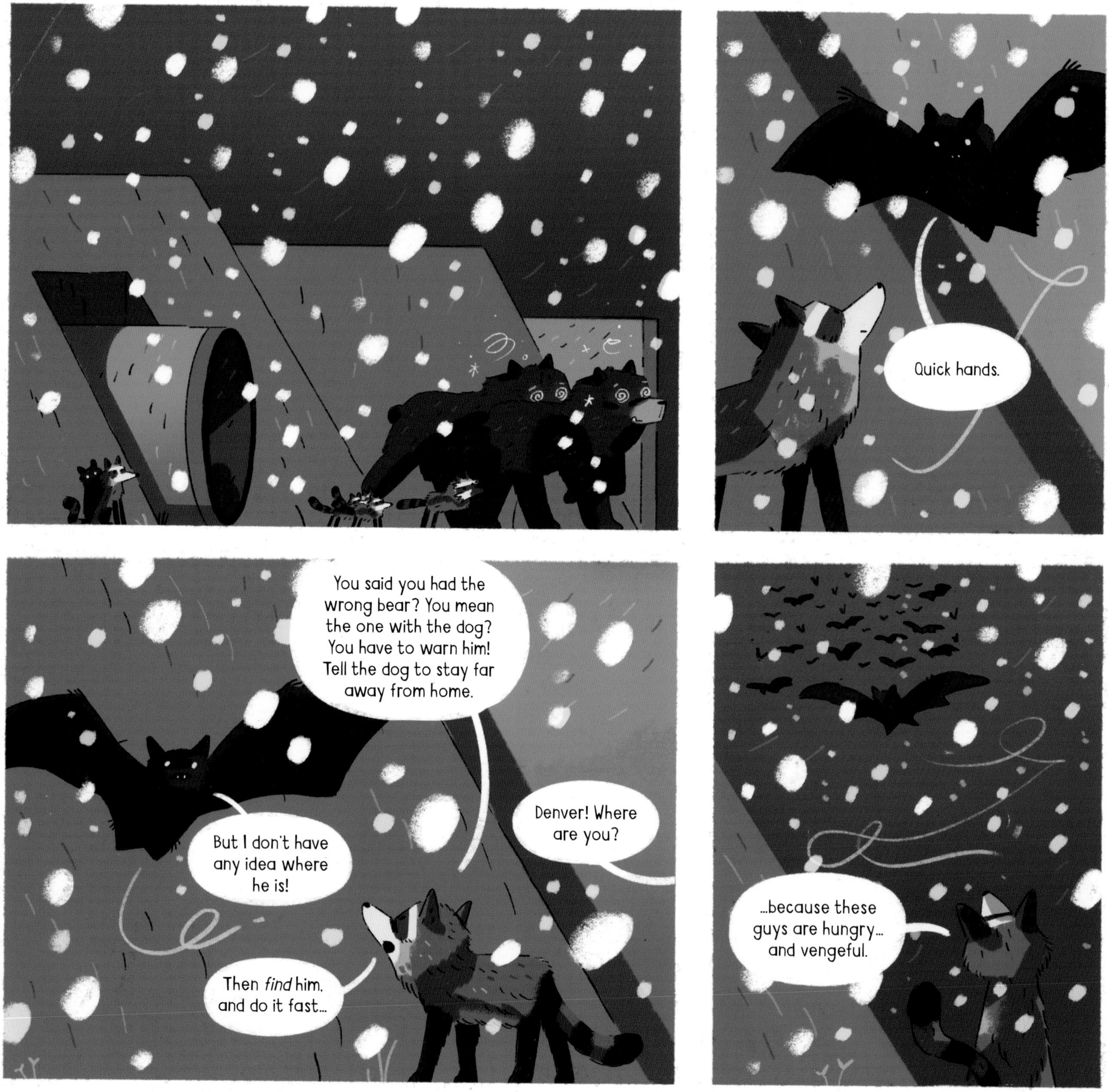
Quick hands.
You said you had the wrong bear? You mean the one with the dog? You have to warn him! Tell the dog to stay far away from home.
But I don't have any idea where he is!
Denver! Where are you?
Then *find* him, and do it fast...
...because these guys are hungry... and vengeful.

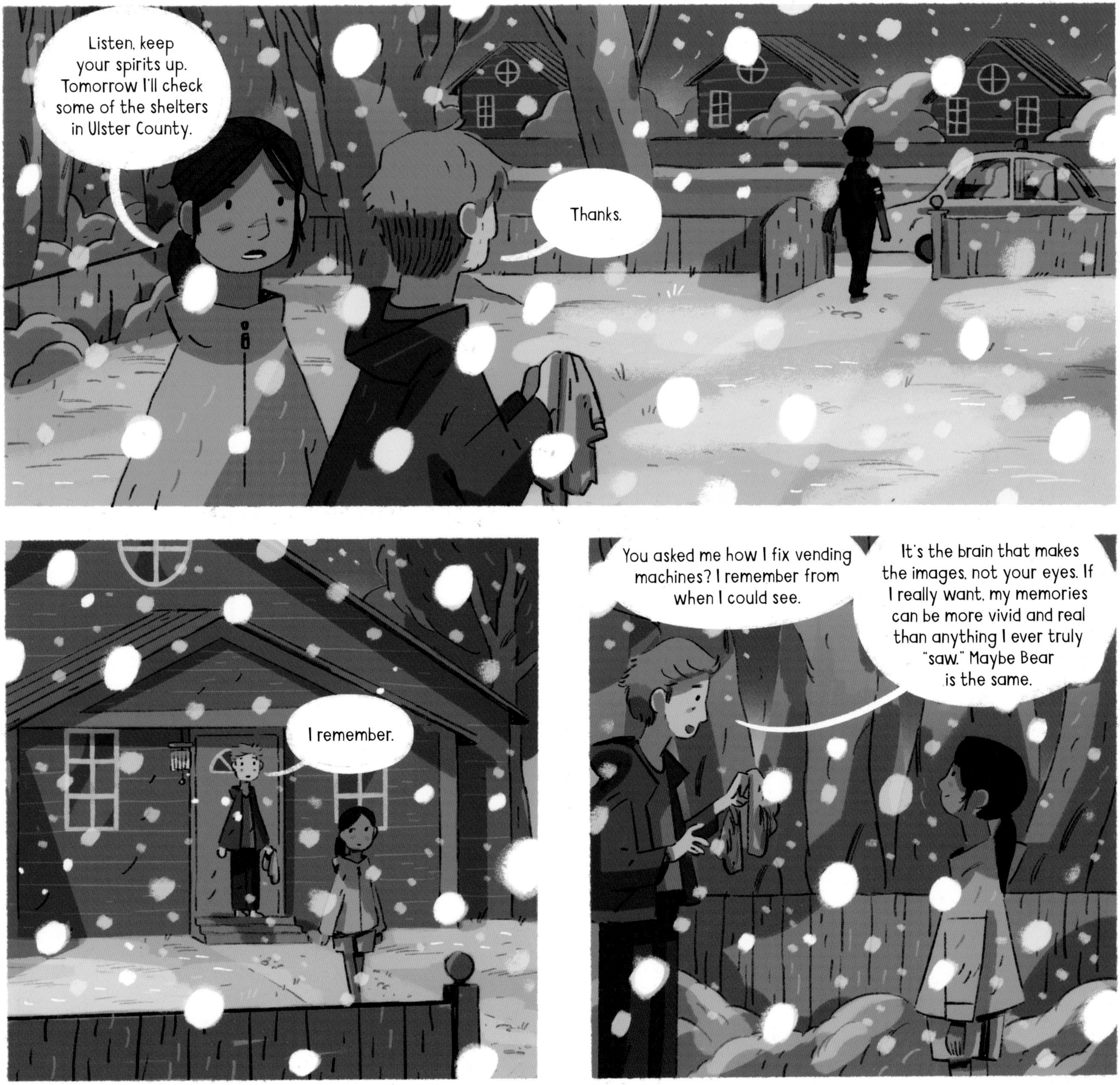

Listen, keep your spirits up. Tomorrow I'll check some of the shelters in Ulster County.
Thanks.
I remember.
You asked me how I fix vending machines? I remember from when I could see.
It's the brain that makes the images, not your eyes. If I really want, my memories can be more vivid and real than anything I ever truly "saw." Maybe Bear is the same.

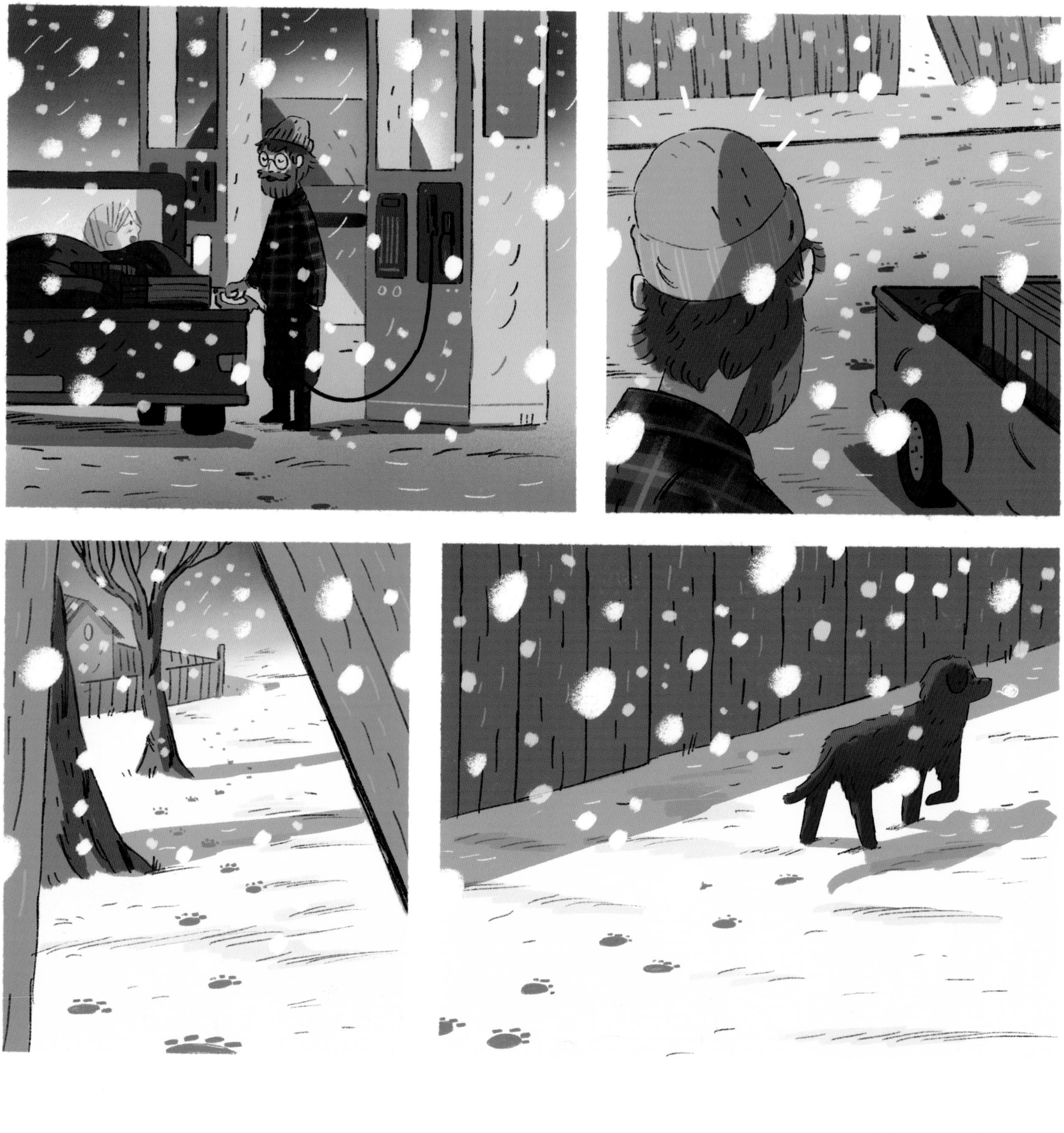

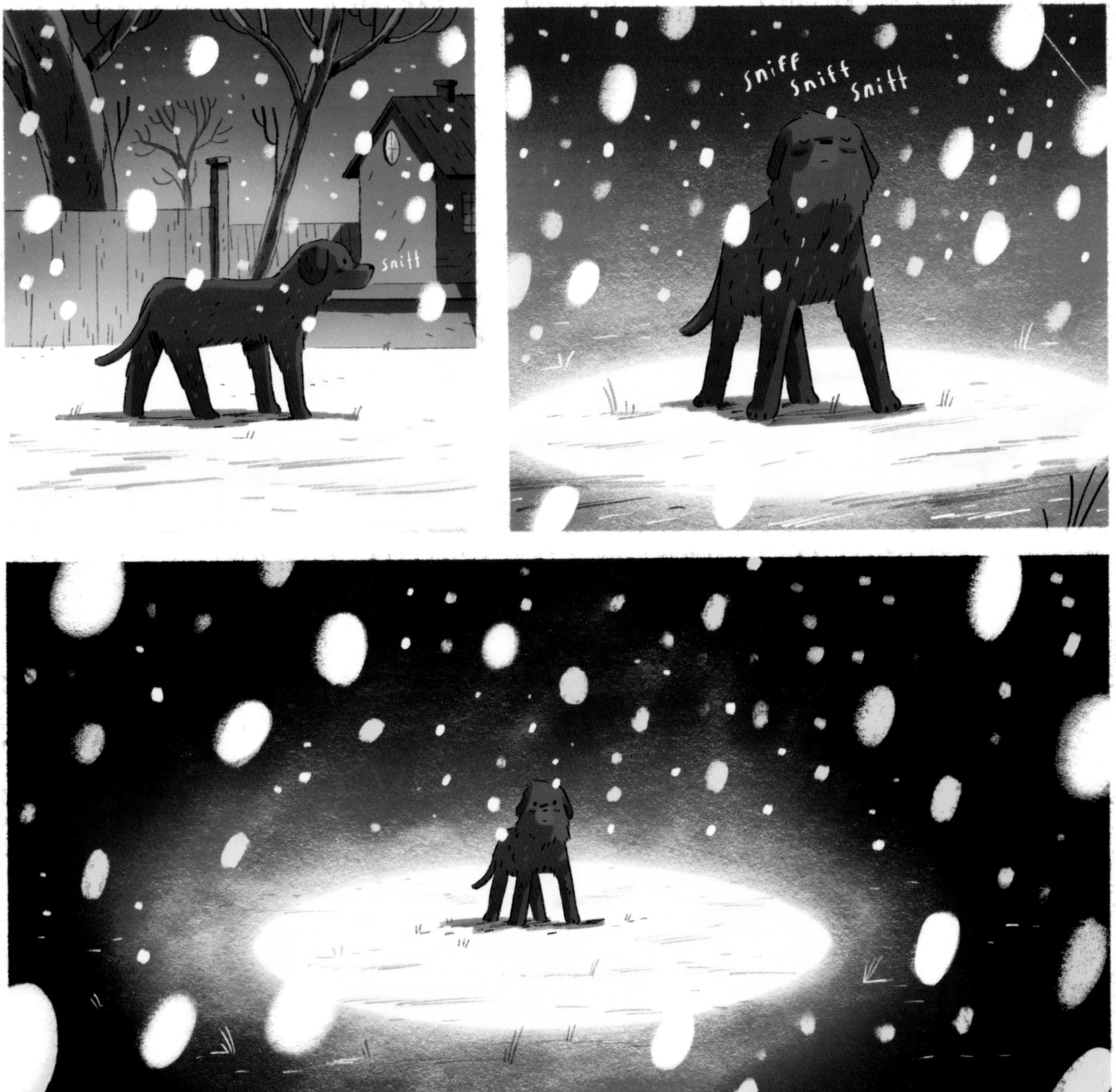
sniff
sniff
sniff
sniff

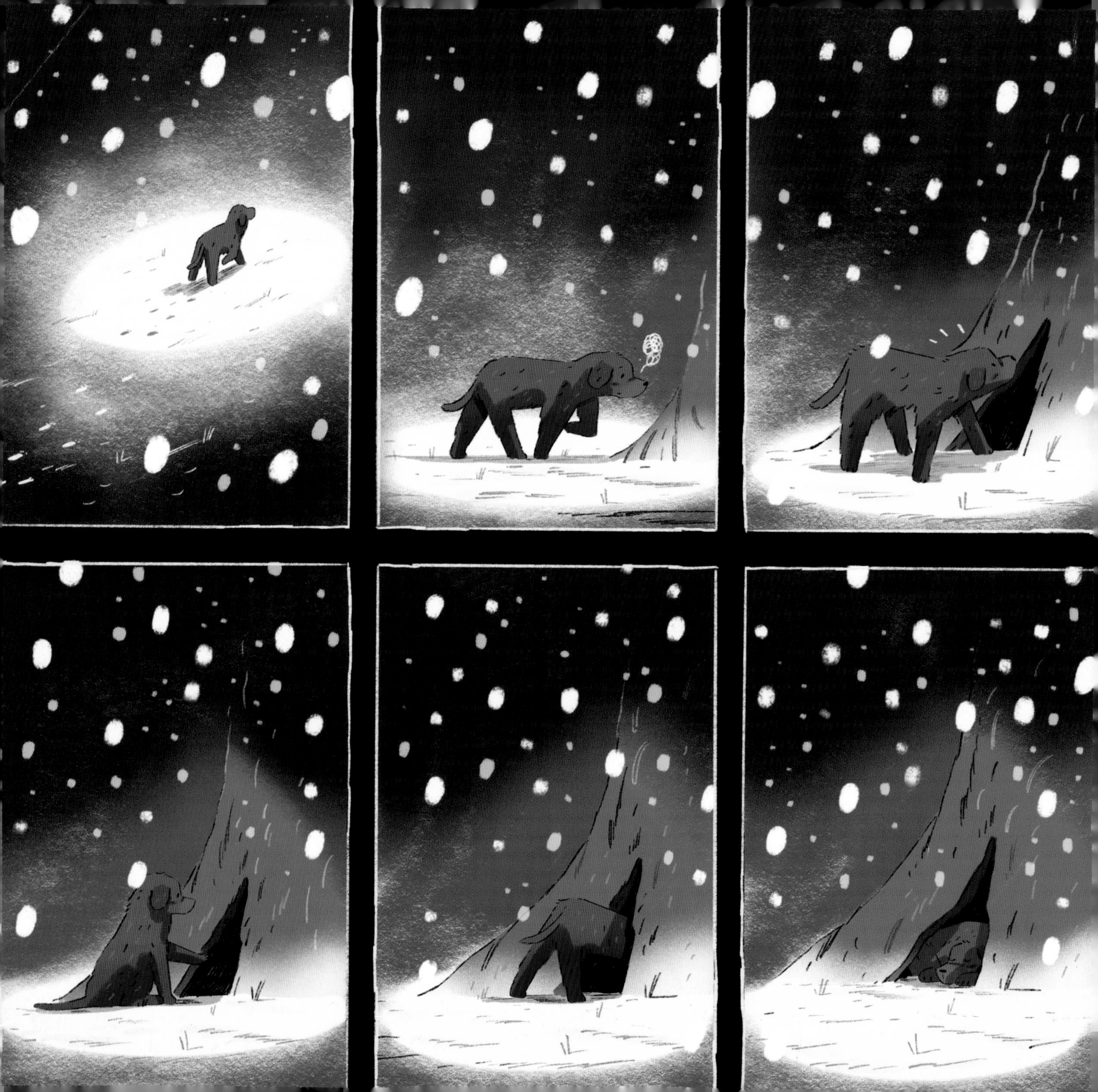

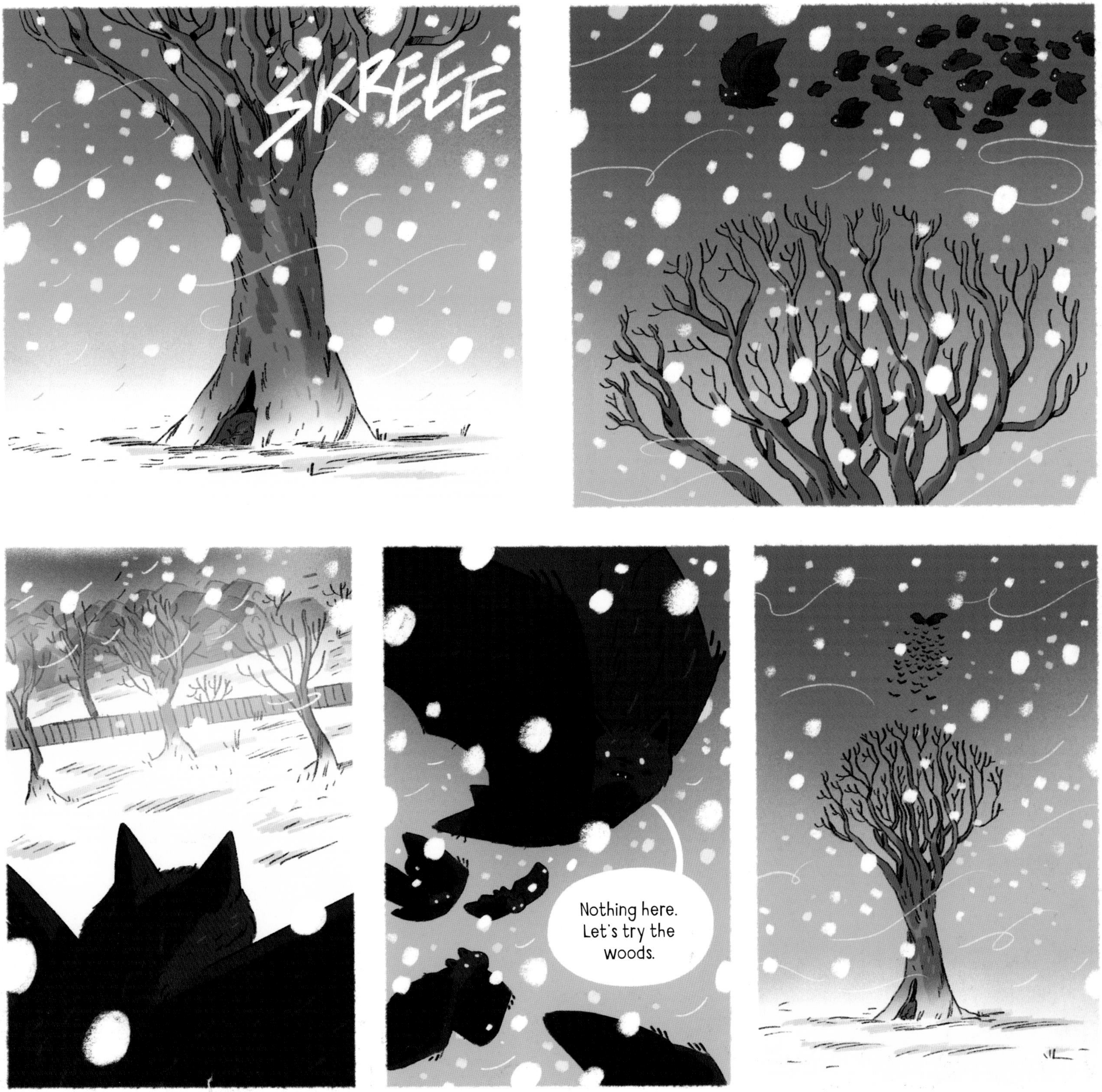
SKREEE
Nothing here. Let's try the woods.

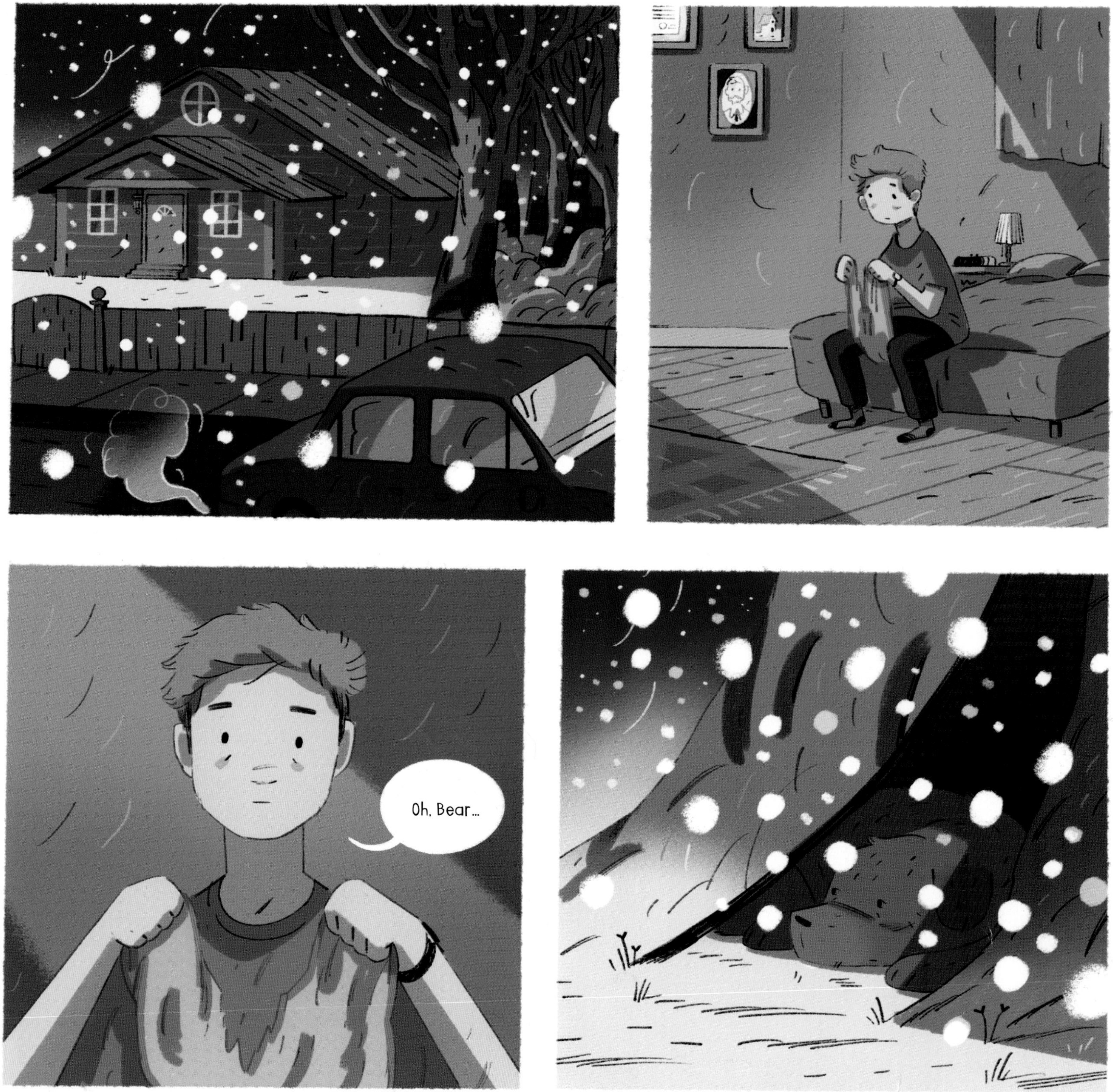
Oh, Bear...

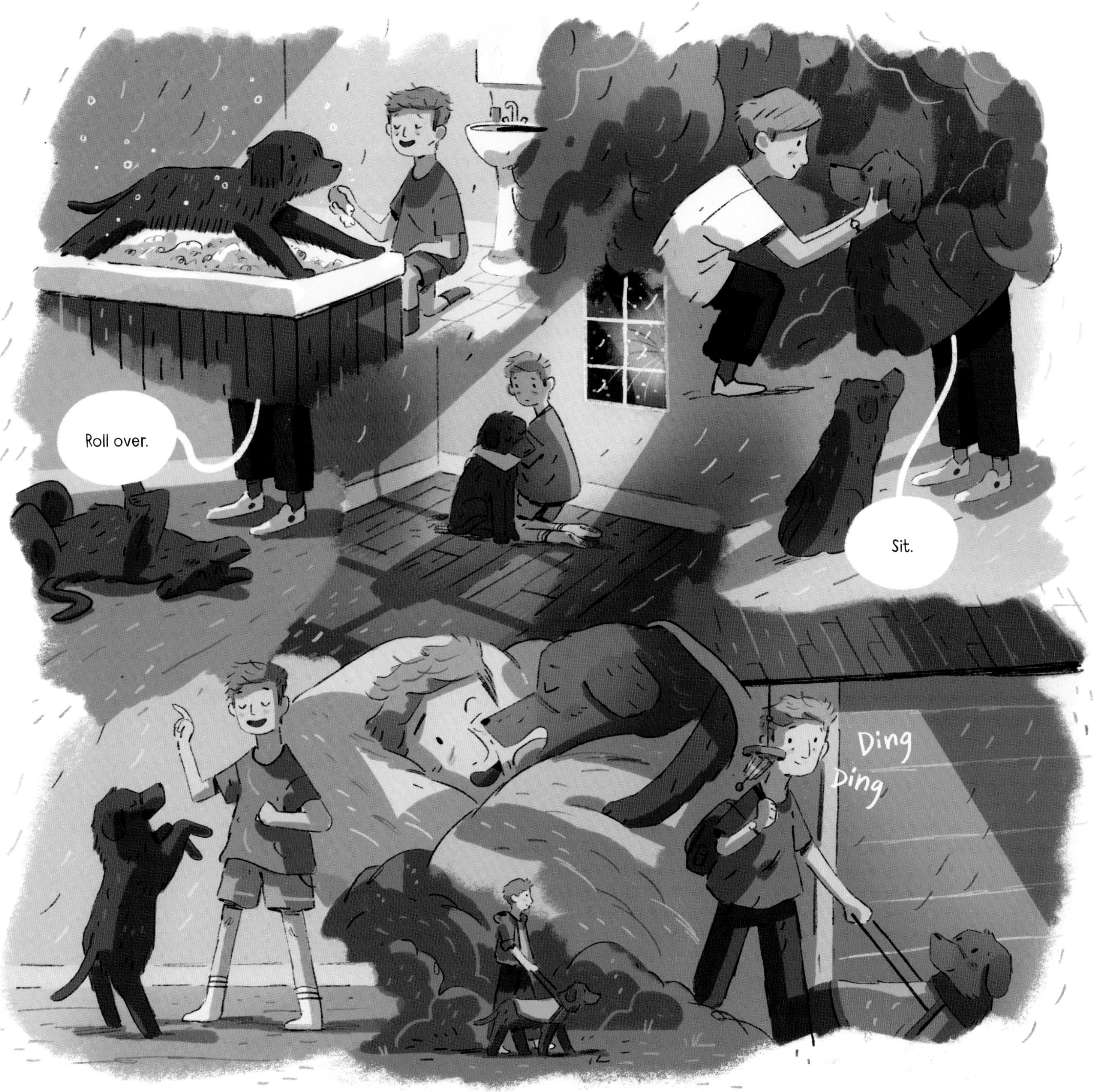
Roll over.
Sit.
Ding
Ding

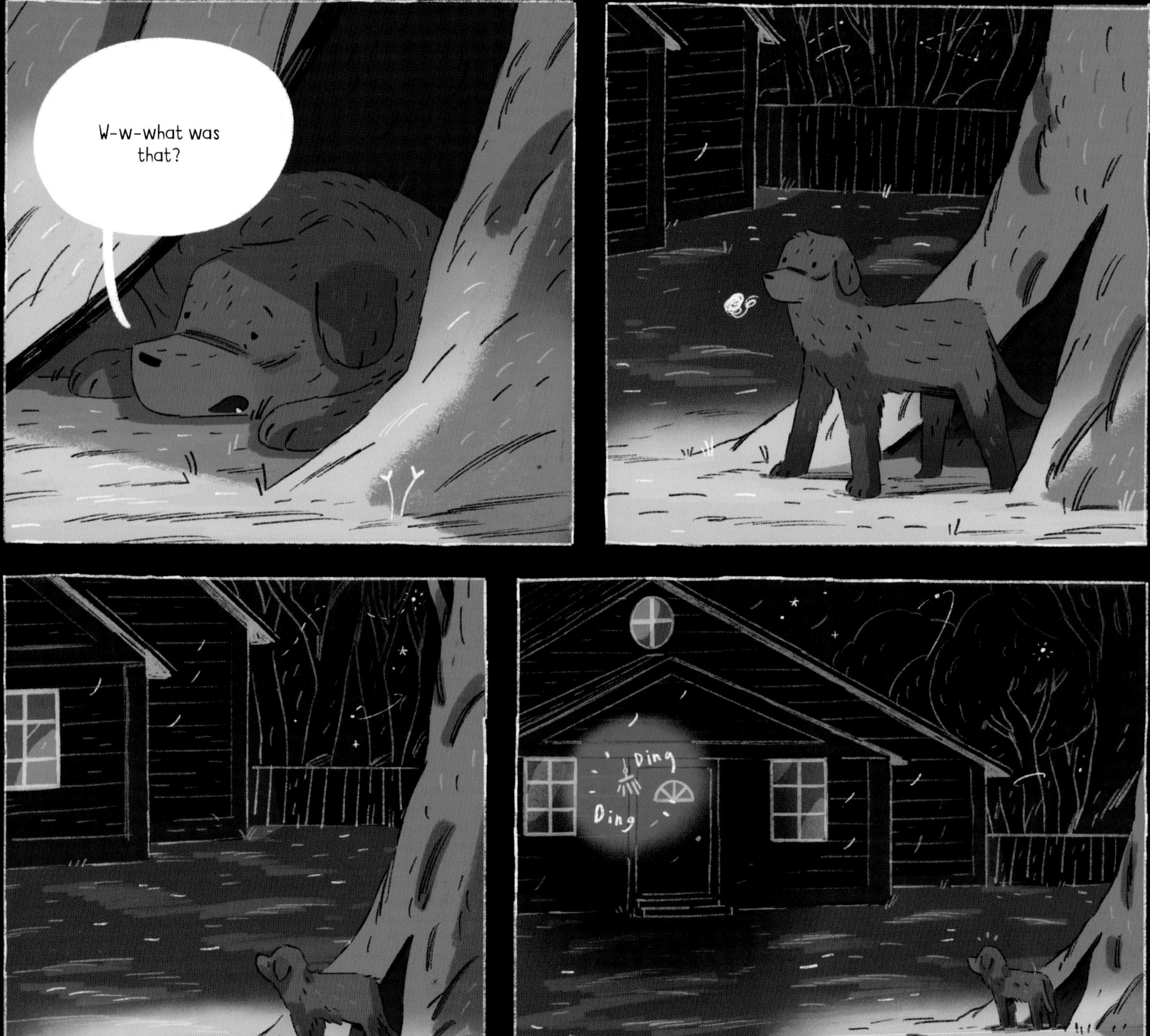
W-w-what was that?
Ding
Ding

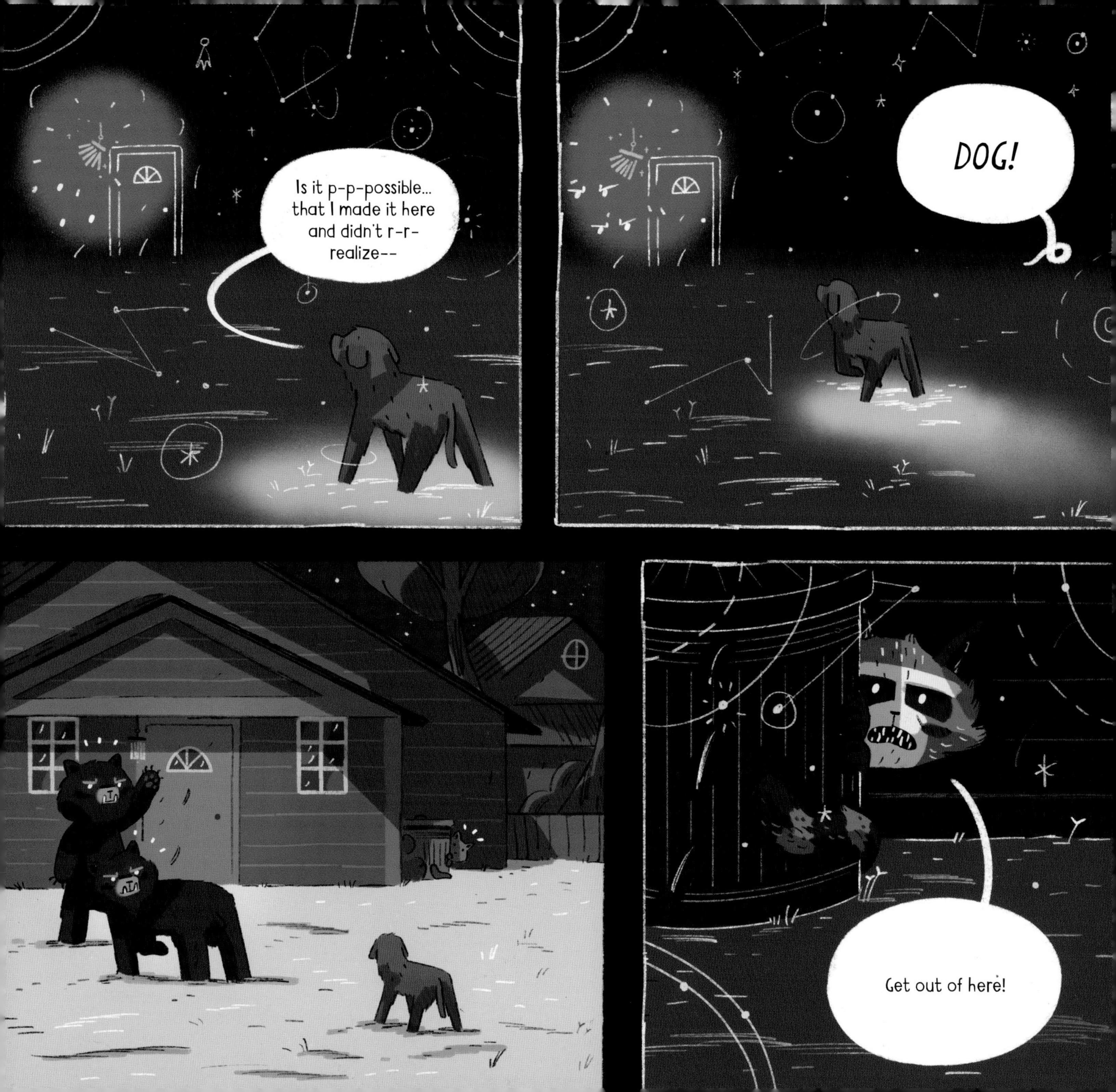
Is it p-p-possible... that I made it here and didn't r-r-realize--
DOG!
Get out of here!

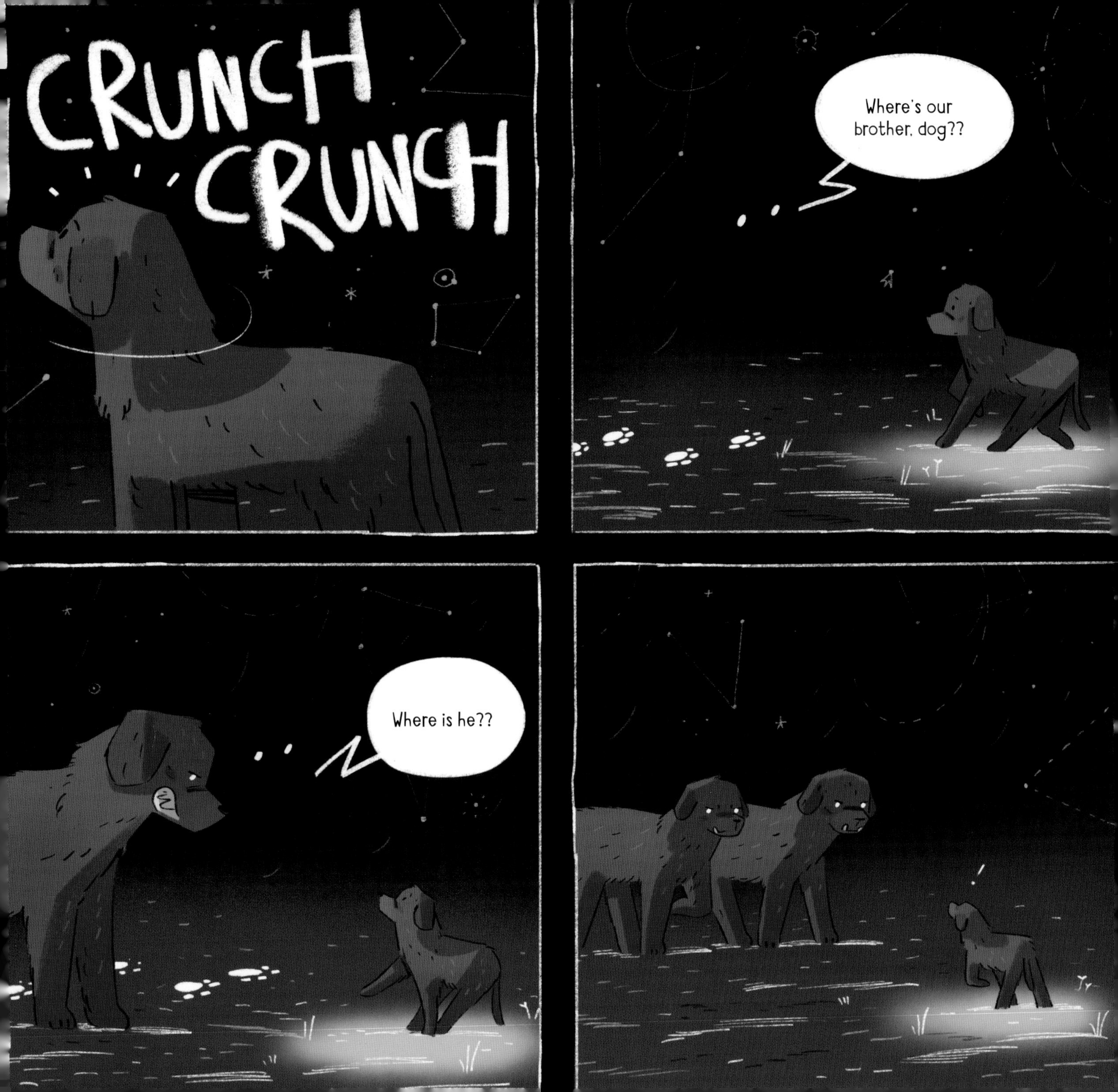
CRUNCH
CRUNCH
Where's our brother, dog??
Where is he??
!

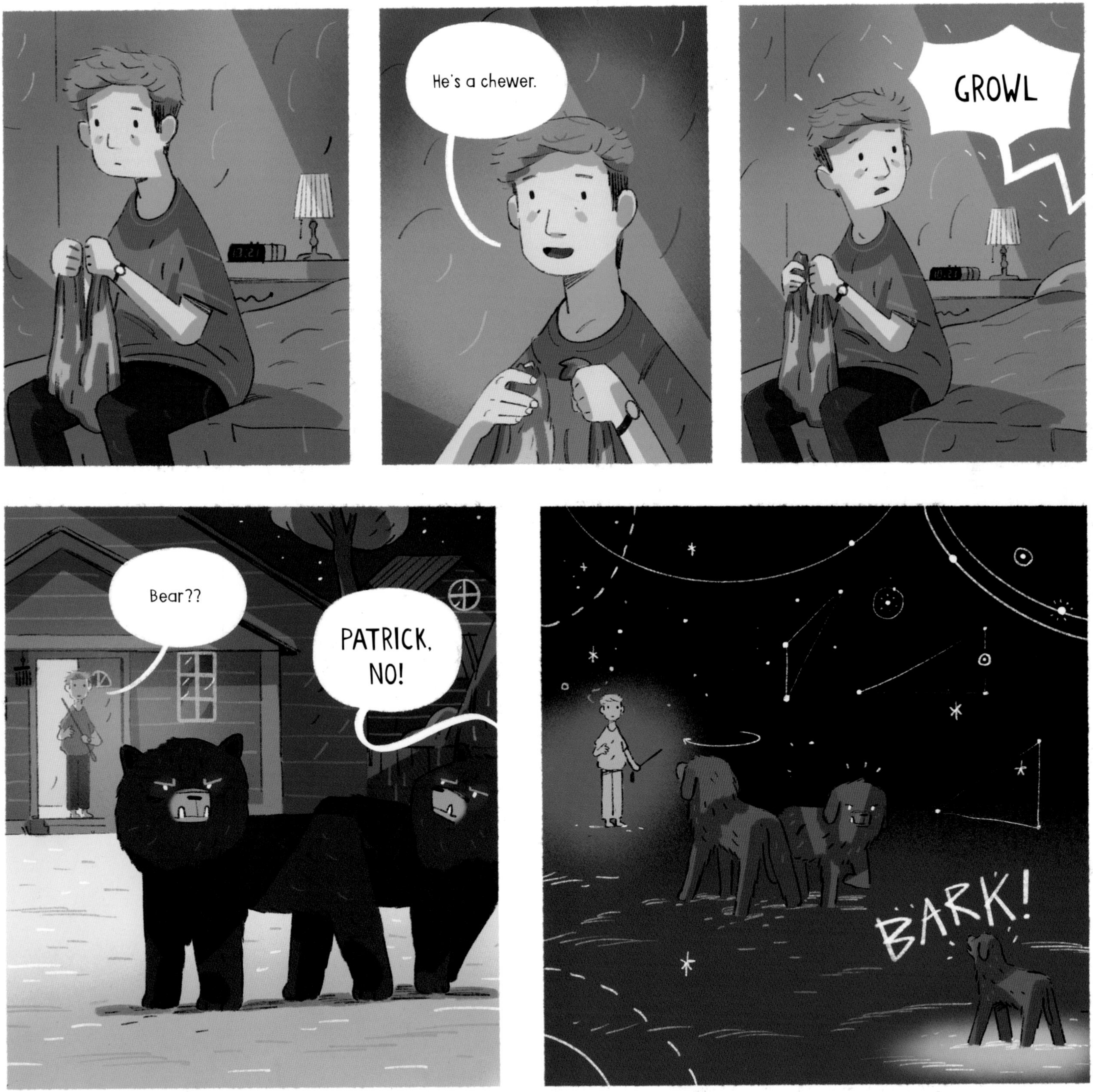
He's a chewer.
GROWL
Bear??
PATRICK, NO!
BARK!

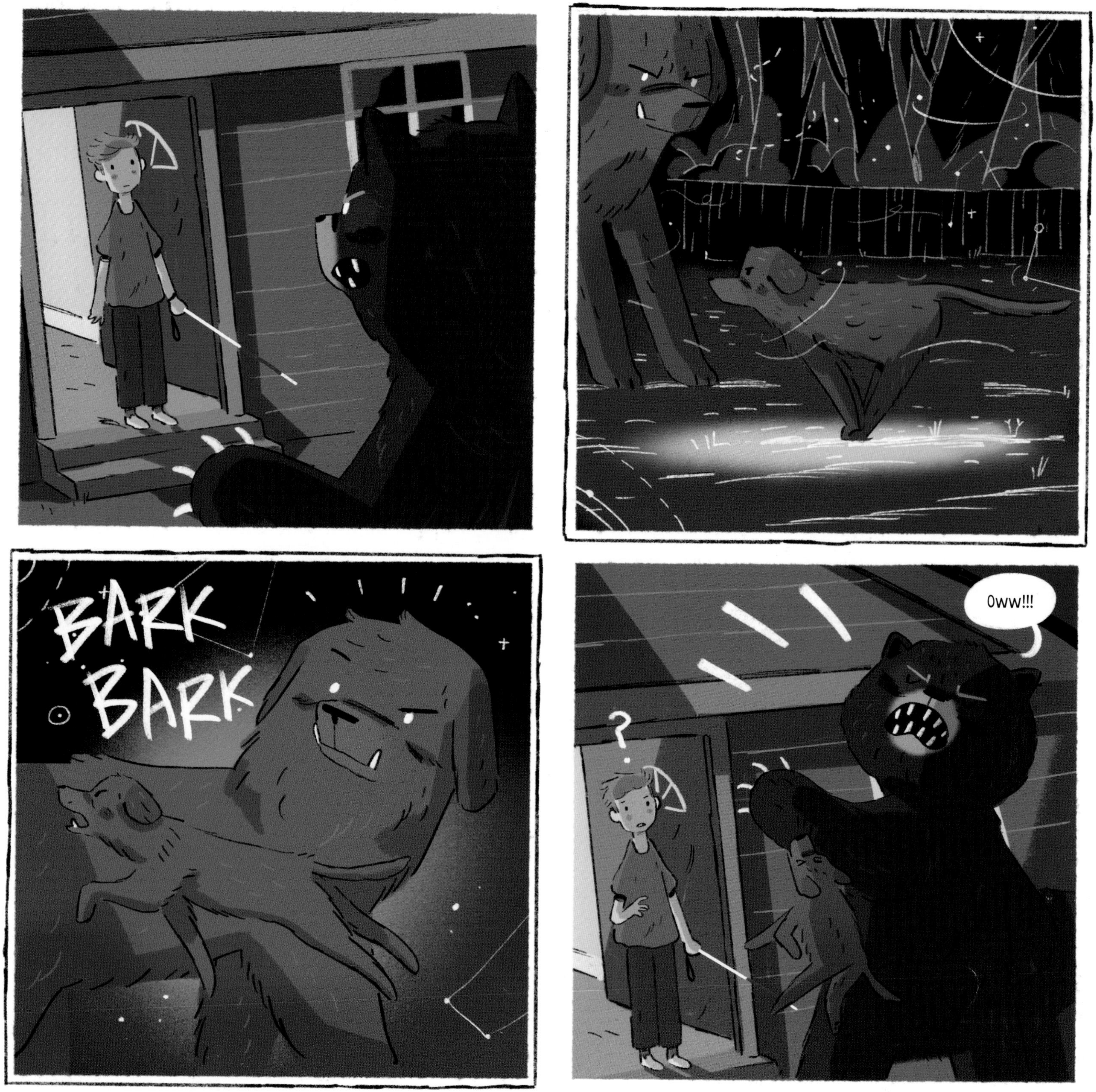
BARK
BARK
Oww!!!

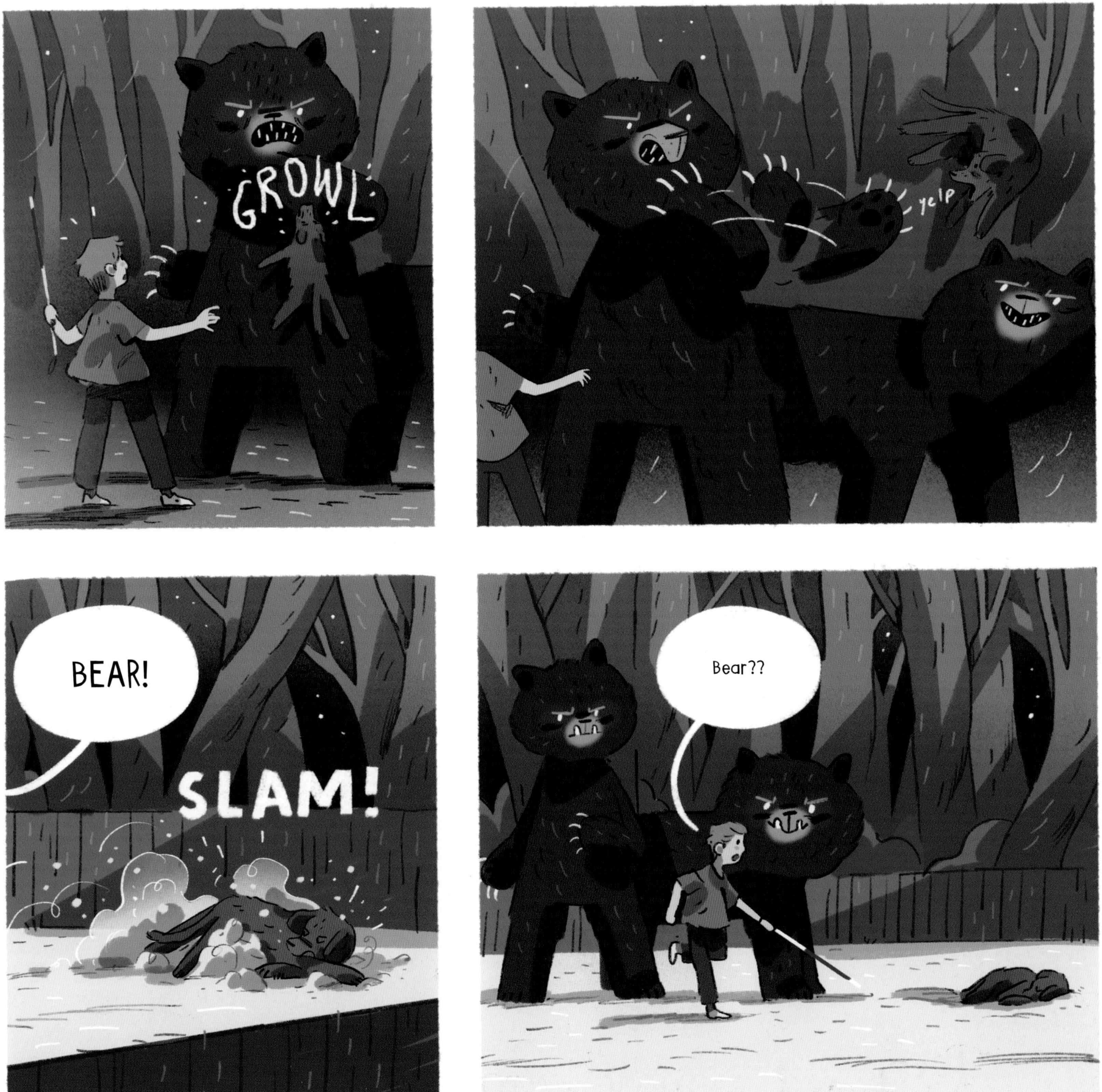
GROWL
yelp
BEAR!
SLAM!
Bear??

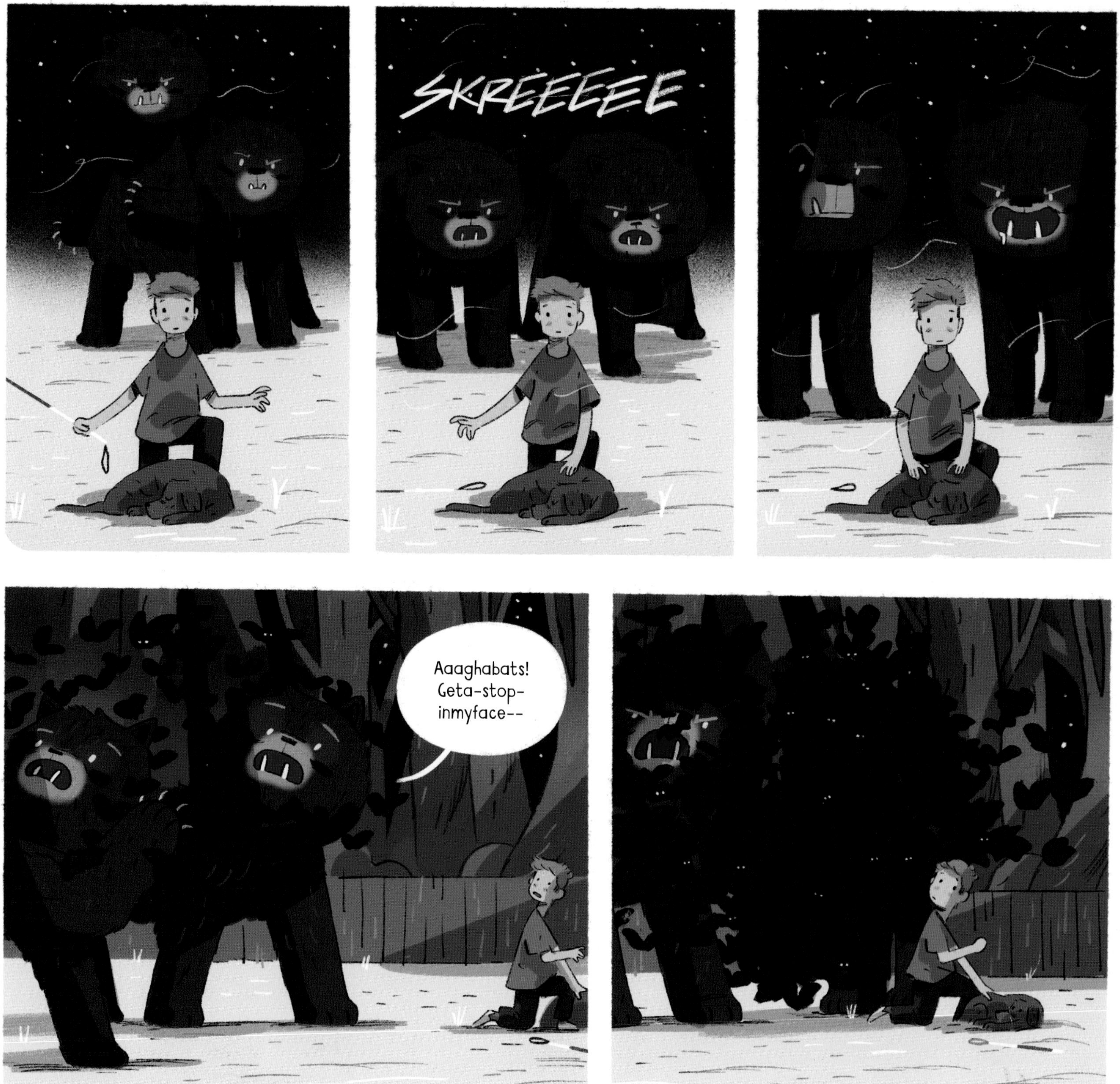
SKREEEEEE
Aaaghabats! Geta-stop-inmyface--

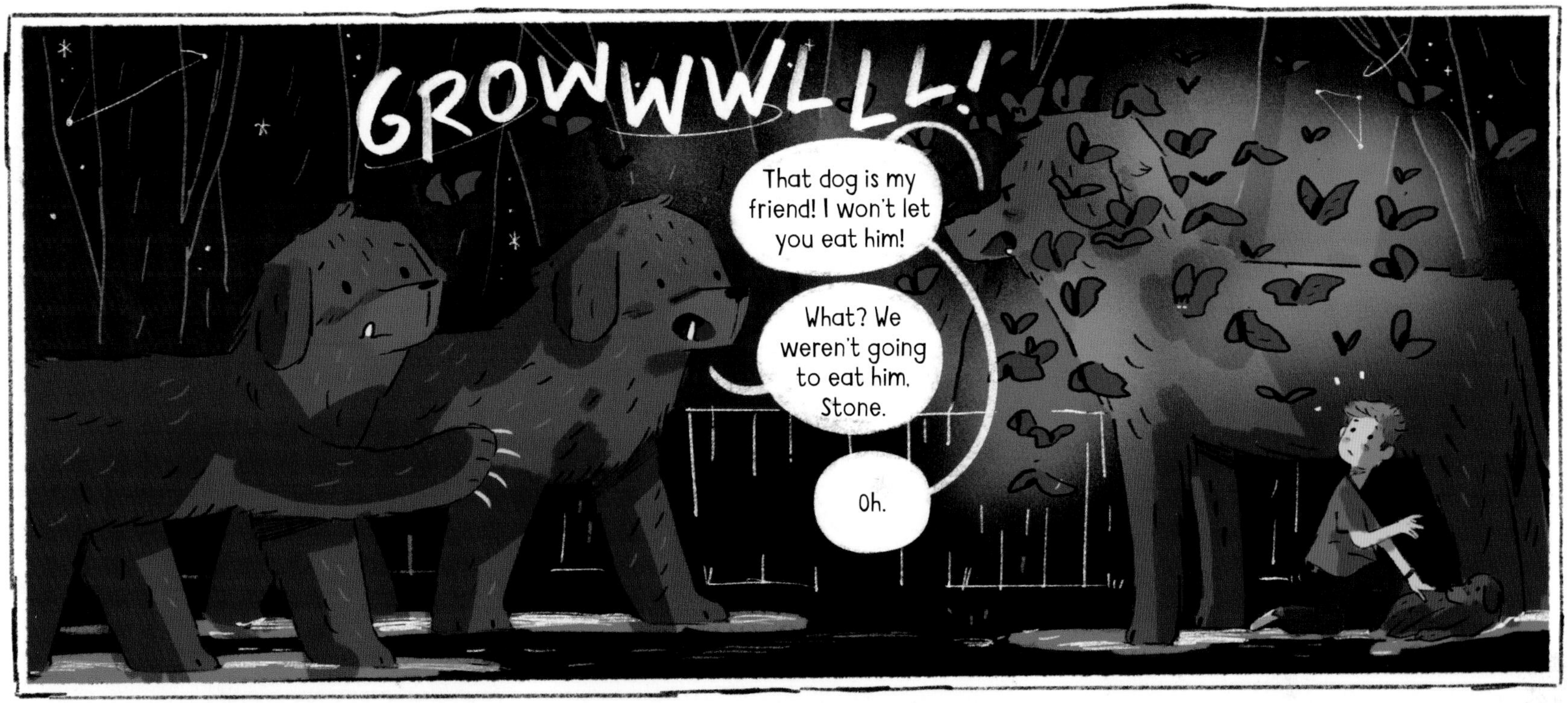
GROWWWLLLL!
That dog is my friend! I won't let you eat him!
What? We weren't going to eat him, Stone.
Oh.
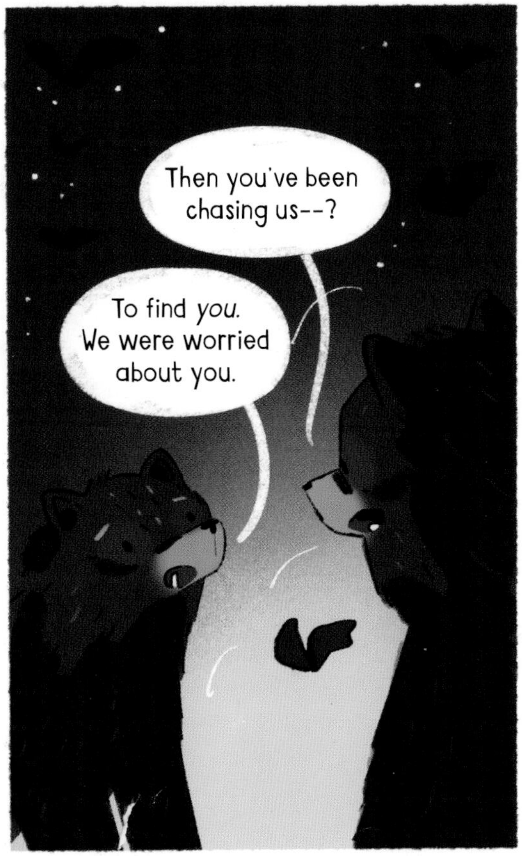
Then you've been chasing us--?
To find *you.* We were worried about you.
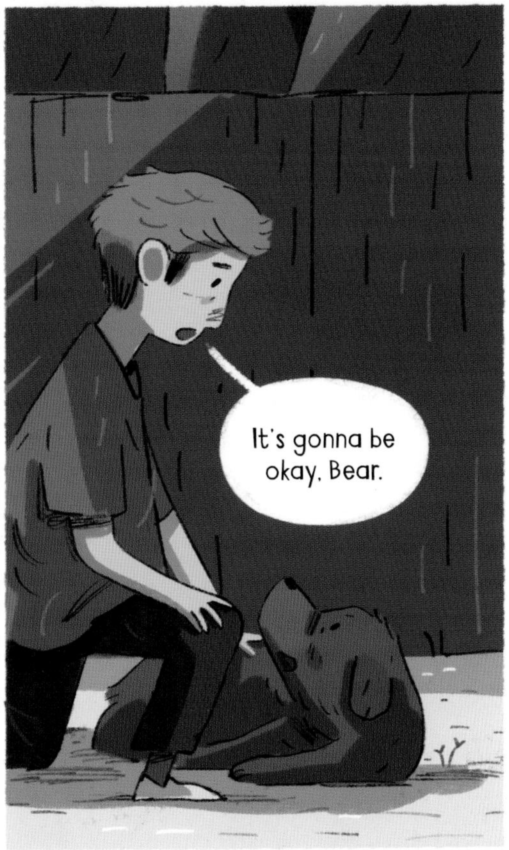
It's gonna be okay, Bear.
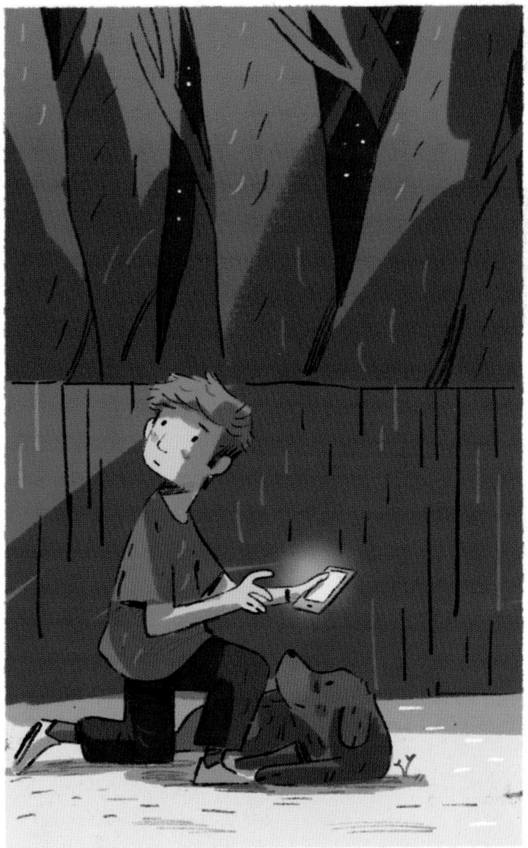

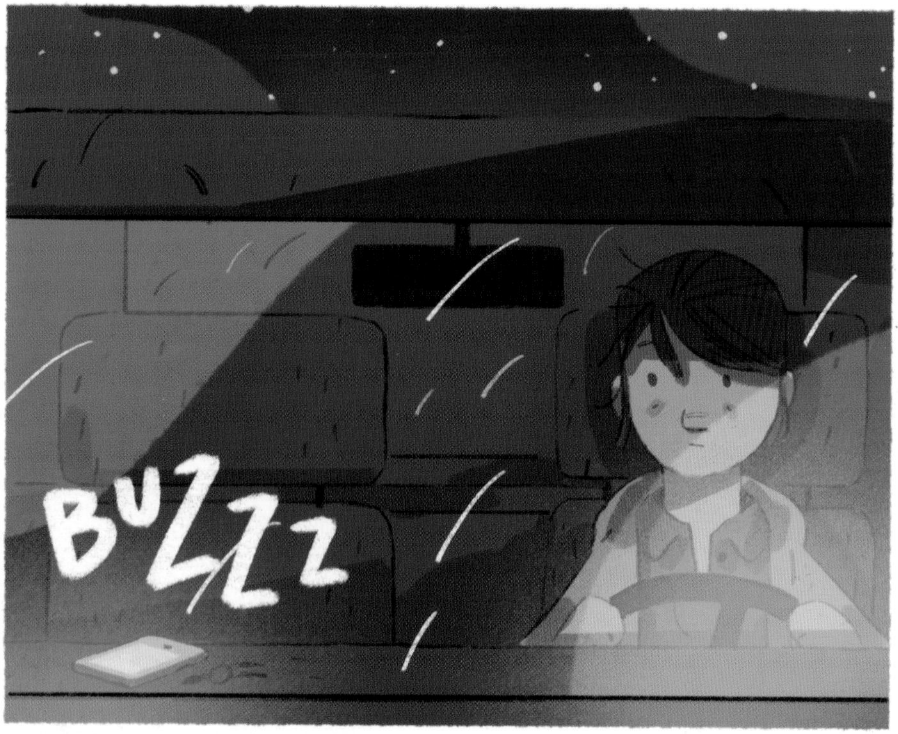
BUZZZ
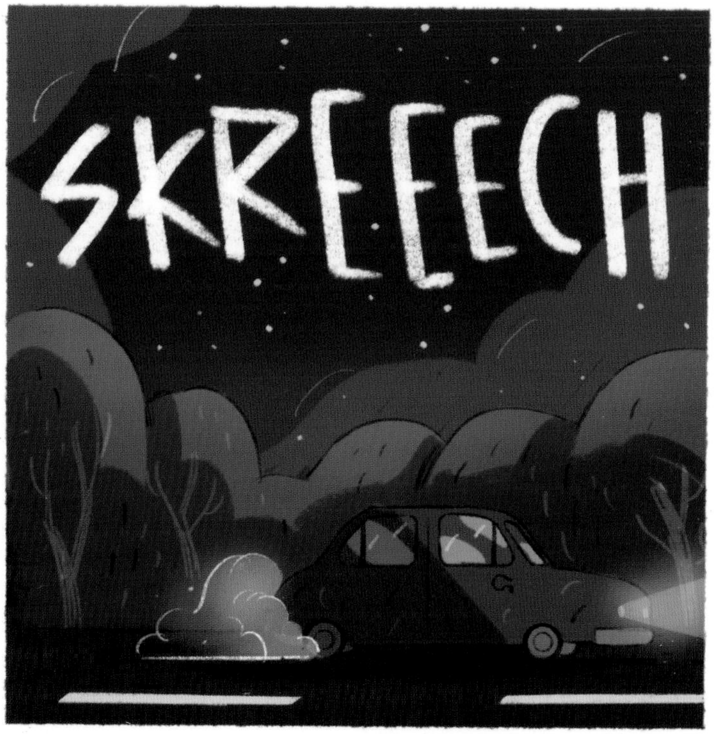
SKREEECH
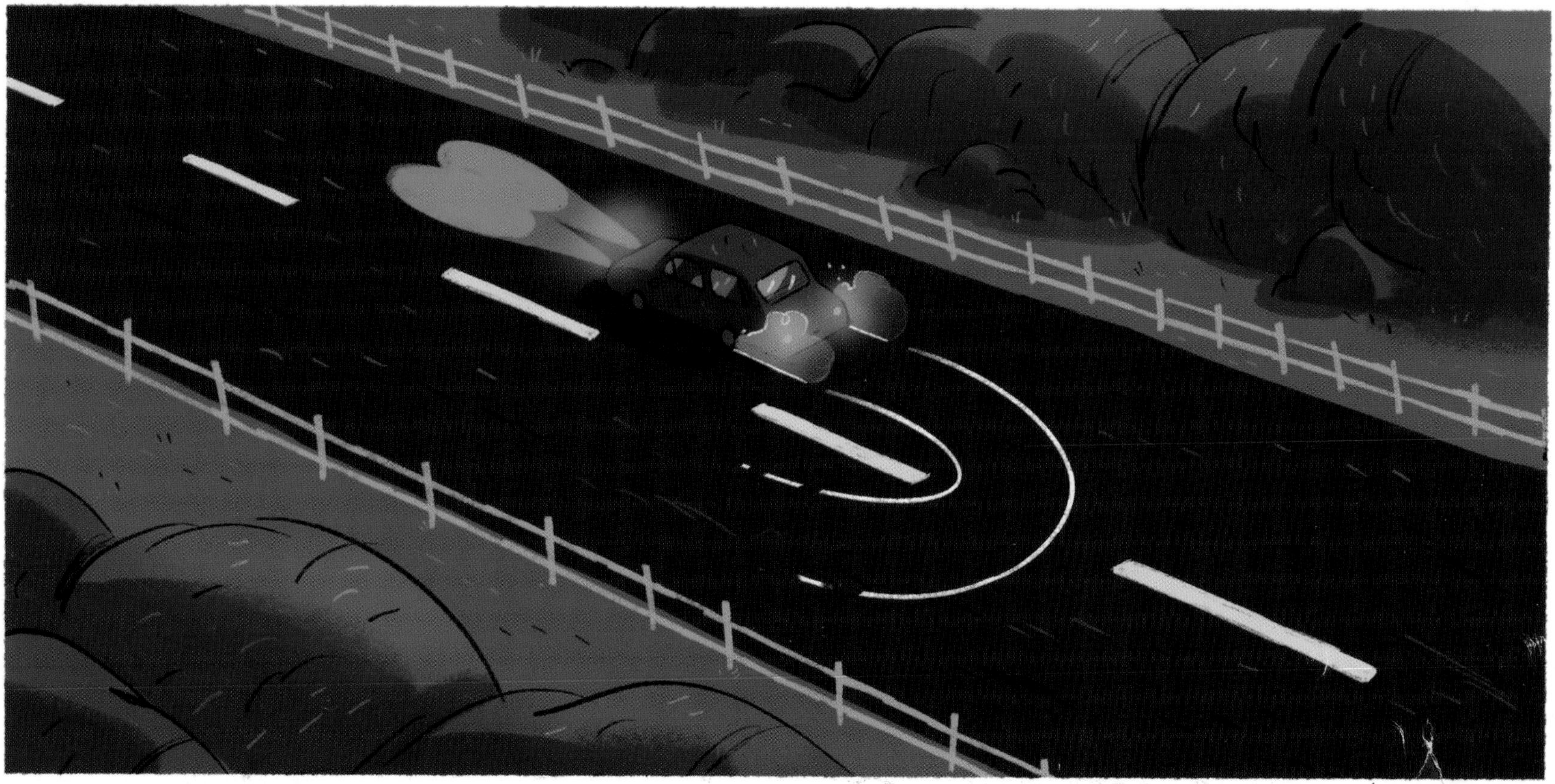

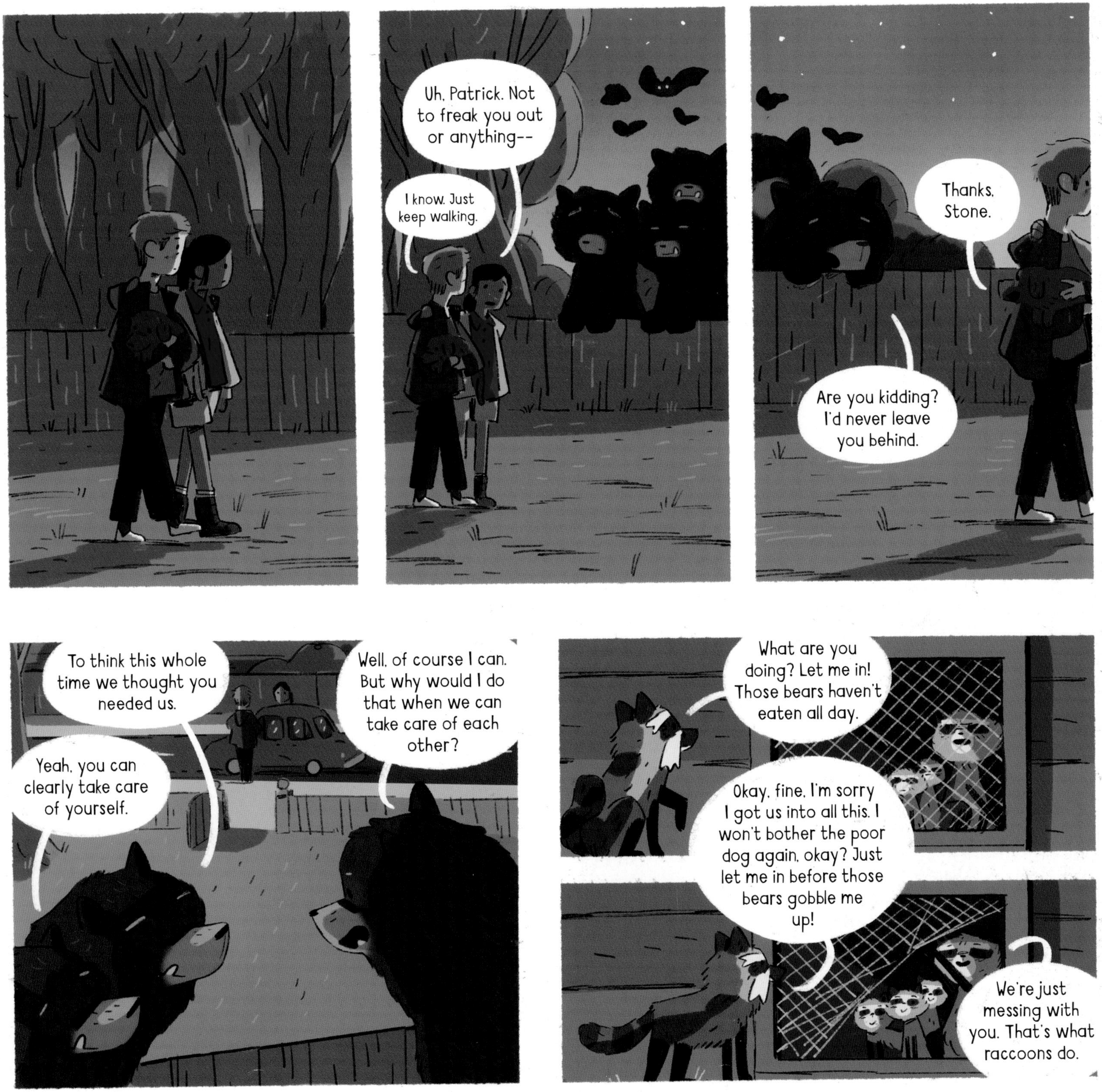
Uh, Patrick. Not to freak you out or anything--
I know. Just keep walking.
Thanks, Stone.
Are you kidding? I'd never leave you behind.
To think this whole time we thought you needed us.
Yeah, you can clearly take care of yourself.
Well, of course I can. But why would I do that when we can take care of each other?
What are you doing? Let me in! Those bears haven't eaten all day.
Okay, fine, I'm sorry I got us into all this. I won't bother the poor dog again, okay? Just let me in before those bears gobble me up!
We're just messing with you. That's what raccoons do.

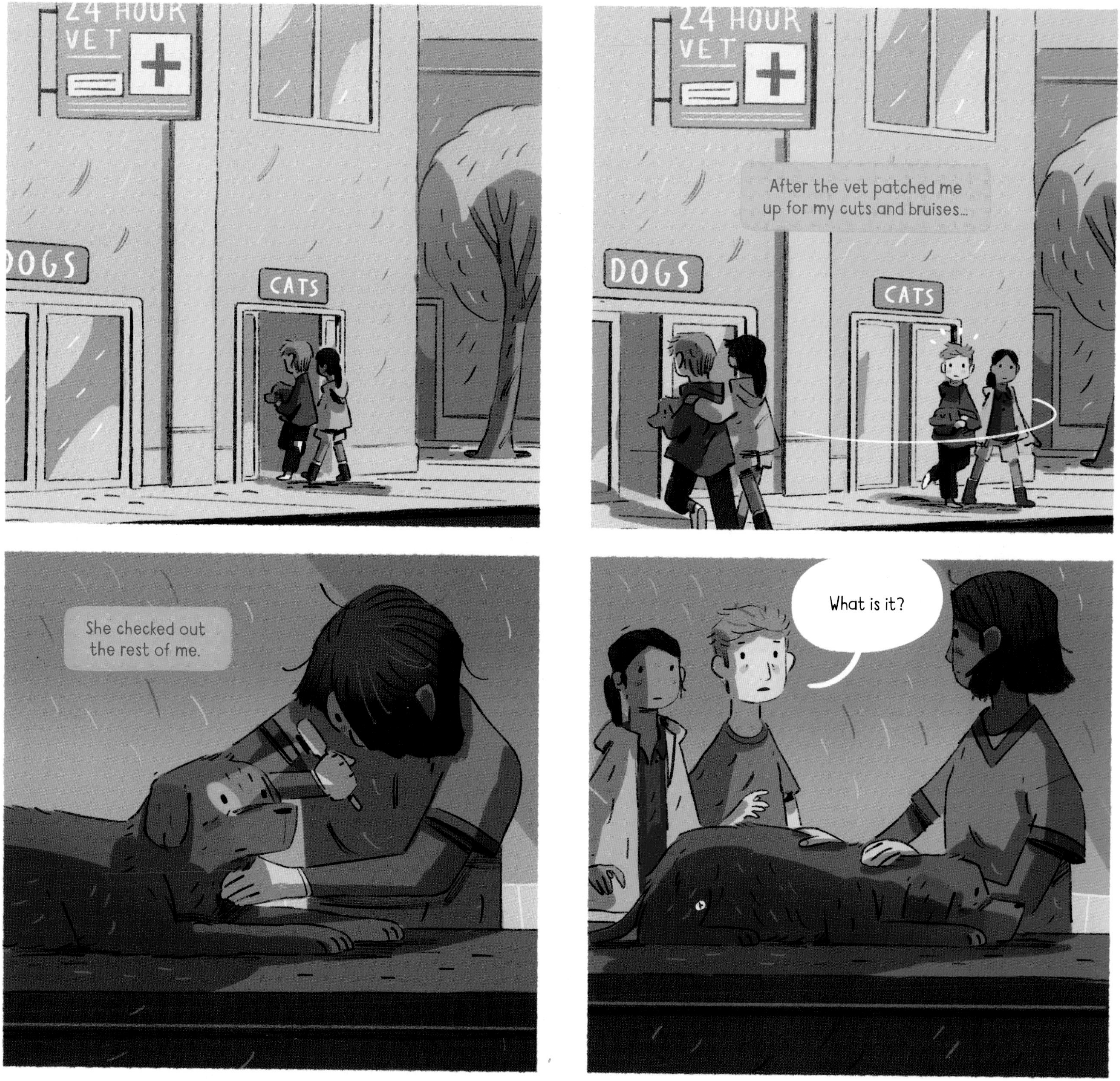
24 HOUR VET
CATS
24 HOUR VET
After the vet patched me up for my cuts and bruises...
DOGS
CATS
She checked out the rest of me.
What is it?

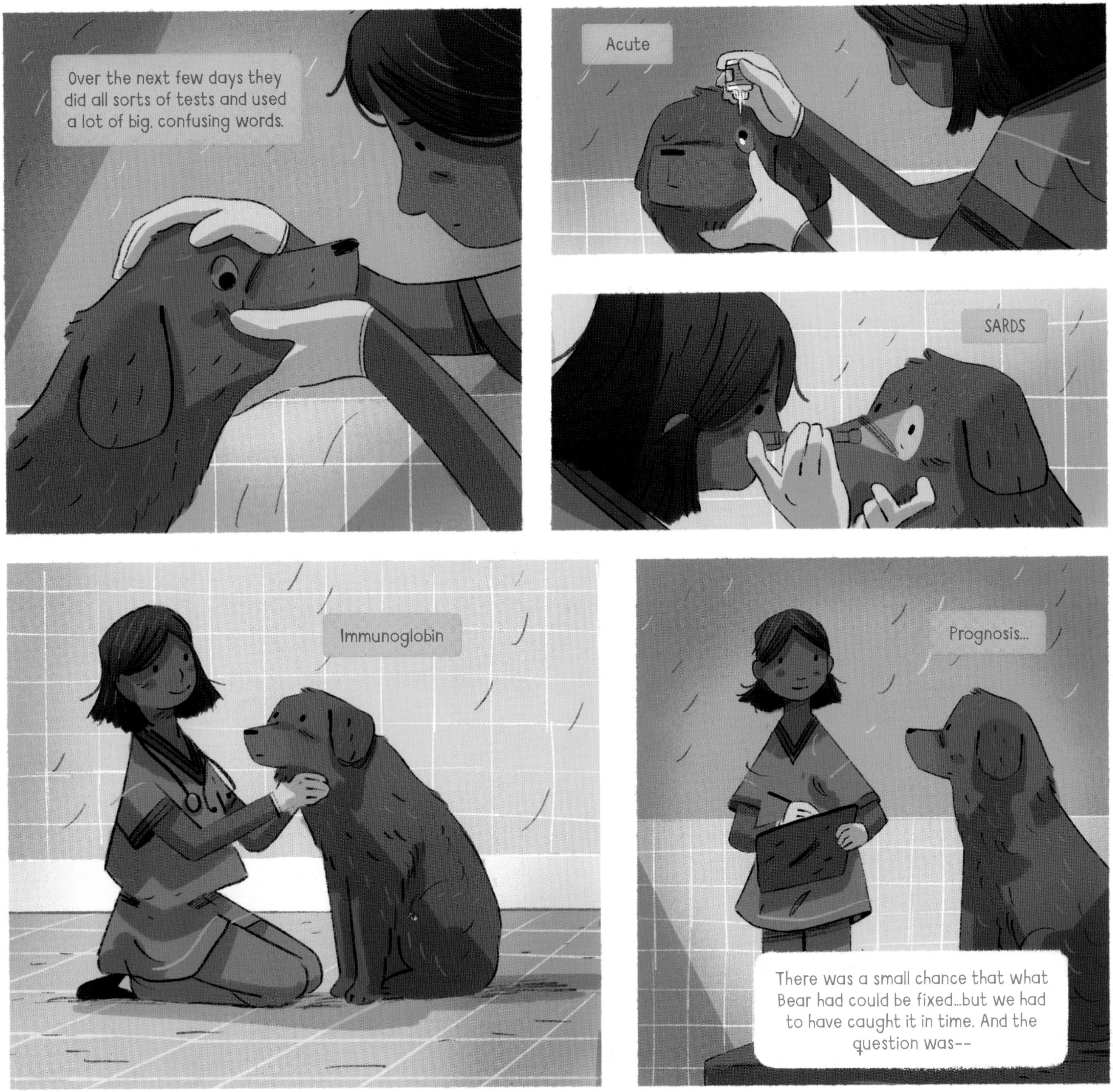
Over the next few days they did all sorts of tests and used a lot of big, confusing words.
Acute
SARDS
Immunoglobin
Prognosis...
There was a small chance that what Bear had could be fixed...but we had to have caught it in time. And the question was--

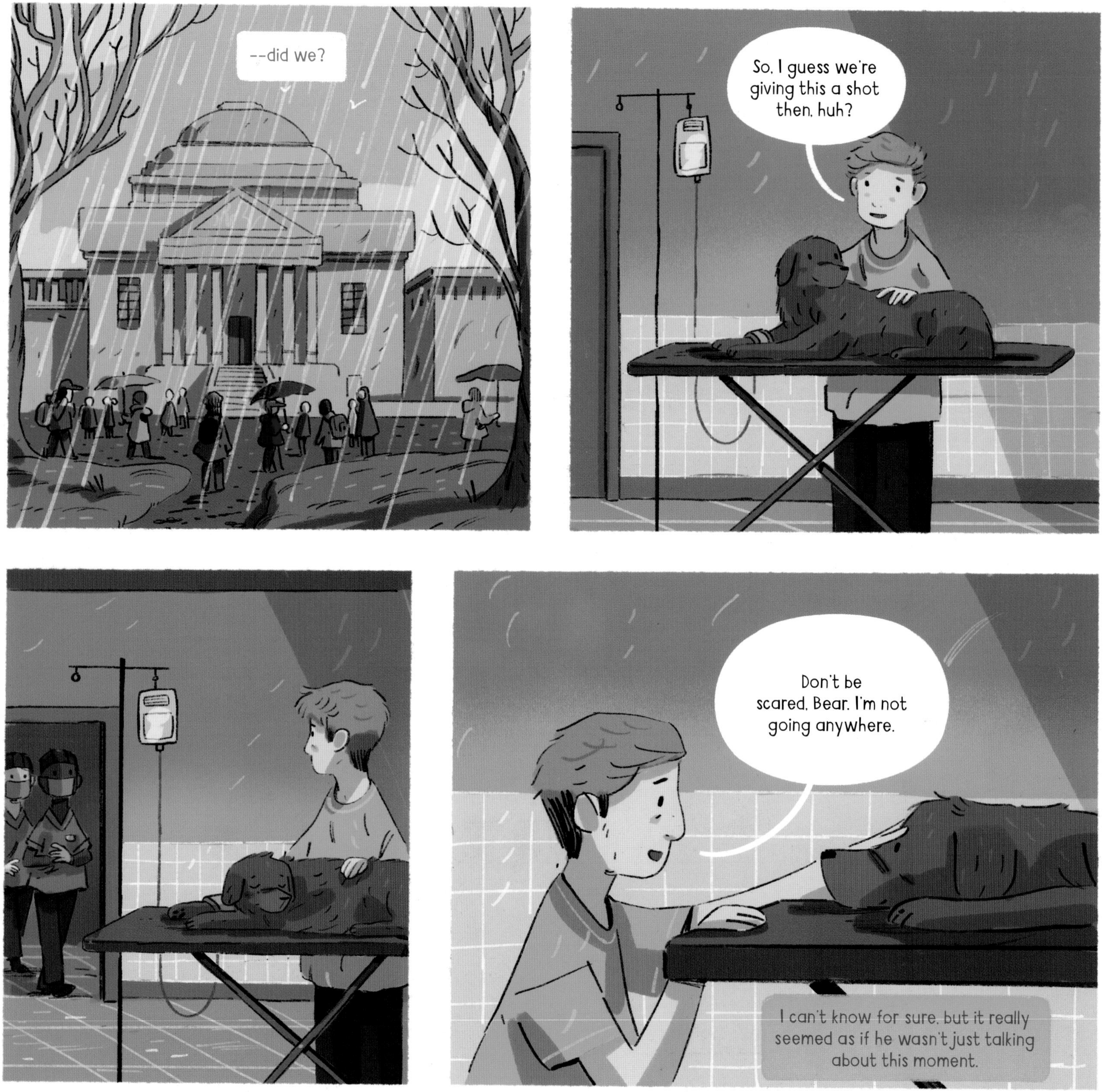
--did we?
So, I guess we're giving this a shot then, huh?
Don't be scared, Bear. I'm not going anywhere.
I can't know for sure, but it really seemed as if he wasn't just talking about this moment.

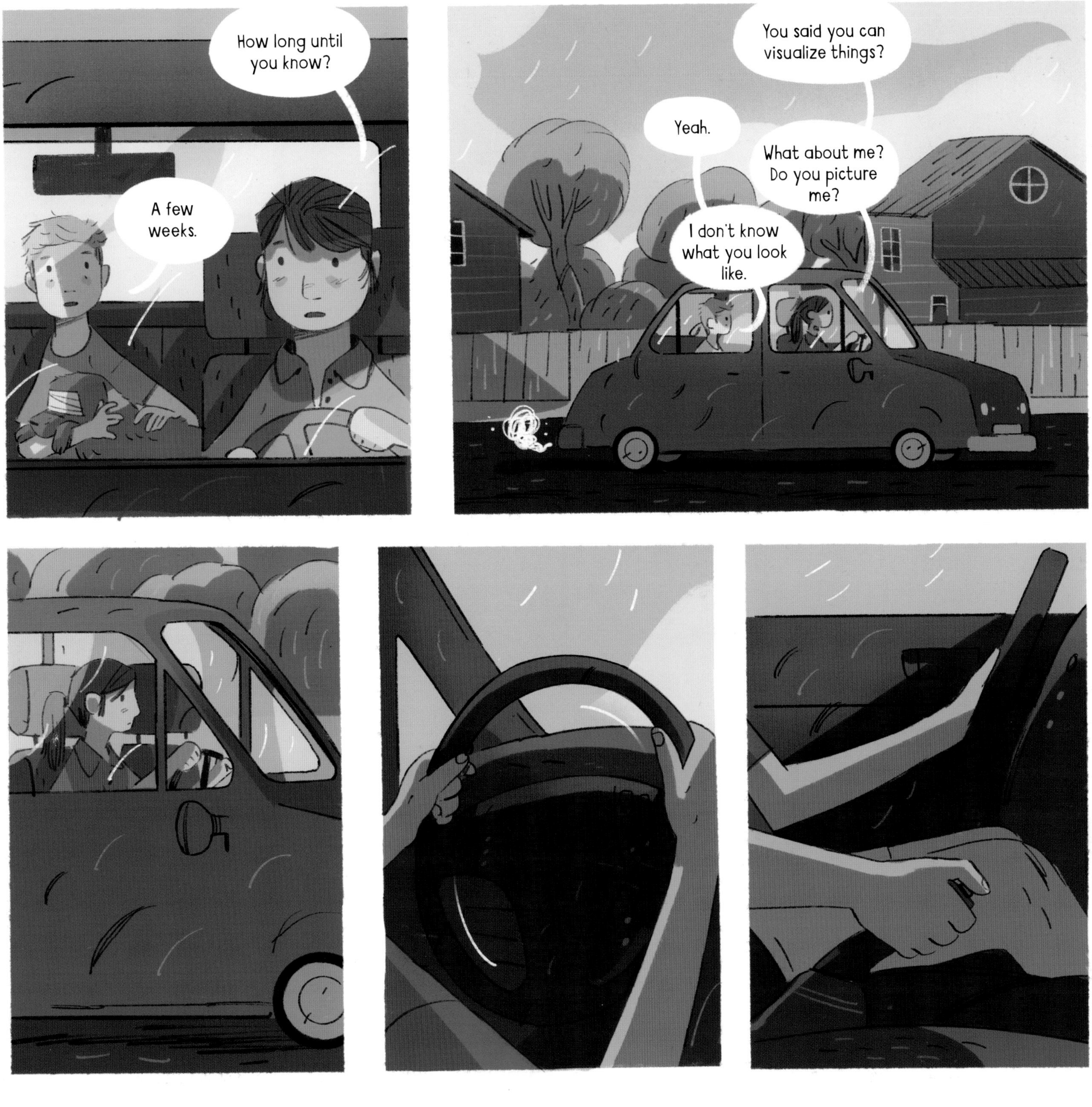
How long until you know?
A few weeks.
You said you can visualize things?
Yeah.
What about me? Do you picture me?
I don't know what you look like.

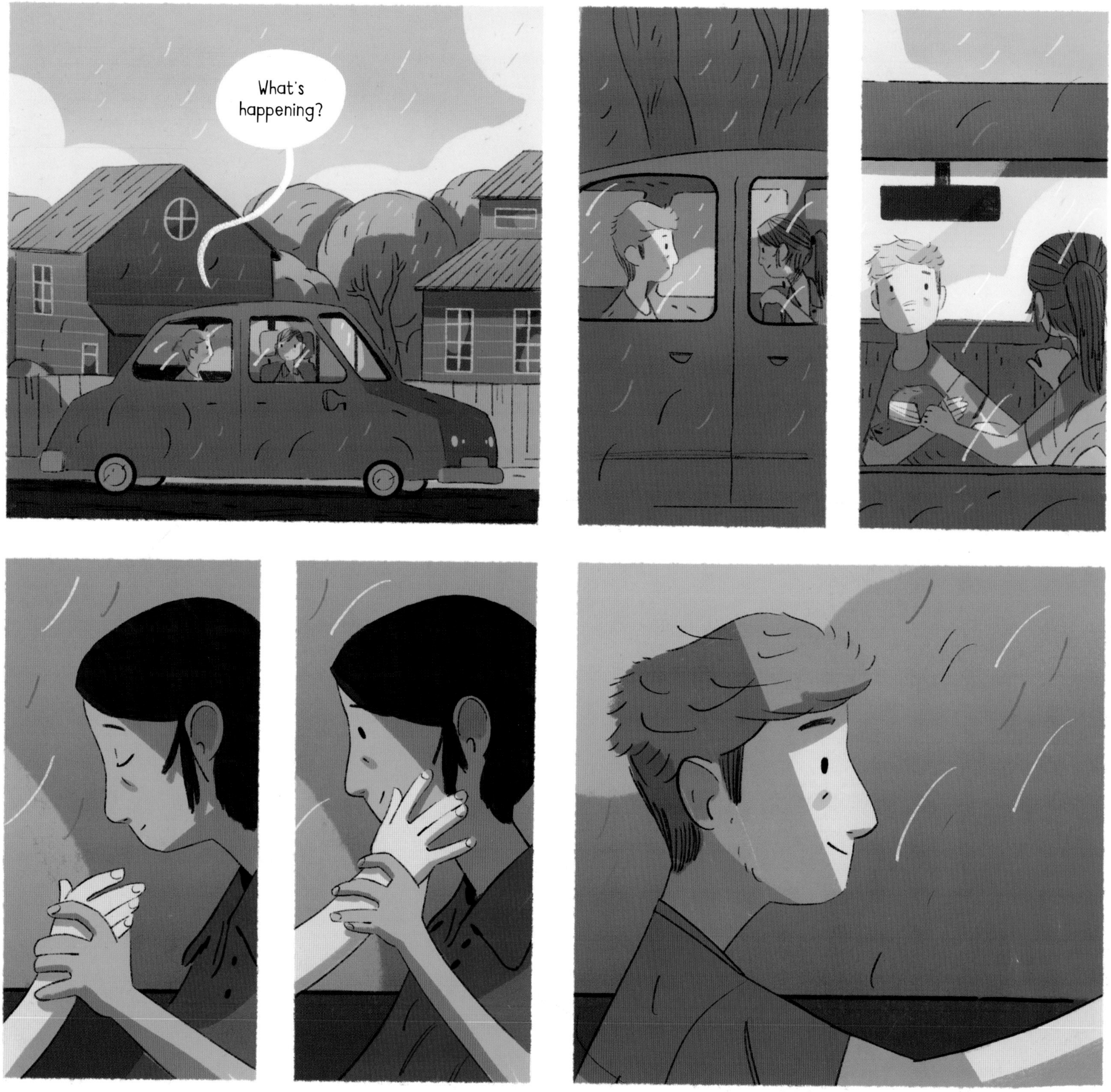
What's happening?

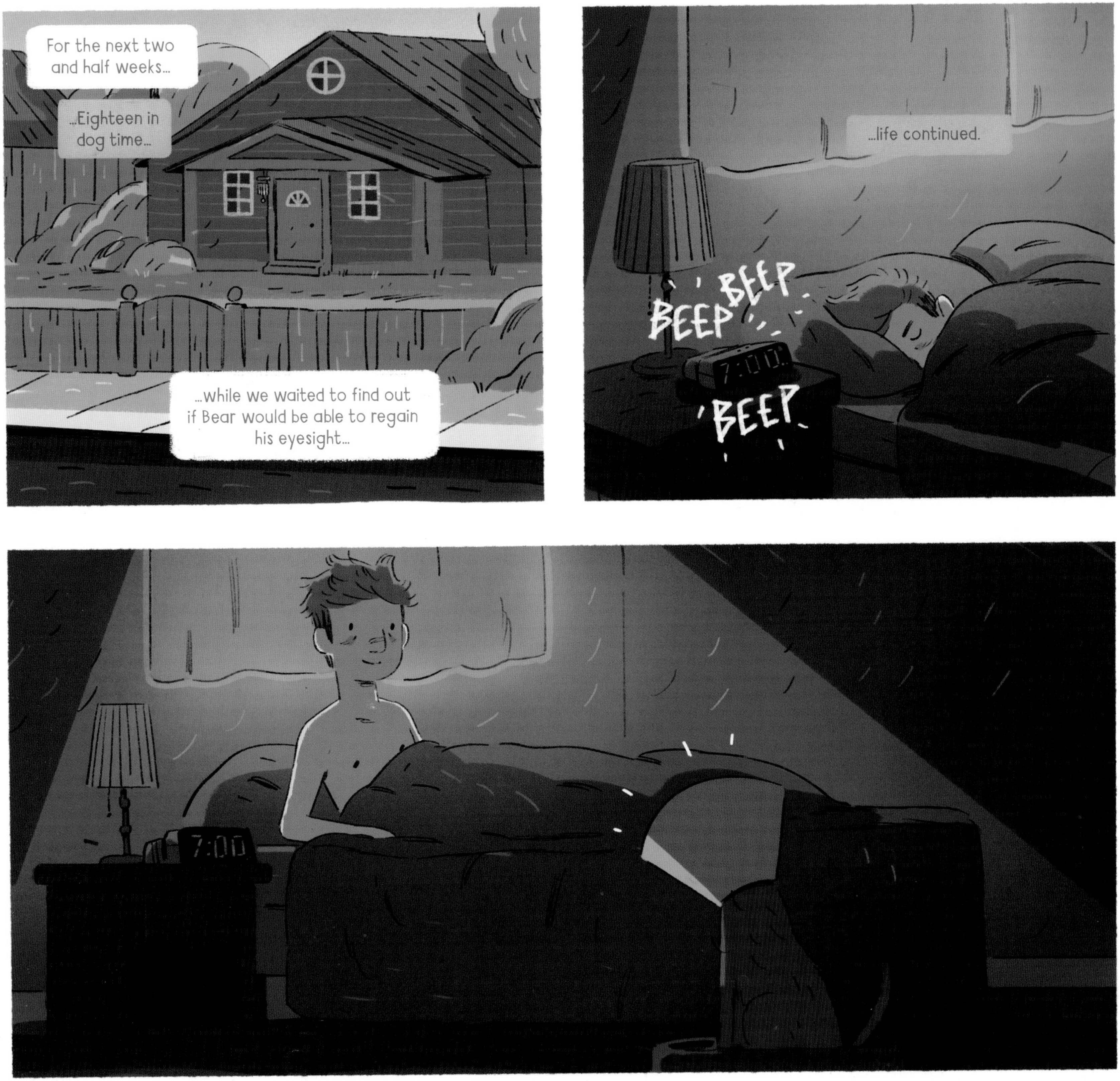
For the next two and half weeks...
...Eighteen in dog time...
...while we waited to find out if Bear would be able to regain his eyesight...
...life continued.
BEEP
BEEP
BEEP
7:00
7:00

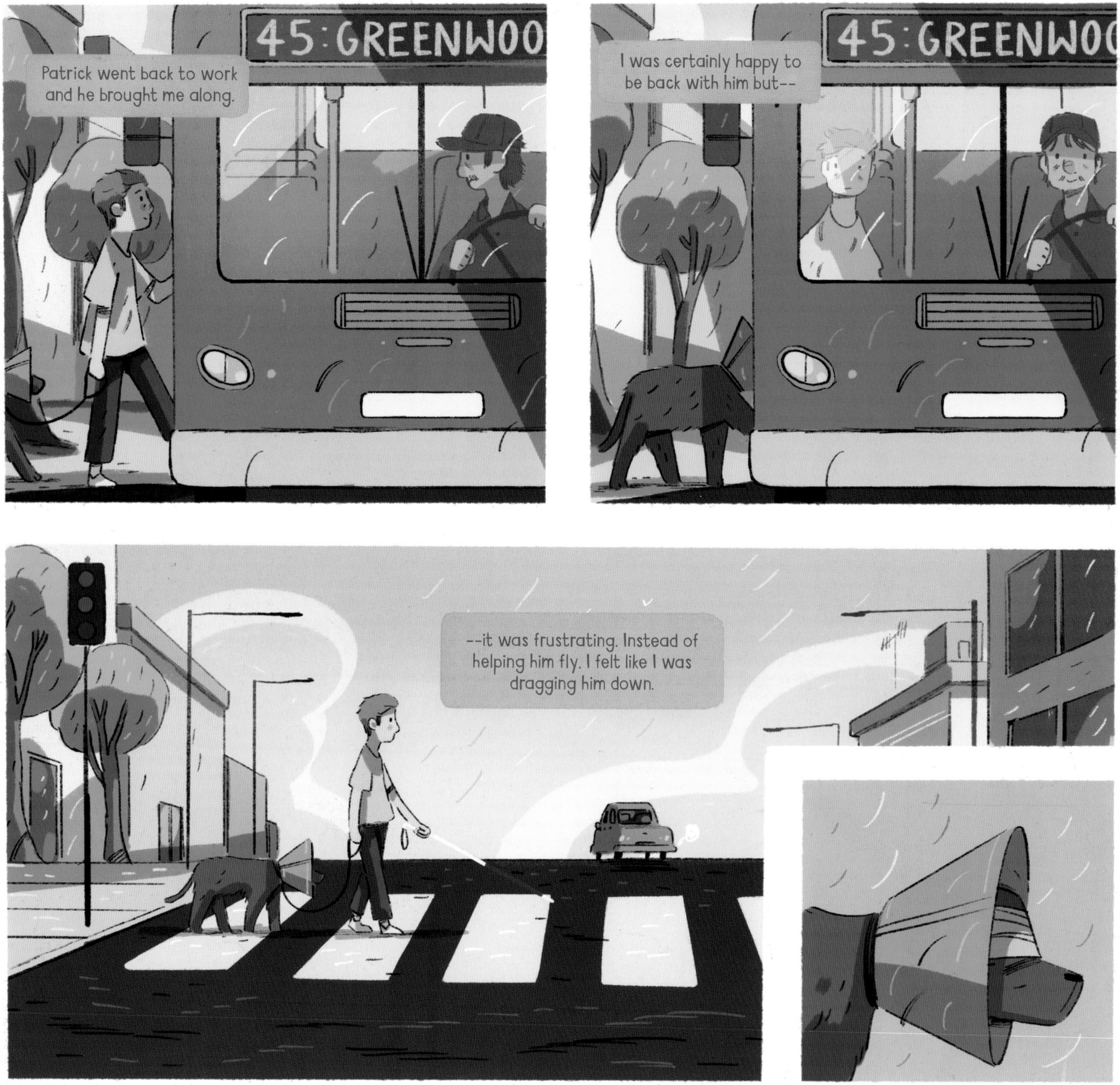
45: GREENWOO
Patrick went back to work and he brought me along.
45: GREENWOO
I was certainly happy to be back with him but--
--it was frustrating. Instead of helping him fly, I felt like I was dragging him down.

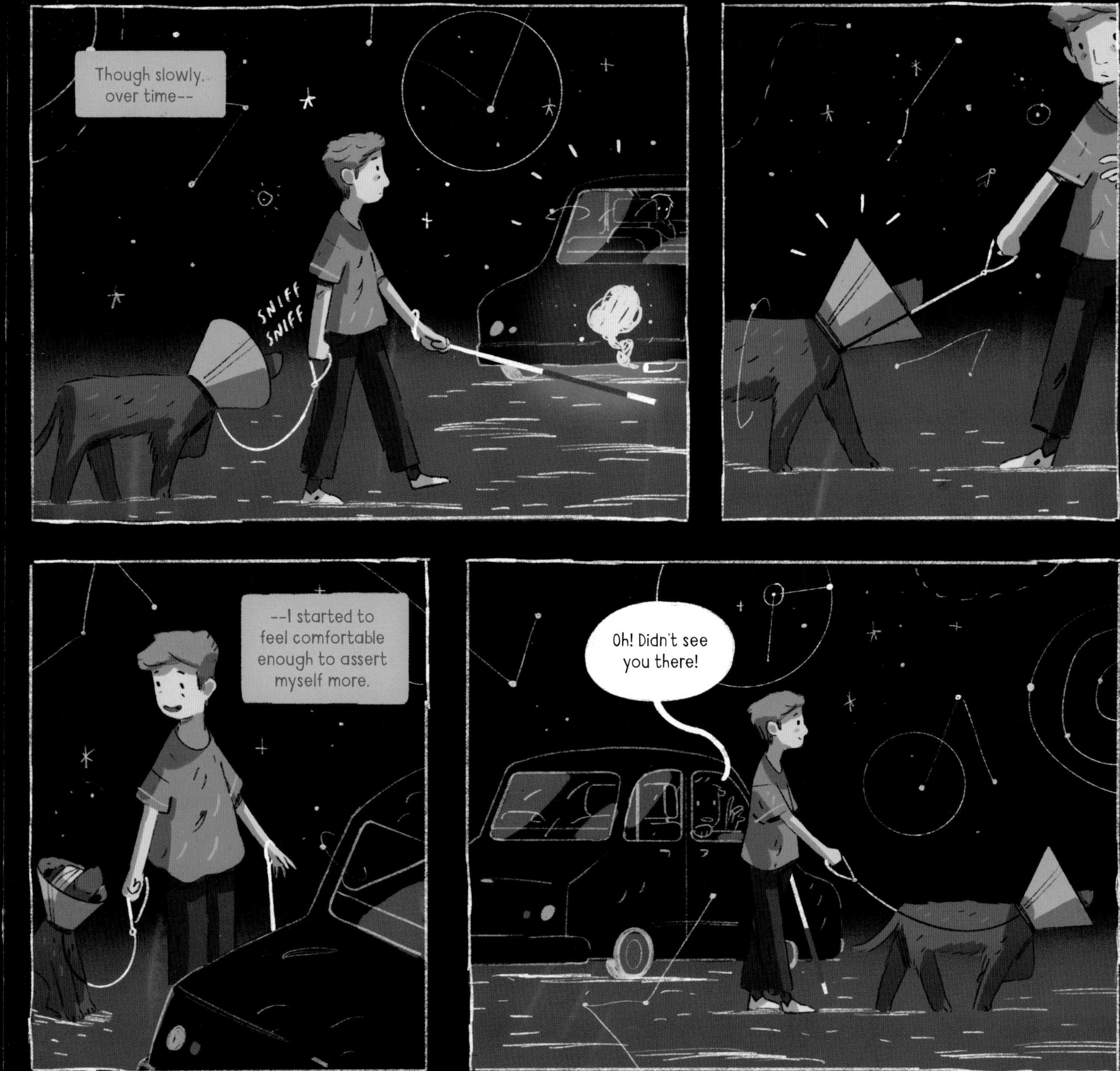
Though slowly, over time--
SNIFF SNIFF
--I started to feel comfortable enough to assert myself more.
Oh! Didn't see you there!

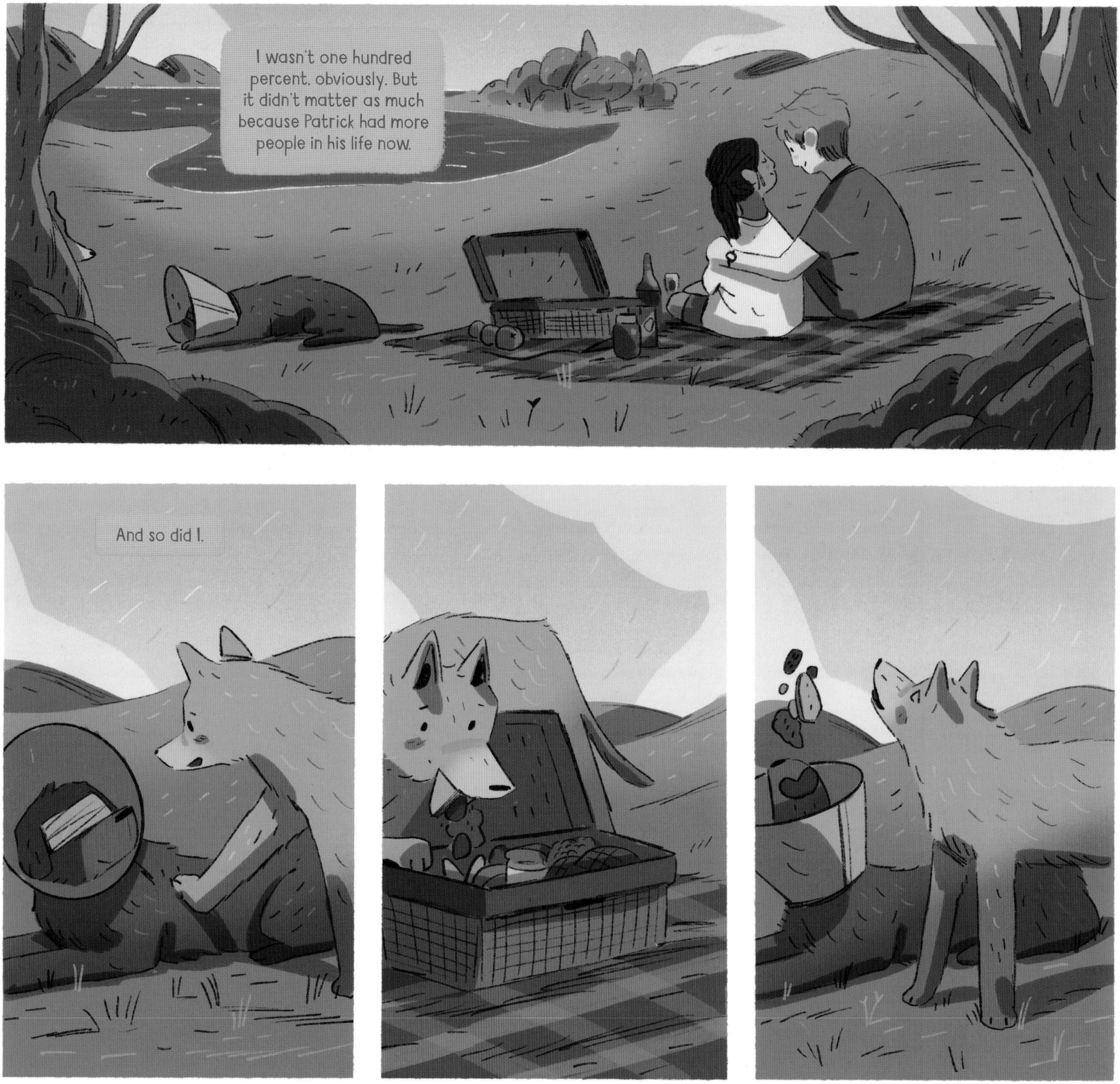
I wasn't one hundred percent, obviously. But it didn't matter as much because Patrick had more people in his life now.
And so did I.

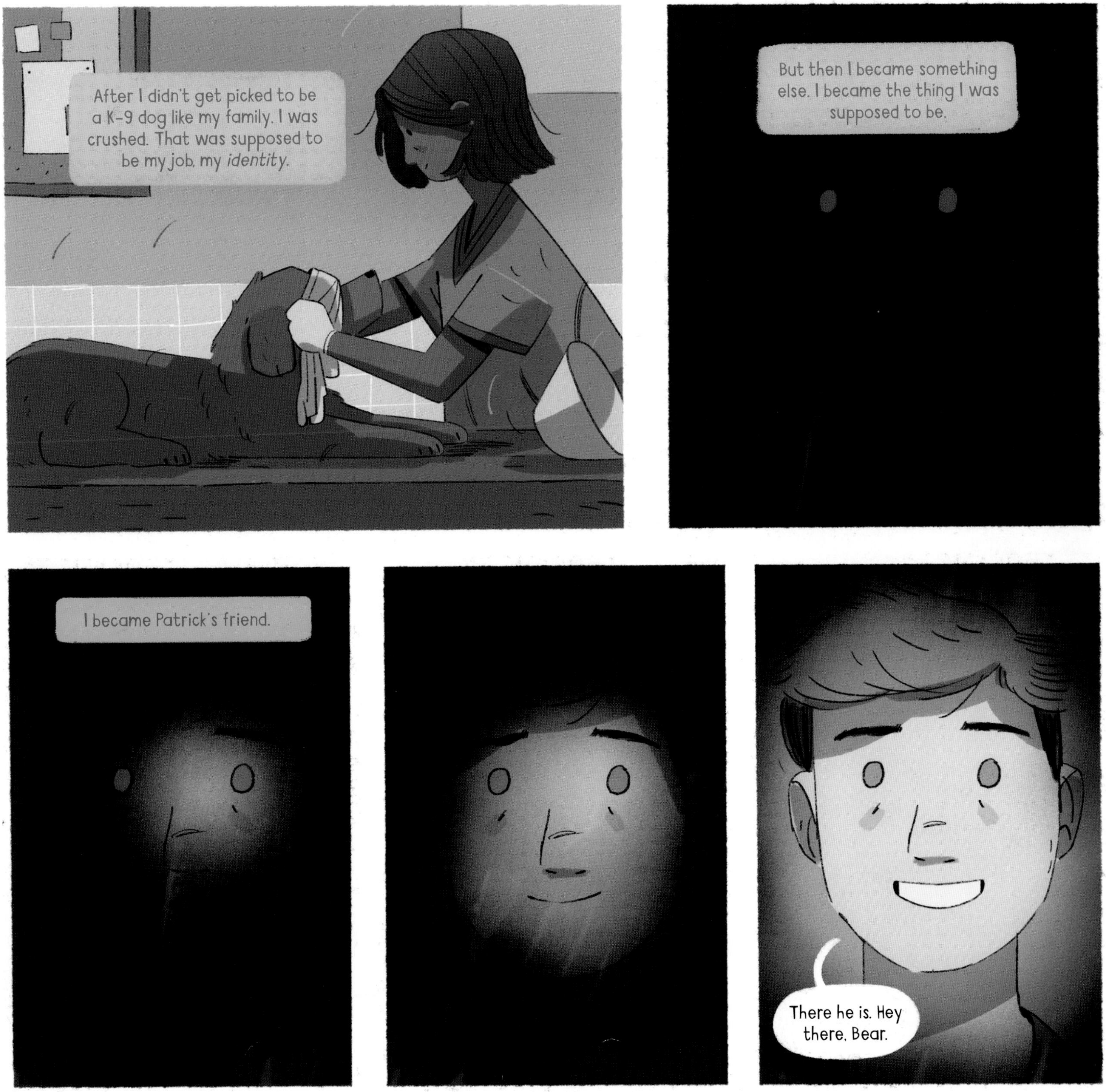
After I didn't get picked to be a K-9 dog like my family, I was crushed. That was supposed to be my job, my *identity*.
But then I became something else. I became the thing I was supposed to be.
I became Patrick's friend.
There he is. Hey there, Bear.

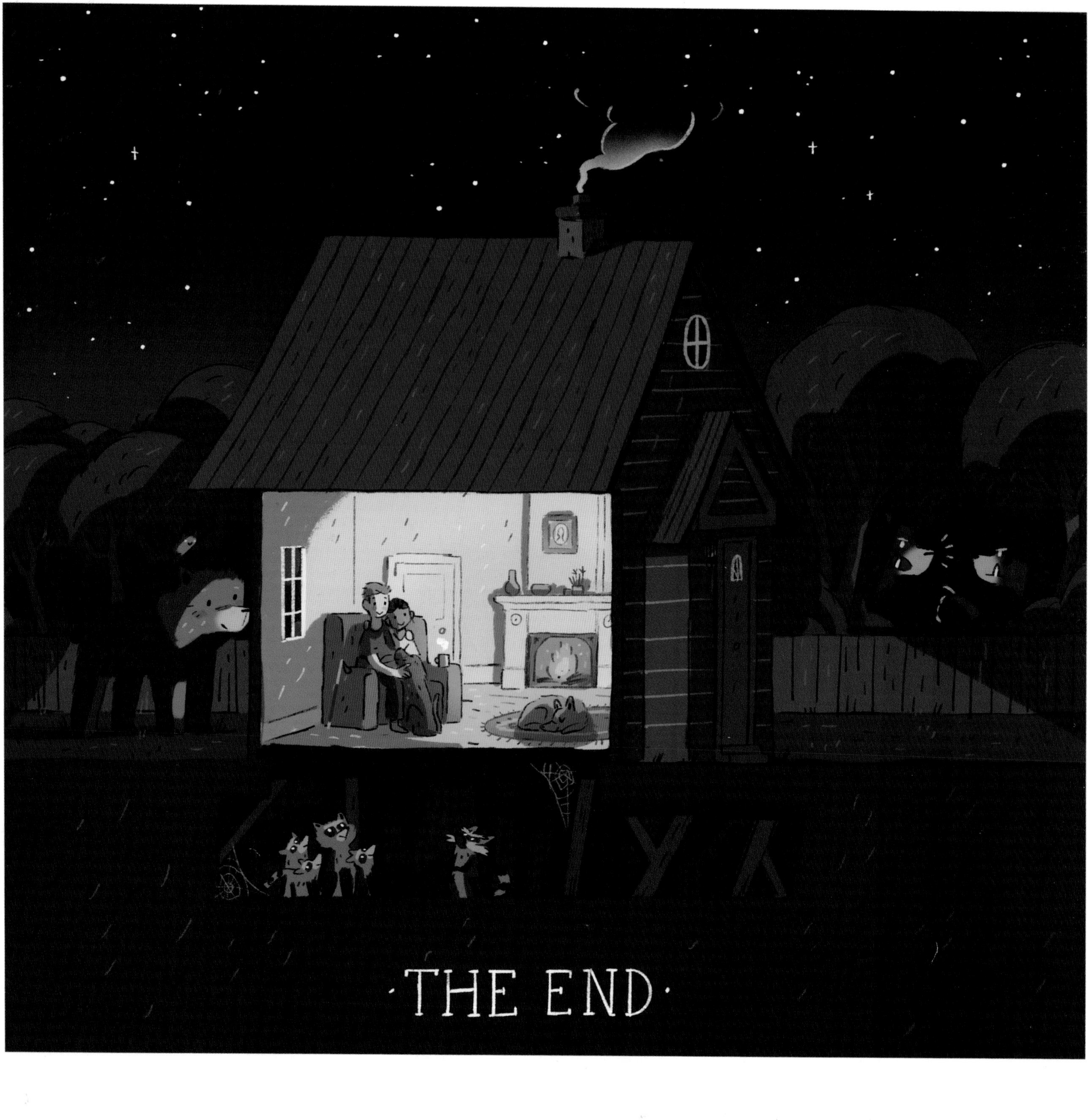
·THE END·

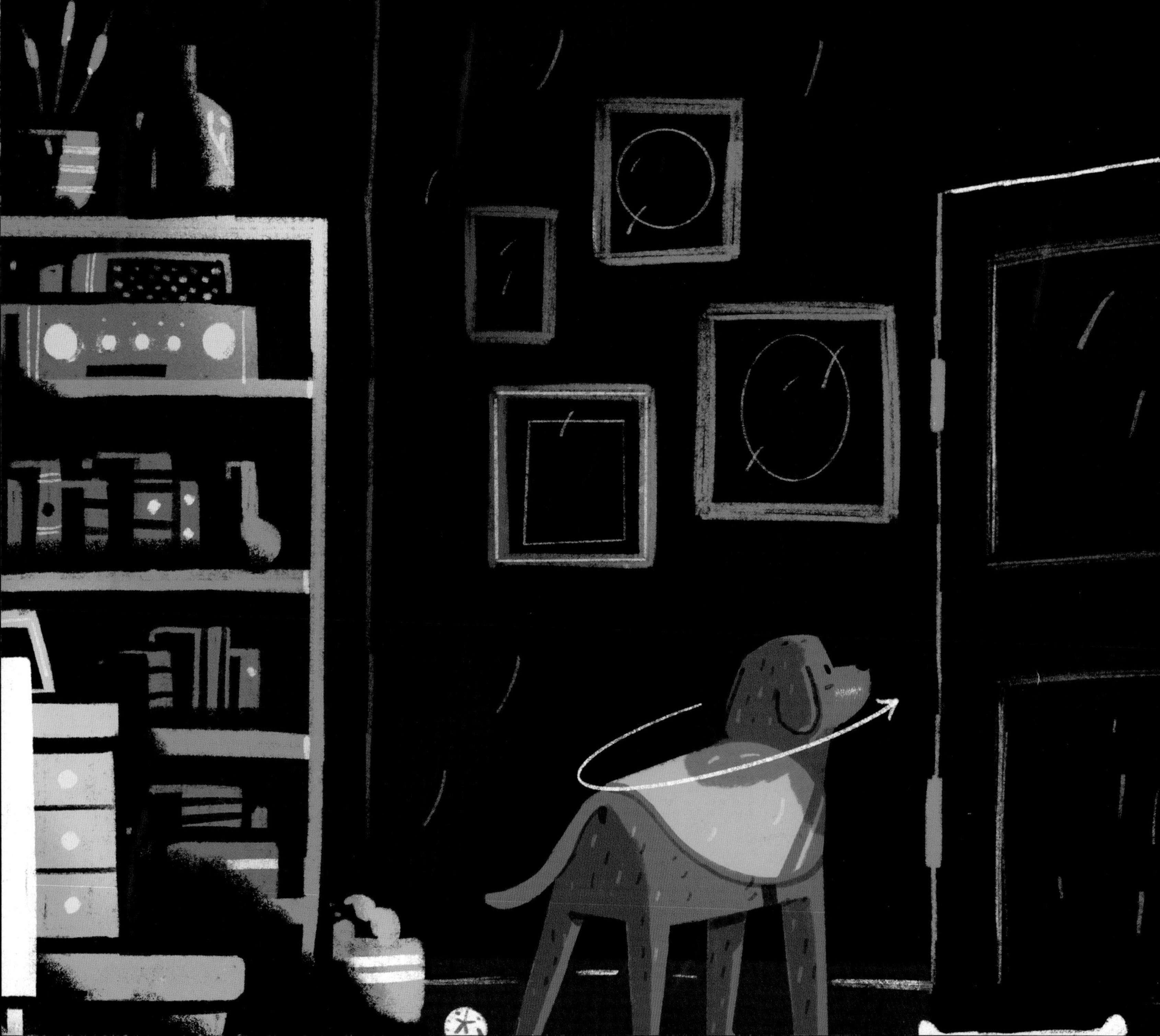

Those who have lost their sight can create images in their brain based on memory, context clues, and their imagination. Although some choose not to, most blind people picture aspects of their world in this way. Neurologist and author, Oliver Sacks, referred to this as "inner vision."

John Bramblitt, a terrific visual artist and one of many people who generously gave interviews as research for this book, describes it this way: "We think our eyes are where our sight comes from, but the eyes are just sending chemical and electrical responses back and it's the *brain* that is actually making the images. So, whenever you lose your eyesight, your brain is still sort of like in dream mode, it's still putting up images."

A story about a blind character that shows the world through his visual perspective felt like a unique opportunity to tell an imaginative story. And making it from the point of view of a guide dog added a whole other level of emotion and distinctiveness. The limited perspective of Bear lent itself to off-kilter interpretations about his surroundings, again something that was inspired by the true experiences of blind people. Bramblitt adds, "So, if I heard a car, in my mind, I might have an image of a car just on a random street. It's just like a dream image. In reality, it could be a motorcycle, it could be a red truck, it could be a car on a TV that's just playing somewhere. It doesn't necessarily relate to reality or anything." Hence, Bear picturing a drainage pipe as a large Meerschaum smoking pipe, or a black bear's den as having club chairs and a bookshelf.

I was lucky to have an illustrator such as Joe Todd-Stanton to bring Bear's story to wondrous, creative life. My hope is that readers of this book will take away what I did when I researched and wrote this—that the way we see the world depends not just on what we've seen, but what experiences we have had, and most importantly who we are.

Ben Queen
Los Angeles, California

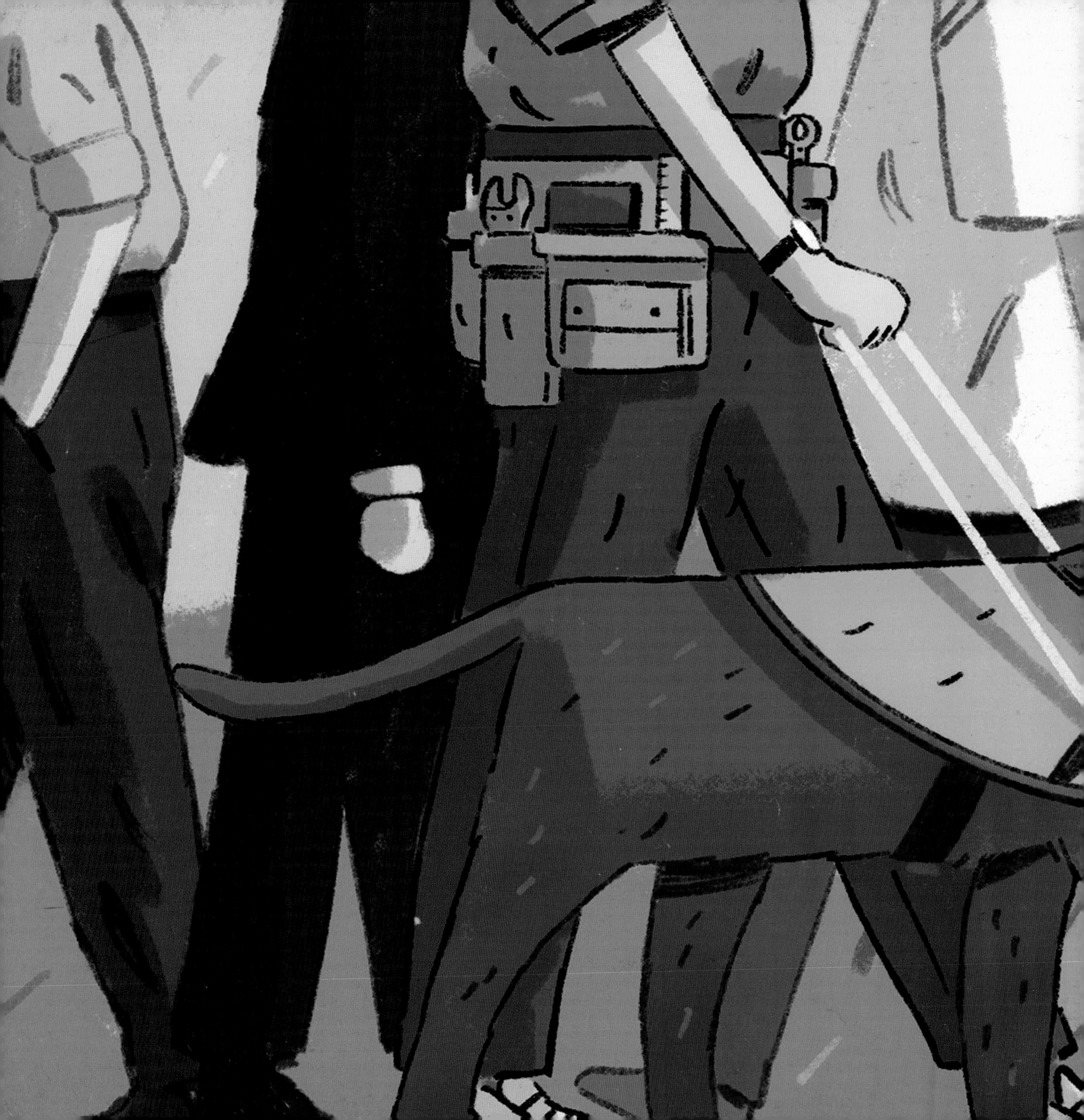

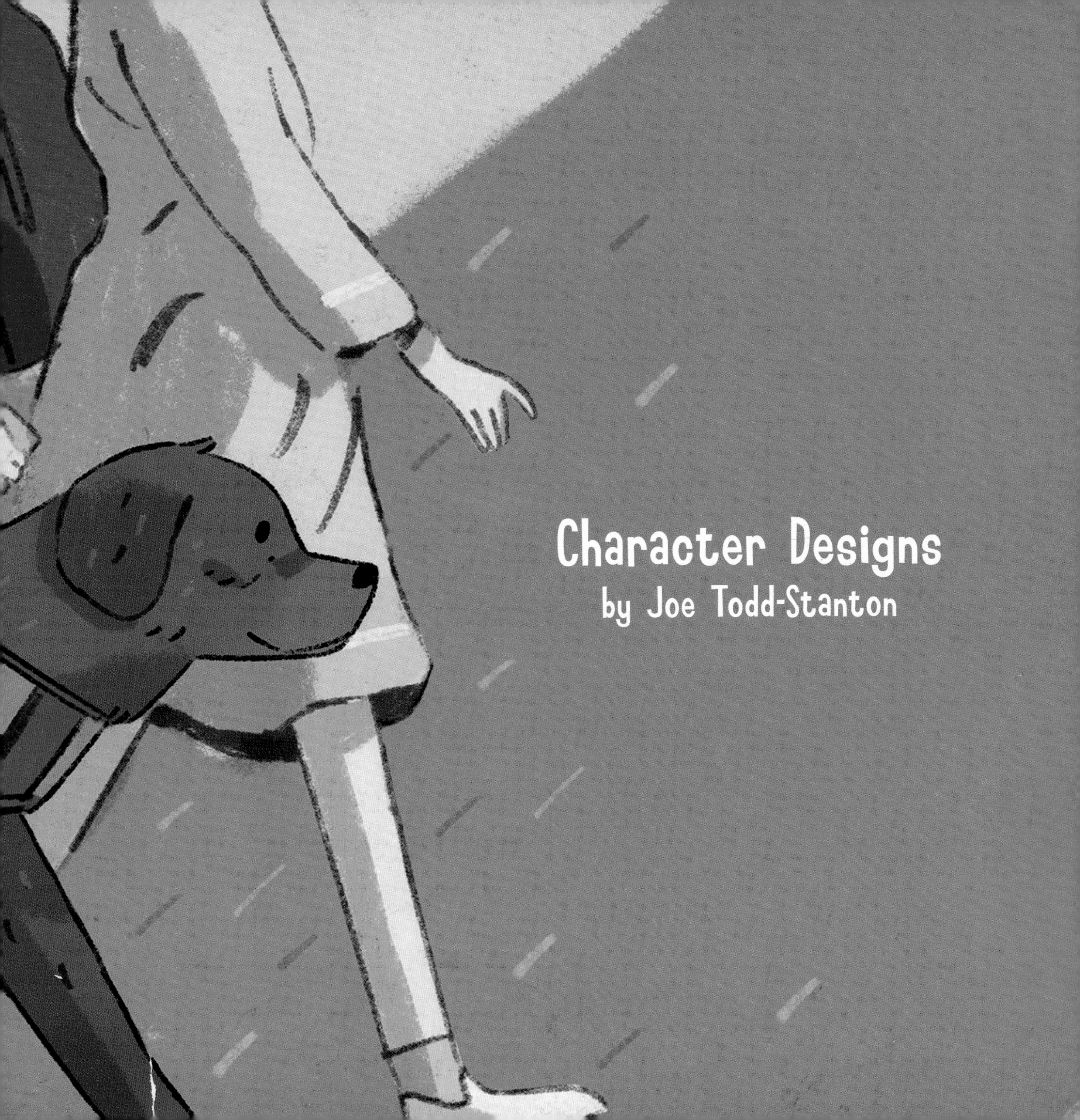

Character Designs

by Joe Todd-Stanton

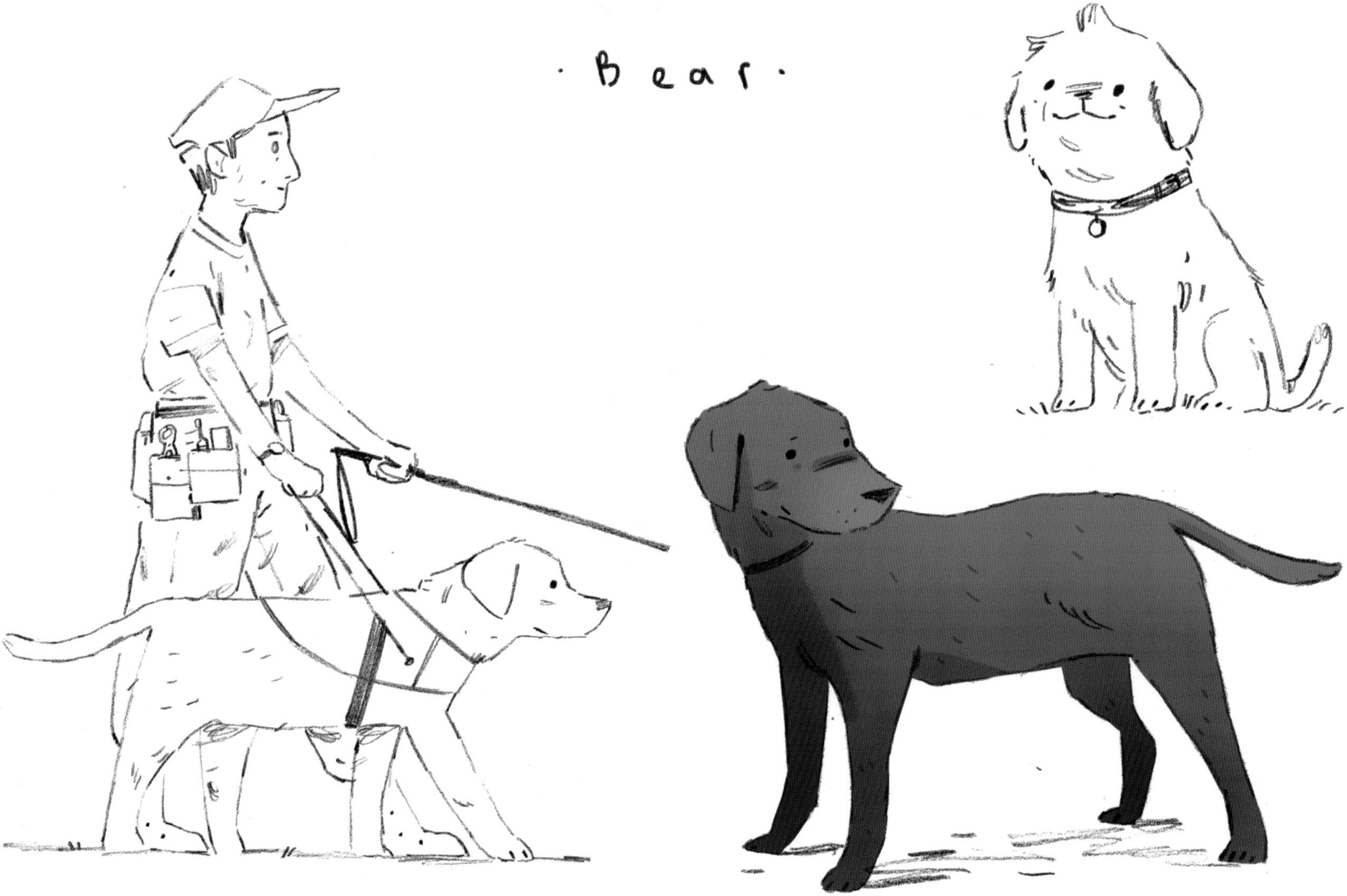
· Bear ·

· Patrick ·

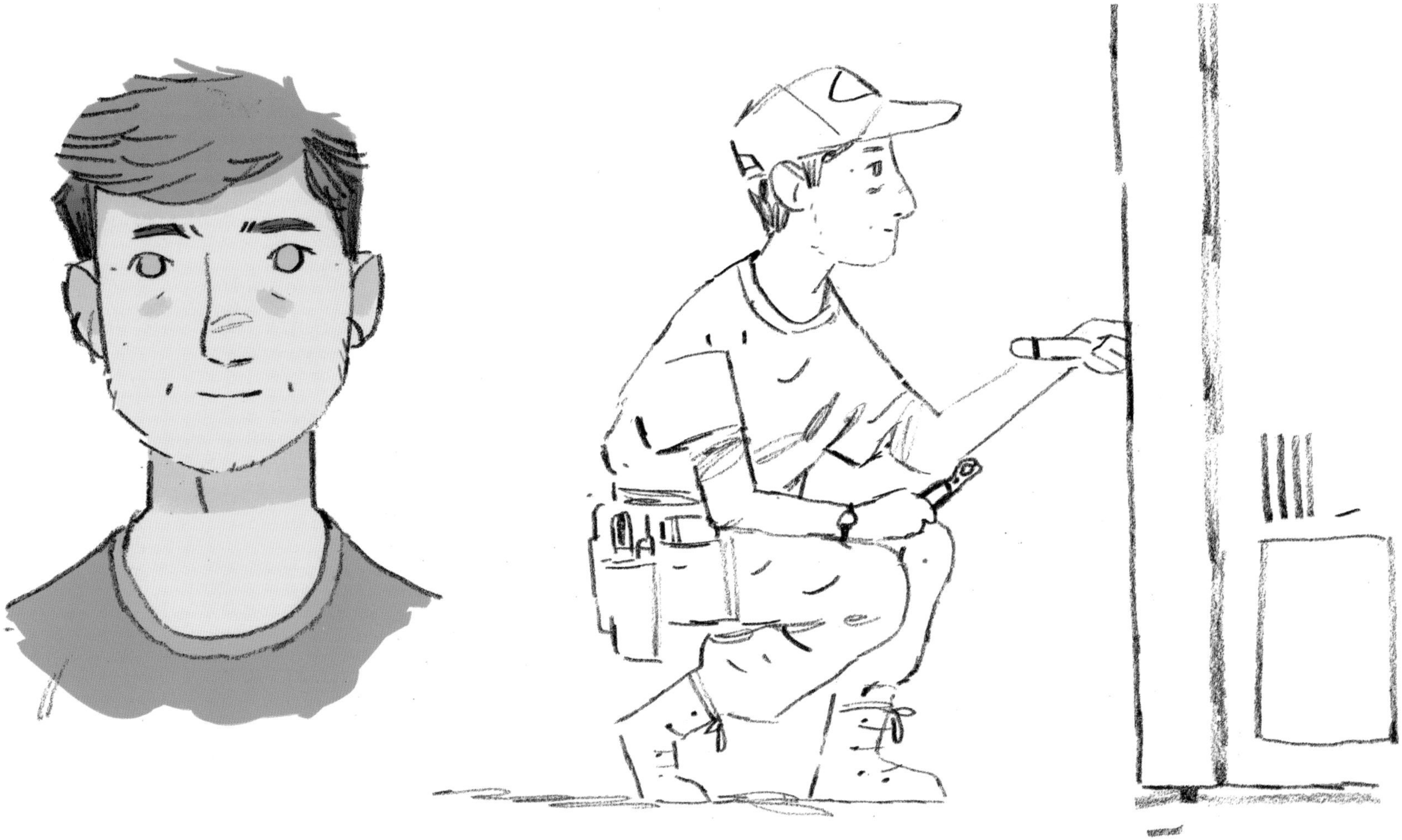

· M e g ·

POLICE

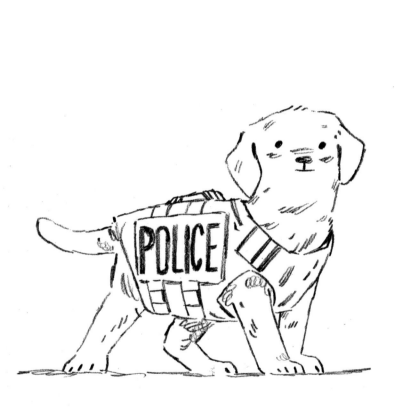

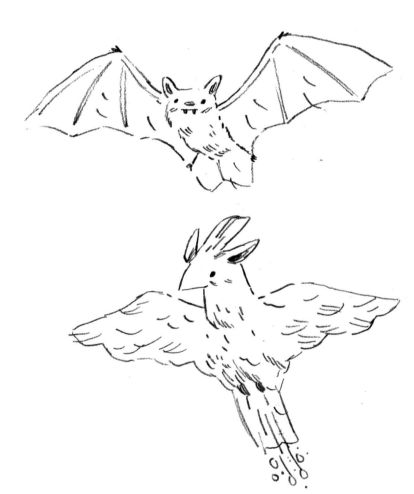

Jake & Andromeda

Stone.

. Jasper & Flint.

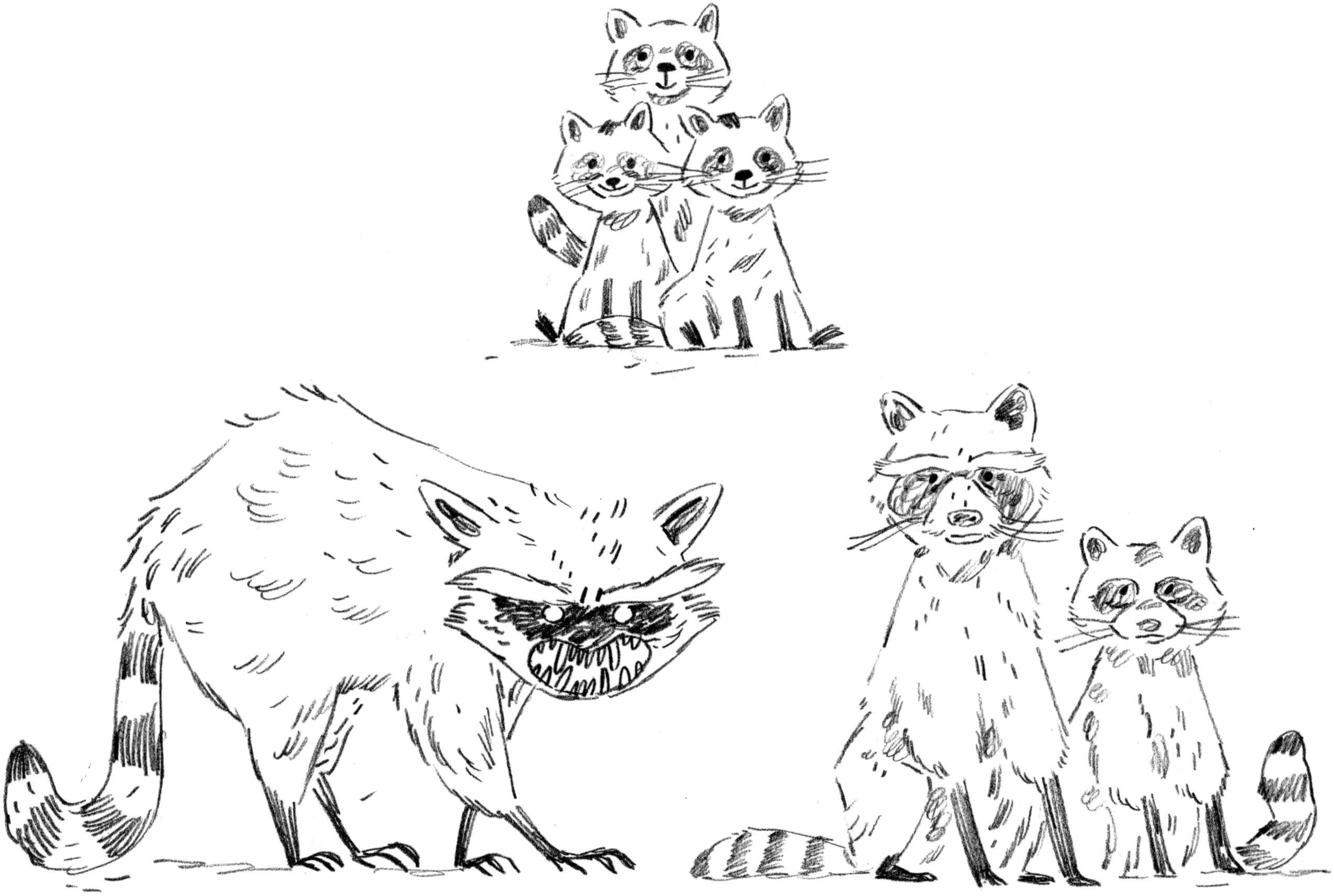

·uncle, Denver & the triplets·

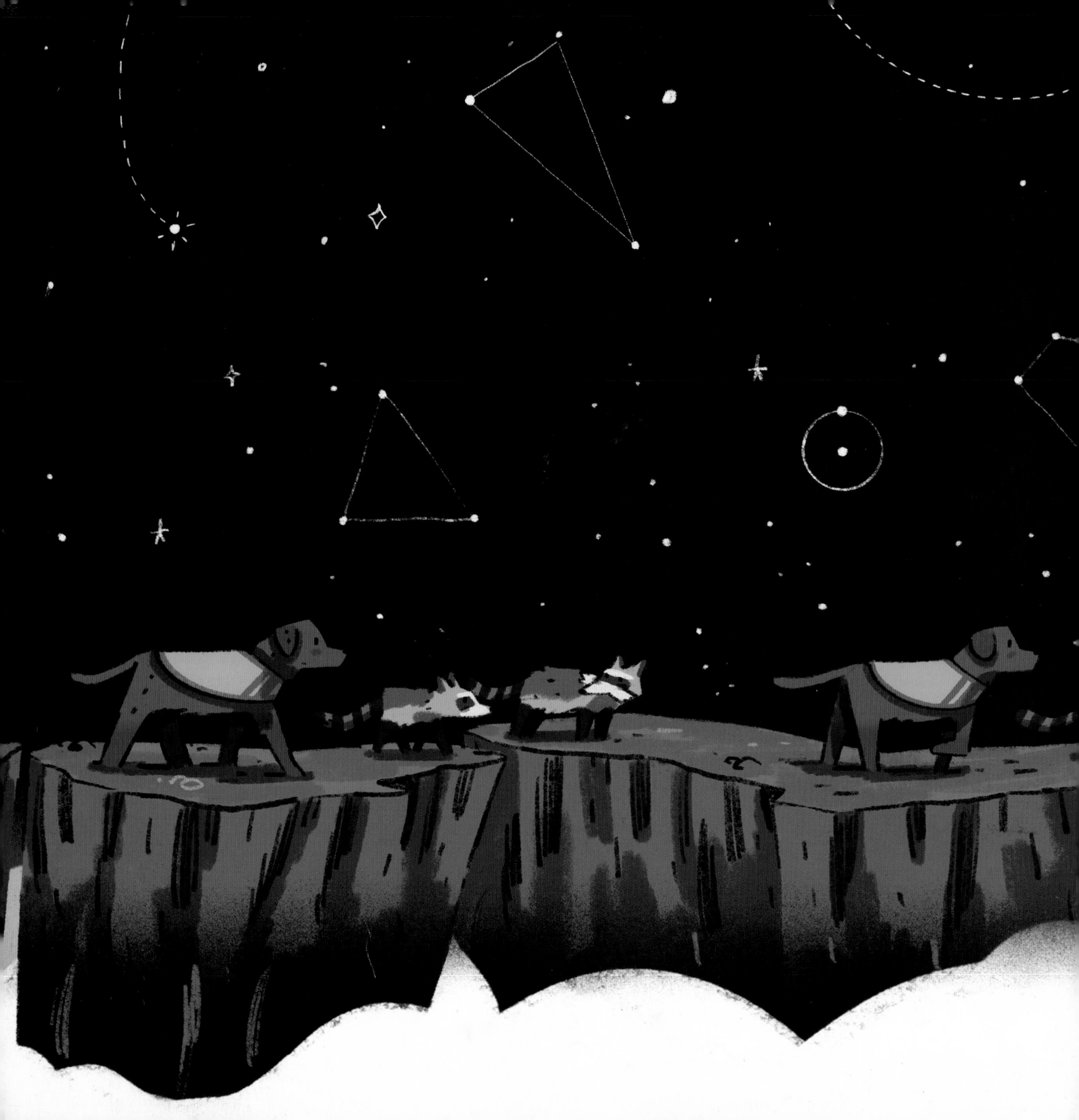

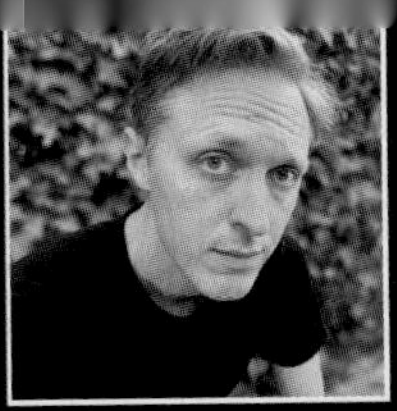

Ben Queen was the creator and executive producer of the NBC half-hour comedies *A to Z* and *Powerless*. He previously wrote the Disney-Pixar films *Cars 2* and *Cars 3*, as well as created and executive produced the Fox action drama *Drive*. He currently lives in Los Angeles with his family and a cat.

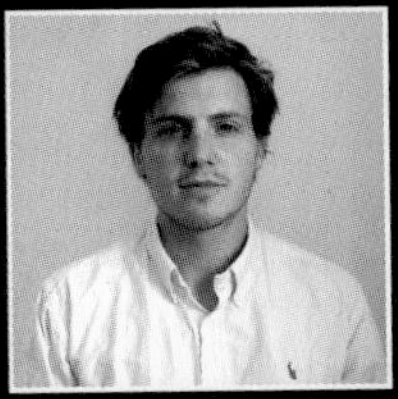

Joe Todd-Stanton grew up in Brighton and was taught how to draw by his mum. He has since been commissioned to work for clients such as Oxford University Press, Bloomsbury Publishing, and Penguin Random House. He has also written and illustrated his own series of books called *Brownstone's Mythical Collection*.

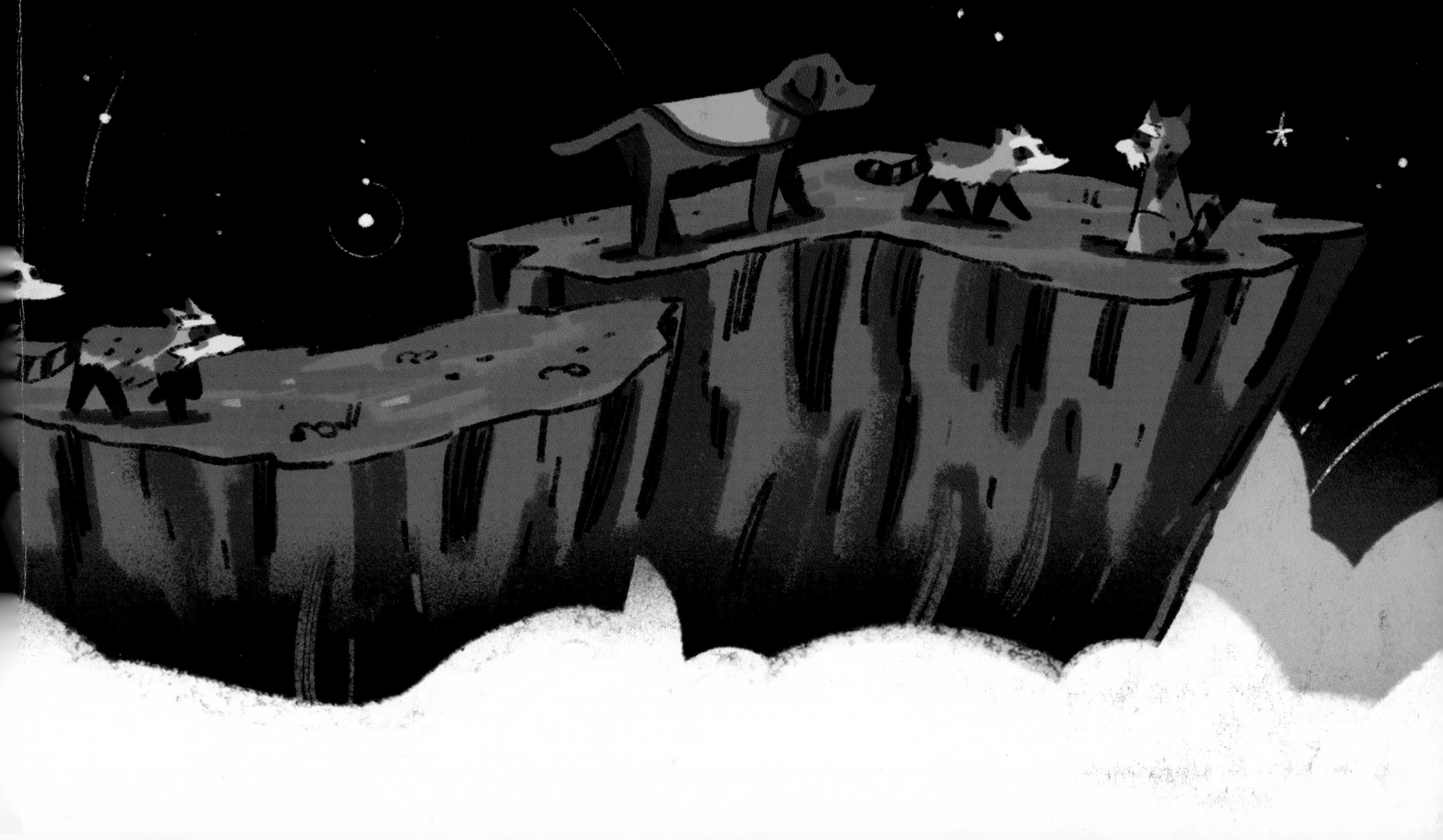

DISCOVER
GROUNDBREAKING TITLES

ASAF HANUKA
THE REALIST

LONG WALK TO VALHALLA
ADAM SMITH MATTHEW FOX

THE MARCH OF THE CRABS
THE CRABBY CONDITION
ARTHUR DE PINS

Jane
ALINE BROSH McKENNA
RAMÓN K. PÉREZ

ROYDEN LEPP
RUST
VOLUME ONE
VISITOR IN THE FIELD

MOUSE GUARD
THE BLACK AXE
DAVID PETERSEN

The Realist
Asaf Hanuka
ISBN: 978-1-60886-688-5 | $24.99 US

The Realist: Plug and Play
Asaf Hanuka
ISBN: 978-1-60886-953-4 | $24.99 US

Long Walk to Valhalla
Adam Smith, Matt Fox
ISBN: 978-1-60886-692-2 | $24.99 US

The March of The Crabs
Arthur De Pins
Volume 1: The Crabby Condition
ISBN: 978-1-60886-689-2 | $19.99 US
Volume 2: The Empire of the Crabs
ISBN: 978-1-68415-014-4 | $19.99 US

Jane
Aline Brosh McKenna, Ramón K. Pérez
ISBN: 978-1-60886-981-7 | $24.99 US

Rust
Royden Lepp
Volume 0: The Boy Soldier
ISBN: 978-1-60886-806-3 | $10.99 US
Volume 1: Visitor in the Field
ISBN: 978-1-60886-894-0 | $14.99 US
Volume 2: Secrets of the Cell
ISBN: 978-1-60886-895-7 | $14.99 US

Mouse Guard
David Petersen
Mouse Guard: Fall 1152
ISBN: 978-1-93238-657-8 | $24.95 US
Mouse Guard: Winter 1152
ISBN: 978-1-93238-674-5 | $24.95 US
Mouse Guard: The Black Axe
ISBN: 978-1-93639-306-0 | $24.95 US

The Cloud
K.I. Zachopoulos, Vincenzo Balzano
ISBN: 978-1-60886-725-7 | $24.99 US

Cursed Pirate Girl Coloring Book
Jeremy A. Bastian
ISBN: 978-1-60886-947-3 | $16.99 US

ARCHAIA

AVAILABLE AT YOUR LOCAL COMICS SHOP AND BOOKSTORE
To find a comics shop in your area, visit www.comicshoplocator.com
WWW.**BOOM-STUDIOS**.COM

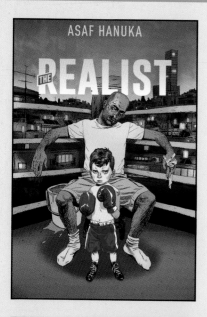

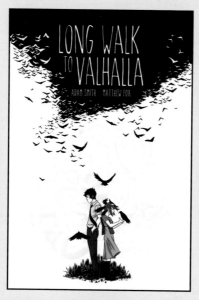

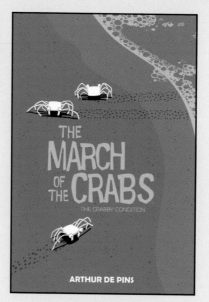

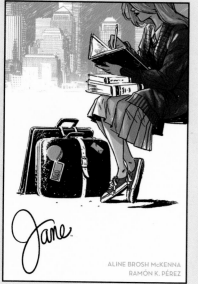

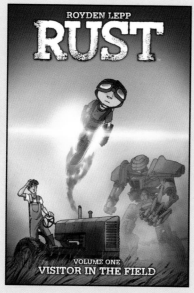

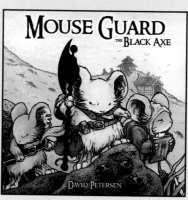

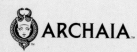

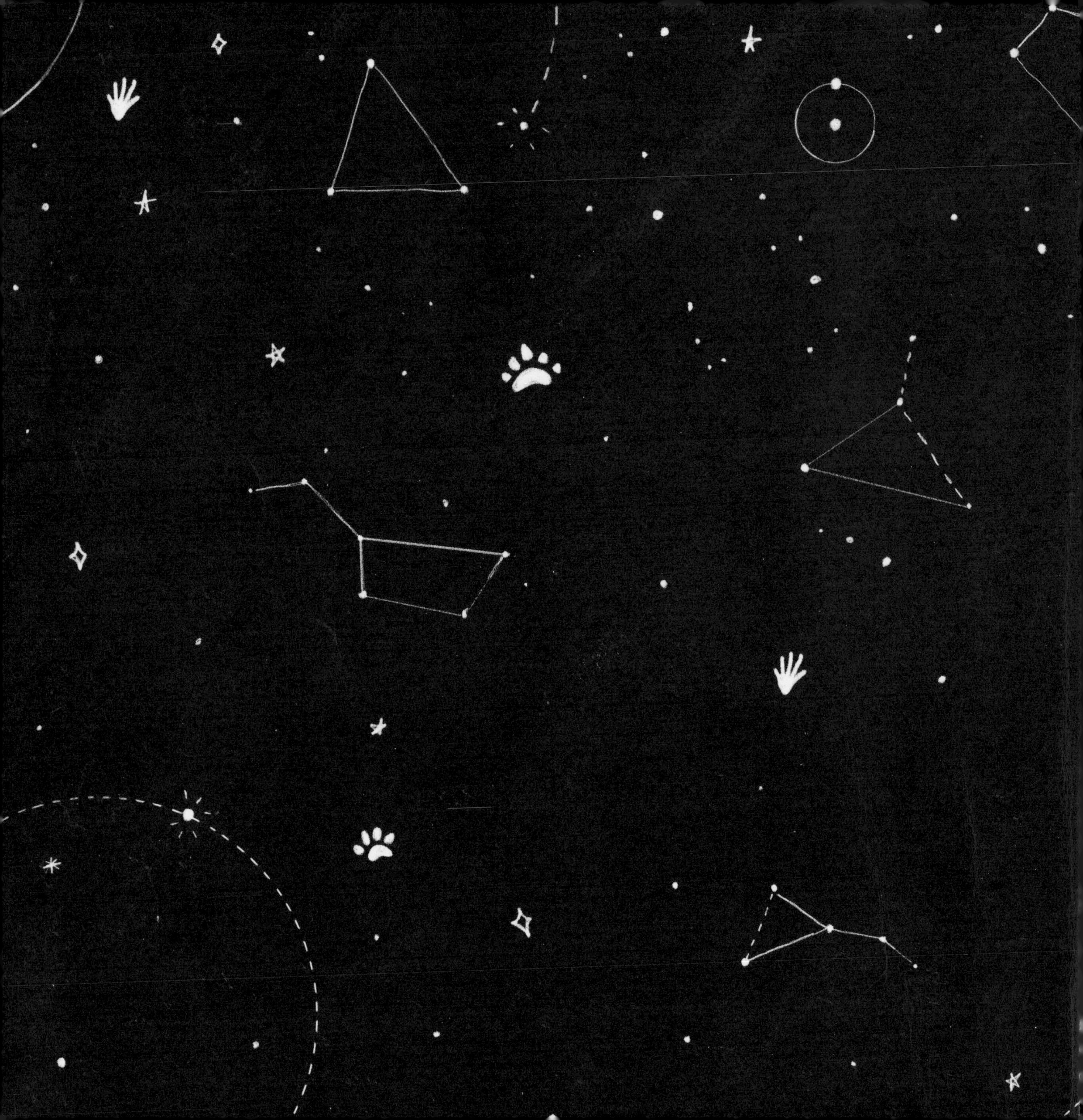